"EXCUSE ___ ✧ ___ WATCH WHERE YOU'RE GOING. AS BIG AS MY BEHIND IS I KNOW YOU SAW IT BACK THERE."

Marvin did a quick, barely noticeable body scan. Now that she'd mentioned it, that ass was an attention grabber. His mother called them Carter-catchers, because they all were butt men. Marvin didn't know whether to be insulted or to fall in love. He decided on staying focused, read her name tag, and stepped behind her.

"You can't say sorry?" she asked.

"I could, but I'm not. You stepped back at the same time I moved forward. So I could be the one copping an attitude right now and saying you ran into me. And with all this going on"—Marvin paused, emphasizing his body—"I can see why."

The woman's shocked expression made him laugh. Clearly, she wasn't used to getting what she served out dished right back to her.

"What's your name?" She leaned forward to read the label stuck to his shirt. "Marvin Carter. Figures."

"What do you mean?"

"Common name for a common brother. Trying to work my nerves on the very first day."

"Oh, I get it. Working those jaws helps calm your nerves. Might as well get your digs in now, because more than likely this first day of the competition is going to be your last."

A collective, combined groan and gasp went up from those who heard him. He watched her raise her brow and take a breath. "Darling," she said, her voice changing from a loud, caustic tone to one that was soft, almost loving. "I'm going to slice you and the rest of this competition up just like a loaf of fresh bread."

Also by Zuri Day

Lies Lovers Tell

Body by Night

Lessons from a Younger Lover

What Love Tastes Like

Lovin' Blue

Love in Play

Heat Wave
(with Donna Hill and Niobia Bryant)

The One That I Want
(with Donna Hill and Cheris Hodges)

The Morgan Men Series

Love on the Run

A Good Dose of Pleasure

Bad Boy Seduction

The Blue-Collar Lover Series

Driving Heat

Packing Heat

Sweet Heat

Published by Kensington Publishing Corp.

Sweet
HEAT

A BLUE-COLLAR LOVER NOVEL

ZURI
DAY

Dafina
BOOKS

Kensington Publishing Corp.

www.kensingtonbooks.com

DAFINA BOOKS are published by

Kensington Publishing Corp.
119 West 40th Street
New York, NY 10018

Copyright © 2019 by Zuri Day

All Kensington Titles, Imprints, and Distributed Lines are available at special quantity discounts for bulk purchases for sales promotions, premiums, fund-raising, and educational or institutional use. Special book excerpts or customized printings can also be created to fit specific needs. For details, write or phone the office of the Kensington special sales manager: Kensington Publishing Corp., 119 West 40th Street, New York, NY 10018, attn: Special Sales Department, Phone: 1-800-221-2647.

Dafina and the Dafina logo Reg. U.S. Pat. & TM Off.

ISBN-13: 978-1-61773-429-8
ISBN-10: 1-61773-429-2
First Kensington Mass Market Edition: July 2019

ISBN-13: 978-1-61773-430-4 (ebook)
ISBN-10: 1-61773-430-6 (ebook)

10 9 8 7 6 5 4 3 2

Printed in the United States of America

To all foodies and thick chicks everywhere. Cheers!

Acknowledgments

DayDreamers who've been with me for a while know that when I'm not writing I'm a chef in my own mind! Because of that, this book was especially delightful to write. Thanks to my ace Kensington team for indulging my fantasies—Selena James, who wears an "S" on her chest, my editing eyes Rebecca Raskin and Robin Cook, Janice Rossi for the PERFECT cover, Steven Zacharius for loving Zuri the mostest, EVERYONE at the K . . . love you bunches. To all the cooks and chefs who've inspired me, starting with my mama, my beautiful sister-authors (you know who you are), and to all of the beautiful DayDreamers . . . the wind beneath my writer wings! Fix a plate, pour a drink . . . and enjoy.

1

"Mama, taste this."

Marvin Carter entered his parents' living room bearing gifts, this baker's take on a Southern favorite. Traditionally a gooey, white, sugary filling covered in caramel and rolled in chopped pecans, Marvin placed all of the above between the layers of a triple-tiered dark chocolate cake and topped it with a caramel pecan frosting. Enough sugar for Type 3, 4, or 5 diabetes, if such a thing existed, but eaten in moderation it was better than sex.

Elizabeth Carter, whom everybody called Liz, and her husband, Willie, sat in matching La-Z-Boy recliners engrossed in a marathon of *Family Feud*.

"Shh! Quiet, boy." Liz leaned forward, as if she couldn't see the fifty-five-inch screen. "I've got to help this family win twenty thousand dollars."

"I don't have a dog in the hunt," Willie drawled, examining the contents of the saucer Marvin gave him. "Was just thinking about something sweet, too. This smells good, boy."

"It sure does," Liz agreed, her attention drawn away from the television by the tantalizing aroma wafting toward her from the saucer Marvin passed under her nose.

"Cake!" she yelled, responding to the TV prompt, smacking Marvin's hand as she threw up a meaty arm.

"Dang, Mama!" Marvin jumped back, barely saving his creation from a meeting with the carpet.

"Didn't you hear Steve ask her to name something sweet you might eat at a kid's birthday party? You inspired me, Marvin. I think we're going to win!"

Aware that he was no competition for Steve Harvey, Marvin waited until the game was over. Cake was that category's number-one answer. Indeed, the family on TV walked away with the prize.

"Now," Liz said, huffing with excitement as she settled back against the couch. "What do you have over there smelling so good?"

"My version of a pecan log roll." He handed her the saucer.

"A log roll?" Liz looked at her husband.

"You never had one?" Willie asked her.

"A big old log roll?" Her look turned suggestive. "You shared yours with me just last night."

"Stop it, girl." A brusquely delivered comment, but a smile spread across Willie's face as slowly as a squeeze of molasses down a stack of pancakes.

Marvin was not amused. "Mom, when it comes to

what you and Daddy do behind closed doors, please spare me the details."

"If we'd spared those you wouldn't be here." She took a bite of the dessert. Marvin watched, waited. She took another forkful, chewed more slowly this time.

"Lord Jesus." She shook her head, licked frosting off the fork.

"Boy, you have outdone yourself this time." She continued a running commentary, softly, as if to herself, and didn't stop eating until the last piece was gone. His parents now preoccupied with the unexpected dessert treat, Marvin went back into the kitchen to get a slice for himself.

Liz watched Marvin return to the living room and sit down. She eyed his plate hungrily. "Why didn't you bring me another slice?"

"You didn't ask for one."

"She don't need one, son," Willie drawled. "She's supposed to be trying to lose a pound or two."

"Yeah, but not tonight," she mumbled, then smiled sweetly when Marvin got up and reached for her saucer, quickly returning with another, smaller slice.

"Thank you, baby." Liz quickly downed another forkful of goodness. "Can't call it a roll anyway, since it's a slice. That don't make sense."

He shrugged. "It's inspired from a recipe for what's called a pecan log roll. I think it comes from the South. But you're right. Maybe I'll call it a pecan log cake, or a Southern pecan log cake."

"Or you could shape the cake like a log," Willie

offered, which from this retired army sergeant was rare culinary input.

"Baby, at the end of the day you can call it whatever you want. Cake, log, whatever . . . it's heaven on a saucer. Almost as good as Willie's was last night."

Marvin eyed Liz and scowled.

"Oh, I'm sorry. Forgot you didn't want to know about your daddy's woody."

"Good Lord, Liz." Willie shook his head.

Both were used to Liz Carter's tawdry outbursts. But neither ever stopped being shocked and amazed.

"What?" Liz innocently asked. "Everybody knows you've got one of the best logs—"

"Hello!"

"Anybody home?"

Saved by the doorbell and two of Marvin's brothers. Byron and Douglas came through the unlocked door without waiting to be let in.

Douglas walked over to Marvin, now seated on the couch. "What's that?"

"A pecan log roll," Liz answered, with the type of authority where one would think she'd made it.

"Pecan log cake," Marvin corrected.

"A Southern pecan log cake," Willie added, his Mississippi drawl an obvious reason why he approved of the geographic nod.

"Got any more?" Byron asked.

Marvin nodded. "In the kitchen."

Byron and Douglas made a beeline for the kitchen island.

"You ever had a pecan log roll, Daddy?"

Willie nodded. "Come to think of it, I believe so. Years ago, when we visited relatives in Arkansas. There was a roadside store that was known for their candy—sweet, sticky white stuff and caramel rolled in pecans. Everything you've got in here." He forked the small bite remaining on the plate. "Only this is better."

Byron and Doug came around the corner stuffing their faces. "You did your thing with this one, Marv," Byron said. "Can I take some home with me? I want Cynthia to try it."

"Make a move for that door with my cake and I'll cut you," Liz warned.

"It's worth the risk," Doug quickly countered. "I definitely want Jan to try a piece."

They joined Marvin on the couch.

"You heard about that cooking contest?" Byron asked. "You should enter it."

"Through the Food and Cooking Network?"

Byron shrugged. "I don't know who's doing it. Just heard some women talking on the bus."

"Probably Food Network. I'm not interested. Been there, done that with several of their contests over the years. Sent in audition tapes. Never heard back. So I'm good."

"You sure? One of the women said that this was the chance she'd been waiting for and declared that the fifty-thousand-dollar prize might as well already be in her pocket. That there was no way anyone else would win."

"Fifty thousand dollars!"

A choir couldn't have exclaimed more harmoniously than Liz, Willie, and Marvin.

"That's what she said. Look it up online. It's happening here in LA, and from what she said, sounds like it's happening soon."

"I'll check it out." Marvin stood and headed to the kitchen, empty saucer in hand.

Liz scooped up the last crumbs of her second helping off the saucer and placed it on a side table. She looked at Byron and Doug. "What are y'all up to?"

"I came over to borrow Daddy's power tools," Doug said. "Building a mini-studio for Jan. She thinks I'm building a man cave, but it's her birthday surprise."

Jan was Doug's wife, a former postal worker who was now a Grammy-nominated singer.

"I was just in the neighborhood," Byron said. "Saw Doug when I was coming down Slauson Avenue. Called him up and learned he was headed over here."

"What brought you out of your rich-folk neighborhood?"

"Get out of here with that," Byron said with a grin.

Ever since he'd given in to his wife's pleading and moved to the upscale home she'd been offered as her parents' wedding gift, he'd endured his family's ribbing, often accompanied by someone

humming a 1970s TV-show theme song, "Movin'
On Up."

"You know I've been volunteering over at the
Boys and Girls Club, right?"

"No, didn't know that."

"Yeah, a friend of mine asked me to help coach
the basketball team. Said they needed more positive role models."

"That's a good move, son," Willie said, with a
slow nod. "Proud of you for that."

Marvin returned carrying two containers, a large
one for Byron and a smaller one for Doug.

"Here's some cake for your families."

"Why'd he get a bigger one?" Doug asked, an-
noyed.

"Because he gave me the tip that's going to net
me fifty grand. Once I take that first-place prize, I'll
bake each one of y'all a cake."

Naomi Carson was a thick chick with a well-
proportioned body and a pretty face. Until she
scowled. Like now, when a ringing doorbell inter-
fered with her cooking. She turned off the burner
and headed toward the door, just as the bell rang
again.

"Coming!"

She looked through the peephole and smirked.
"I knew it was you." She opened the door, then
turned back around and sashayed into the kitchen
without awaiting a reply.

"Hello to you too, grouch." Naomi's cousin and

best friend Kristy stepped inside and closed the door behind her. She followed Naomi into the kitchen. "Is that any way to treat a dinner guest?"

"It is when said guest arrives early and jeopardizes my beurre blanc."

"Burr who?"

"Beurre blanc. A white butter sauce."

"Then why didn't you call it that?"

"I did," Naomi deadpanned before returning her focus to the saucepan.

Kristy was nonplussed. She and Naomi had been friends almost from the womb. They were next-door neighbors growing up, until Naomi's world got flipped and she moved in with her grandma. They bonded while sharing secrets, making pinky promises, and assuaging their mutual love for food. She probably knew Naomi's moods better than anyone but Naomi's grandmother Nana, and knew that when it came to cooking, no one better stood in front of a stove.

"Is that what smells so good?" Kristy walked over and placed her nose near the pot.

"Get your nose out of there. Might have a loose booger drop in my sauce and get mistaken for a caper." She elbowed Kristy out of the way and reached for a jar on the counter. Unscrewing the lid, she gave her friend a cautionary glance and made a point of examining the creamy concoction before shaking a few capers from the jar into the pot.

"I do not have a cold and even if I did, there would be no loose boogers or anything else hanging out in my nostrils. That's just plain nasty and not the best visual to put out there right before a meal."

"As if a distasteful comment would ruin your appetite. Girl, if that was the case growing up around your mama, you would have been passing up every other meal and be skinny as a rail."

"It would take more than passing up a couple meals for me to drop all this weight." Kristy sighed as she eased onto a bar chair opposite the counter where Naomi worked. "I need to, though. On my last visit to the doctor, he told me my blood pressure was higher than Mommy's. If it doesn't go down, he wants to put me on medication. But I don't want to have to take pills the rest of my life. I think that's part of what makes Mommy so hard to live with sometimes. Talking foul and cursing like a sailor. Because on most days she just doesn't feel good."

Naomi nodded as she pulled on a mitt and removed a glass baking dish from the oven. She placed it on the stove, poured the sauce over the baked fish fillets, and put the dish back inside the oven. She pulled a covered cast-iron skillet from the bottom oven rack, set it on top of the stove, and turned off the oven. When she lifted the lid a symphony of aromas wafted up and over the counter and teased Kristy's nose.

"Oh my gosh! That is what I smelled when I walked in here." She slid off the stool and headed toward the stove. "What—"

"Back!" Naomi demanded. Holding a cooking fork like a sword, she danced on the balls of her feet and made stabbing motions. "Away from my laboratory lest you ruin my concoctions with your boogery nose."

"Ew, Nay, shut up with that!" Kristy backed up with a frown-filled face. "What is up with you today and this fixation? I think you might need to go and blow your nose."

Naomi laughed. "I have no idea what started that, but agree that I need to give it a rest. Want you to sit back down though, because the food is ready. No, actually I can put you to work. Get two plates out of the cabinets. Silverware is in there." She nodded toward a drawer on the opposite counter.

"Like I don't know my way around this kitchen. I've only been in it a million times."

"There are cans of soda in the fridge. I'll take a strawberry. No, a grape."

Kristy placed cans of soda next to each plate on the counter. She retrieved silverware and napkins, sat back down and opened her drink.

"Oh, those are pork chops. I see that now."

"Not just chops, my special kind of stuffed pork chops. I'm calling them Pork-U-Pines because they're stuffed with minced kale, goat cheese, and tiny bits of pineapple, then brushed with a maple glaze."

She carefully lifted the perfectly done, juicy, cheese-oozing chop from the skillet and placed it on a platter, "I baked the vegetables in the same skillet so they'd be flavored by the meat."

After removing the other chops, she scooped up several heaping spoonsful of slightly charred carrots and potatoes and arranged them around the meat that took center stage, or in this case, center platter. She chopped several sprigs of fresh parsley and sprinkled it over the dish. Back at the stove she carefully lifted out the glass baking dish containing fillets of fish over a bed of rice, all covered with the white sauce. After taking pictures of the dishes with her cell phone, she placed helpings of each on the plates.

She stepped back, crossed her arms as she leaned against the counter. "Okay, taste the fish first."

"Why can't I try the pork chop?"

"The pork chop is spicier, more robust. If you eat it first, you won't be able to taste the delicate seasonings in the fish dish."

Kristy sank a fork into the fish dish, making sure to get some of the fish, sauce, and rice. She took the bite and ate slowly, her expression thoughtful as she chewed. She took another bite, set down the fork and reached for her napkin. "Pretty good," she said and took a drink of soda.

"Pretty good? That's all?"

"Pretty good from me on a dish like that is saying something. I only like fried catfish or fish sticks, and even those only every now and then. Now this pork chop . . ." She picked up her fork. "May I taste it now?"

"Sure, Kristy."

Kristy fixed her with a big smile as she picked up her knife and cut off a bite-sized piece. Seconds after placing the fork into her mouth she jumped up from the bar chair.

Naomi started. "What's the matter?"

Kristy started dancing. "I'm shouting hallelujah because that bite just made me happy!"

Naomi laughed, finally walking over and sitting in front of her plate. "No doubt you'd go with the pork chop if made to choose."

Kristy returned to her seat. "I don't like kale and didn't even know goats made cheese, but this dish right here!" She pointed to it with her fork, continuing to eat. "So good! Where's what's-his-name, Victor?"

"What made you think of that fool?"

"Because this dish is inspired by something or someone. I thought maybe it was him."

"That dish was inspired by the Cooking Channel and my imagination. I haven't talked to Vic in a while."

"Why, Nay? He was cute!"

"Yeah, he was fine but couldn't stuff my pork chop, if you know what I mean."

Kristy almost spewed her bite across the counter. "You. Are. Stupid!"

"No. Horny, though."

"Maybe you'll meet somebody through that contest."

"The only meat on my mind next week will be the piece I put in the judge's hand to get past the general call and on to the preliminaries."

"What's a general call?"

Naomi shrugged as she chewed a bite. "I'm thinking like a cattle call, but will find out for sure next week. So you liked the pork chop the best, hands down? Not that your answer is unbiased, but . . . you're my only opinion until Nana gets home."

"That pork chop could cure cancer."

The high praise almost made Naomi blush.

"I mean that, honey. It was everything. But I thought you told me the prize was a food truck."

"It is, plus fifty thousand cash to help with start-up costs."

"Hmm."

Naomi looked up, convinced there was a wealth of opinion behind that one word. "What?"

"Nothing."

"Nothing, what?"

"I thought you'd focus on your pies to win. What do you call them?"

"My savory slice pies?"

"Yeah. Those are good. I can see a lot of people coming to a food truck for those."

"That's simple cooking. The judges are going to be culinary experts. They're going to be looking for recipes that call for skill, finesse."

"They're going to be looking for food that tastes good, that folk want to buy. Now I'm sure that baked fish is better for my waistline, but if you can find a way to put that chop on some dough and get people to thinking about more than pizza when they hear the word *slice*? You'll win that contest."

Kristy ate, shared her two cents, and left. Nana came home from Wednesday-night Bible study and raved about the pork and the fish. Naomi watched TV and went to bed. But she couldn't sleep. Kristy's words wouldn't let her. They'd prompted her to think more about uniqueness and niche as much as the way the food tasted. The unusual idea that would set her apart from hundreds, maybe thousands who'd be there next Saturday for the contest's open call. Just after one in the morning, Naomi gave up on sleep, headed for the kitchen, and in the words of her bestie tried to figure out how to put that chop on a slice.

2

Marvin entered the Los Angeles Convention Center's South Hall and welcomed the blast of cool air that greeted him. April had brought an unusual amount of rain to Southern California, and if this second Saturday was any indication, it looked as though May would bring the heat. After discovering that the contest Byron had mentioned was on the Chow Channel, the newest network to focus on food, Marvin had decided to enter after all. He thought maybe a new network would lead to a different outcome than what had happened with his previous attempts. Plus, as Liz had said, the only way to win a contest was to enter it. So here he was. Marvin lifted his purple-and gold-Lakers ball cap to wipe away sweat, walked over to a list of instructions displayed on a large screen, and then scanned the auditorium for the letter designating which aisle he should enter. He ambled amid at least a thousand others doing the same. With the kind of prizes being offered, he'd figured the turnout would be huge. It was. Looked like every cook in California had come after that prize money. Maybe some from Oregon and Nevada, too.

He spied a large letter C on the room's opposite side and began working his way through the noisy masses to get there. Each entrant had been asked to bring a single serving of a dish that best represented who they were as a cook or chef. After a week of baking samples, to his family's delight, and taking votes, he'd brought three individually packaged slices of the pecan log cake. While his brother Byron's wife had fought diligently on behalf of his sweet potato soufflé, Marvin's latest creation was the overwhelming favorite. It was Liz's suggestion to bring several slices in case one got dropped and another got stolen. Forms of sabotage, she'd suggested. Best not to take chances.

Aisle C was crowded, Ca–Cl on one side. Cm–Cz on the other. He reached his area and walked toward a loud-talking woman as she took a step back.

Sassy attitude swung around. "Excuse you, dough boy. Watch where you're going. As big as my behind is, I know you saw it back there."

Had she just called him dough boy, as though she knew him like that? A picture of indignation, getting with Marvin in a way that reminded him of his mama? He did a quick, barely noticeable body scan. Now that she'd mentioned it, that ass was an attention grabber. Liz called them Carter-catchers, because they all were butt men. Marvin didn't know whether to be insulted or to fall in love. He decided on staying focused, read her name tag and stepped behind her.

"You can't say sorry?"

"I could, but I'm not. You stepped back at the same time I moved forward. So I could be the one copping an attitude right now and saying you ran into me. And with all this going on"—he paused, emphasizing his body—"I can see why."

The woman's shocked expression made him laugh. Clearly, she wasn't used to getting what she served out dished right back to her.

"What's your name?" She leaned forward to read the label stuck to his shirt. "Marvin Carter. Figures."

"What do you mean?"

"Common name for a common brother. Trying to work my nerves on the very first day."

"Oh, I get it. Working those jaws helps calm your nerves. Might as well get your digs in now, because more than likely this first day of the competition is going to be your last."

A collective, combined groan and gasp went up from those who heard him. He watched her raise her brow and take a breath. "Darling," she said, her voice changing from a loud, caustic tone to one that was soft, almost loving. "I'm going to slice you and the rest of this competition up just like a loaf of fresh bread."

"The bread you slice," Marvin countered, "will be the award-winning loaf I baked and gave to you as a consolation prize."

Chuckles, oohs and aahs commenced from contestants who stood nearby and more who gathered, egging them on.

"Yes, but that award your mama gave you for cooking in her kitchen doesn't count. It was cute," she hurriedly continued, having gained the audience and the upper hand. Her eyes beamed and he noticed a dimple when she smiled. "But it doesn't count."

"Obviously you can't either," Marvin said, his demeanor relaxed, pausing long enough to let her take the bait.

"How do you figure?"

She'd chomped on the hook like he knew she would. Time to reel her in. "Because if you could"—he read her name tag—"Naomi Carson, you would have already counted yourself out."

This woman didn't know he'd grown up in a house with four boisterous brothers and Liz Carter, the ace trash-talker. He could hang with her all day long. Good thing, too, because Naomi wasn't done.

"So, you're up on your numbers. How about your ABCs? Because you are About. To Be. Chopped." A hand motion was added for emphasis.

"I hope you can cook. I really do. Because your chances of making it as a comedian are slim to none."

"Boy, bye. I'm done with you. Let's let our food do the talking. We'll see who's got jokes when the day is over."

"All right, Ms. Carson. I'll accept your truce for now."

Naomi's smile widened as she looked around her. "Y'all see how he backed down when I mentioned food?" She looked at him. "All right, Mr. Carter." She held out her hand. "Truce."

He shook a hand that was silky soft to the touch. Their eyes met. His dick jumped. Damn, she had nice lips. All that trash-talking out of such a pretty face. Marvin had never subscribed to society's beauty standards. He'd dated every size, race, and age, but he had a special thing for big, pretty girls. Probably because his first love was fluffy. Average man would tell you that there was nothing like some fluffy love! *Umph!* He almost groaned aloud. Best get his mind fixated on something other than her body.

He nodded toward the stainless steel container she held. "What did you bring?"

"A slice of heaven."

"You're a pastry chef?"

"No, but when it comes to dessert I can hold my own. This is a savory dish, though."

"What, a pizza?"

"Sorta kinda."

"Pretty simple, don't you think?"

"You tell me." Naomi opened a peephole in the specially sealed container.

Marvin bent down to take a peek. Bent down for a sniff. Came up frowning and fanning his nose. "What is that?"

Naomi smirked. "You know what? I don't even know you and I can't stand you. Even at room temperature you know that smells delicious." She smelled it herself. "That is some good cooking right there." She looked at the woman in the line next to theirs. "Here, smell it."

She complied. "Smells good. Goat cheese, right?"

"Yes."

"And pork?"

Naomi nodded, then turned to Marvin. "The cheese is probably what you smelled but couldn't identify."

"Girl, I know goat cheese when I smell it. I know doodoo when I smell it, too——"

"Oh my gosh!" Naomi burst out laughing, along with some others. "I can't with you!"

Marvin laughed, too. "I'm just messing with you. Let me check that out again."

"No, because you're probably going to spit in it or try some other way to sabotage me."

"Check this out, Naomi." He flipped back the cover to the peephole on the stainless container he held, the same as Naomi's, a specially made container with a vacuum seal, which was sent out by the contest organizers, designed specifically to keep prepared food fresh and bacteria-free. Marvin held it out to her first, and then to a few others. Comments came from all sides.

"Wow, that looks good!"

"What is that?"

"I want a piece."

"Why don't you let me break open that container for you? I'm a judge. No, really. I'm in line and all but . . . as a decoy."

Marvin looked at the guy three people behind him who looked all of sixteen. "You don't look old enough to drive, let alone judge."

The contestant went red all the way to his platinum-blond roots. "I might be only eighteen and just graduated high school, but I know my way around a kitchen."

Naomi waited until the chatter died down. "It looks all right."

Marvin gave her a look. "You know you want a bite of what's in here."

"Only because I didn't have breakfast. It's a box cake, right?"

"Aw!" Marvin gasped and reached for his heart. "She said a box cake." He looked around. "Did y'all hear that?"

"I heard it," said the young teen.

Marvin turned around. "Hey, what's your name, man?"

"Ryan." They shook hands.

"So later on, Ryan, when I win this whole thing, you'll be my witness to this woman's insults, and how deep she pushed the knife."

Marvin covered the peephole. "I don't even see how your dish is going to get tested. How are they going to taste savory dishes containing pork, eggs, and whatnot, without the threat of getting salmonella poisoning?"

"The special container, obviously," Ryan said.

"Plus, we're going first," Naomi added.

Marvin looked at her. "How do you know?"

"Oh, so you can't cook and can't read either."

It was Marvin's turn to chuckle. "Why are you being so mean to a brother?"

"Mean? *Moi?* You call mine a doodoo dish and I'm the cruel one?"

"You're right. Probably shouldn't have said that."

"Don't get soft on me now. Because I'm still going to go hard if you meet me in the kitchen."

"No doubt. But that was kind of rude. I apologize. So the savory dishes go up first?"

"We'll split up in the next room. Entrées or dishes that require heat will be one group. Desserts will be another, and so on. Our dishes have to be at a certain temperature to be considered safe. With all of these people lined up in here, there's no telling who is judging. Probably regular folk just like us."

"Guinea pigs," Marvin joked.

"Gangsters," Naomi countered. "Anybody willing to taste food from a stranger brought off the street has a large pair of cojones. That's a mafia move."

The sound of a microphone being handled caused everyone's attention to shift to a raised platform at the front of the large room.

"Hey, that's Da Chen!" Marvin lowered his voice and leaned toward Naomi's ear. "He won his truck off of the Great Truck Championship a couple years ago. That brother can cook!"

Naomi shushed him. "I want you to be sure and hear these instructions. So that when you lose and see me driving around town in the first prize, you'll know exactly how it happened."

3

"Good afternoon, Los Angeles! Good afternoon,
food truck fanatics!"

The contestants responded to the exuberant
greeting with excited applause.

"Some of you might not know me. I'm Da
Chen—"

"We know you, Da!" a male voice boomed.

"We love you, Da Chen!" a female yelled.

"We love your food!" another man said. The
audience clapped and laughed.

Da Chen bowed slightly, his hands crossed over
his chest. He was a slight man, around five nine, but
his body was toned. Handsome, with olive skin and
coal-black hair, the shoulder-length tresses held
back with a leather band, Da scanned the crowd.

"Thank you. That is kind. Thank you. I don't
have much time to welcome you, but I was invited
here because just a few short years ago I was just like
you, a chef with a dream. I was working as a sous
chef for a very popular, well-known restaurant here

in the city. Hard work. Long hours. I loved it. But I didn't have much of a life outside of it. Which, by the way, won't change much if you want to be a successful food truck owner. What was different was the ability to chart my own course, set my own menu and hours. Be my own boss. Someone sent me a link from FNC—the Food and Cooking Network—seeking cooks and chefs to enter a food truck contest."

Applause and cheers went up.

"Oh, you guys saw that? Then you know it turned out pretty good for me. Which is why I'm excited to be one of the people judging the ten finalists, the shows that will be taped for possible cable or Internet distribution. I'm glad that they asked me to come here today and have the chance to meet all of you. Because after today, there will only be one hundred of you moving on to the first of four preliminary rounds of Food Truck Bucks!"

Marvin felt Naomi's eyes on him amid the groans and murmurs around. He turned and laughed at the expression on her face. "Don't look at me all sad like I'm leaving. You're the one who might get cut."

"I don't think so."

"That's cool. We'll both be here next week then. Because I'm not going anywhere!"

They returned their attention to the stage. Da Chen wrapped up his enthusiastic welcome and was followed by one of the organizers who gave more specific instructions on how the day would unfold. The large crowd of hopefuls were divided into several groups based on their dish, as Naomi had mentioned. He turned to speak with someone to his right. When he turned back she was gone. He didn't know which direction, and tried not to feel let down that she'd left without so much as a wish of good luck. *Woman with that kind of mouth, I should be glad she's gone.* Right? That's what he told himself. Soon, he was swept up in the large group of cooks who'd brought desserts as their taster. Inside the smaller room the group was further divided by type of pastry: cakes, pies, cookies, etc. Once split up, Marvin scoped out his immediate competition. Looked to be about a hundred people. He recognized a few from the culinary school he'd attended years ago and a few more from restaurants he'd regularly frequented over the years. Most made eye contact, acknowledged that they knew him. A couple he felt ignored him, or looked over him like they didn't remember who he was. From Marvin that idea earned a chuckle and a scoff. He was many things to many people, but easily forgettable wasn't one of them. The next sixty seconds proved that out.

"Marvin Carter!"

He turned in the direction of the familiar voice. "Is that Abbey Abs? What's up, teach?" He held out his arms for the culinary instructor who approached. They enjoyed a hearty embrace.

"Are you trying to get a food truck?"

"No." Abbey chuckled. "The only cooking I want to do is at home or in a classroom. I'm one of the contest coordinators."

"Really? Cool! Then I'm moving on to the second round no problem, right?"

"Probably, but that will be determined by the judges, not me. You're a great cook, Marvin. A shame you dropped out of school."

"Couldn't be helped. Got a job offer. Had to take it."

"A job cooking?"

Marvin nodded.

"Where?"

"A place called the Soul Spot."

"Never heard of it."

"Few in the Valley probably have. It's popular on the south side of town among the clubbing, drinking crowd. On Fridays and Saturdays it stays open until two a.m."

"How's the food?"

"Excellent when I'm cooking."

"Are you the head chef, line cook, what?"

"This place doesn't have chefs. I'm the assistant cook. Next to the top guy, the son of the owner."

"Sounds a bit below your pay grade, guy. But a good enough place to start, I guess, get some experience under your belt."

"I thought so. Plus, promises were made when I took the position."

"Were they kept?"

"We'll see."

Abbey saw a producer waving her over. She turned to Marvin. "It's great to see you again," she murmured while leaning in for another hug. She wrapped her arms around his middle and squeezed tightly. Marvin retreated, a little taken aback.

"Boy, how I've missed those hugs." Her eyes seared him in a way that suggested hugs weren't the only thing she'd thought about. "You know you were my favorite student. My life has definitely been duller without you in it."

Is she flirting with me? Marvin took another step back. "Good to see you too, Abbey."

She turned to leave. "Is your number the same?"

"Yep."

"I'll call you. Maybe we can catch up over a drink, or I can come to where you're working."

"That sounds cool."

Marvin watched her hurry over to the producer now joined by a couple others. Before he had a chance to digest what had just happened, it was time for his food to get tasted.

He approached one of ten rectangular tables, each with a three-person panel sitting behind it— all recent graduates of California culinary schools, the contestants had been told. Retired instructors and mom-and-pop restaurant owners made up the first round of judges. In the center of the table was a stand that held two cardboard cutouts—a knife, and a chef hat. He gave his container to an assistant who used a special tool to open the hermetically sealed lid, cut the slice of cake, and placed a bite-sized piece on each of three paper saucers before placing one in front of each judge. While this happened, they questioned him. After the routine

ones—name, years cooking, place of employment—
came one that caused Marvin to stop and think.

"Why do you want to win, and why do you think
you should?"

"The second question is easiest," he said after a
pause. "So I'll answer it first. I'm a great cook, and
a passionate one. Cooking gives me life. My food
will add years to yours. When I was a kid, cooking,
especially baking, kept me out of trouble. Didn't
make me too cool with the other boys in the
neighborhood"—he stopped as the judges smiled
or laughed—"but it gave me something to do, kept
me focused. I want to be able to offer that to other
young boys, and once I win the food truck, plan to
offer internships to interested teens. I guess in
saying all that I answered both questions. Because
that is why I want to win, and why I think I should."

"I like that answer. Describe what you've prepared for us."

Marvin looked into the eyes of the woman who'd
spoken. He guessed her to be around his mother's
age, and talked to her in the warm, engaging way
he would speak to Liz, or one of his aunts.

"It's what I've named the Southern pecan log
cake."

He went on to describe the ingredients and what
inspired him to make the dish, then stood silently
as they tasted it, secretly smiled as they asked for a
second bite.

"The caramel," a young male judge began, leaning back against a hard plastic chair. "Is that melted
down from a toffee candy?"

"Oh, no. That's from scratch."

"It's delicious," the woman said.

"One of the best desserts we've tasted so far," the third judge said.

"There's no need for further discussion." The older woman plucked the chef's hat out of the stand. "Congratulations, Marvin. You're on to the next round."

"Yes! Thank you!"

All day long Marvin's demeanor had been one of utmost confidence. But the relief he felt at holding the chef's hat in his hand was proof that he'd not been 100 percent sure he'd make it to the next round. His excitement and gratitude were genuine. He bounced out of the room and headed across the hall to where the judges said he'd receive further instructions. About thirty contestants who'd made the cut milled around the room. Naomi was there, head down, texting on her phone. He walked over.

"I see you stole somebody's chef hat," he said, nodding at the cardboard hat on her lap.

"Haha. I don't think so." Naomi looked up and noticed the same type of cardboard hat in his hand. "I see you did though."

He sat down beside her. "I told you I was getting through."

"Yes, exactly what I told you."

"Congratulations."

She looked at him, her expression unreadable.

"Why are you looking at me like that?"

"I'm waiting for the punchline," Naomi replied. "Or the put down. Or both."

"Not this time. I'm being serious."

"First time?"

Marvin raised a brow. "You've got a smart mouth."

"Thank you."

"I'm really happy you made it through to the next round."

"Thank you." A more genuine smile caused Naomi's dimple to wink at him and sent sunshine to Marvin's heart.

"I can't wait until that first Saturday in June," she said. "That's when the real work starts."

"Lucky for you to have a couple more weeks to practice on your customers, or friends, or wherever you cook."

Naomi placed her cell phone in her purse. "Where do you work?"

"The Soul Spot."

"Oh, yeah?"

He nodded. "What about you. Where do you cook?"

"Nana's kitchen."

"Where's that?"

"At Nana's house. She's my grandmother."

"Oh." They both laughed. "So you're what they call an amateur."

"Nope. I'm what they call a sistah who can cook her ass off. When not doing that I'm working as the assistant manager at a 99 Cents Store."

"That's cool. What makes you think you can run a food truck?"

"I can do anything I put my mind to. Plus, cooking makes me happy. I'm good at it. And I want to work for myself. Be my own boss. Know what I mean?"

"I know exactly what you mean." Marvin got a text. He looked at it and stood.

"That your girlfriend?"

"Is that your way of asking if I have one?"

"It's my way of asking who texted."

"Why are you being nosy?"

"Never mind. I don't give a damn who it is anyway."

Marvin chuckled. "Yes, you do. But the text was from one of my brothers, about the Inglewood Alliance Block Party."

"The one coming up on Memorial Day?"

Marvin smiled. "So you know about it."

"Of course. As does anybody else who's read the *LA Chronicle* or listened to KJLH anytime in the past decade or longer. She adopted a deep male voice. "Everybody—"

"Rockin' the Block!" They finished together, laughing at the familiar tagline.

"You ever been?"

"A couple times. You cook for that event?"

"I grew up with that event. My mom is one of the organizers. You coming this year?"

Naomi shook her head. "I'll be with friends at the Mirage in Vegas, hanging out with Boyz II Men."

"Cool. Then I guess I'll see you in a couple weeks."

"I guess so. See you later."

Marvin took a couple steps, then turned around. "And as for whether or not I have a girlfriend, the answer is no." He walked out the door without looking back, and missed another one of Naomi's sunshine smiles.

4

Naomi found her car and pulled out of the parking structure. She rarely came downtown and was glad to be leaving before it got dark. For a city second only to New York in population, this part of downtown seemed nearly empty, at least on this particular Saturday night. There weren't many out walking, and those who were looked like she'd not feel too comfortable passing by them without pepper spray. She reached the light, but when it turned green she didn't veer left and get on the freeway. She kept straight to Olympic Boulevard and headed home through the city streets, on a bit of a downer even with the cardboard chef eyeing her from the passenger seat.

She engaged her car's Bluetooth and called Kristy.

"Hey, girl!"

"Hey, Tee."

A pause and then, "So, what happened? You

know I've been waiting all day to hear if my idea worked in your favor."

"It did."

"You won?"

"Nobody won yet. But I got through to the next round."

Kristy shrieked. "Way to go, cousin! I knew you should turn that pork chop dish into a slice."

"Yep. You were right."

"Why don't you sound too happy?"

"I don't know. Tired, I guess. I didn't sleep good last night. Don't really feel like going home though. Called to see if you want to go out and do something."

"Girl, I can't. I got a date."

"With who?"

"That guy I met on PlentyOfFish."

"You and those dating websites. I thought you weren't going to do that anymore. After the run-in with Freddie Krueger's brother's uncle."

Kristy laughed. "You can't let one bad apple spoil the whole bag."

"Even one who practically assaulted you the first time you met and then stalked you when you refused to accept his apology and go out again?"

"This one's different. We've been talking and texting for over two months. Plus, we're meeting in a public place. I'm not going over to his house till, you know . . ."

"Until you've run a background check, talked to references, met at least three of his family members, and let me meet him . . . right?"

"Dang, Naomi! Paranoid much?"

"Yes, and if you watched the ID channel you would be, too. There's this show called *Web of Lies*—"

"I don't want to hear the details. Have me scared to meet anybody new."

"That's kind of my point. What happened to that other guy you were head over heels for? The one you said was the one?"

"Oh, he is. He just doesn't know it yet. Until he does, I'm keeping myself occupied."

"Come on, Tee. Let's do something. I'm on Olympic and can be at your house in about ten or fifteen minutes."

"I told you I have a date, and I am not passing that up to hang out with a female. Even my favorite. They'll be enough estrogen on our all-girls trip to Vegas."

"True that."

"What did you do down at the convention center all day?"

"What do you mean, what did I do? I entered a cooking contest."

"There weren't any cuties down there for you to go out with afterwards, get a phone number, something?"

Yeah, but he had to work. "Not really. Besides, I didn't go there to get a date. I entered the contest to get some dollar bills, get that truck and move out of Nana's house."

"She know you're leaving?"

"She knew when I moved back in with her that it wasn't to stay, only until she got better."

"You know she's not going to want you to leave."

"She'll be all right. Nana's messing up my love life."

"Girl, what love life? You haven't gone out for months."

"Doesn't mean I don't want to. And what if I do and want to bring him home? Try and tiptoe his ass past her bedroom when you know she hears every creak in that hardwood floor and knows its exact location from the sound."

"Ha! That's the truth."

"You know it! But I'm ready. I'm getting tired of the ménage à moi."

"The what?"

"You know what I'm talking about. The DIY project. Playing the piano. Fanning the fur!"

"Oh."

"Don't say it all drawn out like that, like when you hit a spell that's dry you don't DIY."

"Honey, there are way too many dicks in LA for me to have to doo-wah-diddle all by myself."

"Yeah, but all too often they come with minor inconveniences. You know, like ankle bracelets, STDs, crazy baby mamas, and stalker tendencies."

"You left out wives and P.O.'s. But if he has the right kind of hose that can start up a fire and then put it out, that's sometimes a chance worth taking."

"I hear you, Tee. Don't agree with you, but I do understand. I'm way past ready to cuddle up with something that don't require batteries."

"I can see if Gary has a friend."

"Yeah, one that he can go out with so you can keep me company. I'm almost at Crenshaw."

"I love you, cousin, but not that much."

"Forget you, heifah," Naomi replied, laughing. "Just be sure and send me a picture of Gary, along with his phone number before y'all meet. And try to get his birthdate or driver's license number, so I can do a background check."

"My, would you look at the time!" Kristy's voice rang with pseudo amazement.

"I hate you. Bye."

Kristy's loud guffaw boomed out of the speakers before Naomi ended the call. She wanted to hate her cousin for real right about now, but there was no way that could ever happen. Born just months apart, Kristy was a part of her earliest memories. If she was lucky, her favorite cousin would also be in one of her last.

With no one else to call, or at least no one with whom she wanted to be bothered, Naomi continued down Crenshaw into Inglewood. Marvin was still on her mind, had been since they'd waved goodbye downtown. A little too much, she decided. He was obnoxious, cocky, and rude. Who cared that he had sexy eyes, juicy lips, and that his cockiness was exactly the kind of swagger that she liked in a man? He was an opponent, not an opportunity. Sure, she'd be friendly. It was always good strategy to keep the enemy close. But what she wouldn't be was a friend with benefits. In every movie she'd seen on the subject, sleeping with the enemy ended badly.

She stopped at a corner store near the house to purchase a candy bar, chips, and a six-pack of hard lemonade for tonight's date with the remote. At the counter she thought of Nana and picked up a few scratchers, the closest to gambling Sis. Carson would ever come, or admit to anyway. That and bingo. And the occasional slot machine pull, but only if out of town and away from her church family. Armed with her necessities for the evening, she turned on Seventy-ninth Street and a couple blocks later pulled into the driveway of her grand-mother's Spanish-style bungalow. She parked her black Hyundai behind her grandmother's "spank-ing white"—as Nana called it, though she admitted to not quite knowing in this context what "spank-ing" meant—Buick Regal. She chuckled in spite of her somewhat sour mood. Coming here often had that effect. She could be mad, sad, have premen-strual cramps or have just broken up with a boyfriend, and seeing this house with a Buick in the driveway could produce a smile. To most people those items would simply represent something to drive or a place to live, but for Naomi, they repre-sented love. Nana, whose real name was Nadine, and Naomi's grandfather Claude, had purchased the place over forty years ago. Until the day her Pop-Pop died it was his pride and joy, surpassed only by the latest-model Buick and his Juicy Fruit, Nana's pet name.

Naomi headed toward the front door with every

intention of a quick hello to Nana and a beeline for the fridge in her room. At twenty-five she was grown and made her own money, and teetotaler Nana had never criticized her about drinking, but Naomi still tended to sneak alcohol into the house. What could she say? Some habits were hard to break.

Nana sat in her favorite seat, a cushiony upholstered rocker that had seen better years. Two steps in and Naomi stopped abruptly. "You didn't."

Nana's eyes sparkled. "Yes, I did, too."

"Chicken and dumplings?" Nana nodded. "And banana pudding?"

"Good nose, girl."

"Nana!" Alcoholic beverages forgotten, Naomi rushed over and gave her grandmother a hearty hug and kiss. "What got into you to do all that cooking?"

"Most of it is for church tomorrow. There's always a fellowship after first Sunday's service. You should go with me. A little of the Lord will do you good. What do you have in that bag?"

"What I thought would be dinner." Naomi backed rapidly away. "But this junk food is no competition for your food from scratch. And speaking of, I bought you some scratchers. Be right back!"

Surprisingly, Nana ended up being Naomi's date for the evening. Usually in bed by nine o'clock on a Saturday night, her grandmother spied an old Sidney Poitier movie coming on television and stayed up to watch it. Complete with delightful sidebars during commercials on how her young Claude resembled the young Sidney, only much handsomer, and how some of the scenes in the classic that also starred Katherine Hepburn and Spencer Tracy reminded her of the first visit home when her "cup of strong black coffee" met her somewhat uppity, slightly color-struck Creole clan. Naomi pigged out on Nana's good cooking while drinking her contraband liquor from an innocent-looking, daisy-covered Dollar Tree glass. By the time the movie ended and Naomi went to her room, she'd almost forgotten about that guy named Marvin who'd earlier gotten on her nerves. But when she got into bed and slipped between the covers, memories of that meddlesome man and the scrumptious-smelling cake he'd baked reentered her mind. If he was half as good in the bedroom as he appeared to be in the kitchen . . . Naomi flipped over, punched her pillow and chased the thoughts away. She was trying to win fifty thousand dollars and change her and Nana's life. What a competitor could or couldn't do in the bedroom was none of her business.

Ain't nobody got time for that!

5

Marvin swatted the alarm clock buzzer, second-guessing the decision he'd made at one in the morning to cover the head cook's six a.m. shift on Sunday, the restaurant's busiest day of the week. Seemed like a good idea at the time, maybe because he was still stoked at having made it through yesterday's Food Truck Bucks general call. Plus, Marvin knew the more money he made the faster he could move out of his parents' home and get his own place again. Not that they minded having him there. With their baby boy, Barry, practically living at his girlfriend's house, they'd encouraged Marvin to move back home. He hadn't had much of a choice at the time. When his roommates bailed from the pricey Culver City condo they shared, he'd tried for a couple months to swing the rent on his own. But he couldn't handle two thousand a month on what he was making. Cooking shows made the occupation seem glamorous, but the average cook didn't make Bobby Flay money.

They made paycheck-to-paycheck money. To get anything extra, he had to work extra shifts.

Thirty-two minutes later, he pulled into the Soul Spot restaurant's parking lot and drove to the far corner where employees parked. Not having checked the weather, he wasn't prepared for the slight drizzle that began halfway there. He exited the car and dashed toward the back entrance. Within minutes he'd donned a white apron and cap, and had large pots of water boiling for oatmeal, grits, and rice, ready to feed the large, nonstop Sunday crowd, easily the restaurant's most profitable day.

Ten minutes later, the back doorbell rang. Marvin looked at the camera and hit the buzzer. His line cook slogged through the door, head hanging.

"Hey, Ricky." Marvin did a double take. "Look what the cat drug in."

"Glad the cat helped me, brother, because I probably wouldn't have made it on my own."

"Too much partying last night?"

"Too much brandy." Ricky rubbed his stomach and made a face. "Man! I don't know if I'm going to be able to hang for the whole shift."

"Oh, no. Don't go trying to make a case for leaving early again, Ricky. You know how badly we get slammed on Sundays."

"Why do you think I'm here? I knew Donald had called in sick, like he does every other week. Anybody else and their ass would have been fired. But not the owner's son."

A nod of the head was Marvin's only response. Sometimes walls had ears.

"Everybody knows you should be the head cook in this joint."

"Head chef."

Ricky fixed bloodshot eyes on Marvin's back. Watched him pull a tub of meat from an industrial-sized refrigerator. "What does your check say you are, a chef or a cook?"

"Check says I'm damn near unemployed."

Ricky's boisterous laughter turned into a coughing fit. "Oh, man, I think I'm going to be sick." He dashed out of the kitchen.

"Just what I need," Marvin mumbled. "A drunk sideman."

He pulled on a vinyl glove, dug into the tub of sausage and pulled out a large chunk of meat. He added pepper flakes to the already spicy mix, formed a patty, and slapped it on the grill. The doorbell rang again. He checked the camera and pushed the buzzer, then cracked a couple eggs onto the sizzling iron. Janet entered the kitchen. Ricky returned a short time later.

Marvin set a plated sandwich on the counter. "Eat that."

"What is it?" Ricky asked.

"Where's mine?" was Janet's question.

"It'll help your hangover," Marvin said. He looked at Janet. "Morning, Miss Bossy."

"Morning, moody. Where's my breakfast?"

"In the refrigerator. Bread's over there."

She looked at Ricky. "See how he does me? Biting the hand that fed him."

"You didn't feed me, woman. Told me about the job, though."

"I tried to feed you. But you're scared to come over to my house."

"He needs to be," Ricky said around a mouthful of sausage, egg, and cheese. "You're a man-eater!" He started singing the popular 90s tune. They all burst out laughing.

Marvin alternately teased and tortured Ricky and Janet, but they were his favorite coworkers. Ricky had worked at the restaurant for years, and aside from his penchant for booze, weed, and scandalous women, he was a decent cook. Janet was like a big sister, giving him a hard time every chance she got, but would give him her last dollar if he needed it.

He glanced at the clock. "All right, family. Playtime's over. We open in ten."

Marvin was right. From the moment Janet turned on the OPEN sign and unlocked the front door, a steady stream of customers poured into the dining room. As restaurants went, it was on the small side, seating just sixty-two diners. An hour into being open, every table was full, with a line going outside. Marvin and Ricky knocked out orders in record time, thanks to Marvin's prep work and cooking skills. A limited menu also helped, but the orders kept on coming. Two hours in and Marvin hadn't even glanced out the kitchen to gauge the crowd, much less go out as he often did to chat with family and friends who came by, or to get a stranger's opinion on his food. The dining room was loud, but at just past noon, a melodic burst of laughter floated over the din of other voices. Not just any laugh. One that caused Marvin to pause and look in the direction of the sound. Was it her? He flipped the egg ordered over-easy, gently slipped it onto a spatula, and placed it on top of a plated pile of ground beef, potatoes, and onions all cooked together and simply called smash. He reached a hand into the warmer, tossed on a couple biscuits, and set the plate in the window. "Order up!"

Taking the tip of a towel slung across his shoulder, he wiped his brow while crossing the kitchen and stepped just beyond the door, enough to see but not be seen. Two seconds was all it took and . . . there she was. Gold hoops, yellow maxi, hair pulled up and away from her round, pretty face. Standing and yapping nonstop with a woman beside her. Another big pretty, though not as captivating as Naomi. There was a light about the girl he'd met yesterday that shined through the attitude and hard veneer. She laughed. He smiled. Sunshine. That's what she reminded him of—the sun, round, bright, and hot. Juicy too, though, like a plump, ripe melon.

Janet bumped him on her way to pick up the order. "Back to work! You don't have time to be shopping right now."

Marvin smiled, working the toothpick in his mouth as he returned to the kitchen. *I knew she was feeling me.* At least he hoped so, because while he might deny it if asked outright, he was feeling her.

Janet returned to the kitchen.

"Hey, Janet. Do me a favor."

"What?"

"Go pull that girl in the yellow dress out of the line and get her a table."

"And have twenty hungry Negroes mad at me? Messing with my tip money? I don't think so."

"Come on, Janet. Just stroll down nice and official-like and tell her their table is ready. Anybody asks, say they came in earlier and then came back."

Janet scowled. "You want me to pull her out of line and lie on a Sunday?"

"Won't be your first time. Come on, now. I'll owe you one."

"Don't say I've never done anything for you." She turned and sashayed out of the kitchen. "And you don't owe me one, you owe me several."

A cool Naomi and confused Kristy followed Janet to a table in the corner. Janet placed down their menus and offered a tight smile. "Your server will be here shortly to take your order."

Kristy watched as Janet walked away. "What just happened?"

"What do you mean?" Naomi asked as she scanned the menu.

"Why'd we get pulled out of line like that?"

"Because we're special, that's why."

"I'm serious."

"I am, too." Hearing the concern in her cousin's voice, Naomi looked up. "Marvin probably did it."

"Who's Marvin?"

"A guy I met downtown yesterday."

"At the contest?" Naomi nodded. "So you did meet somebody."

"I met several somebodies. It's no big deal."

"It's a big enough deal for you to drag me out of the house and pay for my meal. A big enough deal for him to spot you and pull you out of line." Naomi shrugged. "Did you give him some?"

"Girl, please."

"Don't *please* me. Stop acting coy and tell me what happened."

"Nothing happened! We were next to each other in line, that's all, because of our last names. His Carter to my Carson."

"Soon to be Carter?"

"You're the one trying to marry every man you meet, not me."

Kristy clucked her tongue. "The way you begged me to come here and eat, I can't tell. Which one is he?"

Naomi looked toward the front. "He's back in the kitchen most likely."

Kristy eyed her cousin with suspicion. "No wonder you were so quick to call this your treat. You probably won't even have to pay for the meal."

"I hope you're right."

"Uh-huh. I know you gave him some, now."

Naomi laughed. "No, I didn't!"

"Take your order."

The stranger's matter-of-fact voice startled them both. Wrapped up in their conversation, neither woman had heard the server approach. Naomi sensed anger in the woman's tone, but dismissed it as an employee having a bad day. She'd had plenty of those herself.

Naomi looked at Kristy. "Do you know what you want?"

"I usually get the number three. Maybe I should try something different." She looked at the server, smiled, and asked politely, "Which one would you suggest?"

"Whichever one you want to eat." No smile. Not polite.

"They all look good," Kristy said, shrinking a little into herself. "I just wanted a suggestion."

"I just gave you one."

There was no mistaking the funk this time. Or her cousin's feelings of intimidation. "Aren't you being a bit rude?" Naomi asked.

"She asked a question. I answered it. Now are you ready to order or not?"

Naomi bristled. "No, but I'm ready to add some kick-ass to that attitude you're serving up."

The petite server dished up a second helping. "Trust me, you don't want none of this."

"Oh, yeah? I don't think you want none of this either." Naomi pushed back and rose to her full five feet seven inches, towering over the worker who'd riled her nerves. A hundred and seventy-five pounds of I'm-not-the-one added volume that increased with every word. "In fact, I don't think you want to wait on this table. Where is the manager?"

"You'd better get out of my face."

"I said get the manager now!"

Zuri Day

Marvin rushed into the dining room. "Ladies, ladies!" He stepped in between Naomi and the worker. "Charlotte, I've got this one."

She looked at him like there was poo on his face. "Oh, so this is another one of your tricks? Should have known." She looked back at Naomi. "No home training."

"I've got your home training. Matter of fact, let me give it to you right—" Naomi reached for Charlotte, but Marvin blocked the blow with a firm grip on her arms. "Ignore her, Naomi. Please. Let's not make more of a scene than has already happened."

Naomi plopped down in her seat, staring in the direction the server had walked.

"Why are you trying to start a brawl in here?"

"I didn't start it. She's the one who brought attitude to the table. Don't nobody talk to my family like that."

Marvin took in Naomi's thundercloud expression with a slight smile. "Family first, huh?"

"Damn right! Family is everything." She looked up. "What's that goofy grin for?"

"Nothing. I apologize for our server's behavior."

Naomi mocked Charlotte. "One of your tricks? I should have known."

"Don't take it personally. She was born unhappy."

"Come at me again like that and she's going to die that way."

"You ain't killing nobody, cousin. Calm your ass down."

"Have you placed your order?" Marvin asked.

"No," Kristy answered. "And if we do, I don't want her anywhere near our food."

"I'll handle it personally. Matter of fact, if you don't mind, let me whip up something just for the two of you. Chef's special. Fair enough?"

"I guess." Naomi sat but was clearly still in a huff.

"There are several orders ahead of you two, so it will be about fifteen, twenty minutes, but I am working on it. Something to drink in the meantime?"

"Yes, preferably something with alcohol," Kristy replied. "So Naomi can go ahead and chill the bump out."

"Sorry, but we don't serve alcohol."

"I know," Kristy replied.

Marvin winked at Kristy and squeezed Naomi's shoulder. "Calm down, Mayweather, so I can stop refereeing and cook you something nice. Deal?"

Mayweather was still too steamed to speak.

"What's your name?" Kristy asked.

"Marvin."

"Thank you, Marvin. Naomi and I appreciate you coming out of the kitchen to help."

"My pleasure." With a short bow, he turned and left.

Kristy tore into Naomi, her voice low and fierce. "Girl, what is the matter with you?"

"Don't start in on me. If you'd taken up for yourself, I wouldn't have had to."

"This isn't grade school, Nay, and we're not on the block. I don't need you to take up for me."

She reached over, gave Naomi's arm a squeeze. "I appreciate it, though."

"Whatever."

"I understand your frustration. He's cute."

"You under . . . he's . . . you think this is about Marvin?"

"I know it is. And you need to get with that brother as soon as possible."

"Why?"

"Because he's got what you need to relieve all that tension you're holding. Something that doesn't require batteries. You feel me?"

Thirty minutes and two fresh-squeezed orange juice drinks later, Marvin approached their table with a loaded tray. French toast, eggs, hash browns, bacon, sausage, and a bowl of freshly sliced fruit. Naomi had calmed down by the time the food arrived. She dug in with relish and heartily ate. It was some of the best food she'd ever tasted.

As they finished up, Marvin came out of the kitchen again. "How was everything?"

"You cooked all of that?" Kristy asked.

"Every bit of it."

"This your restaurant?"

"No." Marvin laughed.

"Well, it should be, because when it comes to cooking, you're the straight-up boss."

"Thank you. Naomi?"

She ran a finger through a small bit of syrup on her plate, licked it and said casually, "It was alright."

Marvin looked pointedly at a plate so clean it

almost looked washed, picked it up, and caught Naomi's eye. "I see."

Everyone laughed at that, even a few from surrounding tables.

"It was good, Marvin," she admitted. "Not enough to beat me in the contest, but enough to where I see that you know how to do your job."

"You are something else."

"Thank you."

Kristy looked disgusted. "She's something else alright."

"Whatever." Naomi looked at Marvin. "Can we get the check, please?"

"I'll take care of that. But only if I can get something from you."

"What?"

He smiled. "Your number."

Naomi sat back as if to ponder the request.

Kristy sat up. "If she won't give you hers, you can have mine."

"Back off, chick," Naomi warned.

"Ha! I thought so. You may act crazy, but you haven't totally lost your mind."

They left the restaurant, thoughts of the incident and Marvin temporarily forgotten after Kristy complained of feeling sick and Naomi played nursemaid. But later that night, Naomi replayed the day's events in her head. She didn't regret defending her cousin, but admitted to herself that she could have used a calmer approach. She admitted something else, too. Something she'd downplayed when Kristy said it. She thought Marvin was cute, and sexy, too. And if he played his cards right, she'd offer him a tasty treat that wasn't on anybody's menu. But only after she'd won the truck and the money. She'd keep her guard up until then.

6

Fourteen hours from the time he'd left the restaurant, Marvin flopped back on the king-size bed, naked as the day he cabbage-patched into the world. Rarely hungry after cooking through a long shift, he'd visited a drive-through, bought an extra-large chocolate shake, and placed the remainder in the freezer while he showered off the day. He'd retrieved it and now had all he'd need for the remainder of the evening—the rest of the shake, a bottle of water, a bag of hot chips, a box of cookies, and the phone where he'd just tapped the speaker button after placing a call.

"This is Naomi. What the hell you want?" Said cheerfully, with the words strung together in a way that made them melodious and made Marvin laugh.

"Girl! That's no way to answer a phone."

"I usually don't, but I knew it was you."

"How'd you know? I didn't give you my phone number."

"I knew."

"Yeah, right. What are you doing?"

"Talking to you."

"Do you have a smart answer for everything?"

"Smart girl. Smart answers. No dumb ones, sorry. Hope you can keep up."

"Dang, Naomi. All that mouth, I know you don't have a man."

"You mean," she said seductively, "with all this mouth . . . how many do I have."

For Marvin it was a double, a triple, a quadruple entendre. He shifted in the bed.

"So was that one of your girls who almost got slapped today?"

A chuckle. "Who, Charlotte?"

"I guess so. It was getting ready to be Charmin on account of how I was going to wipe off the floor with her rude, unprofessional ass."

"Charlotte has . . . issues."

"Are you one of them?"

"She wishes I was."

"I was about to be one, and she wouldn't have liked it at all. You came to the table just in time. Superman's timing couldn't have been any better."

"So . . . you think I'm Superman, huh?"

"You probably think you're Superman," she said.

"I'm just going by what the ladies tell me."

"Oh, Lord, help me! I can fertilize a football field with all the crap you're talking!"

"Yeah, whatever. Why'd you come in today, then?" he asked.

"The same reason everybody else did. Hungry. Wanted to eat."

"How many places did you pass up to get to mine?"

"How many places did all of those other people pass up?"

Marvin laughed, pulled the sheet over himself to ward off the chill. The woman's sarcasm and constant barbs should be getting on his nerves. So why did they make him feel good instead, almost giddy?

"I'll go ahead and say it because you already know. When it comes to a good, down-home breakfast, nobody does it better than the Soul Spot."

"Nobody does it better than them, when I'm cooking."

"Your cooking made my cousin sick."

"What?"

"After we left the restaurant, she got sick."

"Did you?"

"No."

"And y'all ate the same thing, right?"

A pause and then, "Right."

"Then she may have gotten sick, but it wasn't from my food."

"I don't know . . ."

"Well, I do."

"Hmm."

"The French toast you ate today, had you ordered it before?"

"Yes."

"Was it the same or better, tell the truth."

"Well, since you're begging for compliments . . . it was better, and delicious."

"What was different? I want to test your palate, see how well developed it is."

"Then you should have called me earlier, right after I ate. That was breakfast. I've had lunch, dinner, and a couple snacks since then."

"That's the reason? Okay."

"That caramel-pecan syrup was everything. So good. I tasted caramel in that . . . and pecans."

"Girl, you're crazy."

"Thank you."

"And even though we don't allow boxing in the dining room, I like how you took up for your cousin today, your thoughts about family being everything. That's how we Carters roll. You must come from a big family, too."

"Not really."

"Then why do you feel so strongly about family?"

"Maybe that's why, because I have such a small one." She paused. Marvin started to make a joke but detected a subtle shift in the tone of her voice and remained quiet. "I grew up with my grand-mother, mostly. Kristy is my cousin, but we're more like sisters."

"That sounds like a family to me."

"But not a typical one. Parents are missing from the picture."

"Why? It's none of my business and if you don't want to talk about it, I understand."

"No, it's okay." Said in a quiet voice tinged with vulnerability, one that sounded as though it was not okay at all. "My dad left when I was really little, maybe four or five. I barely remember him—what he looked like, or anything else. There's a blurred image of a big guy, loud. One day he came home with a stuffed animal bigger than me. A rainbow-colored unicorn. I was so excited, slept with it and everything. That's my only real memory of him and me interacting. He left shortly after that. I don't know why."

"What about your mom?"

"She died."

That's all she said, in a way that told Marvin that's all she wanted to say. He obliged her, even as the sadness in her tone caused a crack in his heart. A tear just big enough for a bit of her essence to slip inside it. For some of the bricks in his wall against being attracted to her to tumble out.

"What about you? As conceited and self-assured as you act, I'm sure there were plenty women around to spoil you. Squeeze those big jowls you probably had and say, 'Isn't he a cute snuggle bug.'"

"I grew up in a house with four brothers. My dad's an army vet. Wasn't too much snuggling going on."

The shield was firmly back in place, but in that moment he got it. Why she portrayed herself as a loudmouth badass, brimming with confidence and devil-may-care. It was her armor, a shield. One she'd let down so that he could see who she really was. He liked the view.

"But you're the baby, right?"

"No, the fourth of five. And we have a big sister, Anita, who isn't our biological sister but might as well be. She was our next-door neighbor and spent more time in our house than she did in her own. Ironically, she'd lost her mother also. Mom stepped in and filled that space."

"Like Nana."

"That's what you call your grandmother?"

"Yeah. Are you guys close?"

"Very, in age and everything else. Mama wouldn't have it any other way. Growing up, Dad was gone for long stretches of time. He fought in the Middle East. Never talked about it, not to us kids anyway. Mama was determined not to lose us to the streets. Couldn't roam the block at will or be out after dark. So we mostly played with each other. Back then we thought it was unfair and fought just as much as we got along. But looking at it now, that tough love helped us become the men we are now and probably saved all of our lives."

"Your parents still together?"

"Very much so. They've been married over thirty-five years."

"Wow. You don't see that much these days."

"Didn't see it much back then, either. Our block was an exception though. Almost every household was a two-parent family with values, standards, and goals for the kids. Everybody stuck together. Partied together, kids fought and played together, everything."

"Is that how the block party got started?"

"I guess so. Never really gave it much thought. We stayed close to home mainly because it was more fun hanging out on our block and with our families than hanging with anyone else. So, when's the last time you came out to one?"

"A couple years ago. Went with my cousin Kristy, matter of fact. The one with me at the restaurant. So that big festival, with all the stages and the block shut down, just grew out of families hanging out?"

"I think it just . . . happened. A couple neighbors decided to barbecue together one year and then another family joined them. And then another. It kept growing from there. Got so big we eventually got permission to shut down the block and turned it into a street party, one that is now put on by our neighborhood association. My mom has always been very active in it. One of their goals was having a close-knit group that felt like family, where everybody looked after and took care of each other. Where any grown-up had the same authority as a parent and any kid was looked after by any adult as their own. Having the annual street party was something where everyone could participate, and those who'd moved away could come back and catch up. It kept growing and more people kept coming until it became an event not to miss, the way it is now."

"How many women are you messing with?"

"Whoa. That was quite a segue."

"Really? I thought it was a question."

"Why do you want to know?"

"So it's like that, huh? Too many to name."

"Ha! How do you figure?"

"You're dancing around the question harder than Michael Jackson danced onstage. That usually happens when one is avoiding the question that's been asked. I don't care anyway, just making conversation. The only man I'm focused on right now is the one who will give me the keys to a food truck and a check to get started."

"How is someone going to give you the keys to my food truck?"

"You mean my food truck, fool. There's no way you're winning that contest. We might as well get that straight now."

"I agree. We need to get it straight. I'm winning, but I'm going to need an assistant. If you play your cards right, you might get the job."

"Yeah, someone to assist you off the floor after you fall out from losing. But wait, you've got your girlfriends to help with that. Including that old white woman feeling you up yesterday."

"What old white woman?"

"There was more than one?"

Marvin laughed out loud. "You mean Abbey? I'm sure she'd be mad to hear you call her old."

"I don't know her name and she looks old. But I saw you all hugged up with her when I walked past where the desserts were being tested."

"So you were stalking me."

"Don't flatter yourself, dude. I was on my way to the room right across from there, where you came over once you got the hat."

"Abbey isn't old. She's mid-forties, maybe."

"She can tell somebody else that lie. That face has seen at least fifty ball drops, maybe more."

"Ball drops?"

"Yeah, Times Square on New Year's Eve."

"Oh. I think the gray in Abbey's hair makes her look older. She was one of my instructors from culinary school. I don't have a girlfriend right now. You applying?"

"Maybe, but I command a high salary."

"No problem. After winning Food Truck Bucks, I'll have fifty Gs."

"You mean after winning you'll have a job. On my truck."

"Girl, I can't wait to shut that mouth!"

"How are you going to do that?" Naomi's voice turned seductive. "By covering it with your big yap-yap?"

"Hmm, alright now. You might want to be careful, baby girl. Don't play with fire unless you want to get burned."

"I can handle the heat."

"I bet you can. All nice and juicy looking. And not just your lips. In fact, that's what I'm going to call you. Juicy."

"Ah, that's cute. My grandfather used to call Nana 'Juicy Fruit.'"

"For you no fruity, just juicy."

"You can give me nicknames and flirt all you want. I'm still going to win."

Marvin didn't dispute the claim. Why not let her enjoy the fantasy? There was no doubt in his mind that Marvin Carter would win the competition. Maybe he'd get a bonus by winning over Naomi Carson, too. But for now . . . he allowed her to dream.

7

Naomi thought the wait would be endless, but the rest of May flew by in a blur and in no time she awoke to a new month and the first preliminary round of Food Truck Bucks. Her and Marvin had texted back and forth a few times but hadn't talked since that night after the general call. Her dating calendar stayed as barren as the desert, and more than once Naomi had almost called him. But she figured a girlfriend, or friend with benefits, or booty call, or whatever, had kept him busy and she didn't want to come off as a thirsty girl. So Naomi had spent her nights with Mr. Big, her dildo, and had a blast partying in Vegas with her fantasy husband, the lead singer in Boyz II Men. As of today, right now, party time was over. It was time to go to work and win her freedom from the 99 Cents Store and Nana's house. She dressed with care, telling herself it was about putting forward her best face and had nothing to do with the fact that the man she'd missed after just one meeting would be there, too.

"Where are you going, baby? They got you working weekends again?"

Naomi reached the door but stopped and turned at Nana's question. "No, Nana, I'm off today. I'm headed to the convention center. The preliminary rounds happen this month, remember?"

"That's what I thought until you came out of your room just now. That's a pretty fancy outfit for cooking."

"What, this old thing?"

Technically correct if, like a car, a top depreciated the minute it left the store, since Naomi had just bought it last week. The blue and white vertical-striped, wraparound number accentuated her forty double-Ds while slimming the tire around her middle. The thigh-teasing design downplayed her hips, and the three-quarter slacks and sling-back mules helped bolster the illusion that thunder did not clap with her thighs.

"You look very nice, dear."

"Thank you, Nana." She opened the door.

"I'm sure your young man will think so, too."

"Nana, the only person I'm trying to impress is myself!"

"Very good, child, and sounded real convincing. Did you practice in the mirror?"

"You know what . . ." Naomi made a face as she turned to leave. The delightful tinkle of her grandmother's giggle followed her out the door.

She got into the car and backed out of the drive, but didn't turn on the stereo, which was normally the first thing that happened after buckling her belt. She didn't tap the wheel to call Kristy either. For Naomi it was time to think, get focused, be prepared for whatever test or exercise the judges had concocted for this elimination round. The only hint given last week was that there was no need to bring anything from home as they'd be judged on something prepared there. On the spot. But that's as much as they'd say. Not whether it was an appetizer or an entrée. Not how much time they'd have to prepare the meal. Not whether they'd be working alone or in teams. Just be ready to cook. Those were the parting words. Every night after getting home from work, Nana had met Naomi in the kitchen, where they'd stood side by side trying this and preparing that. Admittedly, desserts were her weak spot, so that's where most of the time was spent. After tasting Marvin's pecan log cake, Naomi knew she'd have to create a masterpiece to win it all. She'd kept her comments nonchalant, but that man had put his foot, knee, and thigh into that dish! The thought had been reinforced the next day at the restaurant, when he'd made that batch of caramel-pecan syrup, just for their table. He knew what he was doing. Giving them extras. Being all friendly. Trying to whittle down her defenses and throw her off her game. She'd eat any sweet he put in front of her, but when it came to the competition, Naomi was taking no prisoners!

"Yes! That's right!" Feeling mentally ready to face whatever got thrown to her, she reached over and pressed the button on what had been her theme song for the past year, by a singer named Jan Baker, the woman who'd knocked Beyoncé off the throne and become Naomi's shero. She danced in her seat, zoomed around a couple of Saturday-morning sightseers, and exited off the freeway into downtown, singing as though onstage.

" You be you and I'll be me. I'm the best me I ever could be. Yeah! Don't fit your mold? Don't give a damn. You be who you are and I'll be who I am!'"

Inside the convention center, signs directed Naomi to a different room than had been used last week. This one, she saw, was set up much more as she'd initially imagined. She quickly counted twenty cooking stations, each having a full-size range and a large, island-style prep table with a wooden top. A blender, block of cutting knives, and a mandoline were among the items to the right of the otherwise empty counter. Beneath the prep counter were cookware, bowls of various sizes, and a bevy of cooking utensils. Having scoped out the "rink" where she'd slay the opposition, Naomi looked around for a sign or assistant to tell her where she needed to check in and what she needed to do. About twenty feet away from her was a frantic-looking young woman with tousled brown hair, clutching a tablet, wearing a headset and talking nonstop into the mouthpiece. She wore a white shirt with

FOOD TRUCK BUCKS emblazoned across the back. Naomi walked toward her. The woman looked up when she was about two feet away and pointed to her right without pausing the conversation. Naomi was about to get an attitude until her eyes followed where the worker's finger directed and settled on a rectangular table under a sign that read START HERE. Three women sat beneath the sign wearing tired smiles, pointing out directions and typing on laptops. Naomi walked over, got signed in, and learned that all further instructions would be given out by the host. Finally, she could relax. Grabbing a complimentary bottle of water out of a huge ice-filled container, she downed a swig and for the first time since arriving took in the people around her. Of all the contestants she'd met last week, Marvin was the only one she knew for sure had gone to the next round.

"Naomi!"

Speak of the stranger. She turned to see Marvin, looking so fresh, so clean in black jeans, black Tims, and a starched white shirt. Tails out, like the cool guys wore them. Next to him was the thin, older-looking woman with frizzy, blondish-brown hair and a tight smile suggesting she'd rather Marvin had not called out to her. Looked like Abbey was down for a little swirl. Naomi smiled as she walked to meet them, adding extra sway to her hips just to make no-hip Abbey even more jealous. This even as another part of her thought, *Leave that poor woman alone.*

"Hey, Marvin."

"All right, all right," he said, nodding as he checked her out approvingly. "I see you. Are you ready?"

"Born ready." Naomi's response was to him, but her eyes were on thin frizzy, who she now saw wore an earpiece and shirt like the young woman who'd pointed her in the right direction.

Marvin looked between the two women. "Have you met Abbey?"

"No."

"Naomi, this is Abbey. Abbey, Naomi."

The handshake was as lackluster as the two women's desire to know each other.

"Abbey was an instructor at the culinary school I attended. She's one of the coordinators for the show."

"You knew her beforehand? Isn't that like . . . a conflict of interest or something?"

"I'm not judging," Abbey replied.

"But still . . ." Naomi's eyes and expression filled in the blanks.

"Girl, I don't need anybody's help to beat you."

"Ah, here we go."

"Yep. Here we go."

"Marvin," Abbey interrupted. "I've got to run. Remember to call me later."

"Alright."

"Promise? Because last week you forgot to return my call."

"I was busy, Abs. Today for sure."

"Okay." She hugged Marvin, ignored Naomi, and walked away.

Naomi chuckled. "Alright, Abbey. Go ahead and ignore me because I'm with your man."

"Stop it, Juicy. I'm not her man."

"Not yet."

"Not ever. She's not my type."

"She wishes she was."

"How do you figure?"

"Like you don't know she was flirting." Naomi batted her eyes. "Call me later."

"Stop with all of that, she was just being nice. She wants me to go back and finish school, get my culinary degree."

"Trust and believe she wants to get something, too."

Any comeback Marvin had was interrupted as one of the organizers signaled that the next round of competition was about to begin. Naomi watched a good-looking young man with ruddy skin and a shock of brown hair bounce to the front of the room.

She leaned toward Marvin. "Who's that?"

"I don't know. His face looks familiar . . ."

"Good afternoon, Food Truck Buckaroos! My name is Ted Reynolds, your host for this next round of competition. Some of you may remember me from the show—"

"*Power Games*," Marvin said, under his breath. "I knew I'd seen his face before."

"I was a little younger then," Ted went on, brandishing a toothy smile. "I still take acting roles here and there, but these days my primary employment and my passion is the restaurant Claws that I own with my husband, Joe, back in my hometown of

Bristol, Rhode Island. If any of you are ever in that neck of the woods, feel free to come in for some of the best seafood on the East Coast. But enough about me. I'm here to tell you what you have to do to move forward. Your job is to form a group and prepare dishes that are tastier and more cohesive than the other group. Besides cooking, any idea of the point to this next challenge?"

"Teamwork," someone yelled out.

"Exactly! No matter how well you cook, a successful food business cannot be created alone. You have to be able to lead and motivate as well as you can season and plate. That is why the next round will be a series of team challenges. Each member of the team must make a contribution to the final set of dishes that can be judged alone. What will those be? Not so fast. You'll find out after teams are chosen."

Ted continued his instructions, and explained how the teams would be chosen. The contestants reached into a set of five bags with ten red balls and ten black ones. The reds would be on one side, the blacks on another. Naomi barely heard any of that though. She was too busy trying to strategize how she could position herself to be on Marvin's team, or at least on his side with the same-colored ball. She didn't get either. Her first mistake was deciding to stay standing next to him. Instead of counting off every ten persons, as she'd hoped, they counted off every other person to choose from the bag. When Marvin pulled a red one she wanted one, too. Nope, got the black ball. Life wasn't fair.

It doesn't matter. Some people are going home today, but it won't be me.

She told this to herself, tried to bolster her confidence. She knew she was a good cook. But after tasting his cake last week, she had to admit something if only to herself. Marvin might be just a little bit better.

8

Marvin didn't have to say anything about wanting to lead the challenge of preparing hot and cold appetizers. When the buzzer sounded, signaling their five minutes of planning time, the people on Marvin's team all looked at him. He jumped in as though he'd run a crew all his life. His team gathered around the island. He picked up a Sharpie that lay on a notepad and wrote HOT and COLD at the top in large, bold strokes.

"Let's showcase what we each do best, giving our dishes flavor, texture, color, and presentation. I'm thinking some kind of soup, maybe with home-made croutons—"

A tatted woman with fierce green eyes and streaked, purple hair interrupted. "I've got a killer crispy, crusty cheese cracker that would pair perfectly with tomato."

Marvin held up a finger in agreement. He checked out her arms, covered with ink. "Good idea,

Tat. That's the direction I was thinking. Will it hold up in the soup, though?"

"Yeah. Drop em on top right before we serve the judges. They won't get soggy at all."

"Cool. I've got the soup. What else?" He looked around. "C'mon, y'all. Team effort, let's go!"

"I can do a corn, red bell pepper, green onion, celery salsa to sprinkle over the top. Tossed in a little olive oil and agave, splash of lime. It'll pair well with the tomatoes and cheese."

It was a guy Marvin had met that morning. Waist-length blond locks stuffed under a dreadlocks cap. Bob Marley tee. Gauge-pierced ears. Energy beads around his neck and wrist. Grew up in Oregon. Moved to LA six months ago. His name was Cody, but Marvin rarely used a person's government name. Five minutes into their conversation, Marvin nicknamed him Zen.

"Add freshness and, you know, lighten up the dish."

"I agree. Sounds good, Zen. So we're good on the hot appetizer." Marvin looked around the circle. "Who has a cold dish idea besides salad? Because four out of these five teams will probably be doing that."

A petite Latina with coal-black curly hair wrapped into a topknot suggested mini open-faced sand-wiches with a "faux gras" pâté spread that she'd make. That would be spread on a homemade pita, the contribution of a cook who'd grown up in an

Israeli kibbutz Popsicle chops, delicious handheld treats, rounded out their menu.

Marvin glanced over at Naomi. He was worried. She'd pulled the black ball with a guy named Jeremy that he'd nicknamed Airhead on account of his arrogance and total obliviousness to the fact that he got on everyone's nerves. Looked as though he was captaining the team. *No bueno.* If something went wrong, Marvin believed Airhead wouldn't hesitate to throw Naomi under the bus. He tried to get her attention and send a warning, but the bell sounded for the thirty-minute appetizer round. Marvin grabbed one of three baskets the teams had been supplied and joined the others in a race toward a row of industrial-sized, glass-front refrigerators at the back of the room. Foods had been grouped for easy access. He ran to the end and the two filled with produce. Others beat him in quickness, but he won out in size and determination. Jockeyed with several others for his preferred beefsteak tomatoes, fresh corn, and other vegetables, and handfuls of fresh herbs. He ran to the baskets holding onions, garlic, shallots, and leeks. After that he went for the dairy shelf and the heavy cream needed for his silky tomato soup. Once back at their station he began slicing and dicing, all while directing, coaching, and encouraging the rest of the team. Thirty minutes later, his group presented a well-balanced set of appetizers to the judges and got good ratings. A couple dishes on Airhead's team got dinged—one for needing salt

and the other for dough still raw in the middle—
but they praised Naomi's dumpling. She and Marvin
made it to the next round. He was almost more
relieved for her than himself, but not because he'd
caught feelings for her. Not like that. She was nice
and juicy the way he liked his women. Had a mouth
on her though, and thought she could compete
with him in the kitchen. *The nerve!* Even as he
thought that, he looked around for her and was
disappointed when it became clear she'd already
left the room. Without saying a word? Funny how
one could miss the same mouth that got on one's
nerves.

After a quick chat with some of the other remaining contestants, Marvin looked for Tiffany Reed, the
cook he'd nicknamed Tat. Her croutons were delicious and had helped to set their dish apart. He
wanted to thank her, maybe get the recipe. But
after looking into the last set of rooms used for the
contest, he figured he'd missed her and headed
back down the hall to the exit. On the way he
peeked into the other rooms, just in case he'd
missed Tat the first time. He reached the room
nearest the exit. Someone was in there, but it wasn't
Tat. He jerked his head back, but not quickly
enough.

"Looking for me?"

"Hey, Abs."

He told himself that it was Naomi's teasing that
had him paranoid, that Abbey wasn't really looking

at him like a rib slathered in sauce. He decided to be clear in any case.

"I was looking for one of the girls on my team today. She made some killer grilled-cheese croutons and I wanted to get the recipe."

"I can help you with that."

"Oh, yeah? You tasted them?"

"Don't have to, I've made them."

"If your recipe tastes as good as Tat's did, then you might be able to help me."

"I can help you with a lot of things. They'll taste even better."

Said in such a way that made Marvin uncomfortable, and left no doubt that his former teacher was coming on to him. Marvin ignored the blatant invitation, and hoped Abbey would get the hint.

"Thanks, but I can wait until next week and get it from her. Alright then, Abs. I'll see you later."

"Are you leaving?"

"Yeah, I'm on my way to work."

"I'm heading out, too. Wait and we can go together."

Marvin hid his chagrin and gave a casual look around to see who was near them. The last thing he needed was for Naomi to see him and Abbey together and learn that she was right about Abbey making a move.

"Okay, I'm ready." He held open the door so Abbey could exit first. "What's the name of where you work again? The Soul Spoon?"

"Soul Spot."

"I knew it was Soul-something. Typical soul food menu? Greens, chicken . . ."

"Comfort food, not all of it Southern."

"I'll have to come check it out. You say it's in southern LA?"

"Off of Manchester, not too far from the 405." He gave her the exact address. She plugged it into her phone. "Is that why you wanted me to call you, to get the name of where I work?"

"No." Abbey checked to see if anyone was close by. No one was, but she lowered her voice anyway. "It's about one of the contestants, that Naomi girl. You should steer clear of her."

Marvin frowned. "Why?"

The light changed. Abbey remained quiet as she stepped off the curb. Marvin did, too, and glanced at her a couple times as they walked through the intersection. "Why are you warning me about Naomi?" he repeated, when they reached the other side.

"It's nothing I can put my finger on, but something tells me she'll do anything to try and win this contest, including sabotaging anyone she views as competition."

"I'm not worried about Naomi or anybody else. Besides, how can she sabotage me?"

"By having you engage in behavior that is inappropriate."

Marvin stopped just inside the parking structure. "What kind of inappropriate behavior? I just met that girl."

"I watched her today, watched her as she watched you. You were on separate teams, but she was aware of your every move. Call it women's intuition or a teacher's sixth sense, but I don't trust her motives when it comes to befriending you. Fifty thousand dollars and a food truck is a life-changing grand prize. Some will go to any lengths to eliminate their competition. You, dear one, are a major threat." She placed a hand on his forearm. "So be careful."

Marvin looked pointedly at his arm, then up. "What about you, Abbey? Somebody could see your actions right now and question where you're coming from."

"I'm just a teacher being friendly." Abbey squeezed his arm, her fingers sliding over bare skin before she released it. "Where are you parked?"

"Second floor."

"My car is right there." She held up a key fob and released the lock. "Come on. I'll drive you up."

Marvin almost declined the offer, but curiosity at what she was about to say won out. He followed her to the car and got into the passenger seat. She placed the key in the ignition, but turned to him without starting the car. "You've always been one of my favorite students, Marvin. Not only because you can cook, but because you're handsome and funny and know how to make a woman feel good, even a plain old hag like me."

What the hell? When did I make you feel good . . . and how? He almost told her that she wasn't a hag, but didn't want to sound flirtatious.

"But more than any of that, though, I believe in you and your talent. You could win this thing, Marvin. You deserve to win. Yes, there are talented, more experienced chefs, but you have an innate sense for cooking that can't be taught. The judges see it, too. I probably shouldn't tell you, but your pecan log cake was the most talked about dessert from that first day. There were other impressive dishes. I don't want you to feel you can relax and coast through this thing. But you have what it takes to win. Your winning is all I care about. I want to see you secure a great future for yourself as owner of a premier food truck in a city known for them, maybe even parlay that into your own restaurant.

"People are watching, Marvin, and the competition is strong. Someone could see you and Naomi . . . being friendly, misinterpret what's happening, and find a way to somehow use it against you."

"See what? Use what? I haven't done anything with Naomi that I haven't done with the other contestants—talk, be friendly, joke around."

"You didn't see what I saw earlier today. Naomi's dish was respectable, but there's no way she'll win. Not based on her cooking skills, anyway. Mark my words, she's going to make a move to start something personal. Get you distracted and off of your game. Maybe even disqualified."

"What, contestants can't be friends?"

"There's no specific rule against fraternizing, but there is a chance that if someone thought you were knowingly or even unknowingly helping her in any way, it could jeopardize your chances of winning the contest."

"How would I help her? Unless we're on the same team, and if that were the case we'd be helping each other anyway, right?"

Abbey let out the type of sigh Marvin remembered her using when out of patience with someone who couldn't absorb what she was trying to teach. She started the car; looked straight ahead.

"You probably think I'm meddling. I am. But it's only because I care about you, and your future. I want you to focus on winning, and I'll do whatever I can to help you, within the legal parameters of the contest, of course. I'm not a judge, but I've taught cooking in this town for fifteen years. I know a lot of people in the industry and that comes with a bit of influence." She looked at him. "Do you understand?"

Marvin stared back, his reply slow and deliberate as he waded through the various implications of what she'd said. "I think so."

"Good!" She backed out of the parking space and headed toward the ramp. "I've really missed you, Marvin. You were not only one of my top students, but just such a bright spot in my life. You were young then—what, eighteen when you came to the school?"

"Nineteen."

"And how old are you now?"

"Twenty-seven. How old are you?"

She gasped. "Marvin, you should know it's impolite to ask a woman's age."

"You just asked mine!"

She smiled and tossed back her hair in a way that caused him to look past the frizzy, unkempt style, past the bright yellow organizer tee and khaki cargoes, and notice bright green eyes, a spray of freckles across her nose and the hint of a dimple on her right cheek. He'd not really paid attention to her like that before, but looking at her now, Marvin realized she wasn't a bad-looking woman. She had potential. She might even be younger than Naomi imagined.

"I'm forty-three."

"That's not old. Why are you hiding it?"

Abbey shrugged. "I live in LA. No one here tells their real age." Abbey reached the second level. "Which row are you?"

"Last one, on the end." Marvin pointed out the way. "Black SUV. Right there."

She stopped behind it and looked at Marvin. "Don't forget what we discussed. Don't share it either. Stay focused on winning this competition."

Marvin nodded. "I'll do that."

"Good."

He got out of the car. "Thanks, Abs."

She winked. "See you later, handsome."

Marvin walked to his car almost in a daze. Naomi had told him to watch out for Abbey, and now Abbey had just told him to watch out for Naomi! He wished it hadn't, but what Abbey said made him think about Naomi in a different light. What if Abbey was right, and Naomi was just coming on to him to try and get the advantage? What if she'd warned him about Abbey so he'd put up a wall and not listen to something Abbey found out about her? But what if Naomi was right and Abbey was just trying to block what she saw happening between the two of them? He thought he'd been cool with his feelings toward Naomi, but maybe to someone like Abbey the attraction had been obvious. If someone like Abbey could tell he was feeling Naomi then Naomi had to know, too. And what if there was an ulterior motive, as Abbey believed? What if all of Naomi's flirting was just a game to try and catch him off guard, maybe get him kicked off the show?

By the time he pulled into the Soul Spot parking lot, Marvin had made a decision. He was going to keep the atmosphere friendly between him and Naomi, but not take the attraction to another level until after the contest was over. At least, that's what he thought. But when an image of Naomi's luscious backside rose up in his mind's eye, Marvin's determination wavered. There were three more weeks to the competition, and if she lost, Naomi might not want to be with him. Marvin honestly didn't know whether or not he could take that chance, or wait that long.

Turns out Naomi was sharing similar feelings in another part of town.

"I need to just do him and get him out of my system."

Naomi paced the narrow section of exposed

carpet in Kristy's living room, the rest of it covered with furniture, boxes and knick-knack-filled baskets. She hadn't calmed down since leaving Marvin last night.

Kristy watched her cousin with slightly concerned, slightly confused eyes. "Why are you treating him differently than other guys? You see something you want, you go after it. That's the Naomi I know. This one here"—Kristy waved her hand at her still pacing cousin—"all nervous and unsure of herself? I don't know who she is."

Naomi walked over to the couch where Kristy returned to folding clothes. She removed a stack of towels from the cushion and placed them in a basket, picked up a decorative pillow—the other item in her way—and plopped down on the well-worn seat. A stack of clothes on the middle cushion fell to the floor. Naomi didn't notice.

Kristy did. "Dang, Nay. Look what you did!"

Naomi bristled at her cousin's sharp tone. "Don't bite my head off. It's just a pile of clothes." Shaking her head, she reached toward the pile. "I don't know what's gotten into you, but it needs to come out. You were bitchy while in Vegas and now it seems the bitch is back."

"She never left."

"What's the matter? Gary still mad that you went to Vegas without him?"

Kristy shrugged. "I don't care about him, and the man I really want doesn't care about me."

"I told you to quit being a side chick. If a man

can't take you out in the daytime, your ass shouldn't take him in at night."

"Mind your business," Kristy replied, in a more cordial voice. "I know what I'm doing."

"If you say so." Naomi continued refolding the clothes that had fallen, and in the silence that followed, rearranged her judgmental attitude, too, before changing the subject.

"I really like Marvin." There. She'd finally said it. Honestly, the truth felt kind of good rolling off her tongue. "The first time I've felt this way in a long time."

"I can see you being attracted to him. But you're sounding like he has you whipped, and to hear you tell it, y'all haven't screwed."

"We haven't."

"Then you don't even know the man."

"That's just the thing, Tee. I feel like I do. It's crazy, but from the moment we met it was like we'd known each other forever. I was attracted to him, but he got on my nerves. In a good way, though. Like someone you like so much you can't stand them at all. Even when we're arguing it's almost fun. A challenge to see who can one-up the other. He has that magnetic kind of energy, where everyone likes him." She frowned. "And I mean everyone."

Kristy looked up. "He's got a girlfriend?"

"He said he didn't. But he's got a bunch of women who want to be his girlfriend. I can tell that just by what's happened already."

"Like what?"

"Like that girl at the Spot, the one whose attitude was shitty toward us because she likes him. And then there's this coordinator who was his teacher in culinary school trying to push up on him. I really don't need the extra aggravation. I should just ignore him, and focus on winning the contest."

"There you go. Leave him alone, simple as that."

"Leaving him alone isn't simple at all."

"Girl, which one is it? You want him and then you don't want him. You can be with him and then you can't. Make up your mind!"

"I want to be with him, but I don't know if I should. Doing so might mess up my chances of winning the contest. But then after I win he might not want to be with me, and I'll never find out if the dick's good or not."

"Then go on and be with him, Nay. That's the only way you're going to find out."

Kristy huffed as she stood and balanced a large stack of towels in her hands before heading down the hallway to the linen closet.

Naomi watched her retreating back, mad at her cousin's nonchalant attitude. Kristy made it sound so easy. "He probably isn't even that good," Naomi mumbled. "Probably walking around with an enormous ego and an itty-bitty ditty."

A howl from the hallway.

"Oh, you heard that?"

"I sure did." Kristy retraced her steps down the hallway and entered the kitchen.

"Tee-hee!"

"Hey, cuzzo, you want a margarita? I can't make you call Marvin, but I can get you drunk."

Naomi slid off the couch to join Kristy in the kitchen. Getting inebriated sounded like a safe option. Curing a hangover was much easier than nursing a hurting heart.

9

The next morning, Marvin rolled out of bed around ten a.m. and after a quick wash-up headed for the kitchen. On Sundays that was usually exclusively his mama Liz's domain. But his parents were gone. They'd spent the night with Anita at a casino in Palm Springs. Today it was just the boys. It had been a while since he'd cooked for all of his brothers, and even though he'd been over a stove for almost ten hours the night before, he was looking forward to preparing their meal. Known for using them as guinea pigs to test out new recipes, today he planned to stick with American breakfast classics—eggs, bacon, sausage, hash browns, grits, pancakes, and homemade biscuits. Something for everyone.

Marvin placed a tray of thick-cut bacon and another one of sausage into the oven, poured olive oil into a cast-iron skillet, and pulled out a jumbo bag of prepared hash browns from the freezer. He grabbed green peppers and sweet onions from the vegetable bin. After placing those contents on the counter, he scrolled through his iPod library for Tupac's *Greatest Hits*. Bobbing his head to "California Love," he'd just begun dicing the onion when he heard someone at the door. Halfway to the hallway, he heard jangling keys and knew it was his baby bro, Barry. He opened the door and offered a quick shoulder bump before returning to the kitchen and his task.

"Dang, bro!" Barry followed Marvin and the tantalizing aromas. "You've got it smelling good in here!"

"I'm just getting started." Marvin finished dicing the onion, tossed the pieces into the oil, and reached for the large green pepper. "What, that fine chick you brought over to Byron's house don't feed you?"

"Yolanda's skills are used to handle a different kind of appetite."

The brothers continued to banter back and forth, with Marvin continuing to work his cooking magic and Barry wanting to "test" every dish removed from the stove. By the time Douglas, Byron, and another sibling, Nelson, arrived, everything was ready. Marvin set up the food buffet-style on the kitchen counter. He filled a bucket with ice and set out cartons of orange and apple juice. The men grabbed plates and piled them high, grabbed their drink choices, and found seats to chow down.

"I hope the food is to your liking," Barry said after swallowing a bite. "Not the best I've cooked, but—"

Nelson delivered an elbow jab to Barry's arm.

"Shut up, Negro! You didn't cook anything. You can't even boil an egg."

"He can't boil water," Byron added.

"I'll tell you like I told Marvin about my girl Yolanda. My skills are put to better use in another room in the house."

"What?" Doug asked. "The bathroom? Cause you are definitely full of—"

"Not while we're eating!" Byron interjected.

The brothers laughed. Barry appeared unfazed by the good-natured ribbing. "Back off, fellas. Jealousy is an ugly thing."

Marvin spread jelly on his biscuit. "Yeah, well, so is your face!"

Another round of laughter as the siblings enjoyed Marvin's food and each other's company. These brothers and best friends had teased, argued, and fought with each other all of their lives and were closer than they'd ever been.

"This is good, Marv," Nelson said, after shoveling in a forkful of cheesy eggs and following them up with a bite of jellied biscuit. "You really should open up your own place."

"Hey, speaking of having your own, how's that contest going?"

"I don't want to jinx it, Byron, but so far, so good. In a few weeks the dream of having my own spot just might come true."

"How is the winner determined?" Doug asked.

Marvin explained the process. "The final ten will go head-to-head and be taped for television."

"When will it air?" Barry asked.

Marvin shrugged. "Whenever it does, I'll be on it."

Doug reached for a napkin, then poured more apple juice into his glass. "Who's your competition so far?"

"Nobody," Marvin confidently replied. "No, for real, there are a few in the game who will give me a run for my money. A few executive chefs who've run award-winning kitchens. This Cordon Bleu–trained hotshot that claims to have cooked in kitchens all over the world. Naomi thinks she's competition, but she isn't."

"Naomi's the one you're digging?" Byron asked.

"What makes you think that?"

Doug answered. "Because she's the only one you mentioned by name."

"Yeah, whatever," Marvin replied. But the smile on his face more than suggested that Byron was right. "Naomi's cool. But she's also competition. I don't know if dating her is a good idea."

He also told them what Abbey said and asked them what they thought.

Nelson spoke up first. "I don't know, bro. Sounds like your ex-teacher might have her own agenda, blocking you from Naomi so she can have you for herself."

"Which may not be a good move either," Byron said. "Because what if the situation goes south with her? Either of the women could try and sabotage your chances."

"Or try and mess you up because you don't hook up," Doug suggested.

Barry slapped Marvin on the back. "Don't worry, Marv. I know you're not used to handling multiple females simultaneously, but I'm going to help you out. Stay friendly with both of them, but don't sleep with either one until after the show is over. Then make the choice of who you want to be with. Simple as that."

Marvin had to acknowledge that Barry made a lot of sense. Now wasn't the time to make enemies. Abbey was someone Marvin knew he could handle. He could always use the excuse that she was his teacher and might be again, plus they'd always been just friends anyway. Naomi was different. He was attracted to everything about her, wanted to be with her. Not giving in to the temptation to do so wouldn't be simple at all. In fact, he'd learn sooner than later, it would be damn near impossible.

10

The weekend passed quickly and the following Tuesday, his day off, Marvin relished sleeping in. He'd worked the previous ten days straight, two of them double shifts. The extra hours would net him more money, but little else. Even the amount he'd make with the extra hours was little more than a starting salary at other more high-end establishments. Marvin had been at the Soul Spot for three years, basically doing a chef's work on a line cook's pay. The Spot was a good restaurant. Still in business after twenty-five years, which was good for the food industry. But the regulars were getting older and dying, and young people hadn't been as attracted to the food or the space. That's one of the main reasons Donald had hired Marvin, after the father who'd founded the restaurant died. Donald had given Marvin leeway. Made big promises. Donald had promised that in two years, Marvin could take the lead. That he'd never wanted to cook in the first place and was glad someone with Marvin's passion and skill had come along.

Marvin had been thrilled at the prospect and gone right to work. Updated the menu. Suggested affordable décor changes. White paint covered dark brown tables and booths. Bright orange and yellow accents replaced somber navy and maroon. The all-black ensemble was switched out for comfy jeans and brightly colored T-shirts emblazoned with a logo Marvin had had designed for free. He worked hard, even on off days, envisioning a place to work at for the long term and a kitchen he'd one day run.

That was the first twelve months. Business increased. Accolades abounded. But not everyone was happy. Along with the shift in colors and menu choices came a shift in respect from Donald to Marvin. Donald had the title and the family name, but people came to Marvin because he had the answers. Marvin was the real boss.

"Hang in there," Janet had told him. "Donald will be gone in another year."

That was two years ago. The only things left were Donald's promises and regular raises. Unfortunately, Marvin's passion for the Soul Spot had also left the building.

But on this day off, Marvin woke up smiling. He was weeks away from being able to deliver a message to Don-wannabe-Juan, one he'd bitten back too many times to count. *I quit.* A few more challenges, a few more eliminations, and he'd be on the way to living the dream of having a business of his own. Bolstered by that thought and remembering his brother's advice to stay focused, Marvin rolled out of bed and bounced into the shower. Since the first round had focused on appetizers, entrées were the obvious assumption for round two. Competitions like these were known to throw in an unexpected twist or two though, so nothing was certain. His plan was to prepare so that he could handle whatever the judges threw at him. Whatever came up.

Dressed in black jeans, a black Raiders tee, stark white Jordans and mirrored shades, Marvin jumped into his SUV and headed to the nearest mall and Kitchen Etc., his favorite store. On the way he thought about Naomi and her savory slices, then flipped through his mental Rolodex of specialties and pondered how he could prepare them in a way to stand out among the other chefs. Unique pairings was something that always went over well. A smart use of spices or a new take on an old dish garnered high praise and high points. His mind churned on options both savory and sweet. He thought about the bacon-in-dessert craze over the past few years—in ice cream, cupcakes, cookies, scones—and wondered how it would work with yams, one of his favorite root vegetables. By the time he arrived at the store about ten minute later, Marvin had half a dozen or so ideas to work on for the upcoming show.

For sure he knew he needed a cooking thermometer. One of the ideas on the trip over was a sweet-potato puff, a cakey-type ball rolled in powdered sugar and pecans and having some type of unexpected, gooey center of deliciousness inside it. Perhaps one that included bacon or some other unusual savory-sweet pairing he'd not yet thought of. He waved away the enthusiastic salesclerk's offer of assistance, found the thermometer aisle and picked out a couple different ones based on prospective use. He continued to browse, checking out the latest culinary gadgets. More than once he'd found a trendy new device that inspired a dish and hoped that today might be one of those times. Entering an aisle with chef's knives and a variety of other cutting devices, he stopped when a stainless steel mandoline caught his eye. He picked it up, inspected the super-sharp cutting edges, and thought about sweet-potato chips with a savory dip. The way his thought process had been the past week, he was pretty sure that whatever the challenge, a sweet potato would be at the center of his culinary creation.

His peripheral vision caught someone's movement as they entered the aisle. Before he could look up, a familiar voice sounded.

"Are you following me?"

He looked over at Naomi, looking like a sweet and spicy dish herself—baby-doll-style mini barely covering smooth, thick thighs. Wedge heels that showed off strong calves. Cleavage taunting him to take a plunge inside. Abbey's warning and his brother's advice flew straight out his mental window.

"More like the other way around." Marvin's smile came slow and easy as he moved toward her. "You walked into my aisle."

Naomi looked around. "Oh, really, because I don't see your name anywhere."

"But you saw me, though, and came running."

"Oh, that's what happened?"

"Looks like it." He enjoyed a blatant once-over. "Got all dressed up, too, I see. With that short dress showing off those juicy thighs and sweet-looking melons trying to escape from your prison of a bra."

Naomi took a step closer. "Are you concerned that they might get away, volunteering to be the warden that puts them back in their cell?"

"There you go, playing with fire again."

"I like it hot, darling. If anyone runs from the heat, it will be you."

Marvin's eyes narrowed as he looked at the luscious lips from which those challenging words were issued. Lips he could imagine crushing with his own, and doing other things in other places.

"Always running that mouth," he replied, his eyes still glued to her berry-colored kisser.

She licked her lips seductively. "You like it."

Marvin's dick jumped. He laughed and turned to cover the movement. "Girl, quit playing!"

"Who says I'm playing?"

"So you're not playing? You really want some of this Marvin magic?" Marvin ran his hands from shoulder to thigh. "Careful with your answer, Juicy, because if you say yes there's no going back."

"The question isn't whether I want some of your magic, as you call it. The question is whether you're man enough to handle"—she rolled her hips—"all of this."

"Whoa! Watch out there now. All day and all night, baby!"

"Alright then, player. I like your confidence." She pulled out her phone. "What's your address?"

"Can't happen there, babe. I live at home."

"At home as in, with your parents?" Marvin nodded. Naomi frowned. "How old are you?"

"What difference does it make? I'm twenty-seven. My parents needed my help and I moved back home to give it to them."

That was a slightly creative take on the truth, but it was Marvin's version and he was sticking to it.

He pulled out his phone. "Give me your number, and your address." Hearing no answer, he looked up. "That's all right. All talk and no action. A big tease. I knew it would be hard to back up all that junk in your trunk."

Naomi quickly rattled off her address. "Be there tomorrow, seven o'clock sharp. We'll see who can back what up."

"Why tomorrow? Let's wait until the weekend, Sunday. I'm off and can at least take you out to dinner, or to the movies, do something fun."

"Let's handle this situation like grown folk, okay? We both know the kind of fun that's on our minds. Tomorrow," she repeated, turning to walk away as she took two fingers and pointed from her eyes to his. "Your only chance. You don't show up, I'll know why."

Marvin watched Naomi walk away, a contradictory bundle of daring machismo and feminine wiles. He worked on Wednesdays and on top of that was looking forward to his first Sunday off in several weeks. None of that mattered now. Scrolling his contacts, he punched in Donald's number. The boss would no doubt love switching shifts with him and being off the whole weekend. Marvin knew working both Saturday and Sunday, easily the restaurant's busiest days, would be an exhausting, nonstop cooking inferno. But he was pretty sure he knew something else. Naomi Carson would be worth it, and then some.

11

The next afternoon, Naomi stood just outside the 99 Cents Store, taking her break and talking on the phone.

"Tee, cuz, I really messed up this time."

"Why, what happened?"

"I invited Marvin over."

"Ooh, girl, that's great! You're finally going to let a man clear the cobwebs."

Naomi chuckled and slowly shook her head. "You're silly."

"I'm serious. How is that messed up?"

"Did you forget where I live? With Nana?"

"Of course not."

"Obviously Marvin did, because when I got on his case about living with his parents, he didn't say anything about me living with her, even though I told him that first time on the phone."

"It's Wednesday. Doesn't Nana go to Bible study?"

"Yes. That's why I insisted he come over tonight.

He wanted to wait until this weekend when he was off. Make it a real date by going out and everything."

"And?"

"That's not what this is. I don't want to date Marvin!"

"You only want to screw him."

"Exactly."

"So you can focus on winning the food competition."

"Yes. Are you being sarcastic?"

"Are you being stupid? As much as you like this guy? Do you think you can be with Marvin sexually and still keep it casual when you see him in public? Keep your emotions in check and your heart out of the equation?"

"Yes."

Naomi said this with conviction, but wasn't so sure. She glanced at her watch and headed inside the store. "Look, break's over. I've got to go."

"Stop overthinking everything, Naomi. In fact, don't think at all. Just go with the flow and try to have fun. How long has it been?"

"You mean for the real thingy instead of a toy dingy?" They both laughed at that comment. "Too long."

Naomi had tried hard not to remember that tragic fact, that she was in a forced celibacy and hadn't had sex in almost a year. At least not with a human. It made her sound pitiful, undesirable, unwanted. As though something was wrong with her and right with all the women who jumped in a different bed every month, or every week, for sexual thrills. After the bad luck she'd had with the last lover, puny-penis crazy Vic, she'd felt better off sticking with her dildo Mr. Big. She could come, then roll over without thinking about whether or not a man was trying to use her or whether she'd awaken with a present that only penicillin or some other pill could cure. And then there was the minor detail of her living arrangements. Nothing could put a damper on your sex life like living with Grandma.

The afternoon passed quickly. Naomi stopped by the store on the way home; bought some drinks and snacks, just in case he felt like munching. Thought about cooking something but nixed that idea. Nana usually did the cooking on weekdays. Naomi didn't want to rouse suspicion. Yet when six fifteen came and the elder missus was still sitting in her favorite rocker watching a *In the Heat of the Night* rerun, Naomi began to worry. What if Nana didn't go to church that night? She hadn't even given that possibility any consideration. And while she'd not lied about her living arrangements, she hadn't corrected Marvin's assumption that she lived alone. Figured Nana wouldn't be there and didn't see the need. Figured she'd explain if and when asked directly. Which would be in about forty-five minutes if he arrived at seven, as she'd demanded, and Nana answered the door.

She muted the television and left her room.

Went into the kitchen, poured a glass of water and sat on the couch.

"You going to church tonight?"

"Why, you want to go with me?"

"No, not tonight, Nana."

"I don't see why not. You haven't given the Lord His time in a month of Sundays. He gave you that job promotion and you haven't even stopped to say thanks."

"I thanked Him!"

"Not in person, you didn't."

"You're the one who taught me that the Lord is everywhere."

"Yeah, but that don't mean you can't go by His house for a visit every now and then."

"You're right, Nana. But not tonight." Naomi stretched and tried to feign a yawn. "You going?"

"I don't know. Been feeling tired all day today. Hope I'm not coming down with something."

"Sounds like not feeling well is all the more reason to go to church. Doesn't the pastor pray over the sick at the midweek service?"

"Yeah." Nana sighed, picked up the remote and turned off the TV. "You're probably right. Might be the devil trying to stop me from getting my blessing."

Or the Lord trying to keep me from getting mine! Naomi looked at the window, tried to keep her face neutral. Inside she was about to do the happy dance.

Nana got up from her rocker and walked over to kiss Naomi's forehead. "Thanks for encouraging me to go to church. The next time I offer you encouragement, let your reaction be the same."

"Yes, ma'am."

Nana hated to be late for anything, which is why Naomi felt fine telling Marvin to arrive at seven. Yet it was a quarter to seven before Nana's Buick finally pulled out of the driveway. Barely time for Naomi to jump in the shower, then slip into a loose maxi that was easy to remove.

Fourteen minutes later, the doorbell rang.

Marvin not only showed up on time, but by her watch he was one minute early. She took one last look in her bedroom mirror, ran her fingers through a new loose do, and went to the door.

"Didn't know if you'd show up." She stepped back to let him in, then stopped. Where'd you park?"

"In the driveway."

"Do me a favor and park on the street."

"Why?"

"Because I asked you. Park over there," she continued, pointing across the street. "I don't need the nosy neighbors in my business."

"What do you care what the neighbors think?"

"I don't. Now go move your car. Hurry up!"

Marvin gave her a look before turning around to do as she asked. He returned and came through the door with a plastic bag in hand, which he held out to her. "Sorry it isn't in a wine sack. Didn't have time to make two stops."

"No problem. Nice of you to bring something to

drink." She pulled out a bottle of sparkling wine, reading the label as she walked into the kitchen.

Marvin followed behind her. "I figured you'd like Riesling. Most women do because of the—"

"I'm not most women," Naomi interrupted, rounding on him and getting in his face. "But thank you." She gave him a peck on the lips.

That closeness was all the proximity Marvin needed to do what he'd wanted to do ever since he'd first seen her, seen them. Ever since she'd fixed those ample smackers to deliver the sarcastic "excuse you" after he'd bumped her backside. He placed a hand behind her neck and another one around her waist. Pulled her tight, covered her lips with his own and jabbed his tongue into her open opportunity before she could object or say anything at all. Flicked his tongue against hers, a silent yet forceful, even urgent invitation to stop yakking and start smacking. Start snacking. Delicious attacking. To show her what he came working with, and how he could turn her on. He eased the bottle out of her hand, blindly sought the counter to set it on, and once that hand was freed used it to grab the Carter-catcher that had teased him ever since he first saw it; accidently met it before he met her. That juicy, delicious, breathtaking ass. Palmed as much of it as he could, pressed it into his hardening shaft. Felt her nipples begin to pebble against his chest. Girl wasn't wearing a bra. Was there anything beneath that flimsy dress? The question begged an answer. He pulled back just enough to look into her eyes. To see that, like his, hers were heavy with desire.

"Want to take this into your bedroom?"

Naomi obviously thought she could show him better than tell him. Took his hand and led the way. Through his desire-induced haze Marvin vaguely scanned the home he'd barely noticed since Naomi greeted him at the door. Nice place, but he was struck at how different it looked than how he'd imagined her home would be. He'd expected bright, loud, explosive colors that matched her personality. The home had an older, conservative vibe. Had she inherited it from a loved one, maybe recently, like this morning?

No time to think about that now. They were in Naomi's room. Obviously Naomi. Incredibly so. Bright yellow curtains that matched a geometric-patterned comforter. Noticed only because it's what Naomi backed up to and fell on, bringing him with her. Down on the bed wasn't anywhere he didn't want to go. He'd dreamt of how it would feel to be on top of all her loveliness. The best of his fantasies didn't come close. Her breasts and stomach cushioned him in a way that was made for loving. Caused his dick to harden, lengthen, and beg to be freed from its boxer cage. Marvin was ready to oblige it, but he wanted to savor the moment, too. Wanted to slow things down. They had all night. He eased to the side of her, where his hand was free to roam what his torso had just experienced.

"Damn, girl. You're coming with it! Talked that talk and now you're walking the walk."

"Uh-huh, thought I was playing, didn't you?"

"I was hoping you weren't. You're everything and more than I thought you'd be."

"Hmm. Now I see you've got my problem," she responded. Pulled on his shirt. His zipper. His belt.

"What's that?" he asked, placing his hand on hers to still quick, sure movements.

"Too much time talking when there are other uses for that big wet mouth." She returned to the task at hand, ridding him of his garments.

"Why are you rushing though?"

"Because I want some dick, okay? Do you have one or is that a cucumber poking my thigh?"

Marvin burst out laughing, even as he reached for the zipper with which she still struggled. "Definitely not a vegetable," he replied. "That's a roll of pure beef you're feeling. Grade A at that."

He rolled to a sitting position, then reached down to untie and remove his sneakers. Naomi took the opportunity to remove her maxi. Marvin looked over to see her lounging on her side wearing nothing but a thong.

Lord. Have. Mercy. Top-of-the-line juicy on full display. Breasts for days. Wide hips, an expanse of creamy thigh that went into buttocks that he was sure had their own zip code. It was time to quit playing and get down to business. He figured they could have foreplay and pillow talk before the second round. Standing up just long enough to remove his jeans, he crawled onto the bed and eased off his boxers. His thick, curved manhood stood at the ready. So was Marvin. He eased himself down, gently, beside Naomi. Pulled her close and covered her mouth with his own. He treated her soft, cushy body like an instrument—stroking her chords, playing her keys. His tongue went on a journey from her mouth to her neck. Then shoulders, and on down, until it found what it searched for, a plump, dark nipple to pull into his mouth. He did so with relish, even as his hand traveled south to another set of lips. Slid a finger between them and felt her dewy desire. Heard her gasp with delight when he flicked her pearl. All the encouragement he needed to take his mouth to where his fingers had traveled, where they'd felt evidence of a body more than ready. He scooted down. She shifted her body and let her legs fall open. Exposed the small swatch of satin covering her goody box. That sexy black thong, as cute as it was, proved no match for Marvin. A quick yank and it came away from her body. Any protest she'd planned for his tearing her clothes was silenced when he plopped his face between her thighs and began nibbling her heat like a hungry man ready to dine. His tongue flicked her pearl—skillfully, playfully, mercilessly—before parting her thick folds and lapping her love juice like honey from the comb.

He felt her legs begin to shiver. Unintelligible

murmurings cascaded from her lips to his ears as he continued the delicious assault.

"No."

"Yeah, baby. Let it go and take the ride." Just beyond the thighs he held, the thighs that muted sound as they pressed against the sides of his head, came a scratchy kind of drone near the bedroom window.

"No!"

"Um-hmm." Marvin plunged his tongue inside her, over and again. Encouraged her to "come for daddy" after each lick.

Naomi's body bucked, almost lifted off the bed, even as she pried his hands away from her thighs. Her movements were jerky, almost frantic, as though she was coming and going at the same time.

"Stop!"

Marvin did, immediately, and rolled over on his back. Hers wasn't the usual reaction after inducing an earth-shattering climax, but then again, Naomi wasn't your ordinary girl.

"Crap! I knew I heard something."

Marvin opened an eye and saw Naomi on her knees, squatting low, peeking between closed blinds.

"It's Nana!"

"Who's that?"

"My grandmother! She's home early!" Naomi scrambled off the bed and reached for the maxi that lay in the heap of clothes on the floor.

"She lives here?" Marvin asked, reaching for boxers, jeans, tee, and hurriedly pulling them on, during which a vague memory of her telling him that wafted across his mind.

Good thing for that memory, because Naomi didn't answer. She'd raced to the other side of the room, to a dresser that held several perfume bottles on a mirrored tray. Grabbing one, she yanked off the top, began to spray herself and the room. Marvin stepped left to avoid her waving hand but took a blast of Angel Flowers to the chest.

"Dang it, Naomi. Now I smell like a bouquet!"

"Better than smelling like booty," she hissed.

Both turned to the sound of a door opening. Naomi shushed him with her eyes and placed a finger to her puckered mouth. Neither was needed. The terrified expression on her face was enough to shrivel Marvin's dick and shut him all the way up. For several seconds he forgot to breathe. Hell, he'd never felt this frightened in his mama's house, even when he had to hide a naked classmate in his closet overnight.

"Get under the bed!" Her whisper was soft yet frantic. Low but urgent.

"What?"

"Under the bed!" This time pushed through gritted teeth with an expression that translated to got-dammit-I-mean-now.

Why did he have to get under the bed? The door was closed. Did her grandmother have x-ray vision?

"Why?" he quickly mouthed, even as Naomi

placed determined hands on his back and pushed him toward the bed.

"Because your car is out there. She's going to knock!"

Marvin glanced down skeptically at a bed that looked less than a foot off the floor. "I can't fit under there."

"Naomi!"

Naomi's eyes widened. She grabbed Marvin's shirt and he'd later swear she channeled the strength of Hercules because she placed her hands on his shoulders and almost forced him to the floor. Only stiff arms and pride kept him off of his knees.

"Naomi, you back there?"

The sound of heels on hardwood hastened her tugs and his movements.

"Girl, wait!" Marvin glanced around the room. Spotted a door and moved toward it. "I'll get in the closet."

"Girl, you hear me calling you!"

The voice was close. Too close to make a run across the room.

"Yes, ma'am. I'm here!" Naomi shoved him down again. His knee hit the floor with a sound Marvin knew would cost him tomorrow. He did a tuck and roll that would have made a gymnast proud, momentum aided by a final heave-ho when Naomi lowered the bed skirt and plunked down in front of it just as a light tap on the door signaled time was up.

"What in the world is going on in here?" Nana scrunched her nose as she stepped into the room, waving a hand in front of it. "And what did you do, spill a whole bottle of perfume?"

Marvin listened as Naomi hid nerves behind laughter.

"Yes, I mean, no, not the whole bottle. It was on the nightstand and I . . ." She paused and laughed again. Marvin imagined so that she could think of a believable lie. If it weren't for the fact that his knee was throbbing and his nose was becoming way too acquainted with a box-spring coil, he would have enjoyed listening to the show.

"You what?"

"Knocked it off while I was dancing."

"Dancing?"

"Yeah, or trying to." He saw the bed sag as Naomi used it as leverage to get up. *No! Don't sit—!*

Only she did. The old mattress sagged, the springs sank and took away a valuable inch of breathing room. Marvin shifted his head and tried hard not to become claustrophobic. His eyes landed on a pair of what could only be described as old lady legs in old lady shoes. The same as the neighbor who'd inspired his love for baking. Pantyhose that looked a size too big and a shade too light slipped into low-heeled burgundy pumps that sported a bright gold buckle in the middle of a bow. *Hi there, Miss Church Lady.* Oh, she'd been to church. Of that, Marvin had no doubt. He focused on the shoes, tried to relax his shoulders and begged his neck not to cramp.

"Remember that dance routine me and Tee made up when we were little?"

"Y'all haven't been little in a long time." Nana's brow furrowed as her gaze swept the room. "Where were you dancing, on the bed?"

The way they'd been tousling, Marvin imagined that the bed looked like it had hosted a wrestling match.

"Oh, no. I, um, lay down when I got home. Thought I was coming down with something, but I feel better now."

"Girl, you aren't making any kind of sense. Coming down with something one minute, up dancing the next. Knocking stuff over and about to knock yourself out, the way you're looking." The bed shifted. Marvin gained back a much-needed inch of breathing room. He imagined Naomi going over to a mirror he remembered was hanging on her closet door. He shifted his head back and hoped a coil shape hadn't been imprinted on his cheek.

"What are you looking for, Nana?"

"Do I have to be looking for anything to open your closet?"

At the thought of being discovered had he made it to the closet, Marvin's whole body froze up. He hadn't talked to Jesus in a minute but mouthed a thank-you nonetheless.

"No, but people normally have a reason and I

know you can't wear my clothes. Why are you home early anyway? You still not feeling good?"

"No, I'm not. I told the secretary to add my name to the prayer list and then came on home." I'm going to go take some cough medicine and go to bed, try to knock out whatever this is before it takes hold."

Marvin felt his leg going to sleep, even while the knee on that leg throbbed. *Naomi, please take your grandma out of here.*

"Come on, Nana. I'll make some chamomile tea with lots of lemon and honey."

That's right, baby! That's my girl!

"What about some chicken noodle soup? Want some of that, too?"

Marvin saw the lights go out and heard the door close. He wiggled his fingers, moved his legs and waited a couple more minutes before easing his bulk out from beneath the bed.

What does she want me to do?

He eased over to the window and peeked out the blinds. It looked wide enough but was up rather high. He'd have to heave his bulk over it and then try and avoid falling in a rose bush. A mess of thorns on top of coiled-spring imprints? There had to be another way.

There was. It took more than an hour to arrive and Marvin felt like he was in a game of Twister as he dodged squeaky floorboards to reach the front door. A two-hundred-plus-pound brother trying to be light on his feet wasn't easy, especially after spending the better part of an hour under a bed. Once outside he followed Naomi's last request, necessary because she claimed her grandmother had ears like a bat. He put the car in neutral and pushed it two doors down before starting it up and leaving her block. Only after extracting a promise though. To finish what they'd started . . . and soon.

12

Usually Naomi hugged the pillow until the very last second, but the morning after Marvin's close call, she couldn't get out of the house fast enough. Nana had chosen going to bed over having soup, but that didn't stop the continued interrogation when Naomi brought in a large mug filled with tea and a good amount of brandy covered up with loads of lemon and honey. Naomi had suggested turning the tea into a toddy. She needed something to fog her grandmother's suspicious mind and knew if presented as medicine, alcohol was allowed. "To sweat the sick out," her grandmother had explained when asked by Naomi at eight years old. Naomi hoped drinking the toddy would help her grandmother relax, allay her suspicions. It didn't at first. Nana had asked about the spilled perfume, several times, like every time she inhaled and caught a whiff. Asked about Naomi's delayed response when Nana had called out to her. Naomi was glad when a few sips into the healing concoction, her non-drinking granny's eyes drooped with fatigue. Naomi gently removed the cup from Nana's hand and set it on the table before covering her with an extra blanket besides the one already on the bed. With a night to dream, Naomi hoped that Nana would be out of questions and that the night's events would be forgotten.

She didn't get her wish. After returning home almost ten hours later, Naomi found that Nana hadn't forgotten. She didn't have a bunch of questions, though, only two.

"Did you have company while I was gone last night?"

"No, ma'am." Answered hastily, almost distractedly as Naomi beelined it to her room.

Nana had followed her and leaned on the door. "Then who was that man the neighbor swore she saw sneak out of our house and push his car down the street?"

That was two days ago, and Naomi still hadn't fully recovered. Nana hadn't bought the argument that a friend had only dropped by to pick something up so Naomi hadn't considered him company.

"You know I used to be your age," Nana had responded.

"Yes, ma'am."

"You remember that I raised your mama before I raised you, right?"

"I'm sorry that I didn't remember to tell you," Naomi said, hoping an apology would coat the lies and end the inquest.

It didn't. "Who was this man?"

"One of the contestants for the food truck."

"What'd he come over for?"

"A . . . garlic press." That thought courtesy of the 99 Cents Store because they'd just gotten in a supply and Naomi had bought one.

Nana had actually laughed out loud, shook her head and walked away, but not before a weary "Help her, Jesus," slid through the closing door.

Naomi needed help but doubted Jesus would give it to her. After lying to Nana, filling her room with almost-effing fumes and then the house with the fragrance of a thousand flowers, Naomi figured she was probably on her way to hell. Even worse than eternal damnation was the thought that she'd hurt or disappointed her grandma, evident in how last night the air at home was still strained. Naomi hoped that a busy Saturday focused on realizing her dream would help put the nightmare of being found out behind her. Winning the truck and that stack of cash would be her independence. Naomi was nothing if not motivated more than ever to cook for her life. She stood drinking coffee and chatting with a few other contestants, bracing herself for seeing Marvin, when somebody bumped her butt.

"That felt intentional," she said to the girl who'd been a teammate on the last challenge, giving herself a few extra seconds to adopt a cool façade.

The redhead smirked as she looked behind where Naomi stood. "I think it was."

Naomi turned to see Marvin smiling like a Cheshire cat. Her facial expression was bland enough. But her heartbeat raced, her kitty thrummed, and all she could say was, "You."

He laughed and leaned in with a greeting for her ears alone. "Hey, Juicy." And then to the larger crowd, "Hey, everybody. Who am I beating today?"

Marvin had thrown down the gauntlet. The appropriate responses jabbed back.

"Naomi, can I holler at you for a minute?"

She eyed Marvin suspiciously, the initial reaction at seeing him subsiding. "What do you want, my secret ingredient?" She hoped to make him as off-kilter as she felt.

Just briefly his eyes narrowed, darkened, and sent Naomi a message that couldn't be shared in mixed company, or any company for that matter. "Just want to ask you about something, that's all."

They stepped away from the group and over by where craft services was busy setting up a lunch and snack spread.

"I expected you to call me," Marvin said, as soon as he was sure that no one was around.

"And say what?"

"I'm sorry, for starters."

Naomi made a face. "Sorry for what?"

Marvin held up his hand and began counting on his fingers. "For not reminding me that you lived with your grandma. For not letting me know she was on her way home." He slid his eyes over her body and took a step closer. "For limiting me to the drive-through when I'd come for a buffet." He stepped back and arched a brow. "Need I go on?"

She crossed her arms and was ready to deliver a sarcastic response, but aware that eyes were on them, whipped out a smile as though she were joking. "Okay, I'm sorry. But it's not like that was planned. Nana is usually at church until at least nine o'clock, but that night she wasn't feeling good and came home early. You heard me offer to fix her some soup."

"Stuffed under your bed like some clothes out of season, I couldn't hear much of anything."

Naomi almost reached out to touch him, caught herself just in time. "I really am sorry about that. And just so you know, I'm suffering, too. Are you okay?"

"I don't know. Do I have a bedspring engraved on my face?"

"The bed isn't that low, is it?"

"Not until you sat down."

"Oh!" Naomi's hand flew to her mouth. "I didn't even think . . ." She searched his face for evidence as that night's scene replayed in her mind and she imagined her sagging springs kissing his cheek. "Sorry."

Almost believable, except for the giggle.

"Girl, I know that you're not laughing at my pain."

Naomi shook her head, and pressed her lips together to keep the laughter inside.

"Yes, you are." Marvin looked around, a sped-up replay of that night's video playing in his head. "I guess it was kind of funny, my big ass squeezed between those springs and the floor. If I'd so much as farted my cover would have been blown."

They both burst out laughing at that, the situation becoming all the funnier considering how serious the sex had been just seconds before Nana's Buick pulled into the drive.

"Well, what do we have here, a private party?" Neither Naomi nor Marvin had heard Abbey approach. "Marvin, do you have a moment?"

"Um, not right now," he answered, nodding toward Ted. "Looks like we're about to start."

Naomi ignored a tight-lipped Abbey and followed Marvin over to join the other contestants who'd made it to round two of the preliminaries.

"What's your girl's problem?"

"Who, Abbey?"

"Who else? She was looking at you like she wanted to jack you up." Marvin shrugged. Naomi blew it off, too. "What do you think we're doing today?"

"Entrées, I hope. Played around with a couple recipes this week that I'd like the judges to try."

Naomi leaned in close. "That's not all you played around with."

"Don't start nothing you can't finish, girl, like you did the other night." They both watched as actor and show host Ted Reynolds bounded to the stage. Marvin kept his eyes on him but leaned toward Naomi and whispered, "You probably planned it that way because you know you can't hang."

Naomi almost choked on a mouthful of words she had to swallow rather than allow the outburst she craved. The competition had gone from over a thousand to just eighty in two weeks' time. Now was not the time to lose focus.

"Hello Food Truck Buckaroos! Give yourselves a hand for making it to the round of eighty!" He waited for the applause, whistles, and yells to subside. "Today is very important, because as impressive as it is for you to have reached this point, and for as good as you should feel about yourselves and your culinary chops, today may be your last day in this competition. When today's challenge is over, we will have chopped the remaining number in half." He nodded at the collective gasp. "That's right. After today, there will only be forty spots. Does one have your name on it?"

Naomi and Marvin joined the screams of contestants determined to make the cut. They listened as Ted gave the rules for today.

"You're going to pull colored knives to create eight groups of ten. Two knives out of each color group also have bands around the tip. Whoever chooses those knives will become captains, able to choose four players from the remaining group of the same color to form your team. Once that's done, we'll announce today's dish. Let's go!"

The contestants lined up in four rows behind large butcher blocks that held twenty knives with the same thick wooden handle. Each person walked up and pulled out a knife with a colored plastic blade. Naomi and Marvin were in different rows but she watched him ease out a knife from the butcher block—green! Just like her.

Each knife-wielding player quickly assembled with their same-color counterparts. Red, white, black, yellow, blue, and so on until all groups were formed. Naomi eyed the gold band around the tip of Marvin's knife. He was one of the captains. Figured.

Ted retook the stage. "Has everyone found their group?" Affirmatives abounded. "Good. What about the captains? If you have a band around the tip of your . . . knife"—Ted paused for the expected titters—"hold it up!"

In their group it was Marvin and another contestant Naomi hadn't met or worked with before. He had to have talent, otherwise he wouldn't have made the cut of eighty. Still, she wanted to be on Marvin's team. She told herself only the cooking squad. But the memory of Marvin's stiff tongue flicking her pearl made her muscles clutch and rethink that position.

"Alright, captains. There are representatives at each group to record your choices. Captains with one band on your knife go first. The captains with two bands go second."

Marvin stepped out and turned so he could see

the whole group. He studied them only briefly before nodding toward his first choice. "I choose Naomi."

Naomi let out a relieved breath and almost skipped over to join her man, no, teammate. *Fellow contestant. Mortal enemy! Blocker to her future fortune! Stay focused, girl!*

After the teams of five had been chosen, Ted announced the dish. The all-American favorite go-to snack, hamburgers and fries.

Marvin had a plan before he chose Naomi. He gathered the team around him and quickly laid it out. "Okay, listen up. We're doing a barbecued and bacon-stuffed cheeseburger with crispy onions, a poblano pepper relish, and sweet potato chips."

He began delegating jobs to the cooks around him. When he got to Naomi he told her to fry the chips.

"I think we should do hash browns."

Marvin shook his head. "Sweet potatoes present a modern take on a classic."

"Maybe five years ago, but not anymore. Sweet potato fries are everywhere. A new take on the classic hash brown would make a louder statement. Give the judges something they've not had before."

"And may never want to eat again," another of the contestants mumbled.

"I'll bet my spot in this competition on my potatoes," Naomi said, staring down the mutterer until she turned her head.

Marvin looked at her a moment. "Remember you said that."

Naomi nodded, even as her heart began doing the boogie-woogie in her chest. *Why'd I open my big mouth and put all that pressure on myself?*

Ted gave the countdown. Naomi raced toward the vegetable bin, bypassed the crowd pushing for their share of Yukon Gold potatoes and went straight for the russets, which she knew made a lighter, crispier fry. She dumped those at her station and made a beeline for a shelf of waffle makers on the equipment rack. She organized the ingredients on her counter, then peeled potatoes like the devil was chasing her, passed them on to a teammate who shredded them and dumped them into a large bowl filled with cold water. Naomi plugged in the waffle irons, ignoring Miss Mutterer now smirking at her unconventional choice, spread the shredded potatoes out on the table and seasoned them.

She quickly found out Marvin wasn't that convinced either. "Girl, what are you doing?"

"Helping us take first place today."

"With the waffle iron? Waffle hash browns are nothing new."

"No, but my recipe is. Just stay focused on that burger. I've got this over here."

Naomi backed up her words and turned out a stellar dish. The judges swooned over Marvin's "Triple-B Burger" and the barbecue sauce he'd made on the spot. But they heaped piles of praise on Naomi for her "Shredded Strips." The beauty in the recipe's simplicity. The genius of spraying the iron with a lard-based spray, adding onions, and delivering a crispier hash brown from wedges that had been cut into strips and double-fried. They felt the pairing of her "clean" potato with the aggressively seasoned burger was a perfect match. The green team won as the best overall. Naomi's potato lost overall best, second only to Marvin's burger. Disappointing, but she agreed with the result. Marvin's burger was the best ever put between a bun. It was eight of the hardest hours Naomi had ever experienced, but as she walked toward the parking structure she pulled out her phone. There was one more dish she wanted to have before she went home.

13

When taping wrapped, Marvin found himself surrounded by press. Many of the reporters were locals with blogger websites and internet shows, but someone from one of the major food channels gave him a card. He basked in the spotlight, patiently answered all questions asked. While expertly handling the crowd around him he kept an eye out for Naomi, who'd sent a text asking if he wanted to grab a quick bite before he headed to work. He did, and headed toward the exit as soon as those around him dispersed. The room where the contestants had cooked was still a bustle of activity. Marvin noted Da Chen talking to another guy, someone Marvin had seen on one of the cooking channels. Had they seen the contest? Marvin hoped that Da witnessed the Marvin magic. Marvin was in a hurry to see Naomi, but knowing that the industry was all about networking and connections, he headed over to speak to Da and meet the other guy. Halfway there, he was intercepted.

"Marvin!"

"Oh, hey, Abs." She stood directly in his path wearing an expression directly opposite of the one she'd worn earlier when he was with Naomi. "What's up?"

"You, that's what. Getting the star treatment as you absolutely should. Congratulations!"

"Thanks."

"I tasted a piece of your burger. Even lukewarm, it was really very good. I am so proud of you and totally not surprised."

"Thanks, Abs. As one of my former instructors, the compliment from you means a lot."

"Hopefully not just an instructor, but a good friend, too."

Marvin had no idea how she figured they were friends. They'd never talked outside of the classroom and until this contest he hadn't seen her in years.

"I appreciate that, Abbey, but . . ."

"Oh, no, call me Abs!" She leaned closer, her green eyes twinkling. "You're the only person who's ever given me a nickname. My staunchly conservative mom would never have allowed it. But I really like it."

He stepped back, unable to hide his look of surprise. "Whoa, what are you doing?"

"What do you mean?"

"Getting rather close, don't you think?"

"Would you stop being paranoid? I simply stated that you are the only person who's ever given me a nickname. I like it. Makes me feel sexy, and I rarely feel that way."

I'll be sure as hell not do it again. "I give everybody nicknames, Abbey," he said pointedly. "I've done that since hanging with a bunch of kids on my block growing up."

She leaned into him. "I really like it."

"There you go again, invading my personal space."

"What's the matter, Marvin? I don't remember you being so uptight."

"I don't remember you acting like this, all touchy-feely and everything. Sorry if you think I'm overreacting, but I remember you saying how my actions are perceived by others could jeopardize my chances to win. I don't want to do that."

"Glad to hear you remember that, Marvin. Because when I saw you with Naomi earlier today, I thought you'd forgotten."

The very last thing Marvin wanted to do was talk with Abbey about Naomi. He looked up and Da Chen was heading toward the exit. He planned to do the same. "Excuse me. I need to holler at the chef real quick before he gets away."

He didn't wait for an answer, couldn't get away soon enough. The way Abbey looked at him, giggling like a schoolgirl and acting all . . . weird. He hadn't wanted to believe Naomi about Abbey having a thing for him, even after she flirted the other day. But he could no longer deny what Naomi suspected. For Marvin, that revelation was wrong on every level.

Da Chen was talking with a couple reporters but

waved Marvin over when he saw him waiting on the sidelines.

"Magic Marvin!" The two men clasped hands and did the shoulder bump hug. "Is that what you're going to call your truck if you win?"

"I've got to win first, Da, but no, I don't think so, dude. Sounds too much like Magic Mike."

"Even better, set yourself apart by wearing a G-string while you cook!"

"Interesting idea, but I think I'll pass. I want to become a respectable player in the industry, like you."

"Respectable is overrated." Da signed a couple autographs, waved at a group passing by. "If you can have the fame and keep the work to anything less than eighty to a hundred and twenty hours a week? Take it."

"A hundred and twenty hours? Is that even possible?" Marvin's phone buzzed. He pulled it out of his pocket and tapped the face.

"Eighteen-hour days, bro."

Marvin nodded, responding to the text. "Maybe I'll rethink that G-string idea."

Da Chen clapped his back and headed out of the room and down the hall. Marvin was right behind him. He sent another text and then put the phone to his ear. "Hey, Nay, are you in the parking lot?"

Checking his phone for a reply, he continued down the convention center's long corridor to the set of double doors that led outside. It was just after five, and even though he was scheduled to report to work as soon as the contest taping was over, he was glad he'd accepted Naomi's invitation to grab a bite first. Employees could eat free at work, but after working there for so many years he'd burned himself out on everything they cooked. He pulled on a pair of sunglasses and headed toward the street where Naomi said she was parked. He turned the corner, walked almost a block, and finally saw the car he looked for, idling at the curb. He opened the door and slid into the passenger seat.

"Dang, woman. You trying to make me exercise or what?"

"Just getting away from prying eyes."

"Why are you tripping on Abbey?"

"Shoot, she's only one of several women checking you out. Especially after our win. They were on you like white on rice."

"People were looking for you, too."

"I talked to a few folk. But I had other things on my mind." She eyed him pointedly.

"A lot of people are probably hooking up in here. Did you check out Mr. Zen and the Asian sister on the blue team?"

Naomi shook her head. "From the time the buzzer sounded, if it wasn't a potato or a waffle iron, I wasn't looking at it."

She looked Marvin up and down. Glanced into the backseat. Eyed him again.

"What's wrong with you?"

"Nothing." She pulled away from the curb.

"Where are we going?"

"To a place I heard has delicious hot dogs."

"You've got to be kidding. I know you don't eat that unidentifiable meat."

"It's not unidentified. The ingredients are listed right on the package. Usually pork, beef, or turkey. But we need a little more room. Let's take your SUV."

Marvin furrowed his brow. "Why, are we going to eat the dogs or stuff the casings and cook them, too?"

"You ask too many questions. Where's your car?"

Marvin directed her to the second floor of the parking garage. As luck would have it, there was an empty space next to his car.

She pulled in, turned off the engine and fixed him with a sweet smile. "Shall we?" He put his hand on the handle but didn't open the door. "What?" she asked.

"I don't know. Feels like you're up to something."

Naomi laughed. "Stop being paranoid."

She got out of the car first and crossed to Marvin's SUV. He tapped his key fob to unlock her door. She opened it and slipped inside.

Marvin slid into the driver's seat. "You really must be hungry. I was going to get the door for you, but . . ."

He turned the car to the auxiliary position to pair his phone's Bluetooth but instead of turning over the engine he watched, confused, as Naomi slid to her knees and tried to turn around.

"Dang, I thought this SUV would be bigger, but . . ." She looked around. "Push your seat back."

"Why? What are you doing?"

She found the manual handle that controlled her seat and pushed it back. "Looking for something, okay?"

"What, an earring?"

Naomi huffed.

"Okay, dang." He reached for the lever and eased his seat back, too, turned up the sound of his wannabe rapper friend's mixed tape. It had a driving bass beat against a syncopated yell and clap sampled from a 70s R & B band.

Naomi reached for his belt.

Marvin stayed her hand. "What are you doing?"

"What does it look like? I changed my mind about a hot dog and want this sausage instead. Now lean the seat back and try not to look like someone's giving you head."

"Are you sure you want to do this here?" Marvin looked one direction and then the other, imagining stalker Abbey or someone else who shouldn't see them lurking between cars.

Naomi had unbuckled his belt and pulled down the zipper. She slipped her hand inside his boxers and began to massage his appendage. "Are you sure you don't want me to do it?"

Naomi smiled as instead of responding Marvin shifted his leg so she could get better positioned. *That's what I thought.* She pulled the tip of his limp member into her mouth, relishing the power that came from giving oral. Kristy wasn't that into it and would only do it on a reciprocal basis. But truth be told, this was the only hot dog Naomi ate, and her absolute favorite. That it was happening in a public place and in the daytime made it even better. The risk and naughtiness of public sex turned her on. That she was going to take what she wanted right here, right now, caused her nipples to harden as sparks shot through her heat. Moisture lined the lips pressed against her cotton thong. Her muscles clutched, as if remembering the tongue that had pressed up against them. Would giving Marvin pleasure be enough to calm the raging desire she felt for this man? If they had time, if she could find a way to ride him in the front seat, who knew what might happen later.

It wasn't long before Marvin's soldier began to stir, responding to her gentle sucking motion by rising up and getting hard. She steadied him with her hand and continued to lick and suck, enjoying the sounds that confirmed the excellent job she did. Hisses. Groans. Then a hand to the back of her head as she began a rhythmic up-and-down slide, her head moving to the beat of the song playing, one she hadn't heard before but one that couldn't have had a better or more appropriate hook for the moment.

Slip. And Slide. Slip, slip and slide, slide. Dip. And glide. Dip, dip and glide.

She followed instructions very well. Marvin added a layer of creative sound. His moans and whispered instructions delivered on the upbeat.

Yeah. Um. Just like that. Shit.

Naomi knew he was ready to blow when he placed a hand on the back of her head and began pumping with purpose. She welcomed the finale, continued absorbing Marvin's ecstasy until with a last whimper and a final shiver, he exhaled and became still.

Slip. And Slide. Slip, slip and slide . . .

Naomi cursed as legs that had been bent too long in a position that wasn't comfortable in the first place protested that she was trying to move them.

"Help me up!"

Marvin looked down, his expression genuinely perplexed. "Help you up to where?"

Naomi took in his wide-eyed puppy face and limp dick, and her predicament, and laughed at the question she'd asked. "Okay, I know I drained the pump and zapped your energy. I'll give you a minute."

"I don't believe this."

"What? You know it's true. Besides, you try and get all this I'm packing up and moving in one direction while trapped in a space smaller than a carryon bag."

"No, not you. Damn, move. Quick! No, not up! Stay down."

She heard the car start, felt it back up as she made it over the hump in the floor and could stretch out her legs.

"What in the hell, Marvin! Who did you see?"

"You don't even want to know."

"Abbey."

"Yep."

"Did she see you?"

"I don't think so. If she had, she would have

walked over and that would have been a jacked-up situation. Hold on."

"Where are you going? My foot is tingling, it's just about dead!"

"Up to the roof. There's hardly any cars up there."

Naomi, now on the passenger side, got to her knees.

"You can get up now."

"You should have stayed parked." Naomi pushed against the seat and was finally able to plop down in it. "I would have waited until she spoke, then lifted my head and said boo!"

They both cracked up at that.

"Girl, you are something else."

"Just wanted you to know that I'm not running away from nothing."

"Man, if I didn't have to go to work I'd take you to a hotel and get all up in all of that!"

"Promises, promises."

"I'm serious, juicy girl. But for now . . ." Naomi watched him check the time and turn the car toward the exit ramp. "I've got to go."

It wasn't long before they were idling next to Naomi's car.

"What are you doing tomorrow?" Marvin asked.

"You, I hope."

Naomi grabbed her purse and got out of the car without waiting for an answer. She crossed over to her car, started it up and headed out of the parking lot before Marvin had put his car in reverse. On the way out of the structure, she secretly hoped to run into Abbey, while the taste of Marvin's happiness was still on her tongue. She didn't see her or anyone else from the contest. Naomi was a little let down by that. Now that she'd won next best dish of the day, everyone knew what she'd tried to tell them. Naomi Carson was a force to be reckoned with! She'd especially tried to get Marvin to listen, but showing him instead was much more fun. She laughed, thinking about the look on his face when she reached inside his boxers and realization dawned as to the type of hot dog she wanted. He may have thought the move she made today was super hot, but Naomi knew their pot of passion had just begun to boil.

14

One a.m. on a Saturday night, technically Sunday morning, and the Soul Spot was packed. Economically, the decision to extend the café's weekend hours had been a good one. Usually though, around this time, Marvin would begin to feel the fatigue of what could easily be a twelve-to-fourteen-hour day. Not tonight though. For one he hadn't clocked in until after the contest's second-round taping and Naomi's pick-me-up, hitting the kitchen around seven o'clock. For another he'd cooked practically all night by rote, his mind consumed with Naomi. He had to admit that what she did today he never saw coming. The unexpected move was as decadent as it was dangerous, and showed Marvin that Naomi's skills weren't limited to the kitchen. Baby girl could no doubt serve it up in the bedroom, too. With the stolen moments they'd shared being so explosive, he could hardly imagine how a full, uninterrupted night of loving would be. If he had anything to say about the matter, he wouldn't have to imagine for long. Any thought of waiting until the contest was over to start anything was out the window. "Anything" had already begun. He planned to book a room next week and invite Naomi over for a night of loving. Then he planned to win the contest, get the food truck and get his own place.

"Marvin, one of your hoes is here for you."

He whipped around, but Charlotte had delivered that jab and darted out of the kitchen. Good move since he had a mind to remove the towel from around his neck and pop her with it. Of course, none of Willie Carter's boys would actually hurt a woman. But, for a nanosecond, the thought might cross their minds. As it was, Marvin simply turned off the burner, reached for a towel, and wiped his forehead as he headed into the dining room with a big smile on his face.

Big turned small quickly as he approached the last person he expected to see tonight, standing midway in a line that went out the door. "Abbey?"

From her expression he knew she'd seen his demeanor change.

"Who were you expecting, Naomi?"

"Wasn't expecting anybody, least of all you. What are you doing here?"

"What everyone else here came to do—eat."

"Long way to drive for a late-night bite."

"Not when you know a chef who can make one that is super delicious. I kept thinking about that burger you made today. Decided to drive over

and take the chance that you could whip up one
for me."

Marvin quelled the urge to sigh. Instead he
nodded at the long line of other people waiting. "I
can, but it'll take a minute."

"I've got time."

"Up to an hour, maybe?" Marvin knew the line
might move faster, but he really wanted Abbey to go
back home.

"Marvin!"

He could have kissed the assistant cook's ugly
mug, but instead barked a rushed "I'll be back" to
Abbey and headed back to the kitchen. For the next
thirty minutes his cooking looked choreographed—
flipping, turning, stirring, burning. He almost forgot
Abbey was out there, but when he passed the hall
on the way to the bathroom he saw that she'd been
seated. On his way back to the kitchen he stopped
at her table.

"I see you made it to a table."

"Yes, and I've been looking at the plates coming
out, and the people eating. Everybody seems to
really love your food."

"Drunk folk like anything," Marvin said humbly.
But he appreciated the compliment. "So do this,
order the deluxe patty plate with toppings on the
side. That way I'll know it's yours and try and re-
create what I did earlier."

Back in the kitchen, Marvin came as close as he
could. The barbecue sauce came out of a bottle,
bottled jalapenos replaced scorched poblanos,

and a very respectable fried potato replaced
Naomi's hash browns, but Marvin felt he'd done
justice to the memory of the day's Triple-B. Having
only snacked his way through service himself,
he'd plated one for him too, and walked them
out himself.

"Here you go, um, Abbey." He set the plate in
front of Abbey, then sat down on the other side.

"The burger and your company? I feel special.
But what happened to Abs?"

"Oh, yeah . . . that." Marvin took a bite of his
burger and hoped Abbey had forgotten the question by the time he chewed and swallowed.

"This is really good," Abbey said, after using a
knife and fork to cut the burger into more manage-
able pieces and taking a small bite. "What is the different seasoning I'm tasting, it's kind of sweet?"

"You're probably tasting the brown sugar, but it's
a blend I created a while back as a steak rub."

She took another bite. "The cheese is provolone?"
Marvin nodded. "Is that what you used earlier?"

"No," Marvin said, glad to be having a more appropriate conversation with his former culinary
instructor. "That was fontina, but we didn't have
that here."

After a little more food talk, Abbey set down
her silverware and wiped her mouth. "There's
no way I could eat everything on this plate. The
burger alone is huge! But it is all really delicious. Is

this what you see as the ultimate goal, your own restaurant?"

"I don't know. While celebrity chefs make the life look glamorous, I'm under no illusion about how hard it is to run a restaurant."

"There's a reason why more than half of them fail within the first year of opening for business."

"I'm not sure I want my life to be spent in the kitchen for the next ten, twenty years. Winning the food truck would be a way to do what I love while being able to control how much I work."

Abbey rested her chin in the palm of one hand and cupped Marvin's cheek with the other. "I'm so proud of you, Marvin."

Marvin jerked his head away from her hand. "Stop!"

"Wow, sorry."

Hands fell to her lap. Genuine hurt filled her eyes.

Marvin let out a frustrated breath as he glanced around to see who may have seen what happened. His eyes immediately connected with Charlotte's, whose mouth was set in a tattletale smirk.

Great. That's just great.

"I didn't mean to sound that harsh, but I'm at work. You're my teacher, or used to be, and I still see you like that. You're probably just playing around, or maybe this is a touchy-feely side of you that I didn't see back in the day. But your actions are making me uncomfortable. And with you being a part of the contest I'm trying to win, that doesn't feel cool at all."

"Again, I apologize. The last thing I'd want to do is make you feel uneasy around me. But the truth of the matter is . . . I was always attracted to you, Marvin. Being your instructor, I couldn't show it, as the school's rules about fraternization are very clear. I hated when you dropped out of school, and made several phone calls . . . remember?"

"Not really, if I'm being honest." Abbey's shoulders drooped. "Or vaguely, maybe. My life was crazy back then. I like you, too, Abs, I mean Abbey—"

"No, Abs, please! I love it when you call me that."

"See that right there is why I have to stop doing it. I make up nicknames all the time, but it sounds like you've taken that to mean more than it does. I don't want to hurt your feelings or anything—"

"Then don't. I can probably guess what that would be anyway. I'm probably not the type you're used to dating. I don't look like Naomi . . ."

"Look—"

"No." Abbey put up her hand. "I know you like her. I saw the two of you together earlier today."

"You saw . . . what . . . when?"

"I left not long after you did and saw you in her car, or so I thought. But then I entered the parking garage and what looked to be her car was parked with no one there." She shrugged. "I don't see what it is about her . . . I mean . . . did you know her from before?"

Was Abbey really in the hood at two in the morning declaring her love and asking about Naomi? And did she really think he was going to discuss his private life? Marvin felt like he was in the twilight zone. He'd never seen Abbey as anything but a culinary instructor and had no idea she'd been digging on him since he was in her class.

"Naomi and I know some of the same people, but no, I didn't know her before. And while we laugh and flirt around, I'm not trying to get with anybody that has anything to do with the competition. You told me yourself that that's not cool. All I want to do right now is focus on winning and get up out of this hole in the wall, as popular as it is. Speaking of . . ."

He looked at his watch, grabbed his plate and stood. "I need to get back to the kitchen and start closing up."

"Yes, it is late. I need to head back to the Valley." Abbey stood and pulled a wallet out of her purse, and continued to talk as she took out money to pay the bill. "Thanks for the burger and coming to sit with me. I'm glad you're focused on winning the contest, not dating any of the girls there. But after you get the truck, you're going to need investors, equipment, marketing and PR people, staff. Fifty thousand dollars sounds like a lot of money, but it isn't, and you don't want to plug all of your own money into the business anyway.

"Marvin. I was an only child, had older parents.

When they died, I received a sizeable inheritance. I've never been married and I don't have kids. No, I haven't dated much, am rather plain and not at all hip or cool. But I have real feelings for you, and want to see you succeed. I want to help you succeed. And I can. I can help you with everything."

Her look was intense and meaningful as she placed a gentle hand on Marvin's arm before walking out the door. He heard Charlotte's chuckle before turning around, but shut it up with a curt "Don't start."

He finished his shift with Abbey's parting declaration playing on a loop in his brain. He had to admit her boldness surprised him. She'd put it all out there, basically told him she'd bankroll his venture. It was a lot to think about. The generous offer she made occupied his mind all the way home. He remembered the various speakers who came to the culinary school. The upscale appliances provided by top-notch manufacturers along with stainless and copper cookware, the finest knives and every other modern utensil for a chef's dream kitchen. Abbey knew a lot of people. With her money and contacts, Marvin might not have to put any of the fifty-thousand-dollar monetary prize into the business. He could use that as a down payment on a house, one that Abbey would no doubt want to visit, maybe even live in. No doubt, the offer was tempting. But the next morning when he rolled over to a rare Sunday off and an invitation from his brother, Abbey wasn't the woman that came to mind when he thought about who he'd have join him. Naomi was the woman who warmed his heart and other places. Hers was the number he dialed. There were just certain things that no amount of money could buy. A Carter man was one of them.

15

The GPS's automated voice spoke the directions clearly, as though absolutely sure that they were correct. Glad somebody was, because Naomi could swear she was in the wrong neighborhood. One of Marvin's brothers lived in Venice Beach? The only time she'd come down was to bring friends from out of town to let them see the ocean and walk the boardwalk. And while she'd never checked the area's real estate prices, she knew they were expensive. Heck, even urban areas were expensive in metro LA. Nana's house, in the area labeled South Central during the Rodney King riots, was less than fifteen hundred square feet and built over fifty years ago. The last time Nana had it appraised for insurance purposes, the value was placed at $462,500. Not bad for the "hood." Naomi couldn't imagine what the houses cost down here, and one could double whatever that price was if it had an ocean view.

When the GPS informed her that she had arrived,

it was to a gated home across from the ocean. She texted Marvin to confirm where she was and to ask where to park. You'd think if a house cost a million dollars they'd have some designated parking for visitors in front of it. She read the text back from Marvin. Seconds later, the gate opened. So did Naomi's mouth. The house looked straight out of a movie. A two-story modern design with stark white brick and siding and lots of glass. She looked up. *Wait a minute. Are there people on the roof?* No time to solve that mystery. Marvin was outside and waving her over to an empty parking space behind his car. Naomi stood corrected on visitors having to park on the street. Not necessary when one basically had a parking lot behind their gate! She counted at least seven other cars as she pulled her Hyundai behind his SUV.

Marvin walked over and opened her door. "Hey, Juicy."

She got out. "Hey." They hugged. "I thought you said we were going over to your brother's house."

"This is my brother's house."

"What is he, a celebrity or something?"

"No. Byron works for the MTA. He's a bus driver."

"A bus driver?!" Loudly exclaimed at the same time the door opened and a group spilled out. Everyone looked at her. Expressions were mixed. "Oops, I'm sorry. I didn't mean . . ."

"I know you didn't. Come on, let me introduce you."

Another woman stepped outside. Naomi caught

her breath. She had to be the home owner, Naomi reasoned, since the tall, slender woman with long natural hair and flawless skin could also have graced the pages of a fashion magazine. Naomi became conscious of what she was wearing—white skinny jeans (though she knew nothing could really make those thighs look thin), a wraparound top meant to be forgiving in the middle while highlighting her best assets, and wedge-heel sandals. Never one for much makeup, she'd only brushed on a little mascara and applied ruby-colored lip gloss. The braids she'd gotten done two weeks ago had held up fairly well, though an up-close inspection would have been problematic. She'd piled most of the waist-length strands into a loose topknot, with a few curly ones framing her face and the rest draped over her shoulder and down her back. Back home she'd felt her look was fine, even sexy. Now, looking at chicks who could have competed on *America's Next Top Model*, Naomi felt plain, and wished she'd actually gone into Night's fitness centers instead of driving by, at least a time or two. Flustered and about to pass out from trying to hold in her stomach, she accepted Marvin's hand and reached the landing at the same time as the group.

"Hey, bro! About time you got here."

Naomi watched a man obviously related to Marvin grab his hand and pull him into a one-shoulder hug.

"Babe, this is my brother Byron."

"The bus driver," another woman said, a hand over her mouth as she snickered.

"Yeah, I'm a bus driver." He scowled at Naomi. "What of it?"

"Nothing personal," Naomi responded, his sharp comment cutting away a bit of her angst. "It's just now I know why fares keep going up."

Some joined Marvin in laughter while Byron's scowl deepened. "You think I'm taking the money?"

"No, I mean . . . I'm sorry."

"He's just teasing you," Marvin assured her.

Byron clapped Marvin on the shoulder. "I see you've got a live one."

"Just what he needs," the model said, coming up next to Byron. "Don't let my husband bully you. In this family, you've got to hold your own." She held out her hand. "Hi, I'm Cynthia."

"Nice to meet you, Cynthia. I'm Naomi. Your home is beautiful."

"Thank you."

"This is my sister, Anita," Marvin said of the woman who'd laughed when Byron acted angry. "And her boyfriend, Walter."

"Nice to meet you," Anita said, her smile warm and genuine as she forwent a handshake and gave Naomi a hug. "We joke around a lot in this family. It's never personal, okay?"

Still unnerved by her unintended yet unceremonious introduction to the family, Naomi only managed a nervous chuckle in response. Her eyes followed Marvin's and watched the group who'd come out of the house continue across the alley.

"Where are y'all going?" Marvin asked.

"Over to the beach," Byron said over his shoulder. "Everybody else is in there. We'll be back in a minute."

Naomi followed Marvin as he continued up the steps. "Who were those other people?"

"Some of Cynthia's friends from Chicago, her hometown. The guy over there is from New York."

"New York? Really? I've always wanted to go there!"

Marvin stepped back to let Naomi enter the home. She almost gasped out loud. The home's interior was even more stunning than the outside. Shades of blue, gray, tan, and white blended together to create rooms almost too beautiful to occupy. Lavish chandeliers hung in the entryway and dining room, where a generous spread covered the expansive table and nearby buffet. A marble fireplace anchored the far wall. Above it hung a large watercolor painting of Byron, Cynthia, and a smiling baby boy.

A child lives here, birthed by the woman who wore a midriff shirt, showing off a flat stomach? The home was so perfectly pristine and Cynthia so toned that Naomi couldn't imagine either being true.

"They've got kids?" she asked Marvin.

"Just one, but . . ."

His answer was interrupted by a loud guffaw. Naomi turned to see a tall, fine brother coming from the kitchen, side-stepping the attempted swipes of . . .

Jan Baker?

Her nails dug into Marvin's arm as she turned, eyes wide, and mouthed, "Is that really her?"

Jan Baker was the world's latest R & B sensation, someone who, like Adele, Meghan Trainor, and others, celebrated her uniqueness and embraced her womanly curves.

"Yes, that's really Jan Baker," Marvin replied, as Jan caught up with Barry when he stopped in front of Marvin and popped him upside the head with a dish towel.

"I told you to stop sneaking up on me like that. About to make me have a heart attack. And you'd better be glad I didn't drop that whole platter of perfectly grilled salmon!" She turned friendly eyes to Naomi. "I'm sorry to have to show out in front of company, but this Negro . . ." She pulled back the towel. "Is going. To learn. Today!"

She emphasized each part of the phrase with an attempted pop of the towel. Barry ran behind Marvin, who almost got popped, too.

"So if you haven't already guessed it, this is the family jokester and my baby brother Barry. You know who Jan is."

Jan's down-to-earth antics, something similar to what Naomi herself would do, helped calm the frazzled fan down enough to find her voice. "It is so nice to meet you. Girl, I love your music."

Jan held out her hand. "Hi, what's your name?"

"Oh, I'm sorry. Naomi."

"Thank you, Naomi. Nice to meet you."

Barry hugged Jan's neck, pulling tighter as she struggled to get away. "Uh, do you not see me standing here?" he asked Naomi. "I mean, I know she's a star and all, but I don't get a hello?"

Naomi crossed her arms, putting her double Ds front and center. "Not until you stop bothering my favorite singer."

"Tell 'em, girl!" The women high-fived.

Barry dropped his arm and mumbled to Marvin, "Just met and already they're ganging up on me. Where's my girl? Yolanda!"

Marvin gave Naomi a tour of the home and explained how a bus driver could live like a rock star.

"Cynthia's family is wealthy," Marvin said as they passed a window with an ocean view. "This house was their wedding gift to them."

"Wow," Naomi mumbled. "That's a whole other level. My last wedding gift was a set of monogrammed towels and that was a splurge."

"Who are you telling? I got them a George Foreman barbeque grill."

Naomi burst out laughing.

"What's funny? It came with dinner for two coupons prepared by yours truly. I even threw in candles."

"Ah, that's very sweet."

"They loved it."

"Especially since dinner was served . . . here."

"I know. It's a lot, especially for someone like my brother Byron. He's a man's man," Marvin explained. "And a Carter. From the crib, we were

taught to be the provider and take care of home.
He wasn't for the idea at first, but he finally came
around."

The tour continued. Along the way she met
Marvin's next older brother, Nelson, along with his
date, and a few others. All of the men were fine and
the women were gorgeous. They seemed warm
and genuinely glad to meet her, but with each
toned body, designer outfit, and slayed hairstyle,
the normally confident Naomi grew shy and retreated into a quietness that was quite unlike her.
Just as she gave herself a mental shakedown about
how she was just as good as anybody here, they
reached a rooftop fit for the stars who were casually
hanging out in all of that luxury as if they were regular people. Naomi immediately recognized Night
Simmons, the nationally known personal trainer as
popular as Shaun T, whose arm muscles rippled as
he held the rim and floated in a hot tub lined with
shiny gold and rainbow-colored stones. Night had
a slew of gyms around the city. His wife sat on the
Jacuzzi's edge, lazily running her feet through the
water as she talked to another woman beside
her. Naomi couldn't remember her name but
knew her face from the billboards that advertised
Night's gyms. A bartender in an open white shirt
and black slacks stood behind the bar where a reality star and a '90s boys-group member sipped beer
and chatted. Several barely clad women tossed a
beach ball in a nearby pool, while a few couples
danced under a large umbrella to rap music coming
through speakers Naomi couldn't see. A guy with

dreadlocks looked familiar. *The rapper! What's his name?* Naomi's grip on Marvin's hold increased as she forced herself to stop shaking.

Marvin looked at her, concerned. "You alright?"

"Not really. Why didn't you tell me that celebrities would be here? I could have got my hair and nails done, worn something different, been prepared!"

"Because here we treat them like everybody else. Besides, you look amazing. And not all men want thin and crispy. Some of us prefer thick and juicy." He squeezed her "juicy" to emphasize his point.

Naomi appreciated Marvin trying to make her feel good, but after seeing the rappers and actors and models on the roof, she never quite recovered. After the bartender fixed Naomi a strawberry lemonade and gave Marvin a beer, the two went downstairs for something to eat. They fixed plates and got comfy in a glass-enclosed, second-floor sitting room facing the beach. Barry and his girlfriend joined them. Byron returned and chatted a bit before running off again to tend to hosting duties. Some sat, like Nelson and his date. Others just peeked their heads in, like Jan. The vodka-laced drink calmed Naomi's nerves a bit, but she was never able to fully relax. The food was delicious, but she was too self-conscious to enjoy it. Everyone was friendly, but she felt that was because of Marvin. The atmosphere and the guests were all above her pay grade, and while Marvin was attentive and tried to make her comfortable, Naomi couldn't help but feel out of place. When Marvin was pulled away by his brothers, Naomi told him she'd be fine. But she wasn't. Less than thirty minutes into fake smiling and idle chit-chat, and in need of antacids, she found Marvin in a game room that could have been shipped from Las Vegas.

"Wow, check out that pool table! I've never seen one like that."

Marvin looked over. "You play?"

Naomi nodded. "A little bit."

"Cool. Me and you can play next after I beat this clown." He nodded toward Doug, cued up his stick, and dropped a solid into the far right pocket.

Naomi sidled up to him, lowered her voice. "Thanks for inviting me over. This was amazing."

"The day isn't over." Marvin lined up another shot.

"Yeah, but I'm heading out."

This got his attention. He straightened and asked her, "Why, what's the matter?"

"Just a little upset stomach, no big deal."

"Let me finish this game right quick and I'll go with you."

"It's okay. Stay and enjoy your family. We'll talk later."

Marvin looked across the room and saw his sister Anita's date. "Walter! Come finish this game up for me, finish taking Doug out."

After exchanging shoulder bumps with the men in the room and hugging the women, they made the rounds so Marvin could say good-bye to his family. Naomi thanked Cynthia for the invitation and complimented her again on her home. She got up the nerve to ask Jan for a selfie and snuck pics of the rapper and Night, the personal trainer, so she could text them to Kristy and brag. Once outside, she took a deep breath and immediately felt better.

Marvin noticed. "You sure you're alright?"

Naomi nodded. "I'm fine. It was just . . . never mind."

"Where are you going, home?"

Naomi hadn't thought that far ahead. She looked at Marvin, saw the concern on his face. "Why, you going to come over and take care of me?"

"Is Nana home? I don't need any more bedspring tattoos on my face." His eyes dropped to her lips. His expression softened. "Although I can think of a couple ways to make you feel better."

Naomi's stomach tightened as a squiggle traveled from its core to her heat. She remembered the melody Marvin's tongue had played on her honey box, began to instantly feel better and got an idea.

"You really want to help me feel better?"

"What'd I tell you, girl?"

"Then neither one of us is going home just yet. Follow me."

She backed out of the gated parking and pulled ahead to give Marvin room to maneuver. Byron waved to him from the door and then ran out to the car. While they talked, Naomi pulled out her phone and spoke a command, then tapped the directions so the GPS could think for her. Between her time with the stars just now and memories of Marvin's magic that first night, Naomi's mind was a muddled mush. She returned Byron's wave as he backed away from Marvin's car and went back to the house.

Heading down Venice Boulevard, Naomi checked her rearview mirror now and again to make sure Marvin was behind her. At a stop light she started to text him the destination but then decided to let it be a surprise. Long a popular tourist destination, the Venice Beach streets were crowded, with wealth and poverty living side by side. Naomi didn't miss the irony of a homeless man sleeping in front of a trendy-looking boutique. She imagined the price of one of the items in the window could feed that man for a week, or a month, maybe even get him a room for a night or two. And Marvin had family who lived there? For the first time since meeting him Naomi found herself a bit intimidated, even as she found ironies in his life as puzzling as the beach town's economic divide. Like how did one brother live on the beach, another be married to an R & B star, and Marvin be stuck living at home, working at a greasy spoon and competing with her for a food truck and a nice chunk of cash?

By the time Naomi turned off Venice onto Lincoln, heading toward Los Angeles International Airport, LAX, questions about Marvin the man had bypassed those about his family. She realized that considering where both their mouths had been in relation to each other, she knew way too little, and promised herself that by the time the day ended she'd know way more. In the meantime she punched the favorites list on her stereo and turned up the title cut of Jan's latest album—*All This Woman*.

When Kristy sees my picture with her, cousin is going to freak!

Naomi saw a text message come in. At the next stoplight she tapped the icon.

Where are we going?

Naomi sent him a big smile emoji and started singing with Jan. She put the song on repeat and rocked it as Lincoln merged into Sepulveda Boulevard. A short time later she pulled into the entrance to their destination, drove around to the side and parked her car. Marvin pulled his SUV beside her car, turned off his engine and got out.

"I should have known you'd like that song."

"You know it! Can you handle all this woman?" she asked.

"You already know the answer to that."

She sure did, so much so that a sarcastic comment refused to come out of her mouth.

He looked over at the building. "I wondered where you were going."

"Now you know."

"Hotel. Motel."

They sang together, "Holiday Inn!"

She laughed as Marvin did a spin and started dancing toward a side entrance. Naomi went over to check them in, but after finding out she hadn't prepaid the room, Marvin insisted on handling the bill.

"Considering how I'm about to tear all that up"—he checked out her ass—"it's the least I can do."

"Alright now, don't write a promissory note that your pen can't sign!"

"Baby, I'm full of ink . . . you feel me?"

"No, but I'm getting ready to." They entered the elevator. She pushed up on him. "And this time there will be no interruptions."

16

Marvin reached the room, tried to play it cool as he slid the key card into the slot. Inside though, he was doing the running man. He'd wanted to be with Naomi since that very first day when she tried to dis him in line. They stepped inside the room. It was nice and cool, but Marvin still felt a bead of sweat roll down his neck. He adjusted his collar, watching Naomi check out the room. She closed the curtains, then walked by him toward the bathroom.

"When I come back out, you'd better be ready."

The saucily delivered words were a complete turn-on. He eyed her as she sashayed into the bathroom, that big round ass taunting him with each bounce. She quickly turned while closing the door and caught him staring. Her confident laugh told him everything. She knew what she was working with, and knew he loved every inch.

Yeah, it's about to be on!

Marvin undid his belt, unzipped his pants, then sat on the bed and took off his Jordans. In stockinged feet he walked over to where cool air flowed from a vent, unbuttoned his shirt and pulled it off. He grabbed his tee and pulled it over his head. Then he heard the shower. He eyed the bathroom door, a smile slowly spreading across his face. He let his jeans drop to the floor. Pulled off his boxers and stepped out of both. Thoughts of Naomi in the shower, all that juicy wet and sudsy, made him harden like steel. His shaft went before him like a curved baton seeking its majorette to go for a twirl. Marvin didn't plan to do any marching, but he was sure there would be sound.

He gently opened the door and eased inside. The curtain was pulled, the mirror foggy as wisps of steam wafted toward Marvin's body.

He stepped to the curtain. "Nay."

A gasp and then the curtain was ripped back, revealing Naomi in all of her naked glory. "Why are you sneaking in here, scaring somebody? I could have slipped and fell."

"Stop yapping, woman," Marvin replied, all calm and authoritative as he adjusted the water temperature, stepped in the shower and backed her up against the tile.

"Shut me up," Naomi dared, rubbing her sudsy titties against his chest.

"Okay." Marvin eased the bar from Naomi's hand, soaped the washcloth and looked deep into her eyes as he ran it over her body. Across her breasts and down her stomach, around to her butt and over her thighs.

"Spread your legs."

He watched Naomi's expression as she started to say something smart, saw it change when he eased the cloth between her lower lips, let his finger graze her pearl as he washed her there.

"Umm."

The groan low in his throat, Marvin dropped the towel and played her box with his fingers, placed his middle one deep into her heat.

"Ah!" Naomi's eyes fluttered closed as she ground herself against him. He smiled, noting that within sixty seconds his talkative, take-charge baby girl had offered up her body and exchanged words for sounds. He slid a finger to that plump rump he loved, between those thick cheeks to her sensitive spot.

"Ooh," she squealed and wrapped her arms around him, swiped his mouth with her tongue and then plunged it inside. His tongue met hers, they twirled and danced. He lathered her body and then rubbed his body against hers to soap his own. He felt her reach for him and stepped out of her grasp. She had him harder than an AK and ready to shoot. But Marvin was nowhere near ready to fire. These two lovers had a long way to go.

He broke the kiss, suckled her breasts, then stepped back and placed a hand on her leg, just behind her knee.

"What are you doing?" she managed, soft and breathless.

"Lift your leg," he demanded.

"What?"

He lifted it for her and placed her foot on the rim of the tub. She stood there, exposed, her eyes widening with understanding as he began to kneel. Eye level to the dish he was about to taste, he steadied a hand on each hip, licked his lips and slowly raised his eyes to hers. This time he caught her watching, felt her shudder, and smiled. Just the thought of what he was about to do had her preening. He wanted to fuck her mind as well as her body. Leave such an impression that from here on out he could simply look at her and make her pussy drip. Carter men were known for being unforgettable. He had to represent!

And he did. Parting the doors to paradise, he licked and sucked and nibbled until she screamed out his name. Lifted her out of the shower (his back would feel it tomorrow but brother felt like King Kong today), and after reaching the bed stopped only long enough to grab a condom before following her to the sheets and screwing her senseless. Soon their bodies were wet again, skin gleaming with the sweat of their passion. Marvin held on for as long as he could, then released his ecstasy with a couple of grunts and one long shudder before rolling off Naomi and onto his back. All he could say was, "Damn."

Catching his breath, Marvin tried to pull Naomi into a snuggle.

She resisted. "I'm over here sweating like a sow in Spanx. Give me a minute."

"Told you I was going to pull out the whip appeal. You thought I was playing?" Marvin wore a satisfied expression as his chest led the way across the room, where he adjusted the wall thermostat. "Put it on you until you were wringing wet!"

"Please, fool! Half of this is your sweat!"

"Probably." They both laughed. Marvin grabbed the two complimentary waters off of the counter and gave one to Naomi. "I still put it on you, didn't I, girl?"

"You sure did," Naomi replied, her voice both breathy and syrupy sweet. "The kitchen isn't the only place you know how to work a hot link. It wasn't a jumbo foot-long but . . ."

"But what?" Marvin rejoined her in bed. He took the sheet and began wiping her off. He'd put everything including his still jacked-up knee into insuring her sexual satisfaction, and while his mask of bravado suggested otherwise, he wasn't entirely sure he'd accomplished the job.

He wiped the sweat from under an ample titty, then rested his sheet-clenching hand on her stomach. "What, you didn't cum?"

"You didn't hear me shouting, feel me shaking?"

He released the sheet, sat back and away from her. "Could have been faking. You know how women do."

"Do I seem like the type of woman to fake anything?"

From the corner of his eye, Marvin saw Naomi cross her arms over those big breasts he loved so much. Since she always had one, the attitude she showed didn't prove a thing.

"Baby, I felt that orgasm all the way down to my toes. It's not the size of the boat, but the motion of the ocean. You didn't know?"

"Of course I knew that!"

But really, he didn't. He wanted to, but the first girl he slept with—the one who laughed and called his penis a little twinkie—had left him scarred.

"Just want to make sure you're feeling better."

Naomi scooted over and laid her head on his shoulder. "My stuff is still pulsating. That good dick cured everything wrong with me today and anything that might pop up tomorrow!"

The room, maybe the world, became quiet with her declaration. Marvin played it cool, slid his gaze toward her face all casual-like to check her out. He looked for the twinkle in her eye, the one that said she was joking as was often the case. But her eyes were soft, almost loving. Getting together had meant to be casual, two adults wanting sex with no strings attached. But what he'd experienced since that night at Nana's house seemed more than casual. The look in Naomi's eyes just now looked more serious. Had they bypassed infatuation and jumped into true feelings? Could he afford to do that with a competitor in a contest where there could only be one winner? And was there any way

to hide what both were feeling from Abbey's
prying eyes?

No.

Thoughts of his former teacher and the contest
was like a wave of reality over their sex-made sand-
castle. He shifted farther away from Naomi, where
his shoulder could no longer support her head.

"What's the matter?"

"Nothing, just thinking."

"About what?"

He finished off the bottle of water, adjusted the
pillow and turned toward Naomi. "What was up
with you earlier? At my brother's house?"

"What do you mean?"

Marvin ran a hand down her thigh and then
rested it there. "I kept wondering who was the shy,
unsure chick who was walking beside me and wondering where was loud-mouthed Naomi?"

"I told you. The celebrities made me nervous."

He harrumphed. "I've seen you around celebrities, the ones working the contest. None of them
seemed to affect you like that. I didn't think my
family and their friends would be any different."

"That's just it. They weren't strangers in a huge
room full of contestants and a camera crew. We
were in a home, up close and personal, where I
could literally reach out and touch the idols I've
seen on TV. To be in the kitchen with Jan Baker,
who wrote the big girl's anthem? Then have Night,
the country's most popular personal trainer, walk
into a room? That was a lot to handle, baby, and

considering that I was blindsided, I think I did pretty well."

"You did fine. I noticed because I know you. And like I said earlier, for me and my brothers, people are people, period. No matter the job title. It's the way we were raised."

Marvin repositioned a pillow and rested his head against it. "I remember a block party when I was like . . . seven or eight years old. This up-and-coming rapper was the headliner on the young adult stage. I loved that dude! He was the epitome of manhood, swagger, and cool, all wrapped into one. The next day at our usual Sunday dinner, I went on and on about how great he was and how I wanted to be just like him. I'll never forget how Daddy reacted."

"What did he say?"

"That it was okay to admire, but not to put folk higher. Then he used the tone of voice that usually preceded a whupping and told me that he'd better not ever hear me say I wanted to be anybody other than a Carter ever again."

"Did you get a whupping?"

"No, but I would have preferred a hundred switches to the hurt in his eyes that I'd ever want to be anybody other than his son."

Marvin slid a glance toward Naomi. "So what you think is me being conceited or big-headed is just me knowing that nobody can do Marv Carter better than me."

A brief pause, then Naomi said, "So you're blaming your big head on your daddy?"

Marvin perched on his elbow, ready to defend the Carter name, but he looked over to see the teasing gleam in Naomi's eye that he'd come to love, followed by her carefree, throaty laughter.

"You were getting ready to jump all over that, huh?"

"Naw . . ."

"Yes, you were, and I don't blame you. He sounds like a good daddy."

"Best one out there." The room had cooled off, so when Marvin pulled Naomi closer she didn't resist.

"How did your family meet all of those famous people? And not just meet but marry them?"

Marvin shrugged. "It just happened."

"But how?"

"Doug met Jan at the post office."

Naomi glanced over. "What, she went there to mail a letter?"

"They worked together."

"You're lying."

"Real talk."

"What?" Long and drawn out, like WTH and STFU at the same time. "I thought she used to be a secretary or something."

"She worked the counter at the Normandie Branch."

"Your brother still work there?"

"No. He quit after Jan blew up and asked him to be her manager."

"Hard to believe that just a few short years ago she had a regular job. I can't even imagine that now."

"Neither could she. Doug teases her by saying that if she hadn't quit he'd eventually have had to fire her."

"So she used to work a regular job, just like me."

"That's what I mean when I said they're just people. Mama says celebrities are just regular people who caught a break. That's the only difference between someone singing on TV and a hundred people who do it ten times better from choir stands and living rooms."

"Dreams really can come true."

"They can and do, baby girl. You'll see it happen when a brand-new food truck is parked in my driveway."

"What are you going to do, steal it from in front of Nana's house?"

"Whatever, girl."

"Because there can only be one contest winner and that will be me."

"We'll see."

"What about the model?"

"Model?"

"The one who owns the house in Venice."

"Oh, Cynthia." Marvin chuckled. "She'd appreciate hearing you say that, and she could for sure rock a runway. But she's not a model. She works for nonprofits. In fact, she heads up Jan's foundation."

"So how did Cynthia and . . ."

"Byron."

"How'd they meet?"

"That's a funny story." Marvin told her about it,

and also about how the famous personal trainer's wife was best friends with Jan, which is why they'd been invited over. "Hollywood and that whole world is smaller than you might think," he ended. "Everyone either knows the other person or knows someone who does. What about you? In one day you met almost half of my family, and instead of introducing me to your relatives I had my ass pushed under a bed!"

"You know why I had to do that."

"I'm just teasing. Had it been my house and Mama, trust, I would have done the same thing. Only difference is she would have found you. Three older brothers have shown her all the right places to look."

"Oh my God, that would be so embarrassing. I can't imagine getting caught like that."

"It may not have turned out as bad as you think. Depending on your actions, Mama would have cussed you out and then asked you to stay for dinner. My family is crazy like that. So what about you? It's your grandmother, Nana, and who else?"

A loud grumble rose up between them.

"Dang, girl! Was that your stomach?"

"Yes. I guess my appetite finally came back."

"You want to go grab something and bring it back here?"

"No." Naomi climbed off the bed and retrieved her clothes from the bathroom. "I need to go have a talk with Nana. Things haven't been right since I lied about you being there."

"She knows?"

"Unfortunately."

"How?"

"A neighbor saw you leave the house and push your car down the street."

"Why can't folks mind their business? So how did you explain it?"

"I didn't, at least not at first." Naomi had pulled on her pants and top and now sat on the bed with her shoes in her hand, reliving the unfortunate incident yet again as she told Marvin. "The subject didn't come up until the next evening. I was tired after working all day and just wanted to grab a bite to eat and go to bed. That's why the question caught me off guard. She asked if I'd had company the day before, and I said no. Only then did she tell me about Miss Josephine who lives across the street having seen you leave the house and push your car down the street."

"Damn! Nosy neighbors."

"Especially Miss J. She eats and sleeps by that window. I should have known she'd see you."

"Sounds like Mama's neighbor. I bet she's old, huh?"

"She's lived on the block for like a hundred years. A bird don't fly down the street without her knowing about it."

Naomi placed her sandals on the floor and worked her feet into them. "So after that, I told Nana that you came by but you didn't stay, and that you were only there to get something related to the contest."

"Did she believe you?"

"Hell, no."

Marvin laughed.

"That's not funny!"

"Yes, it is. You can't fool those grandmas, man. Like Mama says, they've walked around the block once and run around it twice."

"Exactly, which is why I rarely lie to Nana, and having done so doesn't feel good. So I'm going to go home, fix dinner if she hasn't already, and tell her you came over and fucked me in her house."

"Naomi!"

It was Naomi's turn to laugh. "I'm just kidding. I won't say it quite like that."

"Dang, your grandmother knows I sneaked into her house. I'll never be able to show my face there, now."

"Yes, you will. Nana meets all my friends."

"Then maybe you shouldn't say anything yet. Because after I win the contest you might not want to remain my friend."

"I'll take my chances."

"For real though, we're going to have to keep this on the low while we're competing. I don't want anybody to be able to use our friendship as a way to get us disqualified."

"Why, is there something in the rules saying contestants can't date?"

"No, but still. It can be viewed as a conflict. I

know it will be hard, but try not to fall in love with me until after I get the truck."

"Please, you're the one who'd better watch it. My ass has you hypnotized."

"Ha! You got me. I can't even lie about that."

They continued talking while getting dressed, speculating about what challenges the judges would cook up next and figuring out how soon the two could hook up again. That they wanted it to happen sooner rather than later was one thing on which the two could definitely agree. Naomi played it a little coy, but Marvin made it clear that he wanted more of her juicy loving. Truth be told, he liked being around her, in and out of bed, and wondered how that would play out once the contest was over. Driving home, Marvin wondered why he didn't tell Naomi his main reason for wanting to keep their dating a secret for now. Because of Abbey's warning, maybe even her offer, too. At first he felt it was a little bit shady, but by the time he reached the house he was convinced not telling Naomi was no big deal. What a woman didn't know wouldn't hurt her, right? Time would tell.

17

Naomi did a lot of thinking on her way home, too. Thought about how not even a month ago she was single with no prospects and replacing batteries in a worn-out dildo, and less than twenty-four hours ago had enjoyed some of the best sex with a live penis that she'd ever had. She replayed the whole day in her mind—from the stars at Venice Beach to the heavenly humping that happened on the hotel bed—and even with the nerves and feelings of discomfort during part of the day's adventures, hanging out with Marvin had been pretty much amazing. So much so that the thought of a casual romp or two that ended when the contest did seemed totally impossible. She wanted more of Marvin. The sex. Camaraderie. Competition. Food. Everything. But was that even possible? Naomi thought back to what he'd said as they parted, about keeping their dating a secret until the contest was over, and thought . . . *maybe*. Wasn't that what the word "until" meant? That they'd secretly date until after the contest and then take their dating public? Meaning that Marvin saw what they had continuing, too? If so, that was even more of a reason to sit down with Nana and set the record straight. When it came to men, Nana could spot game faster than Bolt could run the hundred, could read a man's face and forecast your future together without the guy having to open his mouth. It had caused more than one argument in Naomi's teenage years, basically because Nana disapproved of every boy Naomi dated. That Naomi wasn't with any of those jokers proved that her grandmother's assessments had been right.

Naomi reached the house and was relieved to not see Nana's car in the drive. She felt like cooking and knew that a difficult talk was better digested paired with a good Southern meal. She parked her car in front of the house and reached for her phone.

"Hey, Nana, it's me. Where are you?" Shutting off the Bluetooth, she placed the phone under her ear, grabbed her purse and got out. "What program is happening over there? The pastor's anniversary?" She shifted the phone and dug for her keys. "I know you're going to enjoy that. You love his preaching. Who?" Opening the door, Naomi tossed her purse on the couch, tapped the speaker button and continued into the kitchen. "Miss Josephine. When did she start going to church?"

Probably after getting all up in my business when what she really needed to do was mind her own!

"What do you mean *start*? Josie's been a Christian longer than you've been alive. Been attending church ever since we've been neighbors, and that's been for over forty years. If you ever came to church with me, you'd know."

"Dang, Nana, it hasn't been that long."

"When was the last time?"

"I don't know." She did, but it would prove Nana's point.

"Well, I do. It was Easter. And the time before that was Christmas. You're one of those twice-a-year holiday Christians, visiting only on the day Jesus was born and on the day He died."

Nana proved the point herself.

"What are you doing right now? Service is just about to start and I can save you a seat."

"That's why I called, actually. I'm cooking dinner, so I hope when you get back home you're ready to eat."

"Well, since you've turned down the offer to fellowship I guess it's good that you're being of service. In fact, I'll invite Josie and my other friends to join us. Since you won't come to church, we'll bring the church to you!"

Naomi swallowed a groan, but between ending the call and checking the fridge she decided to change her attitude. Nana was right. Naomi should go to church more often. Maybe if she did, more of her prayers might get answered, like the one she'd sent up while signing up for the contest, and the other one she'd hurriedly uttered before making those hash browns. Maybe a prayer would be what helped her win it all, even snag a man as a bonus. Naomi stopped right then, a frozen roast in hand, and whispered an appeal.

"God, please help me win the contest, and if he's as good a dude as he seems to be, please let things work out with me and Marvin. Okay, that's it. Thank you. Amen."

Naomi decided to attend church with Nana in the very near future and in the rare moment of piety to forgive the nosy Miss J, too. She then sent a text, and seconds later received a reply that made her already sunny mood brighten even more. Marvin would join them for dinner. Knowing he'd be there, she paid the details of her stellar cooking even more attention. She pulled out seasonings and a cutting board and within thirty minutes placed a beautifully marinated piece of meat into the oven, surrounded by chopped vegetables and set to a temperature that would allow the dish to cook low and slow. Then, continuing to feel unusually happy, like she could burst out laughing for no reason, Naomi decided to turn the evening into a true dinner party by formally setting the table and buying something slightly alcoholic, something Nana's friends might drink. Maybe they'd convince Nana to have a sip. She knew her confession would go down better with the pork roast, but thought a little inebriation couldn't hurt either. After double-checking the oven temp, Naomi hopped into her car and headed to the 99 Cents Store near her house, where with her discount and ten dollars, she could get everything she needed for the evening and still have change left over. Almost two hours later, as she viewed her impromptu celebratory handiwork, Naomi second-guessed her decision to have a party. But after a series of text exchanges ten minutes later, she changed her mind again. Nana had criticized her paltry church attendance, but it seemed that maybe God, in His mercy, hadn't yet given up on her and might even be willing to help her out a bit.

Naomi had just pulled a pan of homemade cookies out of the oven when she heard the front door open.

Nana called out just as Miss Josephine exclaimed, "Lord have mercy, it smells good in here!"

A voice Naomi didn't recognize echoed the sentiment and added, "Well, now, if this isn't fancy."

Naomi walked into the dining room just as her Nana called out again.

"Here I am, Nana." She hugged her grandmother and turned to Miss J. "Hello, Miss Josephine." And to the remaining two women, "Good evening."

"What's all this?" Nana asked.

"Since we're having guests I decided to set a formal table."

Naomi watched Nana take in the white tablecloth, yellow candles, glasses of lemon water, and sunflower placemats with matching napkins. She could almost hear her sharp granny's wheels turning.

"Does this have something to do with that contest you're in?"

"Maybe a little bit. Come on, ladies, have a seat.

Help yourself to the pitcher of sangria. It has a little kick to it, but not too much. Nana, can I speak to you for a minute?"

Naomi grabbed her grandmother's hand, led her past the kitchen and down the hall to the bathroom, where she pulled her inside and closed the door.

"Nana, I wasn't totally honest with you the other day and feel really bad about it. My friend from the contest wasn't over here to pick up a utensil. He came over to see me. His name is Marvin. I really like him, and invited him over for dinner."

"Uh-huh."

"I guess I wanted him to think that this was my house. I mean, I'd told him that you live here, but he forgot, and when I realized that, I didn't correct him. So when you came home early I just . . . panicked . . . and didn't tell you the truth. We didn't . . ."

The rest of the sentence died as Nana's eyes narrowed in disbelief or suspicion, Naomi wasn't sure which.

"I'm sorry."

"I'm glad your conscience bothered you enough to tell me the truth. Not that I hadn't figured it out within two seconds of stepping into your room."

Naomi's eyes widened in the same way Nana's had narrowed. "You knew?"

"Kids always think they're the smartest ones born, forgetting that those older than them were once kids, too. I knew that disheveled bed and cloud of perfume didn't come from you being a dancing klutz. I thought whoever you had over was in the closet. So where was he?"

Naomi looked appropriately sheepish. "Under the bed."

"That was my second thought, but I didn't think a grown man could fit under there."

"It wasn't easy."

"You ought to be ashamed of yourself." Twinkling eyes softened the gruffness of Nana's declaration.

"I am, that's why I told you. Because Miss J saw his car."

"I saw it, too. Heard the boards creak when he left."

Naomi's mouth opened, but no sound came out.

"Nadine! Where are you hiding? Do you need help?"

Both grandmother and granddaughter looked toward the door.

"Everything's fine," Nana said through the door. "That's Josie, probably already tipsy. She always was a guzzler, never did learn how to sip. Let me go and attend to my guests." Just before opening the bathroom door she turned to Naomi. "And just so you know, once upon a time I had a very similar conversation to this one with your mama. It happened about nine months before you were born."

With a wink, Nana left the bathroom . . . and Naomi still speechless.

Within seconds she gathered herself enough to return to the kitchen and retrieve the salads, smiling as she listened to Nana's friends comment on how the simple yet specific touches had added sophistication and charm to the room. She knew that not even the humble Nadine "Nana" Alberts Carson could ignore such glorified compliments. Placing the salad plates on a large plastic tray, Naomi reentered the dining room.

"This is a beet salad," Naomi explained as she placed the appetizer in front of each guest. She took a seat and continued, becoming more comfortable as she talked. Cooking, discussing, and/or eating food were all in her comfort zones and what she enjoyed. "It's made with beets, of course, goat cheese, almonds, and arugula, then tossed in a Dijon mustard and balsamic vinaigrette. I hope you're hungry!"

"Didn't you invite somebody?" Nana asked.

"Yes, but he knew you guys would get here first and asked that we start without him."

Naomi took a few bites and then returned to the kitchen to check on the second course. While doing so, she listened to the critics' voices as they ate her food.

"This is good, baby," Nana called out.

"Thank you!"

"I like it, too." Margaret said.

At sixty-five, Margaret was the youngest of the guests Nana had invited, and to Naomi sounded like the most adventurous. After returning the roast to the warm oven, she rejoined them at the table.

Sue Cartwright, a member of Nana's Baptist congregation who'd just turned the big seven-0, sounded thoughtful as she spoke around a mouthful. "I'm only familiar with iceberg and romaine lettuce. This is different, but mixed with the dressing you made, I like it."

"I like my greens cooked," was Miss J's truthful answer, as she set down her fork and wiped her mouth on a napkin. Naomi expected no less. Nor was she surprised at Miss J's next question. "Who else is coming?" she asked, nodding at the empty chair next to Naomi, before looking at her directly.

Naomi swallowed a bite. "A friend."

"Who, Kristy?"

The doorbell rang.

"No, not Tee, Miss J." Naomi excused herself from the table. "I'll be right back."

Her heartbeat increased as she walked through the door and peeped through the hole, although she was already sure of who was on the other side.

She opened the door. "Hey, Marvin." She stepped back so that he could enter, and then accepted his hug. "We just started on the appetizer. Come on in."

The room that just seconds before had hummed with conversation and the clang of silverware on china was pin-drop quiet. Naomi dropped Marvin's hand before entering, but was very aware of his presence behind her.

"Nana, ladies, this is Marvin, one of the competitors in the contest I entered. Food Truck Bucks."

"Hello, everybody."

Naomi watched as Marvin worked the room like a politician up for reelection. He stepped first to her grandmother and held out his hand. "You must be Naomi's grandmother Nana."

"Why, yes I am."

"Mrs. Carson, I know we're not related, but do you mind if I call you Nana, too? My grandmother lives in Mississippi. We don't see her much, and your warmth and ageless beauty remind me of her."

"Ooh, did you hear that?" one of the ladies asked no one in particular. "He said she is a beauty."

Miss Josephine's focus had been different. "I just heard him mention age."

Meanwhile, a clearly impressed Nana nodded her head.

"Nana, thanks for letting me come over." He leaned down and pressed a kiss to her forehead. Naomi could have sworn she saw a blush to Nana's cheek. He offered a handshake and smile to the others as he crossed to his seat.

"Something sure smells good," he said, once he reached his seat and sat down. "Nana, when it comes to the kitchen, I'm sure you taught Naomi everything she knows."

"W-w-well . . ."

Naomi remained standing, taking in the phenomena that a woman she'd known her entire life, and had seen talk a blue streak ten feet long, was stuttering her words.

"Let me get your plate," Naomi told Marvin, and broke the awkward silence. As she headed toward the kitchen and heard Miss Josephine's question, she experienced a brief moment where she wished the quiet had remained.

"Are you the young man I saw leaving here the

other night? The one who had to push his car to get it started?"

Naomi stopped, frozen. Had there been a sink-hole in the middle of Nana's kitchen, she would have gladly disappeared through it. Then she heard Marvin's answer, delivered on the waves of self-conscious yet endearing laughter, and fell just a little bit more in love.

"You must be Miss Josephine."

"How'd you know?"

"Because Naomi told me that you'd observed me pushing my car to get it started and told Mrs. Carson, Nana. I told her that you reminded me of the lady who used to live next to my mother, the one who inspired my love for baking. She made it her business to know everybody else's business, along with a few more single, retired ladies. They provided better security than the LAPD. Nothing got past them on our block. By the time I graduated, neighborhood crime was almost nonexistent. We need more women like you."

Naomi brought out his salad and finished her own, glad not to have to carry the conversation. Marvin handled those older women like rare art, admiring, complimenting, and giving them the respect due an elder. He regaled them with tales of growing up in Inglewood, of his father's war stories and his mother left to raise five boys. He removed the salad plates while she brought out the entrée, which had been plated on a porcelain serving dish. Everyone oohed and aahed at the tender meat, the nicely seasoned potatoes and carrots, the crispy char on the garlic and onions, and how perfectly the accompanying Texas toast sopped up all that juice. Right after she'd delivered small bowls of vanilla ice cream topped with warm oatmeal cookies, Marvin surprised her again.

"I'm sorry to bring this up in front of mixed company, but Nana, I owe you an apology. The other night I came over without asking your permission. I know that wasn't right because it isn't how I was raised. When you came home early, me and Naomi freaked out. I thought about what my mother would do and hid under the bed."

He nodded at Miss Josephine's wide-eyed expression. "I know it's hard to imagine getting this two-hundred-plus body between Naomi's bed and the floor, but not as hard as actually doing it with only seconds to spare. My back is still recovering from trying to hide, and if I never again see a bedspring, it'll be too soon."

Margaret whooped. "Lord! I've heard everything now."

"We didn't get all the way into things, if you know what I mean, but I still felt guilty."

"Not many young men would do what you did just now," Nana said. "Naomi knows I don't like her having men in the house with the door closed. I know she's grown, but as long as she is under my roof she has to go by my rules."

"You're absolutely right, and I'm very sorry for seeming disrespectful, even though that wasn't my intent. Can you forgive me for coming over without making sure it was alright with you?"

Nana was so impressed that Naomi thought she'd not only forgive Marvin but invite him to spend the night. That didn't happen, but as the women enjoyed coffee and Marvin helped her clean the kitchen, Naomi knew one thing for absolute sure. Marvin Carter was a keeper, almost worth as much as a first-place win in Food Truck Bucks. She knew it was a long shot for her to take home both prizes, but she also knew that nothing beat a failure but a try.

18

The next week passed without Marvin seeing
Naomi. She was never far from his mind though,
something that intrigued and irked him at the same
time. The separation wasn't his choice. It couldn't
be helped. Donald fired a new cook and then went
on vacation. The girl hadn't been qualified to begin
with and should have lost her job. Being the boss,
Donald should have postponed his vacation until a
replacement was found. But that would have been
too much like right. So for the past week Marvin
had worked like a slave, but after taxes came out
of his paycheck, had little to prove it. Phone calls
revealed that Naomi had been busy, too, running
between houses to care for her cousin and grandmother, who'd both been afflicted with the same
stomach virus. He'd heard the worry and vulnerability in Naomi's voice when they talked, and goaded
her to try and boost her spirits and bring back the
strong personality he'd met that first day. "Don't let
a virus be the excuse for why you drop out of the

race, instead of the real reason—that you can't beat me." Whether it was those words or something else, when he arrived at the convention center the following Saturday, Naomi's was one of the first faces he saw.

"Hey, Juicy. You look good today."

"Hey, Magic Marvin." They enjoyed a brief hug. "Flattery will get you everywhere, but it won't distract me."

"Always accusing me of ulterior motives when I'm just speaking the truth and trying to be nice."

"In that case, thank you."

"That's better. You're welcome. How's your cousin? And Nana?"

"They're both doing better, but I worry about Nana. She says she's feeling better, but sometimes I think she tells me what she thinks I want to hear."

"Did you take her to the doctor and have her checked out?"

"I wanted to, but she wouldn't hear of it, said there wasn't a cure for getting old."

Marvin instinctively wrapped his arms around her. "Hang in there, baby. Everything is going to be okay."

He felt her take a deep breath before she pushed him away. "It sure will," Naomi said, bravado back in her voice. "As soon as I kick your butt and take this prize!"

"We'll see about that," Marvin countered, while secretly wishing they could both win. If it weren't for the fact that winning the contest would jumpstart his future, he'd win and then give her the prize.

Before Marvin had time to wrestle with that unexpected emotion, round three of the preliminaries began. Instead of Ted, Da Chen was on stage surrounded by a group of people holding signs. The contestants took their seats, curiosity in their faces. Like them, Marvin wondered who the group was and what was on the signs each one of them held, until he recognized one of them as the owner of a food truck. Marvin smiled, hoping they'd get a chance to actually cook on one. Da Chen took the mike without having to ask for quiet. The participants held a collective breath as tension and expectation fairly crackled through the room.

"Wow, it's quiet in here. You guys look nervous. I know you're feeling the pressure, but relax. You're going to live, I promise. You believe me?"

A smattering of responses floated across the room.

"Up until now, the focus has been on your cooking chops, but the name of this competition is what?" Da put a hand to his ear.

"Food Truck Bucks!"

"That's right, so today we're going to focus on the food truck. Onstage are fifteen owners of some of LA's most successful and popular food trucks. The name of their food truck is written on the sign they're holding. Stephanie, one of the show's producers, is handing out envelopes to each of you. Don't open them yet. Once everyone has an envelope, you'll open them up and match your name with the food truck owner standing on stage. The two of you will cook on their truck today and will be required to add a dish of your choice that will complement their current menu. Then you'll go out on the streets of LA where you'll have three-and-a-half hours to shop, cook, and sell your dish. The ten teams that come back with the most money will move on to the fourth and final round. That means there are five teams here today that won't be here next week."

Once everyone had an envelope, Da held up his hand. "Your time will begin as soon as the envelopes are opened and that time . . . starts . . . now!"

He brought down his hand and a mini chaos ensued. Participants scrambled to find the other person holding the same food truck name, then hurried to that owner. Marvin was hoping to get Phil, the owner he knew had hamburgers on his menu. He was also hoping the gods would smile and he'd get paired with Naomi. Neither happened. He ended up with a truck that sold Mexican food, and when he looked Naomi was nowhere in sight. Still, four hours later when everyone returned to the center and the results came in, neither Marvin nor Naomi had sold the most of their dish, but both lived to cook another week.

"I see you made it," he said when they reconnected.

"Barely," Naomi responded. "When I got a truck that sold cupcakes, I almost died."

"Man, you got desserts?" Marvin asked. "I would have taken first prize with that one. Life isn't fair."

"What did you get?" Naomi asked. Marvin told her. "So what did you make, a barbecued taco?"

"Yep."

"Quit playing."

"I'm not. I used a barbecue base for the ground beef, added black-eyed peas, sautéed kale for my greens, and covered it with cheese."

"Dang, I was playing, but that actually sounds good."

"It was." Marvin saw movement in his peripheral vision, took Naomi's arm and guided them toward the exit. "Don't look around, but trouble's coming. Let's go outside."

"Who was it?" Naomi whispered.

"Take one guess."

"Abbey's still chasing you? Why don't you go ahead and give her some of that Marvin magic?"

"Because I'd rather give it to you."

Once outside, Marvin donned his shades as he breathed in the warm June air. He and Naomi fell into a comfortable silence as they walked across the street to the parking structure. It was a beautiful day, he'd made it to the final preliminary round, he was off tonight and felt like celebrating.

"What are you getting ready to do?"

"I don't know, why?"

"I thought about doing something together to celebrate making it into the final round."

"You don't have to work?"

"I've been doing that for the past ten days straight."

"What do you feel like doing?"

Marvin's eyes took a slow journey from Naomi's silky braids to her gladiator sandals. "Getting my groove on with you. But later though, after we find somewhere to kick it in the city, do something fun."

"Like a club or something?"

"No, I never was much into that scene. Do you bowl?"

"No, do you?"

"Heck yeah. But you play pool, right?"

"I do alright."

"Do you skate?"

Naomi smiled. "Since I was eight or nine years old."

"Then let's go skating!"

"Are you sure you can keep up?"

"Girl, I'll skate rings around you."

"We're going to see."

"We sure will."

"Where do you want to go?" Naomi rattled off a list of options.

"See, I knew you weren't a true rink rat. Because if you were, the first place you would have mentioned was BRS in Long Beach."

"Never heard of it."

"When was the last time you went skating?"

"About five years ago."

"No wonder. Bounce/Roll/Skate has only been open a couple years. I can follow you home if you'd like, and then you can ride with me."

"I need to spend a little time with Nana. Text me the address and I'll meet you later, around nine o'clock. Is that cool?"

"That's cool."

They reached Naomi's car. Marvin kept walking toward his. "I'll see you in a few. Prepare to be amazed."

A couple hours later a freshly showered and shaved Marvin pulled into the crowded BRS parking lot just as a text came in from Naomi saying she'd be late. He texted back and asked her shoe size. After shooting off a couple more texts and hanging out on social media a bit, he went inside, played a couple video games and rented their skates. Naomi arrived a short time later. Marvin's heart did a little flip-flop at the sight of her—stretch jeans, a Raiders tee covering her luscious melons, a sight so mouthwatering that Marvin, a Seahawks fan, forgave her lack of good sense when it came to choosing football apparel. Her braids were pulled back, revealing a fresh face, no makeup, which she didn't need. Naomi's butterscotch skin was blemish-free and soft as a baby's bottom. Not that he'd felt many, but that's what he'd heard. He found himself wishing that instead of going skating he'd suggested they spend the night doing horizontal aerobics.

"About time you got here."

"At least I texted you, dude. You need to calm down." They hugged. "Can't believe you're so anxious to get showed up on the floor anyway."

"That's what's going to happen?"

"Watch and see."

"No, I'm going to skate and see."

They walked over to a bench, stored their shoes and put on their skates. Marvin finished first, stood and tried out a quick spin.

Naomi noticed. "Quit showing out." She finished tying her skate and stood, slower and more cautiously than her nimble partner. She took a tentative step and wobbled.

Marvin was right there, placed a firm grip on her arm to keep her upright. "Okay, Miss Champion Skater. Don't want to fall on your rump before you hit the actual rink."

"Don't get your gloat on just yet. It's been a minute; I have to get my skating legs back."

"Is that going to be your excuse after I skate circles around you? That it's been a long time since you skated?"

"No, it's going to be the reason I knock you upside the head, because you have a big mouth."

Naomi used Marvin's body to push off of, and headed toward the rink. His laugh followed and told her he wasn't far behind. The music was loud and the floor was crowded. Kids, teens, and young adults created gusts of wind as they whizzed past them. It didn't take long for Naomi to get her groove back, Marvin noted, and soon they were bobbing and dancing as freely as the others. When the DJ slowed down the beat with a Drake throwback, Marvin placed one hand around Naomi's waist, grabbed her hand with his other and led the dance. Naomi proved to be light on her feet as he twirled her around, held her while skating backwards, and then settled them into a rhythm that matched the beat.

After a few games of pool where Marvin won more but Naomi talked more smack, she followed him to the city's Shoreline Village. Naomi had a couple drinks, Marvin tossed back a beer, and they split a couple appetizers. Then Marvin suggested something naughty. Naomi liked to be nasty. So she rode with him to a secluded spot a mile down from the popular shoreline. They left his SUV and found a tree-covered cove. Both removed their bottoms and kept on their tops. Right there, beneath a starlit, inky sky, backlit by the moon, with the cool breeze of the Pacific cooling their gyrating bodies, Marvin stamped his love on Naomi's heat, sending the message with his body better than he could with words—she was the best he ever had.

19

Rush-hour traffic was its usual LA crazy, so it took almost an hour for Naomi to drive from where she worked on the Wilshire Corridor to El Segundo, a beach community by the airport. Being at Byron and Cynthia's luxury home recently had her expecting another residence well outside of her price range. But she pulled up to an old, modest building on a quiet street where parking was at a premium. It took ten minutes to find a space that didn't require running a marathon to get back to Marvin's building. The space she'd found was less than two blocks away. But with the unusually warm June sun beating down on her, Naomi felt she needed a shower by the time she reached the apartment and knocked on the door.

Marvin answered it wearing a chef's apron and looking almost as good as whatever he was cooking smelled. The sarcastic comment about having to park so far away died on her lips, replaced by the intense desire to kiss him. Which she did, and he did, pulling her inside the cozy abode and kicking the door closed without breaking contact. After a couple minutes, they came up for air.

"Now that's how I like to be greeted," he murmured.

"You told me to come ready," Naomi answered.

Reaching for her hand, Marvin walked them into the kitchen, where a drink that looked cool, frothy, and inviting sat on the counter. He picked it up and handed it to her. "Figured you'd be thirsty," he said, and then turned back to the stove.

Naomi moved the straw to her lips and sucked in a fruity taste of heaven. She moaned, took another sip, and pressed the cool glass against her forehead. "This is a pretty delicious greeting, too. What-all's in it?"

Marvin shook his head without turning from the stove. "Can't reveal my secrets. Might have to use it as a weapon against you."

"You can use whatever weapon you want to, including the one you handled so skillfully yesterday afternoon. But that food truck is mine."

"Here she comes with the jokes."

She sidled up beside him, pinched his butt, and then hugged him from behind. "What are you making?"

"I don't know yet. But the ingredients floated around in my head all day. Figured I'd put them in a pot and see how it comes together."

"So I'm your guinea pig?"

"Luckiest one in LA County! Cute, too." He

leaned back, swiped his tongue across her mouth. "And super juicy."

"You're stupid!"

"You like it."

"Not going to lie, I sure do. Oh, and I forgot to say it when we were talking last night . . . but thank you."

He glanced over his shoulder. "For what?"

"For how you treated my grandmother and her friends. Complimenting them and making them feel special, something that probably doesn't happen too often. I can't speak for all of them, but Miss Josephine and Nana lost their husbands a long time ago. If Nana has dated since, it was definitely on the down low, and I don't think Miss Josephine has seen a penis since Jesse Jackson was at the Democratic convention trying to keep hope alive."

"Ha! I must have missed that broadcast, but then again, I'm not much into politics."

"Me neither, but my nana loves Jesse Jackson. She was barely interested in the internet until I introduced her to YouTube and the search box. That first night she held me captive for almost two hours, watching a bunch of stuff that happened before either you or I were born."

They continued to chat. Marvin cooked. Naomi drank her smoothie. Two-thirds of the way into it, she stopped and cocked her head.

"Does this have alcohol in it? I feel a little tipsy."

Marvin offered up a sly smile and a shrug. "Maybe."

"Baby, you don't need to use alcohol to help get

me in the mood. I already want a little more of that Marvin magic."

"Trust me, we're going to get to all of that. But first things first. This is almost done. Do me a favor and grab plates from the cabinet behind you. Silverware is in one of those drawers just below."

Naomi set down the fruity smoothie-like drink and walked over to the cabinets. "Whose place is this?"

"One of my brothers'."

"It's nice, but not what I expected for a place by the beach."

"You thought it was going to be like Byron's house in Venice Beach?"

"Maybe not that extravagant. That house was amazing."

"Nelson doesn't make that kind of money. He works at the airport."

"Oh really? Doing what?"

"Baggage claim for US Airlines."

"He's one of the ones who jack up my luggage by tossing it around like those girls did the beach ball the other day?"

"Probably."

"Dang, you should have at least tried to deny it on your brother's behalf."

"I've heard stories."

"So . . . does he get those discount tickets?"

"Buddy passes?" Marvin nodded. "These days, with fewer airlines and less flights, they can be tricky to use. But depending on the time of year and where you're going, they can work out."

"Cool. So where are you taking me?"

"Nowhere until after we eat. And since this food is done and you still haven't set the table . . ."

"I'm going! Dang."

"Matter of fact, just set the silverware and drinks. I'll plate it up in here."

Naomi set the plates she held next to where Marvin was cooking and found the silverware, keeping up the conversation as she quickly set the table. "You know what? This place is small and simple, but it's nice. I bet it still costs a lot since it's at the beach."

"Nelson's half is over a thousand, close to thirteen hundred. Not counting utilities."

"That's crazy. You'd almost have to have a room-mate to live down here."

"It works for him. There's soda in the fridge. I want ice in mine."

Naomi found the glasses, pulled two from the cabinet, and fixed their drinks. Not seeing napkins, she pulled two paper towel sheets from the roll, folded them in half and put them and the drinks on the table.

"The roommate is a flight attendant who's rarely home. So he lucked out."

She leaned against the doorjamb of the kitchen entrance. "And how did we luck out where he isn't home right now?"

"He's at work. But he gets off at midnight, so time's a ticking." Marvin turned off the burner and placed the steaming pot on a trivet. "Now, go sit down so I can feed you."

"Ooh, daddy, I like it when you talk all strong like that."

Naomi sat at the dining table in the open-concept space. Marvin entered carrying two piping-hot plates. He placed one in front of Naomi, then sat next to her and set his own plate down.

Naomi leaned toward the spiraling heat and inhaled. "This smells so good! It reminds me of something . . ."

"Beef stroganoff."

"Yes, the kind you can make with Hamburger Helper. Is that what you did?"

"Ha ha ha."

Both picked up their forks and began to eat.

Naomi felt Marvin's eyes on her but continued to eat with abandon.

"Go ahead. Say it."

"Say what?"

"That's the best piece of steak you've ever put in your mouth."

"It's alright."

His laugh was hearty, head thrown back for emphasis. "Yes, you're eating it like it's just alright."

She took a few more bites and set down her fork. "It's so good. What did you do differently? Is it the sauce?"

"That and a few more things."

"You deconstructed it, for one thing."

"Deconstructed. Listen to you, trying to sound like you know what you're talking about."

"You know I do." She rolled her eyes. "The mushrooms and onions were sautéed by themselves instead of being added to the sauce. That upped their profile. And the bell peppers. Stroganoffs I've tasted didn't have peppers."

"What, no peppers in that Hamburger Helper box?"

"Whatever. Like you had a chef growing up."

"We did." He paused, laughed at her obvious disbelief. "Me. And you're right. The most popular recipes don't use them. I added the peppers for another layer of flavor."

"But I see you roasted yours first." Naomi briefly studied a strip of pepper before it disappeared into her mouth.

"Maybe."

She punched his arm. "You get on my nerves! Nobody needs your secrets to try and beat you. You and everybody else in the contest lost your chance at first place the minute I stepped into the room!"

"Is that so?"

"Most certainly so."

"We'll see if you can back up all that jaw-jacking on Saturday. But hurry up and finish eating because I want you to back that thang up"—he motioned toward her ass, then cupped his crotch—"to something else."

"Are you sure you're ready?" Naomi licked gravy from her finger before putting it in her mouth. "What you've made is pretty tasty, but I have an even yummier dish."

The two rambunctious lovers didn't even take the time to clear the table. Or go to the bedroom. As soon as plates were clean and forks laid down, Marvin feasted on the dessert between her thighs that Naomi offered up right there on the dining room table. Once she regained strength in her legs, she slid from the table to the floor and returned the favor. They went from sixty-nine to seventy-seven and made up a couple numbers of their own. One thing was for sure. With Marvin, Naomi had met her sexual match. Later on, as she wearily crawled into bed back at home, all she could think about was how much she was going to miss him if their friendship ended once she won the food truck. But she'd give up a good fuck for a truck and some bucks. She had to keep her eye on the prize.

20

One of the cooks was out sick, so Marvin worked doubles for the next two days. On Thursday he didn't have to be at work until three, so he was home watching television when Nelson stopped by.

Nelson walked over to where Marvin sat. "What's up, man?"

"You got it."

No matter how often the brothers saw each other, they always offered a fist bump, a one-shoulder hug, a handshake, or all three. With Marvin seated, Nelson capped him on the side of the head. Marvin punched his arm before they ended the greeting with a brothers' handshake. Willie wasn't one for showing a lot of affection, but Liz had enough touchy-feely for both of them and had passed that trait on to the boys.

Nelson joined Marvin on the couch. "The girl with you at Byron's the other day . . . y'all dating?"

Marvin made a face, motioned toward the hallway. Nelson continued in the same tone, at the same volume. "Oh, Mama's here? She don't know about your girl?"

Before Marvin could form a comeback, Liz walked into the room. "No, I don't know about his girl, but since he's obviously touting her all over town, seems like I need to know about her."

Liz plopped into the "her" of a his-and-her recliner set, and pushed the lever to raise up her legs.

"Well?"

"She's not my girl," Marvin began, giving Nelson the eye. "She's someone I met at the convention center, another contestant. We're just hanging out."

"Is this a strategy or something? You hoping your peter in the bed will trump her pork in the pot?"

Nelson cracked up while Marvin looked properly mortified.

"Mama, if you'd seen the Carter-catcher Naomi is working with, you'd know she is more than a friend."

That the Carters were butt men had been a long-standing fact. Marvin slowly shook his head. Some people just couldn't keep their mouths shut. His brother fell into that group.

Liz looked at Marvin but talked to Nelson. "You said she's in the contest?"

"That's what Marvin told me. Right, Marvin?"

"Isn't that what I just said?"

"And she can cook?" Liz asked, this time talking to Marvin.

"She does alright."

"She's still in the contest," Nelson added, continuing to share what Marvin had told him at Byron's on Sunday. "The field was narrowed from thousands to less than a hundred. So she can't be a slouch."

"A big butt and can cook, too? Son, is your nose wide open? Come on, you can tell your mom."

"Why don't you ask Nelson? He's the one talking my business like he knows it better than I do. He can keep on talking."

Liz shifted in her chair, smiled for the first time since entering the room. "Uh-huh, he's getting riled up. He likes this girl. What did you say her name was, Nelson?"

"Naomi."

"Does she have a sister, Marvin? Because your brother could use some help in the love department. Nelson spends too much time working. He needs to find time to have fun."

"Where's Daddy, Mama?"

Marvin jumped on that segue like boom on a bomb. "Oh, now you want to change the subject since Mama's tipping toward your bedroom. She doesn't know about the date you brought to the party?"

Liz sat up. "Nelson had somebody over at Byron's house?"

"He sure did." Marvin looked at his watch and then at Nelson. "You might as well tell her everything, brother, because if not I'm going to spill it all as soon as I get home from work."

An hour later, Marvin was in the Soul Spot kitchen, leisurely filling an order for a table of four. This time was always slow on weekdays, with the lunch crowd long gone and the dinner crowd not yet there. It allowed Marvin the luxury of paying extra attention to recipes, tweaking spices, and engaging the customers for valuable feedback. The table had ordered a mix of classic soul fare and contemporary cuisine. He moved seamlessly between crispy fried chicken wings and baked barbecued breasts. Cooked mustard and collard greens, and kale and edamame salad—something the owner's son Donald had not been a fan of, but Marvin had pushed to add to the menu. It quickly became one of their best-selling dishes. Fried potatoes and a pecan and sweet potato soufflé. He finished the order, handled a few more, and then went out to see how the customers had enjoyed their food.

In the middle of receiving accolades, the restaurant doors opened and sunshine walked in. A thick chick wearing a loose black shawl over a fitted red jumpsuit. He immediately wondered whether or not he'd missed Naomi's phone call, and quickly decided that it didn't matter. He thanked the foursome at the table for their feedback and walked over to Charlotte's station, where Naomi had been seated.

"Hey."

"Hey."

"This is a surprise."

Naomi shrugged. "I was out. Got hungry. Drove by here."

Marvin offered up a smile that suggested he

didn't totally buy her story but was glad she was there. "You're not supposed to be at work?"

"I'm covering part of a coworker's shift next Sunday afternoon. So she took half of mine today."

"Cool. Check out the menu and let me know what you'd like."

Naomi reached out and ran a finger down Marvin's forearm. "Why don't you let me know what I should like?"

"You already like that." Naomi gave him a look, knowing that what he spoke of was not something on the menu. "Oh, you're talking about food. Give me a minute to handle the table that came in before you and then I'll hook you up."

Naomi pulled out her cell phone, slowly bobbing her head to the old-school R & B that played through the Soul Spot speakers. She didn't know the name of the group asking people to join hands and get on the love train. But she was down with the idea, and knew the perfect cook to handle meals while onboard. She sent a text to Kristy, responded to an email from her job, and then felt the presence of someone precariously close to her personal space.

"Are you ready to order?"

Naomi knew the voice. It was the same chick who'd disrespected her cousin. Charlotte. Naomi had remembered the name by thinking of spiders and webs. *Why didn't Marvin tell me I was sitting in enemy territory?* She took a deep breath and looked up with as placid an expression as she could muster.

"Hi."

"What can I get for you?"

"I'm good."

"These tables are for customers only. You have to order something."

Naomi chuckled and went back to scrolling her phone. "Girl, quit acting like you don't remember me, and like you didn't see Marvin over here talking a few minutes ago. He's taking care of me." Looking up at her, she added, "Okay, Charlotte?"

"Whatever." Charlotte spun around and almost slapped Naomi with the ends of her long, curly weave. Any other time Naomi would not have let that go unchecked, but Marvin had her feeling more like a lover than a fighter. She glanced up and saw Charlotte talking to another waiter while giving Naomi the evil eye. Naomi tapped Marvin's name on her phone and sent him a text.

Don't let that witch Charlotte touch my food.

He responded a few minutes later. **LOL.**

Just as Naomi settled back to groove with another of Nana's favorite men, Marvin Gaye, a boisterous group of teens and twenty-somethings entered the restaurant and took seats at a long rectangular table. She watched Charlotte smile at them, something Naomi thought impossible, before delivering the order to the table beside her. Naomi had to admit that everything looked delicious. Looking at the macaroni and cheese that someone had ordered made her mouth water. Just then Marvin came around the corner carrying a plate.

He set it down in front of her. "Dinner is served."

"I was hoping you'd bring out that mac and cheese. It looks almost as good as mine."

Marvin rolled his eyes. "Here we go."

Naomi leaned into the steam rising from a serving of cabbage plated beside ribs that looked as though they could fall off the bone.

"Are these spicy?"

"A little bit. And those ribs are juicy, just like you." Marvin looked toward the large group and noticed Charlotte walking an order up to the counter. "I'd better get back to work."

Naomi snapped a picture of the plate and sent it to Kristy, along with the tagline, Wish you were here.

Kristy's answer was instant and what Naomi expected. Heifah. Bring me a plate!

Naomi texted Marvin and asked if he would make a to-go order for her cousin, then eagerly picked up her fork. Later she would swear that the plate of food that Marvin served could have given her an orgasm. Everything was that good. The mac-'n'-cheese dish was not only a mound of gooey goodness, but the cracker crumble he'd topped it with added just the right texture and layer of flavor to take it over the top of the taste-bud charts. The cabbage was a little spicy, but she liked how he'd kept the dish simple enough to give the underrated vegetable, and one of her favorites, its due. She also liked that the leaves weren't cooked to within an inch of their lives, as was the case in many Southern kitchens, but were left with enough firmness to hold their own with everything else served. The ribs? All Naomi knew was that she'd do whatever she could to try and make sure he did not cook them during the contest. Because if he did, Naomi was convinced that Marvin would drive away with her truck.

It didn't take long for Naomi to devour the dinner. That she was raised by Nana and not by wolves was one of two reasons she didn't lick the plate. The second reason strolled toward her with a face like she'd just chewed a lemon rind, and dropped the check on the table.

Naomi felt too good to let Charlotte steal her joy. "Thank you," she said, with enough saccharin to cause cancer. "Everything was delicious."

"Yeah, Marvin can cook. Guess that's how he keeps so many girlfriends, a different one for every day of the week."

That was a news flash, but Naomi tried to keep her face neutral. She was only partly successful.

"I know you didn't think you were the only one."

"What I think isn't any of your business, but one thing's for sure. You're not one of the women on his calendar, because if you were you wouldn't be over here hating on me."

Charlotte took the verbal artillery like someone wearing a bulletproof vest. "You're not even good enough for the weekend," she continued calmly. "He reserves those days for women he actually wants to be seen with, the ones where he not only fixes their food but sits down with them to eat it."

In her mind, Naomi saw Charlotte's face smashed into the plate of black-eyed peas the man across from her was eating. But knowing the woman wanted to rile her was why Naomi refused to react. She casually picked up the check Charlotte had dropped and noted that Marvin had only charged her for one meal. He'd obviously paid for her dinner, something that Naomi was tempted to point out, but didn't. She had nothing to prove, especially to a chick who didn't know better than to open her mouth and mess with her tip. But the girl didn't know when to stop talking.

"The one he had come here this past weekend wasn't even all that cute, but still beat you in status."

"You're getting ready to get beat, too," Naomi replied, almost too calmly, while pulling money out of her purse. "And status won't have nothing to do with it."

"Go ahead and catch a case if you want to," Charlotte said, though she'd backed up as she talked. "That'll just leave more time for his other women."

Naomi scooted back her chair and began to rise. Partly because she'd had just about enough of Miss Charlotte's jaw-jacking, and partly because she wanted Marvin to come out and refute the waiter's claims. As if on cue, he came around the corner carrying a to-go bag.

"Here's your cousin's order," he said to Naomi.

"Thank you, babe."

He then turned to the server. "Charlotte, why are you bothering my guest?"

"Not just bothering me," Naomi said. "But lying about you."

"I'm not lying about all his women coming in here. And just for the record," she continued, standing almost behind Marvin as though she needed protection, "I have been on the calendar and I just might be on it again."

She gave Marvin a playful shove as she walked away.

Naomi didn't care about that. She wanted to know that the girl was lying.

"You've effed her?"

Marvin frowned. "Is that what she told you?"

"She told me a bunch of stuff. Did you?"

Marvin took a quick glance around. "Let's go outside real quick."

They passed the restaurant's window and continued over to Naomi's car in the parking lot. She watched Marvin take the towel draped around his neck and mop his brow. Was it the weather, or was he in the hot seat? Having asked the question twice already, she wasn't going to ask again. Instead she leaned against her car, crossed her arms and waited.

"Whatever she's talking about happened long before I met you."

"So you did screw her. Dang, I hoped she was lying. Now I need to go to the vet. I might be diseased!"

"You mean the doctor."

"No, the vet. That's who treats dogs."

Marvin tried to make light of the matter, grabbed his stomach and bent over as though he'd been punched. "Ow, girl, that really hurt." Naomi turned to open her door. Marvin stopped her. "My doctor will confirm that I have a clean bill of health."

Naomi appeared unconvinced, which bothered Marvin . . . a lot.

"Come on, Juicy. Don't me mad, and don't worry. I was with Charlotte a couple times, like four or five years ago. She wanted a boyfriend. I didn't want the job. That was it. Life went on. I saw her here and there and thought we were cool until she came in here a year ago, saw me working and applied for a job."

"You didn't get with her again, after she was hired?"

"Nope. Didn't want to have any drama at work. She's pretty much had an attitude ever since. I think the only reason she keeps working here is to get on my nerves."

"What about all the women she claimed come to see you, one for every day of the week."

"I have a lot of female friends and they all like to eat. What's with all the questions? I'm not asking for a résumé on your men. You're acting like we're exclusive or something. We're not. We're just kicking it . . . right?"

Naomi stared for a moment, then reached for her door handle. "Yeah, we're just kicking it."

Marvin reached out once again. "Still, you're the only one I'm kicking it with."

"Okay."

Naomi got into her car and drove away with mixed emotions. Marvin was right in saying they weren't exclusive. They'd been too busy screwing to give the meet-ups a definition. But hearing that she was the only one in his life right now definitely made her feel better. The thought of being his one-and-only made her happy, and considering that he was competition, the thought maybe made her happier than it should.

21

Naomi left the Soul Spot and tapped her Bluetooth to call Kristy. "Hey, Tee, I'm on my way over."

"Do you have my food?"

"I didn't think you'd want a whole order. It was a whole lot of food. So I'm bringing my leftovers, a little macaroni and a couple of ribs."

"Quit playing."

"What? You said you wanted to taste it."

"I told you to bring me a plate!"

"I've got your order, girl. Don't raise your pressure."

They both cracked up at Nana's way of advising someone to not get too excited and raise their blood pressure.

"I'll see you in a little bit."

Naomi navigated South Central streets crowded with the end of rush-hour traffic. She reached the low-to-middle-income neighborhood that bordered an area that used to be called "The Jungle," now called the more respectable Baldwin Village. She squeezed her car between an SUV that had taken up almost two parking spaces and a battered Honda, walked up to a row of town houses, and knocked on a door. Kristy's mom answered.

"Hey, Auntie."

"Hello, Nay-Nay."

They hugged as Naomi said, as she almost always did, "You're the only one who still calls me that."

"That my dinner?"

"I didn't know you were here. It's for Tee. Where is she?"

"In her room, I guess. Probably watching back-to-back episodes of *Black-ish* and dreaming she's Anthony Anderson's wife."

Naomi smiled as she took the stairs and tapped on the first door on the right, before cracking it open. "Hey, girl."

"Come on in and bring my food."

Naomi entered the room, saw Anthony talking to his TV wife, Tracee Ross, and laughed out loud.

"What?"

"Auntie said you'd be watching your husband."

"And her son-in-law. She needs to recognize."

Naomi handed the slightly warm sack to Kristy, who pulled out the Styrofoam container. "What happened to that guy you met on the internet? The one you told me about when I called with the news I'd made that first cut?"

"Gary?" Kristy raised the lid, smelled the contents, and picked up a chunk of mac and cheese with her fingers. "He's alright. Guys online always look better on paper than they do in person."

"He didn't look like his picture?"

"His picture wasn't all that, so, no, I wasn't disappointed. He's tall though, I like that. And he has his own place. And a job, like a real one with benefits that you can't get with a criminal record."

Naomi chuckled, and plopped down in a roomy, worn Papasan chair. "Where'd y'all go?"

"To a comedy club, which was different. It was in the Valley. He knew one of the comedians, so we went backstage. Then out to dinner. He wanted to take me to some fancy restaurant, but I told him I don't eat anything I can't pronounce. So we went to the Cheesecake Factory. You know I love that place."

"Looks aren't everything, cousin. From what you say, he sounds like a nice guy."

Kristy picked up another cheesy bite, talked as she chewed. "Nice guys are boring."

"There's a fork in the sack," Naomi deadpanned.

Kristy ignored her, picked up a rib. "When we're by ourselves, that dude makes watching TV static an exciting alternative to his company. He can screw though, so I'm going to keep him around. Um"— Kristy closed her eyes and chewed slowly—"did Marvin cook all of this?"

"Yes."

Kristy reached into the bag, pulled out a fork and tasted the cabbage. "You might be in trouble, sister. This food is good."

"Thanks for the confidence vote, and you're welcome."

"I was going to thank you. Give me a minute."

Kristy picked up a rib and took a healthy bite. She waved the rib in the air and danced on her bed. "Ooh, girl, go get my mama so I can slap her!"

She wanted to be angry but couldn't. Marvin's ribs were really that good.

After finishing half the container, Kristy set it down, wiped her hands, and reached for a drink resting on a side table. "So . . . how's it going?"

"I'm still in it, so I guess it's going okay. Every week is only going to get tougher though. Next week we're doing team challenges and one on our own."

"That's all well and good, but I'm not talking about the contest. I'm talking about you and Marvin."

Naomi shrugged. "We're cool."

"What does that mean?"

"What I said. We're cool, friends, that's it."

"You know you like that man more than any friend. Why are you acting nonchalant and trying to make what y'all are doing so casual? You haven't dated anybody seriously since what's-his-name."

"Who?"

"Rodney, the psycho."

"Whew." Naomi shivered. "Don't talk him up."

Both women quieted for a minute remembering Naomi's longest boyfriend, the one she'd met in middle school and dated until two years ago. He'd gone from goofy and harmless to an obsessive near-stalker. It took Naomi moving back in with her grandmother to finally shake him off her trail.

"Because that's how the relationship is. I realized

that just before coming over here." She told Kristy about the exchange with Charlotte, and the subsequent conversation with Marvin in the parking lot. "I've only known that man a month. Before meeting him, we both had a life. We're in a competition, and who knows what will happen once it's over. And just for the record, before you beat me to it, yes, I've already imagined happily-ever-after and how it would be with his last name."

"Which is?"

"Carter."

"Wow, that's close. You'd only have to change three letters. Wouldn't even have to get new documents, just use white-out or an eraser or something."

"You're a fool, Tee."

"You too, Nay."

Kristy picked up the container of food and resumed eating. "I just want to say this one thing. If you lose, don't get mad at me, because I'm not going to stop eating at the Soul Spot. And I will be visiting his truck."

"I'll probably be with you, cousin. It's all good."

Saturday arrived and with it a new level of anxiety for the remaining contestants. After today, half of those participating will have cooked their last meal. Naomi had overslept and for the first time had arrived at the convention center with only moments to spare. She got a coffee and bagel from the break room and then entered the room where the contestants were prepped before going into the cooking arena. As usual, most of them were clustered in small groups around the room. Many had known each other before the contest. They tended to hang together and not venture too far outside their circle, and also seemed to break down along geographic lines. The Washingtonians and Oregonians and a sprinkling from Colorado and Las Vegas. The Northern Californian Bay Area chefs, the experts in Southern California cuisine and further divided into traditional, modern, those on the cutting edge of molecular gastronomy, and those in the group, like Jeremy, who felt they were in a class all by themselves.

Naomi saw Marvin on the other side of the room, but instead of walking over she joined a group of women sitting near the back row. One of them, a girl named Bridgette, was on last week's winning team with her and Marvin. Even though they'd had a run-in or two, Naomi liked the cook that Marvin had nicknamed Bridge. She'd worked as a chef for over ten years. Naomi could appreciate Bridgette's feeling that she shouldn't have to compete against a non-cook like her. But Bridgette had admitted that someone like Naomi should be easy to beat, and therefore not someone to worry about. Besides, Naomi preferred the enemies who showed their knives, like Bridgette, to the ones who'd offer a compliment while hiding a cleaver, like Abbey. She waved at the women, turned a chair to face them, and sat down.

"Everybody's so quiet and focused. What's going on?"

"You didn't read the board?" one of them asked.

Naomi looked toward the front of the room and a whiteboard where rules, contest changes, and other announcements were posted.

"No. I just got here."

"Go check it out, rookie," Bridgette said, with a cocky smile. "No more hiding behind your team-mates. We stand on our own two feet today."

Naomi didn't make it to the board. One of the producers got everyone's attention and reiterated what most in the room had already read. Today, there would be two challenges. One involving teams. One individual dish. For the first time since bringing their special containers to that first nerve-racking audition, every cook would have a chance to showcase their talents without having to incorporate the opinions of others. Naomi was both pleased and terrified at the same time.

The producer finished the instructions. Contestants walked into the arena. The usually laid-back Ted, who normally joked with contestants before jumping on stage, was today already standing at the microphone, ready to go, within seconds of the doors being shut. The team challenge was straight-forward and much like the others—creative, challenging, and tricky to execute. Four teams of ten were challenged to highlight fried foods and include a dessert. An hour later, one team was elim-inated and just like that, ten dreams ended. Those cooks did not get to showcase their individual dishes. Naomi and Marvin weren't on the same team, but neither of them were on the team that got cut.

Ted then revealed the individual competition. Each cook would have to fix a dish using items found in the pantries of cooks on a budget. Canned food. Pre-seasoned, pre-cooked grains. Frozen vegetables. Dinner in a box. Naomi relaxed. Some people were going home today, but it wouldn't be her. She'd probably cooked everything the judges had gathered, with a grandmother who could prepare canned food in a way that it almost tasted fresh and fix a boxed mashed potato so well, one would swear that spud came out of the ground. The remaining contestants were told that they'd have two minutes to gather ingredients from the pantry and twenty-five minutes to cook their dish. They were also given a number that corresponded to one of thirty countertop stoves that had been set up for this individual battle. Naomi saw Marvin look over at her with a confident expression. She matched his and raised it ten.

One of the judges raised her hand. "Your time begins . . . right now!"

Thirty determined cooks sprinted toward several pantries. Naomi and Marvin joined the others who pushed, shoved, and grabbed for cans of fruit, vegetables, tomatoes, and soups. Naomi grabbed corn and green beans, hit up two more cabinets and the fridge, then ran to a table filled with cheap dried herbs and spices. Back at her stovetop, she hurriedly placed a pan on the stove, added vegetable oil, and began cubing a less expensive version of a flank steak. She glanced over at Marvin, two stations and one row ahead of her, who had a bag of chicken wings.

"Marvin!" He looked over. "I see you went the easy route," she said, for once being the first one to get in a dig.

"What do you have?"

"Steak."

He chuckled. "Good luck with getting that tender in twenty-five minutes."

"I won't need twenty-five," Naomi confidently responded as she held up a meat mallet. "I can do it in ten and knock some sense into your head."

Those who heard it laughed at Naomi's comment, then they all got down to the business of trying to secure their spot on TV. When the dishes were presented, the judges loved Naomi's hearty beef stew. They raved about Marvin's inventive chicken wings à la king, a deconstructed version of the classic dish where a creamy, well-seasoned concoction of noodles and veggies was topped with perfectly crisp drumettes.

"I wanted to not like this dish," one of the fussier, Michelin-starred judges told Marvin. "I found the thought of having to eat the chicken with my hands as opposed to the classical one-dish presentation was off-putting." He paused, smiled. "But, man, that chicken was so gosh-darn good, I would have eaten it with toes, if necessary."

Ten cooks were eliminated, including Zen and others who'd become friends. The mood became more somber with each elimination, and this time when Marvin and Naomi headed to the parking lot, there was little joking.

"And then there were twenty," Marvin quietly said.

"Yep, and after next week there will only be ten."

"And then it's showtime." He put a friendly arm around her. "Good luck."

Naomi looked over, expecting to see a smirk to show that he was joking. But he wasn't. He was serious.

"Thanks. Good luck to you, too."

The two became quiet, as a similar thought ran through each of their minds. By luck, skill, or miracle, perhaps all three, they both were still standing. They both had a shot at winning. But there could only be one. Both could feel the keys to the food truck in their hand, and the money in their pocket.

22

Naomi reached the double doors to the convention center and smoothed a hand over her stomach. She felt flutters and told herself it was nerves from anticipating the final round in the preliminary stage of competition, not from the thought of seeing Marvin again. With Naomi playing nurse to Nana, she hadn't seen Marvin since last week's competition. But those nasty text messages they'd exchanged had almost led to pulling out the dildo last night. Naomi had tried not to be bothered by what had happened the week before last at the Soul Spot, but unfortunately Charlotte's taunting had stayed with her. Who else liked Marvin? Who else might be checking him out? He was a natural flirt, and while he wasn't an ugly brother, he wasn't so fine that he was intimidating. An average body, cute face, swagger and charm added up to Marvin being a chick magnet. Which meant that what Charlotte said could be more accurate than Naomi wanted to think. She had confidence, but Naomi was a big girl. She knew there were women who were cuter, slimmer, and more appealing. Did she want to have to constantly compete with that?

Glancing at her reflection in a glass pane, Naomi noticed her stomach preceding her and adjusted the jumpsuit across her expansive middle. The hope was that her girls would keep the focus from the breast up and her big booty would keep others checking her out from the hips down. Either way, it was too late for her to change her mind. The contest was beginning in less than an hour and she didn't have anything else to wear, so best to throw a jacket of confidence over the fat-rolls-revealing one-piece and keep it moving. She entered the large room filled with contestants and scanned the crowd. Her eyes fell on Marvin, holding court as usual, with a mostly female audience who were all cracking up.

Naomi walked over. "Hey, everybody!" She slapped Marvin on the back. "What's so funny?"

"The guy and his nicknames," Tat said, a moniker given by Marvin because of several tattoos she sported. "It's crazy how they're so spot-on."

Naomi cocked her head. "What's my nickname?" She knew he wouldn't share the personal one he'd given her.

"You know your name, girl. Juicy!"

The reaction ranged from gasps to guffaws. Naomi was stunned; the way Marvin looked at her

when he said it made the big girl who'd criticized
her reflection minutes ago feel all kinds of sexy.

"Why are y'all tripping? What's the problem?
Okay, wait. I'm using it as you would about something interesting or exciting, like a juicy story. Spicy
like those potato strips that helped us win last week."

"Oh," Tat said.

Naomi was impressed. She hadn't thought of
any of those meanings, and from the parts of her
anatomy Marvin usually squeezed when he said it,
Naomi knew those weren't always the definitions on
his mind.

"Not that she isn't the other kind of juicy, too."

Naomi did a little shimmy and a pivot turn. Marvin
followed suit. Soon they were striking poses. Clap-
ping and catcalling from those around them ensued.
Other contestants joined in. A couple producers
took notice and soon a cameraman was filming the
impromptu dance session. There was only one
person who seemed to not be enjoying the camaraderie as much as the others. No one noticed.
Host Ted Reynolds stepped to the microphone and
soon the remaining contestants were counting off
to be divided into groups of four for a team competition, after which two groups would go home. It
would be the largest elimination yet, the final preliminary round when the twenty contestants who
remained would be whittled down to the ten finalists going head-to-head for the championship. It
would be filmed for television and broadcast over
the Labor Day weekend on Chow TV.

Naomi prayed that she'd get on the same team as

Marvin, but that didn't happen. He ended up working with Tat and a couple others that had become friends over the past three weeks. Naomi ended up with Airhead, so named by Marvin because Jeremy Evans believed he was God's gift to kitchens all over the world. He downplayed Marvin's talents—along with almost everyone else's—and was clearly unhappy with Naomi in his group. The challenge was to create a complete meal containing a protein, a vegetable, and a starch. They were given ten minutes to plan and thirty-five minutes to execute. Disagreement was immediate and vigorous. Believing everyone else would choose meat as their protein, Jeremy wanted to go the vegan or vegetarian route to set them apart.

"That will set us apart alright," Naomi countered, almost before he'd finished the sentence. "We will no longer be a part of this competition. I say we go with either chicken or beef."

"Or we could do pasta with a mushroom sauce. I think going a different route than everyone else is genius, and if we've got dried mushrooms in the pantry they're a great source of protein."

"What about lentils?" someone else said, suggesting a curried Indian dish would stand out.

After a couple more suggestions, Naomi had had enough. "Guys! We only have ten minutes to come up with a menu and five have already gone by. Let's take the top ideas to a vote."

She wasn't surprised when Jeremy's vegetarian idea won out. Clearly some of the contestants had drunk his egotistical Kool-Aid. The next question was how to round out the pasta dish.

Good luck with that.

Then, seemingly out of the blue, an idea popped into Naomi's head. "I'll make some type of bread, a roll that can get down in thirty minutes."

Jeremy immediately shot her down. "No, we've already got a starch with the pasta."

"Did that sound like a question? Because it wasn't."

Naomi didn't wait for anyone's approval. She spun around and headed for the pantry, in search of yeast.

Almost an hour later, the four groups stood in front of the judges. Naomi's heart fluctuated from her throat to her toes. The situation just got real. Two groups were going home. Marvin was in a different group. A strong one with several contestants who'd won individual challenges. After today, half of the cooks in this room would no longer be here. She didn't want to be one of them. They announced the winners. To no one's surprise, Marvin's group was one of the top two teams. Naomi's group on the bottom.

If I go home behind a mushroom . . .

Marvin's group won. They'd gone classic, a beef Wellington (Tat's idea) where they stuffed the vegetable choice—creamed spinach—inside the pastry (Marvin's idea). The other group landed on top because of their daring comfort-food choice—chicken and dumplings—a simple dish they'd elevated to haute cuisine. Naomi wanted to take a piece of raw steak in one hand, a chicken leg in the other, and box Jeremy's ears. When addressing the losing teams and asking what went wrong, Jeremy spoke for their team and threw Naomi under an Amtrak train. She was the only one who'd opposed him, but he cleverly left out that fact. According to Jeremy, they'd lost because she wasn't a team player, had gone against the others' wishes, and made a roll when everyone else felt the fresh herb, lemon, and Parmesan topping he'd wanted her to make would have brought the freshness and acidic quality the judges felt their dish had lacked. That she'd not heard any mention of this topping was a fact the judges would never know. After three weeks of fighting, the loss had taken Naomi's energy and zapped her will. It had been a good run, but you had to know when it was over. Some of these contestants owned restaurants. Naomi wasn't even a professional, just a woman who liked food, with a grandmother who knew how to cook it and passed the knowledge on to her. She was lucky to have gotten this far. While the thought made her misty-eyed, Naomi tried to take comfort in that. She could feel Marvin's eyes on her but refused to look over. One look of compassion, pity, disappointment, or anything similar and she'd very likely break into a Celie-saying-goodbye-to-Nettie ugly cry. *Me and you us will never part . . . !*

Ted's countenance was somber as he took the mike. "Ladies and gentlemen, boys and girls, this is a doozy and a really sad day because some amazing chefs and cooks are going home. But from the beginning we knew that was inevitable. There can only be one winner, and when we return after the holiday, there will only be ten of you here competing in the finals that will be filmed for television. At this point, it is clear that winning involves more than great cooking skills. It also involves a little strategy, and a lot of luck. Today some of you, all excellent chefs, were just unlucky." He paused dramatically before adding, "But I've got news."

Naomi's head shot up. He'd delivered those words in a way that held promise. Maybe only one group was being eliminated. Could it be that she'd get another shot at a new life?

Jesus, given that it's been so long since I've been to Your house, I know I'm coming to You way more and asking far more than I have a right. But if there's any way . . .

Naomi's prayer was interrupted as the gasps, screams, and applause died down and Ted continued. "For two contestants, one from each losing team, your luck will continue. Because there is a component of this contest that we never shared with you, a surprise save. The judges will take a few minutes to deliberate and come back with the names of two people they feel have what it takes to win it all. Those two people will join the other . . ."

Naomi tuned out after that. She watched as a couple people patted Jeremy on the back. One whispered into his ear, and Jeremy nodded. She didn't have to be close by to know what was being said. They knew what she knew. Jeremy would be staying. Naomi wouldn't have been surprised if the judges had come up with the rule just to let him back in the game.

". . . first person who gets a second chance is . . . Naomi Carson!"

If someone asked her how it felt to be shocked with a cattle prod, Naomi would have been able to tell them. She hadn't heard correctly. There were three syllables in both Jeremy and Naomi. Somehow she'd transposed her name over his. No way would they—

"Naomi!" Ted yelled. "Are you here?"

The sound pulled her out of complete paralysis. But she was still dumbfounded, and it showed. "Huh?"

"You'd better get down here, girl, and claim your spot!"

She wasn't hearing things. Ted had actually called her name. She was still in the contest. She danced and shouted her way to the front, where Ted stood next to the judges.

Ted put an arm around her. "You had us worried for a minute, Naomi. We thought you were maybe going to decline the invitation to stay."

"I couldn't believe you called my name."

A movement caught her eye. She and others watched as a totally peeved Jeremy marched out of the room. A few others followed behind him. Ted and the judges observed but said nothing. Instead he focused back on Naomi.

"Judges, tell us why you decided to save Naomi."

One of the judges raised his hand. "I owned a food truck for seven years. It takes more than being able to cook. It's also about being able to connect with people. Make them feel good. But you have to be able to cook, too. Naomi, that was one of the lightest, tastiest, most well executed yeast rolls I've ever put in my mouth."

Reactions to Naomi getting the save were mixed, but there was a group who clearly thought Jeremy should be there instead of her. She tried to ignore the haters and was on her way to hang out with Marvin when one of them approached her. But nothing or nobody could wipe the smile off Naomi's face.

"Hey, Naomi."

"Hi, Abbey." The smile she gave Abbey was sincere.

"I guess congratulations are in order."

"Thank you!"

"You were lucky to get that save today."

"I know. I couldn't believe it."

"Neither could anyone else. Everyone knew Jeremy should have been the one saved from your team. I must say that I was one of them. He co-owns a successful restaurant and is an incredible chef."

"Maybe the judges thought he didn't need a successful restaurant and a food truck."

"That was not for the judges to decide. It was not a fair decision."

Naomi's smile faded. She wished she'd texted Marvin because they were almost to the exit and he was nowhere in sight. She hung back, hoping Abbey would continue out the door. She didn't.

"Waiting on Marvin?"

What's it to you? Naomi so wanted to say that, but it wasn't wise to offend anyone at this stage of the game. "Yes."

"You two got the fun going earlier today. Are you dating?"

"We're just friends. Marvin gets along with everybody."

"Yes, he's really special. Glad to hear you're just pals. He and I couldn't date when he was in school, so I'm happy we're getting close now."

Naomi tried to channel the cool, calm, and collected woman who'd handled Charlotte like a pro, but it had been a long, nerve-racking day.

Maybe if I don't say anything she'll just leave.

Naomi nodded and pulled out her phone.

"It's been great to reconnect with him. We don't get a lot of time together right now but . . ."

Naomi was concentrating so hard on not reacting that she scrolled her phone without seeing a thing. There were only two goals. *Don't say anything. Don't look up.*

"There is a late night here and there. The day you guys won with the bacon-stuffed hamburger? He invited me over to the Soul Spot and made a really special one to put between my buns."

Naomi's head slowly came up. "Oh, really."

"Yes. That was probably too much information."

"What, that he cooked you a hamburger?" Suddenly motor mouth had no gas. "Or did something else happen? Not that it's my business."

"It is rather personal, but . . ."

"But what? You obviously want me to know, so why don't you just come out and tell me what happened?"

"Yes, Abbey . . ."

Naomi turned toward the sound and smiled. She

glanced at a stone-faced Abbey, who looked more shocked than Naomi did earlier after being saved. Marvin's expression was hard to read. Neither had heard him approach.

"I want to hear what you have to say, too, Abbey. Why don't you tell both of us what happened?"

23

The next time Marvin saw Denzel he was going to tell the brother to hand over the Oscar. Because the calm exterior covering up the anger over what he just heard was worthy of an award.

"Hey, Marvin," Naomi said, walking toward him. "Where were you hiding?"

"I was talking to a few folk. Hanging out." He answered Naomi but looked at Abbey, and didn't say another word.

Abbey took a tentative step forward. "That's what we were just saying, weren't we, Naomi. That Marvin gets along with everyone."

Marvin emitted a chuckle that held no humor. "That's not the part I heard."

"What did you hear?"

"You were talking about food. Hamburgers."

"Oh, right. Enjoying that delicious burger you made for me when I came over to the Soul Spot."

"I've been to the spot a few times," Naomi said. "But never by special invitation."

"You don't need a special invitation to eat at what's basically a diner. Don't need a reservation either."

"But Abbey got one." Marvin saw a twinkle in Naomi's eye as she looked at his former teacher. "Didn't you?"

"I don't remember exactly how it happened, whether he suggested it or I did. But it was a great night. It's been wonderful getting to know Marvin better. We didn't get that chance when he was in school."

"But you're getting it now." Naomi turned to Marvin. "She said the two of you were dating."

"I did not say that," Abbey countered.

"Oh, right. You said that—"

"I heard what she said. Not everything, but I heard enough to know that there was creative story-telling happening. Abbey, I don't know what's going on with you, or why you seemed to all of a sudden develop some kind of special interest in me. I don't remember you being this attentive when I was in school.

"Listen, I've tried to be nice. I've tried to say this nicely. I don't like hurting feelings. But this illusion you've got going that there is or can ever be anything between you and me has got to stop. It's going to end today. I respect you as one of my former teachers, just like I respect every other teacher that I've ever had, from kindergarten on up."

He heard Naomi snicker, had meant that last bit to be funny, but remembering that Abbey's obsession was no laughing matter, he held a straight face.

"I don't have any romantic feelings for you. I'm not trying to get with you. I'm not trying to flirt with you. When I'm nice, like when I use a nickname or whatever, it's what I do with everybody. You can ask the other contestants. I have nicknames for all of them. If there is something I've done to make you think I like you or that I'm trying to get with you, I apologize because that is not the case. I don't hate you, at all. But I don't like you the way you want me to. I don't want to date you. I don't want you as a girlfriend—"

"Stop! That's enough. You've said enough."

Marvin and Naomi watched a clearly angry Abbey storm toward the door and push it open. Even on springs it nearly hit the wall.

Marvin heaved a sigh. "Dang, man. I feel bad. I didn't want to do that."

"You had no choice. She's been after you since day one, and no matter what you said or how many times you said it, she didn't get the message. Plus, she was straight-out lying on you. You heard her say that you invited her to your restaurant and then tried to make it sound like there was more to the meeting than what actually happened. That's not cool. If she can lie about that, she can lie about anything."

"Still, I don't like to make anyone feel bad. It's done though, so let's be done with it and talk about that bullet you dodged today."

"Right?!"

"You should have seen your face." Marvin did an

exaggerated version of a shell-shocked Naomi and began cracking up. "Me? What? Oh my God!"

"Shut up!" Naomi tried to punch his shoulder, but Marvin dodged the hit and walked toward the exit. "I did not sound like that!"

They continued talking in the casual, joking manner that had marked their relationship from the beginning. Marvin told her he was happy she was still in the competition because he wanted to be the one who beat her. Naomi countered that she was glad to have been saved just so she could take him down. They'd just reached the corner across from the parking lot when he felt Naomi's mood change.

"Marvin." Her voice was low yet forceful, with no trace of the playfulness that had filled it just seconds before. "Don't look now, but you are not going to believe who I see talking across the street."

"Who?" When Naomi didn't answer quickly, he turned to see for himself. "Who cares about that?" he asked, adding a hand gesture underscoring what he'd seen was no big deal. "It doesn't surprise me that those two would get along."

The light changed and as they crossed the street, Marvin changed the subject.

"Do you have plans for tonight?"

"Maybe, why?"

"Because I was going to invite you to the Soul Spot, reserve you a table and everything."

Naomi laughed. "You're stupid."

She knew he was joking, but seeing Naomi laugh was what Marvin wanted. He also wanted to mask the concern he felt for what the two had seen on the other side of the street. The newly eliminated Jeremy Evans having an animated conversation with Abbey, a consultant for the show he wanted to win, whom he'd just pissed off. He'd made light of it, but seeing those two with their heads together had Marvin worried, especially for Naomi. He couldn't imagine anything good coming from that conversation, and could think of plenty of scenarios that ended badly.

They reached the parking lot's roof. Naomi pulled out her keys and pointed her key fob toward her car. They heard the locks click open.

"What are you getting ready to do, go to work?"

"Yeah." Marvin leaned against his car. "Ouch!"

"It's only eighty-five degrees today," Naomi said, grinning. "You thought that metal wouldn't be hot?"

"You shouldn't be over there laughing. You should be over here trying to make me feel better, licking my booboo or something."

Naomi laughed out loud. "I'll kiss something alright. But not here, and not in the car. Squatting in that car the other day had my legs sore for two days!"

"Now you know how I felt after my date beneath your bed." Marvin looked at his watch. "Man, I really don't feel like going to work. The closer I get to that truck the more I hate working there. What are you getting ready to do?"

"Get in your car after you start it up and turn on the air conditioning. It's hot out here."

"Your air doesn't work?"

"Yes, but that takes gas and I need this quarter of a tank to last me until Wednesday."

"You're crazy, girl," he griped, but opened the passenger door for Naomi and then walked around to his side of the car, fired it up, and blasted the fan. She got in, but kept the door open.

"So what's up for tonight?" he asked again.

"I don't know."

"It's a holiday weekend! You don't have a party to attend? You're not going to hit up the clubs?"

"I know of a couple people doing something. I usually roll with my cousin Kristy. But she recently started dating and now she's Casper."

"You don't have plans for the Fourth?"

"None that excite me."

"Your family isn't doing anything?"

"Yes, but eating bad barbecue and playing rummy with a group of sixty-, seventy-, and eighty-somethings doesn't sound too exciting. Even though this year Nana sweetened the deal with a trip on the church bus to watch the fireworks."

"And bad barbecue? Why don't you cook?"

"Nobody is trying to fight Miss J for the grill tongs and basting brush!"

Marvin leaned over the steering wheel, cracking up.

"Whatever."

He lifted his head and cautiously peeked over at her.

Soon, she giggled, too. "Why do you get on my nerves? You were probably so obnoxious as a little boy." The car finally cooled, and Naomi closed the door. "What am I saying? You're obnoxious now!"

"You like it."

"Whatever. Are y'all having a barbecue?"

Marvin nodded. "Yep. And guess what? You're going to come and help me cook."

"Are you asking me or are you telling me?"

"What if I told you that I'm going to keep some of that sauce, and after the party's over I'm going to act like you're my rib?"

Naomi fixed him with a look. "Then I would tell you that I am so there."

24

Naomi looked at the clock, and then in the mirror. It was seven thirty in the morning on an off day. Yet she was up, dressed, and getting ready to stand over a hot grill in hot weather . . . and she was smiling. Either she was falling in love with Marvin or it was the invasion of the body snatchers and someone had occupied her insides and had her acting bat-shit crazy.

She'd forgotten earrings, and after retrieving a pair of thick red hoops from the jewelry tree, she took a final look in the full-length mirror. The off-the-shoulder red top was simple but sexy and, paired with red wedge sandals and black skinny jeans, looked effortless and stylish. Kristy had done her magic the day before, sweeping Naomi's hair up into a high, long ponytail. Perfect for the eighty-degree weather that had been forecasted. And a great hold-up hairstyle if the heat continued with her and Marvin after the sun went down.

There would be tons of people at the barbecue, and even though she'd be slaving behind a grill, she wanted to look good. Not because she'd be meeting Marvin's family or anything, she told herself, but because she'd soon be on TV, a celebrity who'd gotten her start by winning a food truck. She wanted to leave everyone with a good first impression.

After a spritz of cologne, Naomi unplugged her phone from the charger, placed it inside a fabric handbag that could be slung over her shoulder, and after one last look around her room turned out the light and headed into the kitchen, where she heard Nana cooking, or in her grandmother's words, "rattling pans."

"Morning, Nana." She gave her grandmother a hug. "You're up early this morning."

"So are you." Nana gave Naomi the once-over. "Wanted to get those cakes done before it got too hot outside."

"You say that like we don't have air-conditioning."

"No need putting more stress on it by having on a four-hundred degree oven on top of eighty degrees outside."

"True." Naomi walked over to where chocolate, coconut, and strawberry cakes were cooling on racks. "You've got it smelling good in here. I hope you hold a little back for us to have later."

"You smell good, too. And look real nice. You spending the day with that nice young man who came to dinner?"

"His name is Marvin. His parents and some of their neighbors are holding a Fourth of July barbecue."

"Another block party?"

"Not as large and involved as the annual one held on Memorial Day, but just as fun. You should come."

"And do what? Sit out in the sun and bake like those cakes in an oven? No, me and the ladies decided while sweating and fighting away bugs last year that this year we'd be inside."

"At the church?"

"No." Nana placed a bowl of boiled eggs she'd peeled in the refrigerator. She drained the water off a pot of potatoes, grabbed a peeler and sat down. "One of the ladies moved into a real nice retirement community that has a clubhouse. We're going to meet there. Sue will drive us over to the church when it's time to see the fireworks."

"That's a long day, Nana. Are you up for that?"

"We'll see."

"Take care of yourself and don't party too hard. Stay out of the sun and drink plenty of water."

"Yes, ma'am."

"I'm bugging you because I care. You just started feeling better." Naomi gave Nana a hug.

On the way out the door she heard Nana say, "Take your own advice!"

As she headed toward Inglewood, Naomi felt an unfamiliar feeling in her stomach. Giddiness. She couldn't' remember the last time she'd felt that way about a guy. Like being in love except she wasn't ready to admit that yet. She'd barely known Marvin a month. It wasn't that long ago that she'd finally admitted she even liked him!

There were no such feelings with her last boyfriend. She still wondered what she'd been smoking to ever think Victor was somebody she should date. Almost from the time they met he tried to change her. Lose weight. Wear her hair natural. Stop talking so loudly. Find another job. On top of that he had an average hammer that he didn't know how to swing and wasn't even all that good-looking. That a whole year had gone by before she ended the train wreck made Naomi want to kick her own behind.

Naomi turned on her music app and accessed her favorite channel playing songs from the early- to mid-two-thousands. Hearing 50 Cent's "In da Club" reminded her of Rodney, the boyfriend before Victor and first love of her life. She and Rodney had practically grown up together. Lived on the same block. Attended the same schools. They started dating as seniors in high school and would be off and on for the next several years. Rodney was funny and had rocked her world in the bedroom. But he didn't do much for her outside of that. He was too comfortable being average and content to live his entire life without leaving the state. Naomi wasn't vying for celebrity status or Oprah's money, but she did have a few goals and wanted to expand her life experience beyond the West Coast.

There were a couple other short-lived relationships here and a hook-up or two there, but when it came to love interests, Marvin was definitely the best guy she'd ever dated all the way around. Not only was he funny and kind, with a laid-back swagger, but he wanted to do something with his life. They were super compatible in the bedroom and he had celebrity in-laws. Who could top that? The thought that crossed her mind as she reached Inglewood and the blocks where tents had been erected was one she'd never asked herself with any previous boyfriend. *Will I get along with his mother?* Naomi was about to find out.

Seconds after seeing Marvin's SUV, she saw him coming out of a nearby tent. He waved her forward and directed her to park beside his car in what she now realized was a small parking lot. Like her, Marvin wore black jeans. He'd paired his with a white tee, white sneakers, and a Lakers cap. He wore shades even though it wasn't that bright outside. Naomi's heart skipped a little. Every day it was harder to deny it. She was in deep.

Marvin opened her car door. "You're late!"

"Shut up."

For once, Naomi was thankful for his sarcasm as it took some of the sappy out of her happiness that his mere presence evoked. The strong feelings were almost scary. *I must be about to start my period.* Yes, that was it. Blaming hormones lessened the significance of what she experienced.

Naomi stepped out of the car and into his hug. He smelled of coffee and hickory wood, indicating that he'd already been here awhile. "When'd you get here?"

"A couple hours ago." They began walking toward a side door in the sturdy tent. "You look nice."

"Thank you." Naomi wanted to return the compliment but didn't want to stir up what she'd just tamped down. She breathed in and immediately smelled the undeniable and tantalizing smell of barbecue. "Where are the grills?"

"Everything's inside."

He opened the door and stepped aside so that Naomi could enter.

She did, stopping just inside and looking around. "Wow."

"Surprised?"

"Totally. When you said we'd be cooking in a tent, this is not what came to mind."

"What did you imagine, a tepee?"

"You're so annoying." She playfully slapped his shoulder, and fell in step with him as he walked toward the back of the tent. Walking through one of two entrances to the back room, Naomi was even more awed. An elaborate setup that some kitchens would envy was erected in an orderly fashion. The longest grill Naomi had ever seen took up the entire left wall. Parts of it could be covered with sturdy round lids. Above the grill were large vents, allowing smoke to rise up and out of the structure. In the middle of the room, a rectangular prep station gleamed brightly. A myriad of spices filled a wooden

crate in the middle of the counter. Various utensils
stuck out of large metal containers. Below the
counter, Naomi noted baskets filled with onions,
potatoes, cabbage, carrots, and other vegetables.
Beyond the prep counter was a row of three stainless ranges. The thick grates told Naomi they were
top of the line. On the wall opposite the grill were
a variety of shelves that held cans and bottles, and a
taller one with loaves of bread and packages of
buns that were stacked almost to the ceiling. It was
a lot to take in, but Naomi did so in a matter of
seconds. When she turned, she was surprised to
see Marvin eying her intently, unabashed pride evident through the gleam in his eye.

"It's a pretty bad setup, huh?"

"I can't even lie, Marvin. This is incredible. I've
never worked in a restaurant, but I'd venture to say
this temporary outdoor kitchen probably looks
better than some of them."

"Coming from the restaurant industry, I can confirm that that is true. Come on, let me introduce
you to my father and a couple of my friends helping
us to get the party started."

Taken aback by the sophisticated kitchen, Naomi
hadn't even noticed the table of people sitting in
another room directly behind the room they occupied. A case of nerves assailed her as Marvin took
her hand and led them back to the group, who
looked up as they turned the corner.

"This is Naomi, everybody. She's also a contestant
on Food Truck Bucks and will be helping us out
today. Naomi, this is my dad, Willie Carter."

Naomi looked at the man who'd stood when she entered, and stepped forward to shake his hand.

"Nice to meet you."

He looked like a cup of strong, black coffee with a touch of cream, a tall oak tree that could not be moved or broken. Kind eyes in a weathered face touched her like a kiss on the cheek. He felt like wisdom, stability, and unconditional love, the energy so intense Naomi almost teared up. He felt like the father she'd never had, the grandfather she'd never known. A flurry of thoughts that happened in seconds, before Marvin spoke again.

"The person who wasn't trained properly and didn't stand when you entered as my father did, is one of my parents' neighbors, Ivory."

An obviously confident man slowly uncurled over six feet of good looks to his feet, offered a lopsided smile that Naomi knew had changed a thousand no's to yesses, and held out his hand. "Nice meeting you," he drawled. And to Marvin, "Uncle Willie is old-school. I represent the modern man."

"Don't matter what you represent," Willie responded, his voice as slow and easy as the flow of the Mississippi. "Good manners never go out of style."

The woman getting coffee from a setup near the table whooped. "Tell him, Mr. Carter!"

"That's Janet," Marvin continued. "She also works at the Soul Spot, and this is her best friend, Yvonne. She's helped us out with these barbecues and the past two or three block parties, right?"

Yvonne nodded, as she offered Naomi a smile. "At least. Hope you're ready to work, Naomi. You'll have a good time, but by the end of the night you'll be tired as hell." Her eyes swept Naomi's body. "And I hope you brought another pair of shoes. Those are cute, but in a few hours your feet are going to be very unhappy."

While Naomi was being introduced to those around the table a few others arrived, neighbors and relatives of neighbors, all ready to help. Marvin gathered troops and channeled a general, laying out the menu and delegating jobs to bring it about. Somebody turned on a stereo and soon the kitchen was a whirl of activities. Vegetables chopped or grated. Potatoes and eggs boiled and peeled. Mounds of meat seasoned and marinated. All this to the sounds of 70s magic like Kool & the Gang, Earth, Wind & Fire, and a group Naomi later learned was called Parliament-Funkadelic, who encouraged everyone listening to turn the mother out.

The rest of the neighborhood awakened. More and more people filed in and out of the tent. One of them, a large woman whose presence commanded attention, entered the kitchen. She wore red, white, and blue striped stretch pants and an oversized navy tee-shirt sporting a patriotically dressed Black Betty Boop. Behind her, several young boys pulled wagons bearing foil-covered pans. She barked orders to the young boys. They immediately obeyed, emptying the wagons and placing the trays on rolling shelves that Naomi figured must have been brought in while she was knee-deep in potato salad. Speaking to some and hugging others as she walked through the kitchen, the woman stopped next to Naomi, who was now using what resembled a mini oar to stir a vat of beans. One look into bright brown, expressive eyes that looked just like Marvin's, Naomi knew she was about to meet his mother.

She spoke first. "Good morning."

Liz eyed her slowly, boldly. "Hi, Naomi."

"Oh, Marvin must have pointed me out to you."

"No, your Carter-catcher did. Girl, until I arrived, your ass was the biggest one in here. Wasn't hard to figure out which one was you."

Naomi was taken aback, but the comment was said matter-of-factly, without judgment, and didn't offend. She wiped her hand on a dish towel and held it out. "Miss Liz, right?"

"Just Liz." Liz moved Naomi's hand so she could receive Liz's embrace. "Carters hug." She peeked into the vat. "For the baked beans?"

"Yes, ma'am."

Liz grunted, looked on the counters around her. "Darryl! Bring me a spoon."

Within seconds, one of the boys who'd pulled a wagon ran toward her with one. Liz dipped the spoon into the vat's liquid, blew on it, and then placed it in her mouth. Liz's eyes never left Naomi's as she sampled her dish.

She handed the spoon to Darryl, who ran it to the sink. "You seasoned those?"

"Yes, ma'am."

"Who taught you how to cook?"

"My grandmother, Nana."

"Your grandmother did a very good job."

"Thank you, Miss Liz."

"I said call me Liz, girl. There's no need for formalities. As good as those beans taste, and with that Carter-catcher you're packing? I have a feeling that soon we'll be like family. Oh, and I brought you these. They're my daughter's. Hope they fit."

Naomi opened the plastic bag and saw a pair of flat sandals. Smiling, she pulled one out and examined it. "I think they'll be fine and I think I'm going to need them."

"As someone who's helped prepare more barbecues and parties than I can remember or count, let me tell you something. I know you will."

Liz left. Naomi returned to cooking. She tried to dismiss Liz's compliments and family insinuations. Tried and failed. The longer she was around Marvin and his family, the more she adored them both. The night ended with fireworks, but not the kind that included barbecue sauce as Marvin had promised. Even though he'd cooked all day, Marvin joined his brothers and others to tear everything down. Naomi had to work at nine in the morning. But on the way home she whispered the words that had come to her mind with Marvin's goodbye kiss.

I love you.

25

The next day Naomi was still on a high from her time with the Carters. With her mind filled with so many great memories, the workday flew by. Even having to ignore a creditor's harassing calls hadn't bothered her. Marvin had called a couple times and sent a text, too. She'd texted back that she was at work and would call him later. But once off the clock and in her car, she dialed Kristy first. Her cousin had called several times yesterday, but Naomi hadn't found out until much later. She hoped Kristy had had a good enough time with Gary that she wouldn't be too mad.

"Hey, Tee!"

"Hey."

The lackluster greeting told Naomi that either Kristy hadn't had a good time yesterday or she was in a bad mood today.

"What's wrong?"

"Nothing."

"Doesn't sound like nothing. Are you mad at me?"

"Why didn't you call me back?"

"I'm sorry about that, Tee. You know I helped Marvin at the barbecue yesterday, right? I'd meant to put my phone in my pocket, but we started working literally the minute I got there and stayed so busy that I totally forgot about it until yesterday afternoon. When I finally got my phone and saw you'd called, the party was full-on crazy. I could barely hear myself think. So I thought to call you later, which I'm doing now."

No response.

"Tee, you there?"

"Yeah."

"Why didn't you and Gary come by?"

"We ended up not getting together."

"What?" Now, Naomi felt bad. The thought of her cousin home alone on a holiday when she'd had so much fun didn't feel right at all. "What happened?"

"I got sick."

"Again?"

"What do you mean, again?"

"Why are you snapping at me? You got sick that first night we ate at the Soul Spot, or don't you remember? What was it this time? Cramps, a cold, what?"

"It's worse than that."

"Tee, what's going on? You're scaring me." Naomi knew Kristy had a tendency to not practice safe sex, and didn't get tested either. "I'm on my way home from work. Do I need to stop by?"

"You can if you want to."

"I'm on my way."

Feeling urgency, Naomi weaved in and out of traffic and pushed the boundaries on a few yellow lights. She slowed down when she reached Kristy's block, though. The kids treated the street as though it was their private playground. Sure enough, there was a bunch of boys who'd set up a makeshift ramp in a driveway and were skateboarding off it and flying through the air, about six feet, Naomi guessed, directly in front of her car. Had she been going forty instead of twenty, had she not known that kids always played in the streets . . .

She whipped her car into an available space a few houses down, grabbed her purse and a bag from work, yanked open the door and started fussing before her sandal hit the pavement.

"Boys! What are you doing playing in the street like that? You need to keep that on the sidewalk before you get hit!"

A slew of smart remarks followed her up the steps. She shook her head and decided to ignore them, did a melodic knock on the door. They were just kids who'd obviously not been properly taught. She knew one of the little boys lived right across the street. Mama may have been looking out the window, ready to curse her out if she said too much, instead of teaching her son and his knucklehead friends about the benefits of safety first. A shard of guilt stabbed her conscience. Naomi had no idea how hard it was to raise a child. Some of her friends were single mothers, and Naomi had seen firsthand how difficult life was for them. Maybe there were lessons that hadn't been taught and manners that slipped through the cracks. Who was she to judge? The only person she could control was herself, and one thing was for sure. Naomi wasn't ready to have a child. If and when she allowed Marvin to shed the raincoats, she'd get back on the pill or take a shot. She glanced back as other kids joined the ones in the street. *Maybe I'll do both.*

What is taking Tee so long? Naomi knocked again and then pulled out her phone. She was just about to text Kristy when the door opened.

"Auntie Leese! I didn't expect to see you." Naomi stepped in and hugged Kristy's mom, Lisa. "Are you on vacation?"

"Had to take care of some business at the DMV. Why are you so happy?"

"Is happiness against the law around here?" Naomi crossed over to a table that held a bowl of candy. Unwrapping a piece, she turned around. "That was a joke, Auntie."

"Kristy's upstairs."

Naomi started for the stairs, then stopped and turned. Still wrapped up in yesterday's thrill and preoccupied with the boys she'd scolded and the mothers she'd judged, Naomi hadn't paid much attention when Lisa opened the door. Now that she did, Naomi's own mood shifted.

"You alright, Auntie?"

"Just tired. Go on up."

"Is Tee all right?"

"Go ask her."

Naomi had barely knocked on Kristy's bedroom door before it was yanked open. "It's about time."

"No, you didn't say that. I broke a couple laws to get here when I did." She followed her cousin inside, watched as Kristy plopped on her bed against a slew of pillows.

"I called your butt a half dozen times yesterday."

"You knew I was doing the barbecue. You should have just come over."

"I already told you! I was—"

"Sick, I get it." Naomi sat on the bed, too, noticed an extra-large soda on the nightstand along with cheese and crackers. "Do you feel better now?"

"Kinda, but not really."

Naomi's eyes narrowed as she studied her cousin. She'd been so caught up in the episode of her escapades that she hadn't considered Kristy's at all. "Since you weren't feeling good, why'd you keep calling me?"

"Maybe I wanted you to come over and play doctor."

Naomi laughed. "Those days are long gone. Funny you should mention that though, since for some reason parts of yesterday took me down memory lane. I thought about my exes, including

Rodney. I think he's the man who I played doctor with, probably the first one. And what was his friend's name? The fat boy we called Red, who had all those freckles?"

Naomi watched Kristy produce a hint of a smile. "Mike."

"Mike! Oh my God, remember how when we told him where babies came from he broke down crying!"

Kristy laughed. "He didn't want to believe his whole body had been pushed out of a hoohaw."

"I hope we didn't traumatize that poor boy for life."

"He's probably somewhere practicing gynecology." She reached for her drink, mumbling something else before taking a sip.

"What'd you say?" Naomi asked, still laughing as she felt her phone vibrating.

"I said I could probably use him."

"Time for that pap, girl?" She pulled out her phone and checked the face. It was Marvin.

"No. It's time to confirm whether or not I'm really pregnant."

Phone call forgotten, Naomi couldn't move. When she did it was to turn fully toward her cousin. "You're not playing."

"No, this isn't playing doctors, part two. I didn't tell anybody, but I haven't been feeling good for about a month. Threw up a few times, but it wasn't every day. And sometimes it was more like a gag reflex than actually throwing up. So when it happened I always thought it was either a virus, the stomach flu, some digestive problem, or food poisoning."

Naomi's phone vibrated again. "Hold on, cousin." She answered the phone. "Hey, Marvin, I'm going to have to call you back."

She hung up without waiting for an answer, and put the phone away. "Sorry, Tee. Go on."

"Last week my period didn't come and you know I'm like clockwork. I still didn't want to believe it. But yesterday I was really sick. Really throwing up. Couldn't keep anything on my stomach. Mom heard me tell Gary not to come by, that I wasn't going to go anywhere. She asked me what was wrong. I told her. She asked if I was pregnant and honestly, that thought never crossed my mind. She went to a picnic somewhere and came home with a pregnancy test. It showed positive. I didn't believe it. So this morning I went out and got another one. Same thing. So now . . . I'm pretty sure this is morning sickness and Gary is about to be a daddy."

"Oh my goodness, Kristy. Y'all just started dating! Does he know?"

"Not yet. I want to get an official result before telling him."

"How do you feel? Are you ready for kids?"

Kristy looked over. Naomi watched a myriad of emotions play across her face. "Doesn't matter whether I'm ready for a kid, because one is obviously ready for me."

Naomi's phone rang for the third time in as many minutes. "Man, if that's Marvin again . . ."

"Go ahead and answer it. I have to use the bathroom anyway."

"Hey, Marvin," Naomi answered, concern filling her eyes as she watched Kristy lumber off the bed and head down the hall. During that time Marvin was talking but she hadn't heard a word.

She pressed the speaker button. "I'm sorry, Marvin. What did you say?"

"I asked if you were on your way."

"On my way where?"

A pause and then, "Have you checked your messages?"

"Not lately, why?"

"Because Sean called an emergency meeting."

"For what?"

"Listen to your messages, Naomi. I'll see you when you get here. Oh, and it's not at the convention center. We're at Gower Studios on Sunset. I'll text the address."

"That's okay. I'll GPS it from online."

Frowning, Naomi quickly checked her phone log, then pressed the voicemail icon and put the phone to her ear. She had seven new messages. Five were from the number she'd seen at work but hadn't recognized, the one she assumed was a forgotten creditor. Turns out that number was to a phone in the show producer's office.

New message.

"*Uh, hello, Naomi. This is Sean Owens, one of the*

producers for Food Truck Bucks. Could you give me a call when you get this message? I have a quick question. Thanks."

New message.

"Hello, Naomi, this is Tracy Boyd with Food Truck Bucks. We really need to talk to you, so if you can call as soon as you get this message, we'd really appreciate it."

New message.

Kristy returned to the room "Who's that?" she asked.

Naomi stood, held up a finger and continued to listen.

"Naomi, Tracy again. Listen, sorry to bother you but we have a time-sensitive issue to discuss with you and are trying to schedule a time to meet. Please call back."

Naomi placed the phone in her purse and secured its strap over her shoulder. "That was the producers from the show. They called earlier from a number I didn't recognize. I thought it was a bill collector and didn't check messages."

"What do they want?"

"I don't know, but it must involve all the contestants because Marvin is already down there. I hate to leave you like this . . ."

Kristy walked over to give her a hug. "Go on and handle your business, cousin. I'll be alright."

"If you want me to, I can come back."

"Wait until after my appointment with an ob-gyn. If their results match the other two sticks, I'll really need you then."

Naomi left her cousin's house, heading toward

downtown LA. She couldn't imagine what was so important that they'd called a meeting the day after a holiday and four days before the last challenge. She speculated, but couldn't think of a positive reason. So she turned on the music and did what Nana would have suggested had she been in the car.

Relax, child. Don't raise your pressure.

26

Unless they lived in Hollywood, Los Angeles natives rarely went there. Naomi hadn't been down there in years. Even though her mind was preoccupied with why they were meeting, she drove down Sunset and couldn't help but notice how much Hollywood had changed. Much like those whose dreams lived or died here, the place had gotten another facelift, and this time it looked as though the city had gone all out. Imperfections were shielded with shiny glass and bright neon. Gower Street was much more subdued, the streets almost devoid of human life. She turned into what appeared to be an entrance and up to a manned gate. She introduced herself, told the guard why she was there, and soon was given a pass and directed to a specific building on the huge production lot. Naomi couldn't understand why, but the closer she got to the building he'd indicated, the more nervous she became.

Seconds after finding the building, then the room, and opening the door, the nerves made sense. Sean, Tracy, a production assistant, and a couple other people, were seated around a round conference table. Marvin was there, too, the only contestant in the room. No one was smiling. The palpable tension stopped her better than a wall could do.

"Come on in, Naomi. Have a seat."

"Sorry I didn't get your message. When I didn't recognize the caller, I thought it was a solicitor or scam." She looked over at Marvin. "Hi."

"Hi."

Hi. No smile. No Juicy. Not good.

"What is this about?"

Sean and Tracy looked at each other. Tracy placed her arms on the table and leaned forward. "First of all, guys, thanks for coming. I know it was an inconvenience, especially since we didn't care to elaborate the reason for meeting over the phone. Even in person it will be rather uncomfortable because an accusation has been levied against the two of you and this meeting was called to try and get to the bottom of what's going on."

"Accusations about what?" Marvin asked.

"By whom?" Naomi demanded.

Sean sat up. "Okay, let's stay calm here."

"I am calm," Marvin said, from the same laid-back position he was in when Naomi entered the room.

"You okay, Naomi?" Sean asked.

"I don't know yet. It depends on what you tell me."

Tracy laced her fingers together, rested her hands on the table. "Someone or ones believe that there is some type of collusion going on between the two of you, either to gain an advantage or to help the other out so that at least one of you goes as far as you can."

Naomi sat back in the chair, crossed her arms, and looked out of the window. Marvin didn't move. A couple producers shifted in their seats. The silence screamed.

"Do either of you want to comment on the allegation?"

"Who said it?" Marvin asked.

"We'd rather not say at this time."

"That's not fair. They've identified us and had enough nerve to go to you with whatever story they told you. It's only right that we know who our accusers are."

"In this part of the process," Sean began, "we're just trying to get your side of the story. If this turns into something more, something serious that could lead to your being put off the show, then the names of the accusing party would come into play."

"It was probably Jeremy," Naomi said. "That I was saved from elimination last week drove him crazy. I thought the boy was going to combust right there. Either him or . . ."

Naomi felt Marvin nudge her with his foot. "Never mind."

The room fell quiet again.

After what felt like an eternity but was less than a

few seconds, Sean continued. "Are you two dating? Let's start there."

"Is there a rule that says we can't date?" Naomi asked. "Because there were a lot of pages to the document we had to sign, but I don't remember seeing anything about relationships in there."

"To answer your question, Naomi, while it is discouraged, there are no clear rules that forbid two contestants from becoming romantically involved. However, it is against the rules for two contestants to form a team, if you will, in order to improve the other's chance of winning."

"Or to share information that would somehow give either of you an advantage," Sean added.

"The only advantage Marvin and I have is that we can cook," Naomi said, clearly defensive. "We're not colluding, sharing, cheating, none of that. And even if we did share something, say a recipe or cooking technique or whatever, how would that help us in a challenge? We're either cooking with a team— where we're all sharing—or we're making our own dish at our individual stations. Alone. Where it is against the rules to go over and help somebody else?" She sat back and shook her head. "This is stupid."

Tracy leveled a stare at Naomi. "So you're admitting that the two of you have shared recipes and cooking techniques?"

"No! I'm not admitting that. Those were examples."

"Marvin is a trained, professional cook, while

your experience is that of a home cook. And you have done very well in this competition, Naomi. It would be understandable if you have asked Marvin for advice or he offered to help you out because, as he said, the two of you get along so well."

"Please. If anybody would ask for help, trust me, it would be Marvin asking me. I was trained by the best, baby, a cook extraordinaire named Nadine, otherwise known as my grandmother, otherwise known as Nana. I don't need help cooking. I don't need help beating him or anybody else, and I don't need any help to win that truck!"

The passionate declaration brought out smiles from Ryan and another producer. Even serious Sean's lips turned upward.

Tracy remained stern as she asked her next question. "Is it true that the two of you cooked together yesterday, worked in the same kitchen at a neighborhood event?"

Naomi looked from Tracy to Marvin and back. "Who told you that?"

"Is it true?"

"We helped cook at a Fourth of July event. Folks could get a hamburger, hot dog, or a ten-dollar plate with the holiday works." Marvin counted on his fingers. "Choice of meat—chicken, steak, or ribs. Potato—baked, fried, or potato salad. Greens—mustards, collards, kale, or coleslaw." He looked at Naomi. "What else?"

"Corn, mac-'n'-cheese," she mumbled after a sigh, clearly not ready to kumbayah.

"The works, basically," Marvin said. "Altogether there are about twenty people helping to pull that off. We're not all in the kitchen at the same time, but there were a lot of people cooking yesterday and trust me, there was no time for a cooking tutorial, the one I'd be giving to her." He cocked his head toward Naomi, who sucked her teeth and turned the opposite way.

Marvin chuckled, shifted in the chair. As had happened during the entire meeting, his voice was as calm and relaxed as his posture. "Look, guys. Naomi and I are friends. I've made friends with a lot of people. The contest is intense. You bond in the fire. Naomi and I, we clicked from the very first day that we stood in line right next to each other, because she's Carson and I'm Carter, and she started talking trash about my food. Right away it seemed as though we'd known each other forever, or grew up together or something. So people see us joking, teasing each other, whatever, it's easy to see someone assuming that we are dating or scheming or something like that. But as Ted tells us every week, there can only be one winner. And that will be—"

"Me." Marvin and Naomi simultaneously declared.

The room broke out laughing. Even Tracy smiled.

"Alright, guys," she said, serious once again. "Thanks for coming down and allowing us to hear your point of view. Sorry for the short notice and urgency, but we wanted to hear right away what you had to say because as a matter of procedure all allegations have to be investigated. We will continue to do that, pass everything on to the legal team and give you guys a call as soon as possible confirming that you will indeed be eligible to participate in the televised finals.

"However, I do have to make it clear that should there be any evidence that goes contrary to what you've shared here, anything that can be proven, then you will be disqualified and two new people from the last elimination will go on instead. I know this is a stressful situation to put on you. We're stressed, too, believe me. This certainly isn't the kind of thing we want to deal with and we can't film the final show until this matter is resolved."

"The finals may not happen?" Naomi asked.

"They may not happen on Saturday," Tracy clarified. "We hope they will, but obviously this issue has to be resolved first."

"Until we reach that resolution," Sean began, as he closed the tablet in front of him and reached for its case, "it would be a really good idea for the two of you to keep a low profile with the friendship, not do anymore public functions between now and the end of all this. We can't force it, but if you don't want to provide more ammunition for the person gunning for you, it's something to consider."

The meeting adjourned and while there weren't hugs and kisses, the atmosphere upon exit was much lighter than Naomi had experienced when she arrived. She said goodbye to Marvin, an awkward parting devoid of hugs, playful punches or teasing banter, and headed to her car. Once there she sat, dazed from the one-two punch of the past couple hours. Kristy might be pregnant? Her and Marvin might get the boot? What was going on?

She started her car, passed the gate, and was just about to enter the street when her message indicator dinged.

You want to meet?

Despite the seriousness of the situation, Naomi smiled. Marvin's placid, cordial demeanor hid a rebel and a boss. She texted back.

You heard the judges. Stay away from each other.

Do you always do what people tell you?

They said to lay low.

I want to lay down. With you.

Naomi's smile widened. Between looking but barely touching yesterday and today's drama, she needed a good full-body massage.

Where?

I'll text you. Then several seconds later a final message. And I'm bringing barbecue sauce.

27

A few hours later, Naomi pulled into the parking lot of a hotel near Los Angeles International Airport. She'd had second thoughts about the back-and-forth texts and had called Marvin and voiced her fears.

"Why should we act guilty when we've done nothing wrong? Somebody lies and we get punished? That's not right."

"Not seeing me feels like punishment?" Naomi cooed, warmed by the thought someone felt that way about her.

"Uh-huh," he slowly responded with bass in his voice. "Are you going to break me out of jail?"

Needless to say, she left the house. Dressed in black and feeling like theme music should be accompanying her steps, she quickly crossed the parking lot and entered the lobby. She kept her head lowered, surreptitiously looking for the elevator while trying to look "normal." Finally spotting a set of metal doors, she made a beeline for them, punched the button and prayed for either the doors or the floor to open up, whichever one could hide her the fastest. It wasn't until she entered the elevator, the door closed, and she exhaled that Naomi realized she'd been holding her breath since locking the car.

She found the room number and knocked on the door. It opened within seconds. An arm reached beyond the door, latched on to hers, and pulled her inside. With his arms around her, Marvin backed them both up to the bed. He kissed her, flicked his tongue across the crease of her mouth as a silent bid to enter. Naomi complied. Her tongue went in search of his goodness. She felt Marvin's hands roam her body and squeeze her cheeks. Moaned when he ground his hardening bone against her. Naomi eased onto the bed. Marvin followed her down. He slid his hand beneath her blouse and lightly rubbed his finger across her nipple as the two led their tongues into a leisurely dance. Except Naomi didn't want to do it nice and easy. Her nipples were hard. Her panties were wet. Her body was on fire. She wanted it rough.

"Let me up for a minute," she whispered.

Marvin rolled his body sideways. Naomi sat up and began to undress. Marvin took off his clothes, too. True to his word, there was a squirt bottle on the nightstand with what Naomi assumed contained the spicy sauce used yesterday to lather slabs. She loved oral. Had never deferred the act until later and definitely had never turned it down. But the ache she felt was deep within her core, beyond where his tongue could reach but right where his curved tip landed on the down thrust. When he reached for the bottle, she stopped him.

"Let's do that later," she said, her voice hoarse with desire. "Right now, I want you to fuck me. I need to feel you inside me."

Marvin's hand slid from the bottle to the square foils beside it. He grabbed one. Ripped it open with his teeth and came toward her on his knees. "Put it on me."

Naomi took the condom, placed it on his tip and channeled a porn star, doing something she'd seen on video but never attempted. She unrolled the condom with her mouth and tongue, stroking his manhood into steel-like hardness and Marvin into a man on a mission. He eased off the bed, then placed his arms around Naomi's legs. He pulled her to the edge of the bed. Raising her legs, he ran a finger through her juicy lower lips.

"Ooh," Naomi moaned.

He lifted her legs higher and smacked her ass.

"Ow!"

Before Naomi could process all the sensations, Marvin positioned himself between her legs and gave her another one—his hard shaft slamming into her heat. As if reading her mind, or maybe her body, he wasted no time with gentle half-strokes. Instead he set up a slow rhythm—pounding, thrusting, plunging into her again and again.

Naomi's grabbed the sheets and held on as time and again he hit her spot.

"Yes! Yes!"

Naomi's words turned into unintelligible noises as orgasms exploded on top of each other. The thrusting increased, faster, harder until a loud moan and a series of shudders signaled Marvin's release as well.

Breathing hard, Marvin collapsed on the bed. Naomi rolled over and into his arms. She felt Marvin's wildly beating heartbeat and took several deep breaths as she tried to slow her own. When Naomi's breathing returned to normal, she lifted her head. "Did you even speak to me when I came in the room?"

Marvin responded, his eyes closed. "I had other things on my mind besides talking."

Naomi lay back down, too satiated to argue. After a few moments he turned on his side and kissed her temple. "Hey, Juicy."

"Hey."

"You doing alright?"

"Are you kidding? I'm amazing. I feel like I could float away."

"I'd be flying with you. But I was actually talking about what happened earlier. You were pretty upset."

"Somebody lying on us? Yes, I was upset. I still am." Naomi adjusted the pillows so that she could sit against the headboards. "I know it was Jeremy."

Marvin sat up, too. "I wouldn't put it past him."

"I heard that he was telling people the game was rigged even before he got eliminated. He thinks he knows more than the judges."

"That's because one of them fired him years ago, when his career first started."

"Which one?" Naomi asked. "Who told you?"

"Remember the older guy who looked kind of like Jim Belushi?"

She shook her head. "I don't remember him."

"He didn't make it past the first round. I don't remember his name."

"It doesn't matter. Jeremy wasn't the only one who didn't want me in the competition."

"Who else?"

Naomi gave him a look. "Really?"

"Yes, really. I don't know all your enemies. Was it someone from two weeks ago, when we were on the same team?"

"It's somebody from a few years ago when you were in culinary school."

Marvin thought for a moment. "Abbey?"

"Don't act surprised. That woman can't stand me."

"You're right, but I don't think she'd lie about you."

"I wouldn't put anything past her." Naomi started off the bed.

Marvin stopped her. "Where do you think you're going?"

"To take a shower." She eased off the bed and turned around. "And turn myself into a rib."

"I got the sauce, baby!"

Naomi laughed and walked into the bathroom.

"Hey, Naomi."

"What?" She turned on the shower.

"Mama raved about your beans."

Naomi stuck her head back into the room. "I love your mom!"

"How's Nana doing?"

"She's okay. But I think yesterday was a little much. She was up when I left and out until the nine o'clock fireworks."

"That's a long day."

"Yes, I think she's feeling it. She looked pretty tired when I left her. So I'm not going to stay out too long."

Naomi finished her shower and returned to bed. When Marvin decided to take a quick one, too, she placed a call to Nana. That she got voicemail was no surprise.

"Nana, it's me. Called to check on you, but it looks like you've already gone to bed. I'm out with Marvin, but it won't be for too much longer. Love you."

After being treated like a rib for almost an hour, Naomi and Marvin took a quick shower together, then checked out of the hotel and went their separate ways. Naomi's legs felt like spaghetti noodles and she'd be sore tomorrow. But she'd be smiling. That's what was on her mind when she parked the car and headed inside. The house was dark and quiet. Naomi closed the door softly, turned on the hall light and tiptoed toward her grandmother's room. She opened the door, squinting in the darkness. The white spread adorned with colorful flowers looked untouched. Where was her grandmother?

Naomi stepped into the room and whispered, "Nana?"

Nadine wasn't a light sleeper so Naomi shouldn't have been concerned. But a foreboding feeling crept up her spine as she called out again, louder this time, with no response. Nadine's heartbeat increased as thoughts slammed into her conscience, none of them good.

"Nay, stop tripping." She reached for the light switch and flipped it, turned around and saw Nana lying on the floor.

"Nana!" She raced over to where her grandmother lay next to the bed. "Nana, wake up." Naomi pulled Nadine into her arms. Her grandmother was warm, there was no blood, and when she quickly checked Nadine's wrists, Naomi felt there was a pulse. "Nana, stay with me. Please don't leave me."

Naomi pulled a pillow off the bed and placed it under Nadine's head, then raced to call 9-1-1.

28

The day after his clandestine meeting with Naomi, Marvin bopped into the Soul Spot ready to conquer the world. For weeks, since he met her really, he'd been fighting the strong and ever-growing attraction he felt for the woman he dubbed Juicy. But the past few days had allowed him to see her in whole new ways. He loved that what you saw with Naomi was what you got. That the same person who called him out the first day they met, was the same one who told the Food Truck Bucks producers in nonnegotiable terms the source of her cooking talent.

She was a beast in the kitchen. The annual Fourth of July barbecue's food detail was a challenging one even for veteran cooks. But Naomi had picked up a knife, rolled up her sleeves, and acted as though cooking was what she did every day. Even though she wasn't quite herself in Venice Beach, the family members who'd met her at Byron's house all had good things to say. But his mother's reaction mattered more than anybody's, and when Liz winked at Marvin and said "I like that girl," Marvin decided to step up the romance game. Then came Tuesday and the phone call and subsequent meeting with the Food Truck Bucks producers suggesting it would be good for him not to see her for almost a week. That hitch in the giddy-up almost ruined his plans before he'd laid them out good.

He entered the restaurant through a side door and stepped into the kitchen. He ran into Janet. She looked unhappy.

"Hey, Net. Still recouping from the Fourth?"

"I was over that the next day."

"That's good. It looked like something was bothering you. I thought that might be it."

"No."

"What then?"

"She looked toward the kitchen, and then pulled him out to the hallway. "I'm getting ready to start looking for another job."

"Girl, you can't leave before I do. What's going on?"

"They don't want to pay us. And as busy as this place stays, especially on the weekends, I know they've got the money to bring our salaries closer to industry standards. I've been here five years and my salary has increased less than ten percent. But my responsibilities get bigger. It's not right. Not when Donald is getting paid what he's making and only comes in when he wants to."

"Yeah, my review is coming up in a few months.

If all goes my way, I'll be out of here by then, and looking for people to help me run my truck."

He held up his hand. They high-fived.

"Don't forget the little people."

Marvin gave her a thumbs-up and went into the kitchen. Janet had unwittingly increased his motivation and reminded him just how important it was for him to win that truck. Only someone had lied on him to the producers and he might not get that chance. That thought stayed with Marvin for the next three hours, until his first break. When the backup arrived, Marvin headed outside. Several weeks ago, Abbey had given him her number and begged him to use it. Today, she'd get that call.

He hopped in his SUV and fired it up, turned on the air and Bluetooth. He punched in the number, ready for a confrontation. After the fourth ring, his shoulders slumped and he waited for voicemail.

"Uh, hold on." Marvin heard garbled sounds in the background and imagined Abbey trying to retrieve her phone. "Hello? This is Abbey."

"Hey, Abbey. It's Marvin."

"Marvin."

He could tell that word held a lot of questions. He planned to answer them all, and ask some questions, too.

"What do you want?"

"A couple things. First of all, I want to apologize for the other day. Not for what I said, but the way I said it. I don't like hurting anyone, especially a female, and I know what I said hurt you. So I'm sorry for that."

"Okay."

"The other reason I called is to find out what you told the producers about me."

There was a pause. Marvin wondered if it was because she was surprised by the question, or deciding what type of lie she could tell and appease him.

"Which producer?"

"Any of them."

"They know I taught you at culinary school, that you were a good student. I think I told Tracy that I thought you were cute. Maybe a word here or there about something you fixed at the contest. Stuff like that. Why are you asking?"

"Are you sure that's all you told them? You never mentioned anything to them about me and Naomi and the relationship that you warned me so much about?"

"Why would I tell them that? The very thing I thought would hurt your chances if they found out? No, I didn't talk to them about you and Naomi. That doesn't even make sense. Why? What happened?"

"I didn't say anything happened. I just know there are some things going around about me that aren't true, and in trying to get to the bottom of it I remembered seeing you and Jeremy talking the day he got eliminated and wondered if you had said anything. He can't stand me and he hates Naomi. You don't like Naomi and I'd just hurt your feelings. Either of you alone had enough reason to want to see us out of the competition, but when I saw the two of you together, I knew to watch my back."

"Well, Marvin, it's unfortunate that you feel that way. I may be considered many things, but a traitor is not one of them and even though our friendship was minimal, or nonexistent by your definition, I considered myself to be your friend. And I wouldn't betray a friend like that. Not even one I no longer liked or who had hurt my feelings. That would be wrong, and cruel, and I wouldn't do it, unless I had an awfully good reason, illegal or immoral, something like that. And while you might find this hard to believe, I don't dislike Naomi."

Marvin harrumphed.

"No really, I don't. If you want to know the truth, I envy her. She's everything I could never be. In a society where thin is in and Black people are marginalized, she's loud and proud, confident and daring. She's so out there! I don't know how to explain it, but it's like she doesn't give a hoot what anybody thinks. I've always been a bit of a wallflower, introverted, unsure of myself. Growing up on a farm in Podunk, Iowa, most of mine were four-legged friends. I had strict, religious parents who didn't allow me much latitude, so being socially awkward is an understatement. She's a social butterfly. I didn't like everything she did, or agree with everything she said. But I don't dislike her."

Marvin was stunned, and touched by what Abbey had said about Naomi. "Can I tell her you said that?"

"Oh, gosh, that would be so embarrassing. I don't want to come off as some dork, or something."

"It won't sound that way. You said some really nice things. I think Naomi would appreciate hearing them."

"Well, okay. I guess so."

"Thank you for accepting my apology. Wait, did you accept it?"

"Yes, Marvin. I accept it."

"Good. I believe you regarding me and Naomi and what you did or did not tell the producers. You're good people, Abbey. And even though I'm not attracted to you in a romantic way, I wouldn't mind being friends."

"I'd like that."

"And I'd like to call you Abs again. But not if you're going to turn into a stalker."

The laugh they enjoyed was genuine. Marvin exited the car and returned to work after a productive break. He'd offered an apology, gotten answers, and gained a friend. He still didn't know who was after him, but it was good sometimes to be reminded that life didn't always suck.

29

Naomi sat on a hard, plastic chair in the hospital's nondescript cafeteria, trying to absorb what the doctors had told her just moments ago. She wore the same clothes Marvin had seen her wearing last night when he opened the hotel room door. Stray strands of hair had escaped the high ponytail that just two days ago had been flawless and sleek. Her eyes, red-rimmed and bleary, stared at the gray vinyl floor. There was a Styrofoam cup of coffee in front of her, along with an untouched cinnamon-raisin bagel. Across from her, Kristy mechanically pinched off and ate bites from a glazed twist. Kristy's mom, Lisa, grasped the black coffee that had been her constant companion for the past fourteen hours.

"I know it sounds bad, niecy," Lisa said, her voice low and soothing as though talking to a scared child. "But, unfortunately, heart disease is becoming more and more common especially as people age. Plus, it runs in our family. But you heard the doctor. Implanting a pacemaker isn't major surgery like it used to be. They're going to perform it under local anesthesia. She'll be going home with us today."

"I know what he said," was Naomi's wooden reply. "But somehow the thought of putting a wire into somebody's heart, one attached to a machine, and leaving both the wire and the machine inside her, doesn't sound simple to me. It sounds major."

Kristy reached for the extra-large cup in front of her. "I'm just glad she's still here."

Lisa nodded. "And from what the doctor said, with the help of the pacemaker she can be here for a long time."

"I sure hope so," Naomi said with a sigh. "Because I can't do life without Nana right now."

It was almost ten o'clock before Naomi pulled into Nana's driveway. The surgery itself was over in minutes, but hadn't been performed until a series of tests were completed. An hour ago Nana had been alert and talkative, almost her old self. But on the way home Naomi had looked over, seen her nodding, and become concerned.

"Nana!" she'd yelled, her heart in her chest.

Nana had slowly lifted her head and responded, "Girl, stop yelling. I'm asleep, not dead."

Naomi turned off the engine. "You ready, Nana?"

"For what?"

"To go inside."

"As ready as I'll ever be."

"Hold on, let me come over on that side and help you out."

Naomi jumped out of the car and hurried around to the passenger door. "Here, take my arm."

She helped Nana out of the seat belt and out of the car. Aside from wincing when she inadvertently lowered her left arm, Nana seemed okay. Her steps were slow but sure, and soon Naomi had her undressed and in bed, with pillows propped up around her.

"What can I get for you, Nana? Are you comfortable? Do you need any of that pain medication?"

She watched her grandmother lean her head against the pillow. "I think I'm okay for now."

"Are you hungry?"

"I could probably eat a little something. You know that hospital food isn't any good."

"Okay. Let me see what's in there that I can fix quickly."

"Not much, baby. I don't have a big appetite. Could use some water, though."

Naomi handed her grandmother the remote control, then went into the kitchen. A few minutes later, she returned with glasses of water and orange juice. She retrieved a bed tray from a corner in the room and set it up over her grandmother's lap. After a quick scan of the refrigerator contents, she made her grandmother a plate with small helpings of leftover baked beans and coleslaw, and half a chicken sandwich. Only after delivering the plate to Nana did Naomi feel a slight pang of hunger. As her grandmother's life hung in the balance, Naomi couldn't eat and barely drank. But now that her dear Nana was back, so was her appetite. She fixed a healthy chicken sandwich with coleslaw and mustard as condiments and returned to Nana's room.

Naomi was happily chatting with Nana and halfway through her sandwich when the doorbell rang.

"I know that's Miss J," she told Nana. "Are you up for company?"

"Not really, but go on and let her in. She'll worry herself to death until she sees me and will end up needing a pacemaker herself."

With Miss J at Nana's bedside, Naomi finally went to her room. With only the illumination of the closet light, she pulled off her clothes, pulled on a pair of cotton pj's and crawled into bed. Only then, under the cloak of near darkness, did she release tears held back for almost a day. In the darkness she thanked God for saving her grandmother. She finished the sandwich, and went to sleep.

The Lil Wayne ringtone woke her with a start two hours later. She sat up, frightened and disoriented, until she remembered that she was home and Nana was right down the hall. She reached for her phone on the nightstand, checked the face and offered a groggy hello.

"I woke somebody up," Marvin said, his voice like sunshine in her rainy season.

"Yeah."

"Do you always go to sleep before midnight?"

"I do when I haven't slept the night before."

"Don't try and put the blame on me. I took care

of business and sent you on your way before eleven
o'clock. Don't tell me you went somewhere after that."

"Yeah, I did."

A long pause followed.

"I went to the hospital."

"Why?"

"I came home and found Nana on the floor."

"What happened?"

"The doctors thought she fainted. They ran a
bunch of tests and it turns out she's got heart
disease."

"Ah, man, Nay. I'm so sorry."

"I am, too. The good news is that the doctors
say we caught it early, so there's a better chance of
her heart not continuing to deteriorate. But she
fainted because of a condition with a name that's
longer than this bed I'm lying on, but basically
means that her heart rate is erratic and sometimes
drops real fast and causes her to lose consciousness.
But there'd been other signs, too, only we didn't
recognize them. Nana's pretty active, but she'd
complained of just not feeling good overall, being
tired. She'd talked about getting dizzy a few times.
But we always attributed it to something else. Or
chalked it up to what happens as you get older. I
didn't even know the disease ran in our family.
But it does."

"How long is she going to be in the hospital?"

"She's already back home. They put in a pacemaker and I brought her back last night."

"Dang, they released her that fast?"

"At first, I thought the same thing! I'm thinking if it has something to do with the heart then that is major surgery. But she wasn't even put under for them to perform it. They gave her a local anesthetic and it took about, I say about . . . an hour. Then they kept her another couple hours for observation and that was it. They prescribed medication for the pain. She's got to take it easy for the next four to six weeks, at least, maybe longer because the doctor said everybody heals differently. But the main thing is that she is alive."

"You don't know how happy I am to hear that."

"Oh, yes I do."

"I know how much you love your grandmother, and losing her right before the finals would have been devastating. Do you even think you could have done them?"

"Not at all. In fact, I don't think I'm going to do them even though she survived."

"Are you serious? Why not, babe?"

"For the next few weeks, Nana is going to need someone with her twenty-four seven. She's not supposed to raise her arm too high or lift anything, and Nana's stubborn. Somebody's going to have to keep an eye on that chick at all times. The only person I trust to watch her like that, is me."

"But you're not going to do the final?"

"Um, I think that's what I just said."

"But, Nay, you worked so hard and have come so far. You beat out all of those people, even award-winning chefs like Jeremy Evans. I know you love

your grandmother dearly, but isn't there a way
you can make sure she's taken care of and do the
contest, too?"

"Maybe. But since my mother died when I was
eight years old, it's been me and Nana against the
world. The only mother that I ever really knew,
since mine left so young. My memories of her are
almost like a movie, or an old photo album where
the pictures come in snatches. I zoned out when
Mama died. They said I didn't talk for almost a
month."

"Whew," Marvin loudly exclaimed. "I can't even
imagine what that would be like!"

Only someone like Marvin could take a poi-
gnantly tender moment and make it hilarious.
Naomi laughed for the first time since coming
home last night.

"You know you're stupid, don't you? Oh my God!
I can't stand you."

"I'm sorry, baby. I shouldn't have interrupted
you like that, but the thought of that mouth not
moving. At all. For a month."

"I'm getting ready to hang up this phone."

"Okay, I'll be quiet."

"Thanks for making me laugh. I was getting
ready to go there with that sad memory. I already
did last night when I saw Nana on the floor. So I
don't need to go back. But my life kind of shifted
when I saw her lying there and thought she might
have died. When I ran over to her, and felt a pulse,
nothing else mattered except saving her life. And

now there's nothing more important than keeping her here. Winning it all would be real nice. But when you pull someone you love back from the brink of death, stuff like money, material things, job, status, they really don't seem important at all. Yesterday morning, all of it did. But right now? I don't give a damn."

30

Naomi had told Marvin that she didn't care about the contest's outcome, or if she'd be in it. But when her phone rang that Friday morning, showing the number she now knew belonged to a Food Truck Bucks producer, her heart jumped.

"Hello?"

"Naomi, it's Tracy. How are you doing?"

"I'm okay."

"How's your grandmother?" Naomi's brow creased. "Marvin called and told us that she'd been hospitalized. I hope you don't mind that he told us. He knew you were focused solely on her getting better, as you should be, and didn't think calling us would cross your mind. But with the taping having been initially scheduled for tomorrow, he wanted us to know."

"He's right. I didn't think about it."

"How is she?"

"She's okay, getting better. Trying to tell me how to cook, so that's a good sign."

"I'm really close to my grandma, too, so I have a feeling how relieved you are that she's getting on your nerves."

The women laughed.

"What's happening with those lies somebody told on me and Marvin?" Naomi asked.

"That's another reason I called." Naomi didn't catch the smile in Tracy's voice. Instead, without being aware of it, she held her breath. "The taping has been pushed back one week and will take place next Saturday, not tomorrow."

"You guys are still investigating?"

"The investigation into the allegations waged against you and Marvin has been completed. We found no credible evidence to corroborate their stories, or any proof of anything you and Marvin were doing wrong. You're both in the clear and still very much in the competition for Food Truck Bucks."

"I don't know about finishing the competition, but I'm glad my name was cleared."

"Naomi, what do you mean? Having come all this way and beat out literally thousands to get to the final ten? You've got to be in the finals."

"Up until three days ago, that's what I thought. But almost losing Nana has given me a different perspective. We're all each other has got, and while she's getting better, she still needs somebody to take care of her, and I know those finals are going to take all day. To be honest, I don't even know if I could focus, and concentrate on recipes."

Naomi heard Tracy release an audible sigh. "This is definitely not the conversation I'd planned. Your dropping out would affect production, naturally, and while we'd absolutely hate to lose you, knowing that now instead of this time next week at least gives us a chance to find your replacement. Are you sure that's what you want to do?"

"Given what's happened, it's probably best."

"Again, I'm really sorry to hear that." Almost as an afterthought, Tracy added, "Maybe Jeremy will get a shot at the truck after all."

The call ended shortly after that, Naomi suddenly numbed by the fact that she'd uttered a single sentence and killed a dream. The phone slipped from her hand and landed on the bed. She sat back, looked out the window, and tried to feel okay. Nana needed her more than Naomi needed a food truck. The truck could come later. Nana couldn't be replaced. Naomi told herself this and felt a little better. She'd done what she had to do.

Naomi reached for her phone and tapped the screen. "Nana, what are you doing?"

"About to make some coffee. Why are you calling me from the other room?"

Naomi laughed, got out of bed and headed out to the kitchen. "Because I was staying in bed until I knew you were up." She leaned over and kissed her grandmother. "You know you shouldn't be doing this. Your surgery was just two days ago."

"I know, but I'm already sick of that bed."

"How are you feeling?"

"Like I could walk to church and back. I took one of those pain pills."

"Ha! You say that now. You'll be asleep in an hour. Here, let me get that, Nana." Naomi poured water in the coffeemaker and turned it on. "What do you want for breakfast?"

"What time do you have to be at work?"

"I'm not going to work today. Next week, either."

"Nay, did you quit your job?"

Naomi shook her head. "I took emergency family leave."

"And they're going to hold your job for you?"

"I was looking for a job when I got that one. If they don't, I'll find another."

"I know what you're doing. Betting on winning that food truck, huh?"

Nadine leaned against the counter. "Why don't you go sit down, Nana? I'll bring your coffee."

After fixing two cups with cream and sugar, Naomi took them in the living room and gave one to Nadine before sitting down.

Nadine took a tentative sip, then a more robust one. "You got this just right."

"Good."

"Where are y'all at in that contest? It should be just about over?"

"Yeah, just about. They're doing the final taping next week."

"Are you nervous?"

"No."

"That's good."

"I'm not doing it."

"You're not? But I thought you told me you made it to the finals."

"I did, but I'm not going to leave you here alone."

"I appreciate that, baby. But I don't want you to sacrifice your dream on my account. There are other folk who can check in on me and make sure I'm alright."

"Nobody will take care of you like your own folk. Isn't that what you used to tell me?"

"Sometimes you can't believe everything you hear."

"Nana, you're a mess."

"I'm serious, Naomi. I want you to go to that final and I want you to win. That's what will make me feel better. Knowing that my granddaughter is a business owner. What do you kids say? A boss!"

"There's plenty of time to get a truck, Nana. I'm still going to reach that goal. It'll just take a little longer." Naomi watched her grandmother try to rise from the chair. She hurried over.

"Nana, where are you going?"

"I need to make a call."

"I'll bring the phone to you."

"This is a private matter. I need to pray with someone."

On Sunday, Naomi told Nadine she'd go to church with her. When Nadine said she wasn't

going, Naomi's worry spiked. Nadine Evelyn Alberts
Carson did not miss church. For the rest of the day,
she was Nana's shadow—making sure she took
her medication, checking for signs of pain. By ten
o'clock that night Nadine ordered Naomi out of
her bedroom. When Sunday came and Nana wasn't
an angel, Naomi relaxed. A sense of normalcy
slowly began to return to the house.

Aside from taking care of her grandmother,
Naomi enjoyed being off from work. She saw Kristy
more. They talked almost daily, the way it used to
be. Even though 75 percent of the conversation
was about Kristy's pregnancy, not telling Gary, and
Naomi trying to convince her to tell the baby daddy,
she'd missed that closeness. The two women were
like sisters. They loved each other to the moon and
back. But life had gotten in the way, and without
either of them realizing it, they'd drifted apart.
Naomi hadn't realized how she missed Kristy's daily
interaction until now. A couple times, in the quiet
moments, she questioned her decision to drop out
of the contest. Kristy thought she was crazy, and
when she considered how winning might have
changed her life, she wasn't sure Kristy was wrong.
She felt disappointment at not finishing what she
started, even a little regret. But she wouldn't allow
herself a full-on pity party. She'd made her decision. There was no going back.

On Wednesday morning, Naomi's relative peace
was interrupted by loud knocking on the door. She
was in the kitchen, separating eggs for a cheese and
vegetable soufflé, and didn't appreciate whoever it

was who'd come unannounced. Grabbing a dish towel, she wiped her hands as, halfway to the door, the insistent banging happened again.

"Hold on!" Naomi yelled, not caring that her anger showed. Whoever was hammering on their door like they were the popo was getting ready to get a piece of her mind. She almost yanked open the door without checking the peephole, but thinking it actually might be the police, decided to check it out. She stepped up and looked through it. Her eyes opened, as her mouth dropped. Sure that she was seeing things, she stepped up and looked again.

"Do you want to take a picture?" a voice bellowed, as loud and demanding as Naomi's had been. "Or do you want to act like someone with some sense and open this door!"

Naomi turned the knob and opened the door. A crowd of Carters stood just outside the locked screen door. Naomi didn't recognize all of the faces, but the ones she'd met—Barry, Anita, Cynthia, Marvin of course, and the unforgettable Liz—were all smiling widely, waiting to be let in.

Unlocking the screen door, she again found her voice. "What are all of you doing here?"

"Let us in and we'll tell you." Once inside, Liz put her hand on an ample hip. "A little birdie chirped some news in my ear that I could not believe. They said that you dropped out of the food truck contest because you didn't think there was anybody who could take care of your grandmother better than you."

Naomi's eyes narrowed as she honed in on Marvin.

He lifted his hands while shaking his head. "It wasn't me."

"Is it true?" Liz asked.

"Yes, ma'am. And I'm sure that little birdie told you why. My grandmother was rushed to the ER last week and underwent surgery."

"She got a pacemaker implant, not a heart transplant." Liz relaxed her stance. "Baby, it is admirable that you'd give up everything to take care of your grandmother. In your shoes, I'd hope to do the same thing. But I've seen you in the kitchen. I've tasted your food. We laughed and partied on the Fourth just like we were family. And what families do, is help each other out. So I told that birdie to not worry about a thing, that I was going to round up some folk to be on twenty-four-seven watch this coming Saturday, while you compete in that contest . . . to take second place," she finished, laughing. Everyone joined in. "I'm sorry, darling, but my son's got to win that money!"

As others laughed and high-fived, Naomi let the tears from Liz's words roll down her face. She'd never felt so much genuine love from so many people in the same room, at the same time. In a moment of spontaneity, she reached over and hugged Liz tightly. They rocked back and forth, kissed, and hugged again.

"I can't even believe y'all are standing here, let alone that you would volunteer to help me out. But it's too late. The producers needed an answer so they could replace me, and I'm pretty sure they did."

"They didn't," Marvin said. "And yes, I am the guilty party in that. After you talked to Tracy, she called me, really upset that you were dropping out. I told her not to worry about anything. That I had this situation under control. Carter control, baby."

He stepped forward, pulled Naomi into his arms. "Didn't I tell you that I got you?"

Naomi couldn't answer for crying, just buried her head in his shirt.

"We've all got you, baby," Liz said. The others gathered around.

Naomi regained her composure and lifted her head. "Alright then. I want to thank all of y'all for helping me be able to go and kick Marvin's behind. Because ain't nobody driving off with that truck but me!"

"Ah, here we go," Marvin said, before being drowned out by everybody giving their opinion.

Naomi looked over at Nana, whose eyes were beaming. She walked over and hugged her grandmother.

"Are you the little birdie?" she whispered.

"Maybe." Nadine smiled. "The main thing to remember is that prayer changes things."

31

Marvin walked from the living room to the kitchen and back for no reason. A combination of nerves and excitement made it hard to sit still. Today was the culmination of everything that had happened over the past couple months and more. The one for all the marbles. The finals taping, one that came with a twist none of the finalists saw coming. It wouldn't take place in the cooking arena. The contestants would be challenged to put their skills to the test by cooking in actual food trucks for real-life customers. In a video sent by email three days ago, the cooks had been instructed to recruit and bring up to three assistants to help them shop, prep, and cook for the crowds who'd be in and around LA Live, the sports and entertainment area surrounding the Staples Center. Marvin imagined the event had been marketed, and expected a crush of people in front of his truck. It felt intimidating and empowering all at once. He'd literally be cooking for his life, the kind of life he wanted. One where he took the reins and made the rules.

Because of the limited space, Marvin had decided on having only two assistants and felt good about his menu and the team he'd assembled. Most of the assistance would be prep work anyway, things he could take care of before the crowd arrived. Soul Spot coworker Janet was his first pick. Choosing her was a no-brainer. She wasn't technically trained as a cook, but she followed directions and was a team player. As for the second assistant he'd selected, well, he'd have to wait and see.

Marvin looked over as his number two came around the corner and into the living room. "It's about time," he chided, looking at his watch. "You ready, Mama?"

"I thought I was, but now it looks like I need more time."

Marvin huffed. "To do what?"

"Beat your ass for getting smart. It don't matter what we're getting ready to do, boy. I'm going to be your mama all day long. Okay?"

"Okay, Mama. Put your gun down." Marvin walked over and gave her a kiss. They walked out the front door toward Marvin's freshly washed and shining SUV.

"You look nice," he said.

"Uh-huh. You'd better try and get back in my good graces. Before I take revenge by sneaking a cup of salt into your cake batter."

"Ha! With fifty G's on the line? I don't think so."

Liz looked over. "I don't either." She pulled her seat belt over and buckled it. "Speaking of, remember what I told you."

"About what?"

"About what I get when you win."

He frowned, glanced over at her as he pulled out of the drive. "What do you get?"

"Half."

"Half of what?"

"Your winnings, boy, what else?"

"How do you figure?"

"By using division and dividing by two."

"So I work my behind off for weeks, you come in and assist for a day, and you get half?"

"Spent nine hours in labor to bring you here. Hard hours. And four stitches. So yeah, sounds about right."

Marvin shook his head and turned on the radio. He had no comeback for that.

They arrived at the convention center to organized chaos. Traffic was backed up. Cars were everywhere. Barriers created by orange cones and police cars parked sideways streamlined and forced the traffic into one of two options, to turn right or left. A sign straight ahead read OFFICIAL PARKING ONLY. Marvin inched forward and, after showing the officer the parking label included in the packet he'd received, was directed into the parking structure. He'd arrived early, but still had to go to the third tier before finding a parking space.

He turned off the car and looked at Liz. "You ready, Mama?"

"Are you ready? That's the real question."

"I guess so."

Liz placed a hand on his arm. "You've got to know so, son. I tease you a lot and give you a hard time, but this is serious now, all jokes aside. I believe in you, Marvin, always have. You're a better cook than me—"

"Ah, Mama—"

"You are now. You're one of the best cooks I know, and have cooked some of the best food I've ever eaten. Ain't nobody down there who can cook better than you can. Remember that, and this competition is yours to lose."

Marvin cleared his throat, suddenly tight with emotion. "Thank you, Mama. I appreciate it."

"Win that contest and give me half of the cash. That'll be all the thanks I need."

Marvin chuckled and shook his head as he walked around the vehicle to open the passenger door, glad his sassy mama had returned. Her heartfelt words nearly brought him to tears, the last thing he needed. Today he needed to be able to keep his focus on winning, his nerves under control and his emotions in check. Later would be plenty of time for tears . . . happy ones, he hoped.

Marvin and his mom walked to the side of the convention center and the door where he was supposed to check in. Once there, he was greeted by one of the production assistants, who directed them down a hall that led to VIP parking next door to the building. Marvin stepped through the exit and froze, not expecting the scene before him. Ten colorfully decorated food trucks were lined up in a row. His truck, Sweet Cakes, was on the end to the right. He quickly scanned the row and saw that Naomi's truck, the Savory Slice, was parked next to the last truck on the opposite end. So taken by the trucks he almost missed seeing the large white tent erected just beyond them. Several technicians were laying cable and setting up microphones on the stage while another group set up white wooden chairs.

"You're not going to get any cooking done on these steps, son," Liz said softly. "And I need to find some air-conditioning before this chocolate starts melting."

Her words spurred Marvin down the steps and over to the group of participants already there. Naomi wasn't one of them, but Marvin introduced Liz and Janet to the other contestants and met their assistants. Naomi finally arrived and introduced her aunt Lisa and a coworker, Shelly, to everyone. Tracy arrived with a group of production assistants, a variety of colored T-shirts for all of the contestants and their guests, and a list of instructions that sent the group into an organized frenzy of slicing, dicing, and other food truck prep. When their hour of prep time was over, the ten contestants were called to the stage. Special guests, including some previous contestants, were among the hundred or so of those seated, with several hundred customers just beyond the cordoned-off area waiting for the trucks to be opened for business. A film crew scurried about, reminding Marvin that the finals would be recorded and aired later in the year on Chow TV. He stopped next to Naomi, whom he'd noticed had been unusually quiet.

"Everything okay, sunshine?"

"What happened to Juicy?"

"They've got you in my favorite color, and you're rocking that yellow, I might add. It reminds me of the first time you came to the Spot."

Naomi shrugged and looked away.

"You alright?"

"As much as I'm going to be until this is over. I wanted Nana to be here but . . . she's back home praying for me."

"So you're nervous."

"Yes."

"Wow, I didn't expect you to admit it."

Naomi looked up then, and around her at those listening nearby. "Oh, did you think I meant about beating you? No, I'm nervous because I've never held a fifty-thousand-dollar check before."

Marvin laughed, along with the others. "What are you serving?"

"Five types of slices, including a breakfast slice made on toast and my pork-u-pine original, served on a biscuit-dough crust."

"No sides?"

Naomi shook her head. "I decided to keep it simple and focus on the name of the dish. What about you?"

"My thinking was along those same lines, and also what would be easy for people to hold and eat. So I came up with a couple different breakfast cupcakes served with jelly . . ." He waited for Naomi's reaction.

"You stole my idea!"

He wasn't disappointed. "You inspire me, girl."

"If you win, I want ten. At least."

Marvin didn't get a chance for a comeback. Ted, Da Chen, and a couple other celebrity chefs took the stage. The final ten contestants were introduced, each wearing a different colored T-shirt emblazoned with the name of their truck. The crowd watched Da Chen instruct the cooks, then listened carefully as Ted told them how the winner would be decided.

"Your presence here today is very important," he said, with a boyish charm. "A third of the vote will come from the judges. A third will be based on the cook's overall performance during the entire competition. And a third of the deciding vote will come from you, the buying public, based on which truck makes the most money combined with who gets the highest points for having the best food."

Da continued his instructions. Marvin hardly heard a word. His mind was back in the food truck where Janet and Liz continued to prep. *Are they overcooking the sausage? Cutting the slab bacon too thin? And what about the dough for the cinnamon squares? Did Janet remember to punch it down for the second rising? And what should I do about her observation that buyers might think we only have dessert?*

When Marvin's attention returned to what Da was saying, all he heard was, "Your time starts . . . now!"

The contestants ran to their trucks with only thirty minutes of cook time before service began for the large, hungry crowd. They'd only have two hours of service, so Marvin knew he had to sell as much as he could as quickly as possible. The assistants he'd chosen made him feel a little better. Because of Janet and Liz, he could cook twice as fast. His mother had suggested passing out samples. Brilliant idea. Marvin knew his omelet cupcakes would cook quickly and slid several tins of them into the oven along with the cinnamon roll recipe he'd turned into cinnamon squares. By the time the crowd began milling around them, they had several round platters filled with samples and Liz's booming voice encouraged them over for a taste. The minutes flew by. The line never stopped. Ted kept them informed of the time remaining.

"One hour left! Down to thirty minutes! Only ten minutes remaining!"

Ted started the countdown and the crowd joined in. "Ten, nine . . . three, two, one. That's it! No more customers, no more sales. The Food Truck Bucks contest is over!"

Marvin threw up his hands, almost light-headed from the heat, the pressure, the dizzying pace. His mother grabbed him for a bear hug. He and Janet high-fived. All of them were sweaty and giddy with exhaustion. Janet and Liz walked to the tent and took the seats that had been reserved for the participants' helpers.

Da Chen stepped to the microphone and added his congratulations. "Let's hear it for the final top ten as they make their way to the stage."

Marvin exited the truck, grabbing a towel and wiping away sweat. Until seconds ago, his focus was food. But now he looked for Naomi. She looked as tired as he felt, but still offered a quick, dimpled grin that made his heart flip-flop. It was going to really be a shame if he won and broke her heart. He doubted the wound could be healed with a simple sweet treat. Before those thoughts could dampen his spirits, the participants all converged on each other, hugging and high-fiving as they neared the stage. He reached the steps and waited to give Naomi a special hug.

"This is it, Juicy. How do you think you did?"

"We're getting ready to find out," she muttered as they continued up the stairs.

The assistants were introduced. They waved from the audience. Marvin was stoked to share the moment with Liz. The celebrity judges came on-stage and were interviewed by Myra Montague, a former model who'd turned a popular vlog into one of Chow TV's top cooking shows. Two of LA's top food truck chefs shared a story or two from their time on the streets. Marvin understood that along with it being the final competition, they were producing a show. He also knew the producers needed time to tally the results. None of this made him or the other contestants any less anxious for this to be over and the winner announced. All they wanted was to know who won. All Marvin wanted was to hear his name.

Ten minutes later, Da Chen announced the winner. Marvin's heart pounded as he experienced a moment of being both happy and sad— all at once.

32

"Well, if it isn't Mr. Food Truck Bucks! About time you called back!"

It was late when all the hoopla quieted and Marvin got time alone. The first thing he did was call Naomi. She answered on the first ring.

"Sorry about that."

"I'm just messing with you."

"Are you sure?"

"What do you mean, am I sure?"

"I know how much you wanted to win this."

"You're right. I did. But the right person won today."

"What? You're finally admitting the truth? That I'm the best cook out here?"

"Yes."

Marvin's heart swelled at the hard-earned validation. One word, said so softly and so sincerely it almost took his breath away.

"Congratulations, Marvin."

"Thank you."

"I really am happy for you. After watching you in the tent on the Fourth of July, the way you orchestrated that kitchen, I knew then that you were going to win the contest, and mark my words, yours is going to be one of the most popular and successful trucks in the city."

"Man, I really hope so. I'm going to work my ass off to try and make that a reality."

"So fill me in. What happened after I left? And more important, when will you get the truck and the money!"

Marvin told her about the endless television, internet, and podcast interviews, the photoshoots and meeting with the show producers and their legal team.

"You know about the gag order, that we can't say anything until after the show has aired, which I found out will be during Labor Day weekend."

"On Chow TV, right?"

"Yeah. Between now and then I'll meet with the team who'll be designing my truck, which I won't actually get until October. That's also about the time I'll get whatever's left of the fifty thousand after taxes."

"They take out taxes?"

"The show doesn't, but I took Sean's advice and am working with an accountant to go ahead and give Uncle Sam what's his. I'm not about to do a Wesley Snipes and go to jail over taxes."

"That's smart."

"How's Nana?"

"She's okay. I think she's in more pain than she lets on, especially when she gets up and moves around. That left arm and the area where the pacemaker is implanted is still pretty tender. I try and keep her still as much as possible. If I don't play another game of rummy until my next life it will be too soon."

Marvin laughed out loud. "What about your job at the 99 Cents Store? Are you back to work?"

"Next week, unfortunately, just when I was getting used to the housewife life. But thanks to people like your mother, Miss Liz, I feel a lot better about leaving her. Between your family, Tee, Aunt Lisa, and Nana's church friends, there's a whole army on standby to come in the minute I leave."

"That's really good for me to know."

"You? Why?"

"Because I might want to take a little trip to celebrate, and I just might want to take you with me."

"As if I'd go."

Marvin paused, his sinking heart a real indication of how he'd assumed Naomi would want to be with him, and of how much he wanted her to.

"You wouldn't?"

Hers was the slower answer this time. Marvin waited, not aware that while doing so he held his breath.

"Maybe."

"Maybe, what?"

"Maybe I'll go with you, depending on when, where, and for how long."

"Did anybody ever tell you that you're hard on a brother?"

"Only those too weak to deal with a strong woman like me. Is that you?"

"Hell, no, woman. In the short time you've known me, I'm surprised you had to ask." His tone softened. "I know you're worried about your nana. Give her a hug for me. Tell her I've got some Marvin's Miracle Soup with her name on it."

"Is my name on it, too?"

"No," he said, his voice even softer, and lower. "I've got something else with your name on it."

The sound of her laughter filled his heart with joy, like pulling a perfectly puffed soufflé out of the oven or eating his mama's food. There was a tap at the door. "Hold on, Nay," and then louder, "Who is it?"

The door opened. "Hey, Nay, it's my brother. Let me holler at you later, alright?"

"Okay."

The call ended. Marvin checked the phone's screen to make sure. He understood Naomi's being disappointed and tried not to take her attitude personally. He couldn't imagine how he would have felt for someone else to win the competition, and when it came to attitude, well, that could have been Naomi's middle name.

"What's up, Byron?"

Byron walked into the room and plopped down on a loveseat. "That's what I came in here to find out. Did you win?"

"Win what?"

"So Mama isn't the only one acting crazy," Byron mumbled.

"Oh, the contest."

"Oh, the contest," Byron mimicked, tossing a decorative pillow that landed squarely upside Marvin's head. "Did you win or not?"

"I can't tell you."

"What?"

"If I told you I'd have to kill you and I could never do that. You'll have to wait and see."

"Why?"

"We had to sign a nondisclosure agreement to not share the contest results until the show has aired. Doing otherwise could result in a fine of up to two hundred and fifty thousand dollars."

Byron looked at him thoughtfully. "You won."

"How do you figure?"

"Because you're not in here pouting, or balled up in the fetal position, or drowning your sorrows with a forty ounce."

Marvin laughed. "Fool, nobody in here drinks rotgut liquor."

"You would if you'd lost."

"Think what you will, but my lips are sealed. Besides, you don't have long to wait. The show is going to air in a month, Labor Day weekend."

Byron nodded. "So, that's it? It's back to the Soul Spot?"

"Unfortunately."

"Dang, you hate that place. Maybe you didn't win."

"Ha! You already know . . ."

"Either way, you're going to have to come up with some money. There's a real estate opportunity coming up. I want us brothers to get in on it."

"Real estate? Buying houses? Whose crazy idea is that?"

Byron gave him a look as he rose from the chair and headed toward the door. "You'll have to wait and see."

Marvin spent the evening hanging out with his fam, laughing and joking till past two a.m. He'd taken the next day, which was Sunday, off, but when his phone rang at just after nine the next morning, he was not surprised.

"Let me guess," he began, after answering Ricky's call. "He's sick again."

"Don't know. He's just not here. Neither is Janet."

"Who's with you?"

"The new guy, Lorenzo."

"Who's got the room?"

"Miss Congeniality."

"Charlotte?"

"Who else? You coming?"

Marvin sighed and rolled out of bed. "I'm on my way."

While showering, dressing, and driving to work, he thought about his time at the Soul Spot, the promises made and the ones not kept. He enjoyed the kitchen camaraderie, especially with Janet and Ricky, but couldn't help but feel used at working five, six, sometimes seven days a week and at the end of the day having very little to show for it. He'd had such high hopes when the owner, Donald Jr., had hired him and told him that there was a chance that he'd run the kitchen. Two months later, Donald Jr. dropped out of college and took over the restaurant. At least that's where he drew his paycheck. Nobody knew where Junior actually worked, except it wasn't at the Soul Spot.

It took Marvin less than forty-five minutes to get himself together and arrive at the Soul Spot. There were ten minutes between now and when the restaurant opened. The parking lot was already crowded and a line had begun to form. Marvin hopped out of the car and began walking toward the side door where employees entered when a familiar sports car roared into the parking lot—Donald Jr.'s white Corvette. Dark shades hid the roll of Marvin's eyes as the car stopped and blocked his path.

"What are you doing here?" Donald asked.

"I thought I was covering for you. Does Ricky know you're here?"

Donald shook his head. "I didn't call him. Now that you're here, I won't."

"No, man. I was doing Ricky a favor because he'd have done the same for me. I've covered too many Sundays for you as it is, so go on and do your shift."

"Oh, my bad. I must have framed that as a request." Donald took off his glasses. "It wasn't."

"How do you figure?"

"I'm the boss and I just made a change in the schedule. You're working today."

Everything in Marvin railed at Donald's presumptive statement. Just yesterday he'd been touted as the best cook out of hundreds who'd tried out to win Food Truck Bucks. The public didn't know that yet, but the outcome validated what Marvin had always believed. He could be his own boss. For better or worse, that would start today. He turned on his heel and headed back toward his SUV.

"If you leave this parking lot today, don't bother coming back tomorrow," Donald yelled.

"I won't," Marvin replied, without looking around. He reached his truck and got in, at the same time pulling out his phone to call Janet and let her know about his just-delivered and totally unplanned resignation. He hated to leave Ricky and Janet. They were good cooks and even better coworkers. He definitely hadn't planned for today to be his last at the Soul Spot. He'd intended to work all the way up to Labor Day weekend. Sometimes life didn't go as planned. Today was one of those days.

33

Naomi's alarm went off, jolting her awake the way it had for the past several months. She snatched her phone off the nightstand, clicked on settings and then on alarm. That she was tired of her former heartthrob Lil Wayne screaming at her first thing in the morning was a sure sign that something in her life had shifted. When a song title jumped out at her and she immediately set it as her new morning serenade, she knew what that something was different. A man named Marvin. It had been a week since he won the contest and that long since she'd seen him. She imagined he was busy preparing to be the next star chef on the culinary scene. They'd texted back and forth, joked and flirted, but had only talked once. Naomi might never admit it to Marvin, but she could to herself. She missed him. She restarted the song to play in its entirety, and let Alicia tell Marvin with her ringtone what she almost had the nerve to tell him herself. Almost, but not quite. *No one . . .*

Just as she was getting deep in the groove, the song stopped and hopped back to the chorus. She looked over at her phone, confused until she realized a call was coming in. Seeing the caller's face instantly made her dewy, but just a little bit. She set the phone on her dresser and hit the speaker button while she figured out what to wear.

"I was just thinking about you."

"Oh really." Marvin's voice was low and sexy. "What were you thinking?"

"This and that. What's up?"

"You, obviously. Getting ready for work?"

"You know I don't work on Saturdays."

"I thought that maybe your schedule changed."

"What about you? What time do you go into the Soul Spot?"

"As of last Sunday, I don't work there anymore."

"I thought you were going to work there until the holidays. What happened, Food Truck Bucks changed the rules and cut your check?"

"I wish, couldn't put up with Donald's bullshit anymore. September can't come soon enough. So what are you doing today?"

"Miss J and Sue, who you met at that first dinner, are over watching Nana, so I'm going to meet Kristy for breakfast. Since you're off today, guess it won't be at the Soul Spot."

He gave her the name of another restaurant in

the general vicinity. "What time are y'all planning on getting there? I might meet you."

"Sorry, but this is a girls' morning out."

"Oh, it's like that."

"Yes, Marvin Carter. It's like that."

"Hmm."

A low, slow groan that had Naomi considering a change in plans and partners. But, no, she'd promised Kristy.

"Maybe I'll call you later, and we can hang out," Marvin said. "It's Saturday. We're both off and there is no competition. I think that's a first since we met."

"That might work. Let me make sure Nana is taken care of and I'll get back with you later. Okay?"

"Alright, Juice. Out."

Knowing she might see Marvin later helped Naomi make her wardrobe choice—something cool and comfortable. Since June and July had been scorchers, she wasn't surprised that August had started off hot. Her girls needed room, sister needed air, and she didn't want to have to worry about sweat circles on her clothes. Searching for cotton, she pulled out a strapless purple maxi with a bouquet of flowers that ran from the top of one side of the dress to the bottom of the other. The print pulled the eye toward the side instead of the middle. When it came to looking slimmer, Naomi pulled out all the tricks. After choosing a pair of flat sandals, she added colorful, clunky jewelry, a spritz of cologne, and after sharing a few pleasantries with the ladies, texted her cousin the restaurant Marvin had mentioned and took off in that direction.

On the way she thought about Kristy, the pregnancy, Gary, and how so many aspects of the situation didn't make sense. She chalked her cousin's mood swings up to hormonal fluctuations. But why hadn't she told Gary about the child? Why, aside from her and Lisa, hadn't she told anyone else? The shock had worn off and Kristy now embraced becoming a mother. But all she talked about was wanting a girl so she could dress her up like a China doll. Kristy lived with her mom and did hair out of the home. What if Gary was unwilling to help her? Besides Lisa—and Naomi, however she could—who would help support the baby? That babies are blessings was a popular saying and Naomi wanted to be happy for Kristy. But for all the single mothers she knew, the struggle was real. True enough, Kristy could do the hell out of anyone's hair, but she'd have to braid all night and weave all day to live above the poverty line.

Naomi tried to imagine what she would do in the same situation. She had a full-time job and fairly good benefits, but she lived with her grandmother in a fairly small home. How could she fit a baby into that environment? Turn a drawer into a bassinet? Switch out her queen size for a daybed to make room for strollers and bouncy chairs? Naomi looked down and realized how tightly her hands gripped the wheel. She didn't need to think about having a baby. What she needed to do was make an appointment for next week and get on birth control.

LA traffic was crazy on most days, but Saturday was especially insane. When she pulled into the parking lot of the restaurant Marvin had suggested, she wasn't surprised to see Kristy's car already there. However, her brow did rise when she saw that her cousin was still in it. As hot as it was? *She must have just arrived.*

Naomi found a parking spot, then walked over to where Kristy was slowly easing out of her car. "Good morning, mommy. Why are you moving like a turtle?"

Kristy glared at Naomi, then hefted her considerable frame out of the seat. "Have Marvin put a baby up in you and see how fast you move."

"Girl, please. You're what, four weeks along?"

"Eight, according to my last doctor's appointment."

Naomi looked at Kristy. *Had she even known Gary for that long?*

Naomi could tell that Kristy was grouchy, so instead of voicing a thought that might come off as judgmental, she offered a compliment. "Eight weeks and look at you, girl. You're not even showing."

An eye roll landed where Naomi thought a thank-you might go.

"Why are you tripping? That was a compliment."

"No, it wasn't. You're trying to be funny."

"How is saying 'you're not showing' a dig?"

"Big as my fat ass is? I'll probably never show. Only reason I knew I was pregnant is because my periods came like clockwork before not showing up at all."

Kristy reached for the door and yanked it open. Naomi said nothing as she followed her inside, but pregnant or no, when it came to attitude Naomi was only going to take so much.

They were seated in a booth and handed menus, which they both scanned.

"Who told you about his place?" Kristy asked.

"Marvin. One of his friends works here. He says the food is good and I see that the prices are reasonable. Which is a good thing, chick, because breakfast is on me."

"Ooh, then I might need to go ahead and order lunch, too." The only thing that moved were Naomi's eyes. "You know I'm kidding."

"You'd better be."

The conversation turned more cordial and civil after that. The two women placed their orders. Naomi told Kristy about the finals and how an unexpected twist got her eliminated in the first round.

"I'm sorry, cousin. I know how badly you wanted to win that food truck."

Naomi shushed her cousin and looked quickly around. "What did I tell you?" she whispered. "Shut up about that."

Kristy whispered, too. "Girl, nobody in this restaurant knows who you are or cares what we're talking about. Besides, you don't have to say what I already know."

"Yes, you do know." Naomi continued speaking low as she reached for the glass of water the server put down. "I was disappointed, but not devastated. Marvin is no joke in the kitchen. He deserved to win that truck. And the money."

"How much was it again?"

"Fifty thousand."

"Dang! I know you're going to try and hang on to that man. But after getting that money, he'll probably be looking to upgrade."

It was a thought that Naomi had not considered. The comment stung, and she was surprised by how much.

"If that's what he wants, then nobody can stop him. But I fell in love with Marvin before he won the contest."

"You're in love?"

"Yes, and this is the first time that I've said it out loud."

"Then I hope it works out for you, Nay. That way, at least one of us will be happy."

Misery loved company, and by the time the cousins hugged in the parking lot, Kristy's rain cloud had soaked Naomi's mood. The thought Kristy had planted about Marvin maybe wanting to upgrade women had grown roots, so much so that she almost didn't call him back as promised. But then she remembered their earlier conversation, the laughter and flirting and how good she'd felt when the call ended. Immediately, she tapped her Bluetooth and gave Mr. Feelgood a call.

Marvin's phone rang as he sat in Doug's Culver City living room, less than two miles from where Naomi and Kristy ate breakfast. He hadn't planned it. Doug had called him an hour ago with two words, *family meeting*. That's basically all it took for all who could to drop whatever and meet up. He checked his phone and when he saw who it was, eased up from the couch and went into another room.

"Hey, babe," he said, his voice subdued.

"Hey. Where are you, talking all quiet?"

"With my brothers, at Doug's house."

"Doug as in the one married to my idol? You're at Jan's house?" He noted how the volume rose with each word. "What are y'all doing? Is she there? Can I come over?"

Marvin smiled, realizing just how much he dug this girl. "Jan isn't here and no, you can't come over."

"Why not?"

Marvin imagined those juicy lips in a pretty pout. "Because it's a man's meeting. No women allowed."

"Are you getting back at me for not inviting you to breakfast?"

"Come on, girl. You know better than that. My brothers called a meeting. I came over. Simple as that."

"Okay. How long are you going to be there?"

"I don't know, but I'll call you afterwards. Okay."

Marvin silenced his phone and returned to the room. Byron was still talking.

"The thing is, we have to move now. Leimert Park has been one of the hottest real estate markets in metro LA for the last four or five years, ever since it was announced that the light-rail would pass through it. That this group I'm telling you about was savvy enough to see what was happening, to combine their resources and try and preserve the legacy of that neighborhood, was nothing short of genius. And even with their deep pockets, they could only buy so much. And I'm telling you, their stock is selling quickly. For now, my dude is holding the place for me. But he's not going to be able to hold it long."

"It's crazy you mention Leimert Park, bro," Marvin said in his mellow, unhurried style. "That's where I want to park my food truck for the exact reasons you just mentioned. Not only that, but because it's one of the few historically Black, culturally rich neighborhoods in America. I didn't even know how significant that area was until I started researching the city for where to set up. At one time it was called the Black Greenwich Village, and boasted businesses, restaurants, clubs, art galleries, all owned and patronized by people of color. I think it's a good idea, Byron. I don't have any money to invest in it with you." Then he added, after a pause, "But I've got an opinion and I think we should try and grab something, man. Why not?"

Barry, normally the one least interested in anything besides fitness and women, listened as attentively as the others. "Have you talked to Mama and Daddy?" he asked Byron.

"No, I wanted to start here and see who all was interested. Our parents have done their part. They've secured a nice spot in Inglewood that we'll keep in the family. Now it's our turn. It won't be easy and it will be expensive. There's nothing in that corridor under three fifty."

Nelson whistled, then duck-walked to the door. "Well, that counts me out."

The brothers laughed, clearly enjoying each other's company.

"Are these properties commercial or residential?" Marvin asked.

"Both," Byron answered.

"Which type are we looking at buying?"

"That's why we're here," Doug said. "To discuss the pros and cons of either, or both."

Real estate talk continued for another hour, but eventually wound down. Beer and alcohol came out and those who could hung out until early evening. Marvin continued thinking about actually owning property in Leimert Park. He could envision his food truck being mobbed every day and twice as hard on weekends, parked near the light-rail or the park. Every time he imagined it, Naomi was in the picture. He didn't try and analyze why that was or what to call it. He just wanted to hear her thoughts on his ideas. Every brother with a dream needed a sistah who could envision his dream coming true.

Yours is going to be one of the most popular and successful trucks in the city.

Naomi had said that about his future food truck. That's why he didn't see a future without her in it.

34

When the sound of laughter coming from the dining room had the effect of fingernails on a chalkboard, Naomi knew it was time to go. A group of Nana's church friends had been there for hours. They'd had food delivered, watched movies, and now sat around the table playing Scrabble. When it came to who had the fuller social calendar, her grandmother was winning hands down.

Even with people there to look after Nadine, Naomi had lounged around the house. She'd surfed the web, caught up on social media and got lost on YouTube, partly because there wasn't anything else she felt like doing and partly to wait for Marvin. But it was now several hours past the time they'd talked. Were the brothers still meeting? Even if they were, Marvin could have responded to the message she left on his voicemail or the text she'd sent. At one point she'd checked her phone to make sure the volume was up and the indicators functioned correctly. Her electronic devices worked perfectly. Marvin hadn't called. Obviously something came up that mattered more to him than she did. *Like a beautiful, skinny woman?*

Naomi hated that Kristy's earlier comments had her even giving such a possibility consideration. Worse, she hated the answer that came back to her. *Perhaps.*

That was it. Naomi leapt from the chair with a single destination. Out. Of. There. She'd already changed from the maxi dress to a pair of ripped jeans and a faded Obama T-shirt. Opting for a sexier black tunic tee that flared out at the bottom with pink heart-shaped cutouts and a spray of scattered rhinestones, she switched to rhinestone earrings, replaced sneakers with wedges, waved goodbye to the ladies, and was out the door.

Almost to her car, Naomi remembered something she needed to tell Nana. She hurried back up the stairs and stuck her head in the door.

"Nana!"

"That's my name!"

"Are you going to church tomorrow?"

"I will if you take me."

"What time do I have to be ready?"

There was a pause before Naomi heard her grandmother mumble, "Go see who's out there sounding like Naomi. It's got to be an imposter if they want to go to church."

Naomi walked into a room filled with laughter. She threw her arms around Nadine. "It's me, Nana, and yes, I'm going. I promised God that night I found you that if He'd let you come back to this house, then I'd make a visit to His."

In her car with no destination in mind, Naomi pulled out her phone and scrolled contacts. She hadn't talked to most of her friends in over a month, a circle that grew smaller with each birthday that passed. At the very end of her contact list, a name jumped out. Zena Johnson, a close friend in high school who'd gotten married and lost touch. They'd reconnected through Facebook and promised to meet.

She tapped on the number and two rings later a low and cautious-sounding voice answered the phone. "Hello?"

"Zena, it's Nay."

"Oh, hey, Naomi! I didn't recognize your number!"

"There you are. I was wondering who the pitiful woman was that answered the phone. Sounding all nervous. Hello," Naomi mimicked.

"I normally don't even answer numbers that I don't recognize or are not already programmed in my phone. My ex is sneaky, and I always think it's him trying to reach me."

"I can't believe you got divorced, Zena! You and Anthony were so in love—oh my God, I used to not be able to stand you guys!" Naomi continued through Zena's laughter. "Y'all made a cute couple though. If there was anybody I thought would celebrate fifty years, it was you two. What happened?"

"What didn't happen would be a quicker answer. Wait a minute. Tosha, get out of that! And get your brother. Your aunt Kiki is on her way."

"How many kids do you have?"

"Four."

Naomi screamed.

"I know, girl. That's my reaction most mornings, when I wake up and discover that they're still here."

"Are you back in LA?"

"Right off Vermont."

"Vermont and what cross street?" When Zena told her, Naomi said, "I'm not too far from there."

"Come on over! I'd love to see you. What are you doing tonight?"

"Nothing." Naomi pulled away from the curb. "That's why I called you."

"You should come and go to this party with me. Remember Patrick, the tall, skinny dude with the bubble eyes who used to live across from Loretta. He's having a party. A lot of our classmates might be there."

"I'm on my way."

The first call from Marvin came around eleven thirty. By then she was pissed, having conjured all types of scenarios of what had come up to prevent their getting together. By then she was in a Long Beach club house with about a hundred other people who used to go to CC High. The music was loud. The dance floor was packed. She was on her third cup of "punch," a sweet, fruity concoction dipped from large aluminum trash cans. Who knew what all was in it, but it was icy cold, tasted good, and had her buzzed. She ignored his call.

"Naomi!"

She turned around. Squinted her eyes. "Rodney?"

He walked up with arms outstretched. "Thought I was seeing things. It's been a long time. You're looking good, Nay."

"Thank you."

"You still working at the 99 Cents Store off of Wilshire?"

Had Naomi been sober, this would have been her first clue. He'd just said it had been a long time, yet he knew where she was working. But three drinks in, she didn't catch it. His stalker history penetrated the haze, but that was years ago when they were younger. Surely he'd moved on. It appeared that way. They talked and joked, kept it casual. The conversation wasn't long, maybe ten minutes tops. When he casually mentioned that he might stop by sometime, Naomi gave a vague nod, her attention having already moved on to finding Zena. She took the statement generally, like *how are you doing*, or *see you later*. Most people don't really want to know how you're doing and seeing someone later could mean in the next lifetime. The party was fun and it was good to see old friends. But when Zena finally resurfaced and said she was ready to leave, Naomi was right behind her.

And Rodney was right behind Naomi, but she didn't know. Naomi and Zena reached Zena's car and got in. She started it up. The headlight beams captured someone slinking in the darkness toward another car.

"What's he doing?" Zena asked.

"Who?"

"Rodney."

Naomi leaned back against the headrest. "Probably being weird, as always."

"He's not weird," Zena said with a laugh, looking in the rearview mirror before pulling out of the parking space and heading toward the street. "Always was a little quiet, though."

"You know we dated, right?"

"What? You and Rodney?"

Naomi nodded her head and quickly decided that jerky movements were not in her best interests right now. "Ow."

"You alright, girl?"

"What was in that punch?"

"I don't know," Zena replied. "I knew I'd be driving and only had a wine cooler. How much of it did you drink?"

"More than I should have." Naomi sat up and rubbed her eyes.

"You might need to stay the night with me and the kids. Can't offer you much besides the sofa and some food, but I don't want you out there driving drunk."

"I'll be fine," Naomi said. "But getting something in my stomach is a good idea."

She looked up and saw a California eatery institution. "Hey, stop at that In-N-Out."

Zena shifted lanes and once through the light, pulled into the drive-through. A few seconds later, a black car pulled into the drive-through, too.

"I guess Rodney's hungry, too."

"Huh?"

"He just pulled in a couple cars behind us."

Naomi rubbed her rumbling stomach. "Whatever."

By the time Zena pulled up in front of her home, Naomi felt full and fully alert. The double-cheeseburger and large order of fries washed down with a chocolate shake and large black coffee had been just what she needed. Only once she'd smelled the food did Naomi remember that she hadn't eaten before going to the party. It was an empty stomach, not an overabundance of alcohol, that had made her so tipsy so quickly. Still, she kept her eyes firmly on the road in front of her, being extra cautious the entire ride home. When she pulled into the driveway of Nana's home in Inglewood, she paid no attention to a set of headlights from a car idling at the end of the block. The driver of that car, however, paid the utmost attention to Naomi. Once she'd gone inside and closed the door, the car eased down the street and by her house . . . very slowly.

The next morning, Naomi kept her word to Nana and attended church. She enjoyed the service more than she'd imagined. The choir was excellent and there was a band. Both the drummer and pianist were real cuties, though something about their zealous playing and praising made Naomi wonder if either or both were gay. Not that it mattered. There was only one man on her mind, Marvin. Even if she was still peeved with him, so much so that she'd not listened to the message he'd left some time last night, or the text he'd sent her earlier. You taught people how to treat you, she silently reasoned, and figured she'd let him squirm a few more hours before returning his messages. Show him not to leave her hanging the next time.

Church was over at just after one, but it was almost two before Naomi neared their block. "You sure you don't want to eat out?" she asked Nana. "We could go to M and M's or Harold and Belle's."

"No, baby, not today."

"Are you tired?"

"A little bit. All that shouting wore me out. It was worth it though. Praising the Lord with my grand-baby filled me with joy."

Naomi reached over to squeeze Nana's hand, the grip becoming tighter as she turned the corner and saw a familiar SUV parked in front of their house. "What's he doing here?" she mumbled.

"Who?" Nana asked.

"Marvin," Naomi responded.

"I like that young man," Nana said. "Maybe next Sunday he can come to church, too."

Naomi let the false assumption that attending

church would be a weekly occurrence go unchallenged. Instead, once she'd pulled into the drive, she turned off the engine, got out of the car, and made a beeline for Marvin.

He got out of the car with a smile on his face. "Hey, girl."

"Don't hey me. What are you doing here?"

The smile from seconds ago scampered away from his face. "Didn't you get my messages, or read my texts? I'm treating you ladies to dinner," he continued, rushing toward the passenger door that had just opened.

"Hello, Nana Carson," he said, as she placed her hand in the one he stretched toward her.

"Oh, hi, baby."

Marvin walked Nana slowly down the short sidewalk leading up to her front door. "Naomi, do me a favor," he said over his shoulder. "Grab one of those containers out of the backseat. I'll get the rest."

By the time Marvin had helped Nana into the house and retrieved his goodies from his car seat, Naomi's anger had vanished. Something about the slow-smoked baked ribs now warming in Nana's oven along with stewed kale and cabbage dancing in a spicy tomato sauce made her forget why she was upset, at least until after Nana had left the kitchen, settled into her recliner, and turned on her Sunday lineup of preachers on the religious channel.

"Why didn't you call me back?" Marvin asked her.

"That was my question," she retorted. "For at least half the night."

"So you didn't listen to my message, either? If you had, you would have known that I got caught up with my brothers and time slipped by. When I finally noticed, I couldn't believe it was after midnight, or that you hadn't called again to ask what was up."

"I don't track down men."

"It wasn't like that, Naomi, tracking me down. You know exactly where I was. I can't say the same. Why didn't you call me back after seeing I'd called you?"

"I was out."

"Where?"

"At a party, with a friend."

"Oh, okay. I don't have a problem with that."

"I wouldn't care if you did. I'm grown and can do what I want to do."

Marvin closed the distance between them and shut up further protests with his cushy lips. He swiped his tongue across hers and she sucked it in. He backed her up against the counter and within seconds her nipples had pebbled and her pearl had hardened, her body longing for more.

"Naomi!"

Naomi pushed Marvin away. "Ma'am?"

"Can you bring me some water, please?"

"Yes, ma'am."

Marvin placed a hand on her waist as she walked past. "That wasn't even an appetizer to what I plan on serving up later tonight," he huskily whispered. "That was an amuse-bouche."

Dinner was sublime. Naomi whipped up a salad to start off the meal while Nana rang up their neighbor Miss J and invited her over. The four enjoyed lively conversation, with Nana and Miss J dissecting the sermon the preacher had delivered and sharing juicy church gossip that made Marvin and Naomi crack up. They retired from the dining room to the living room and were giving their food a chance to settle before enjoying Marvin's sock-it-to-me dessert when someone rang the doorbell.

"Who else did you invite?" Nana asked.

"No one," Naomi said, a slight frown accompanying her walk to the door. When she pulled aside the curtain and looked out the window, the frown deepened. She thought about not answering it, but the bell rang again, followed by knuckles on aluminum creating a loud knock.

"Wait a minute," Naomi demanded. She unlocked the door and jerked it open. "What do you want, Rodney? What are you doing at my house?"

Rodney's smile did not reach eyes that looked past Naomi into the living room. "Is that my favorite nana?" he called out.

"Who's that?" Nana asked, straining to see beyond the glass.

"It's Rodney, ma'am." He opened the screen door and pulled a surprised Naomi into an embrace that looked casual but used arms of steel. "Hey, baby."

"Boy, get off me," she said through gritted teeth. She pushed against his shoulders. "Let me go!"

Rodney laughed as he stepped around her, then saw Marvin and stopped. "Oh, so this is why you're trippin'?" he asked Naomi, without waiting for an answer.

"How you doing, Nana?" He leaned down to hug her. "You still feeding the homeless, I see."

"Ain't nobody round here homeless," Nana said, slapping his shoulder. "Lessen it's you. Where have you been? I haven't seen you in years."

"Me and baby girl just reconnected," he answered, making a move toward Naomi, who promptly joined Marvin on the couch.

"He was at the party I went to, Nana," Naomi explained. "We hardly reconnected."

"What did you call what we did for half the evening?" he asked, then sniffed. "That your food, Nana? Something sure smells good in here."

"Marvin cooked dinner," Naomi said, happy to bring her man into the conversation. "Unlike you, he was invited over."

"Is that so?" Rodney laughed in a way that said he knew she was lying and made Naomi wonder just when Rodney had arrived at the house. Had he been there when she confronted Marvin outside?

I guess Rodney's hungry, too. He just pulled in a couple cars behind us.

Zena's observations now seemed haunting. Had

he followed her home and been parked there since last night?

"There's plenty if you're hungry," Miss J offered, showing Naomi that not only was her neighbor nosy but presumptuous, too.

"He won't be staying," Naomi replied.

Rodney crossed to the couch and sat next to Naomi. "I am a little hungry, baby. Fix me a plate."

"I'm not fixing anything, Rodney. You need to leave."

"Ooh, Lord." Miss J fanned her face with her hand, finally getting the message that this was not a friendly visit.

Marvin leaned forward, his voice low and calm. "Did you hear her, homey? She said you need to leave."

Rodney jumped up, his demeanor going from friendly to fiery in less than two ticks. "Or what, fool?" His hands balled into fists. "I don't know you and you sure don't know me."

"Nor do I want to."

"This is my woman. Fuck what you heard."

"What's wrong with you?" Naomi stood. "Are you high?"

Rodney grabbed Naomi's arm, which brought Marvin to his feet. Rodney pulled Naomi backwards, whispered something in her ear.

"You're crazy!" she told Rodney.

"Crazy in love," Rodney smoothly responded, his body language relaxed once again. "Go on, now. Tell this fool who's welcome and who needs to leave."

"Who are you calling a fool? I'm not going anywhere."

Rodney's grip tightened on Naomi's arm, his harshly whispered threat of having a weapon and not being afraid to use it still ringing in her ears. Her eyes were pleading as she spoke to Marvin. "I'll call you later, Marvin, okay?"

"What? You want me to leave?"

"No, but—"

"That's exactly what she wants," Rodney said before she could finish.

"Is that what you want?" Marvin asked again.

Naomi nodded. "I'll call you later."

Marvin looked at her for a long moment. "Don't bother," he said finally. "Miss J, Nana Carson, thanks for the company."

Naomi couldn't bear to watch him leave. She heard footsteps, then silence, as she imagined a last look in her direction. The screen door opened and quietly closed. Just like that, Marvin had gone, and took part of her heart with him.

Naomi tried to pull away from Rodney. His hold remained tight until the sound of a car starting was heard outside. Slowly, his hold on her arm loosened. She jerked away and began rubbing both the ache from his hold and the chill from Marvin's absence.

"Are you going to fix me a plate?" Rodney asked.

"Sure, Rodney," Naomi responded, thinking

about her cell phone on the kitchen counter. "You want something to drink, too?"

She watched a satisfied smile spread across his face as he returned to the couch. "Yeah, what you got?"

"Tea or cola," she replied.

"Cola," he said, and then to Nana, "It sure is good to see you again."

Naomi's hands shook as she reached for a plastic cup in the cabinet, filled it with ice and poured in soda. She returned to the living room and handed Rodney the cup. "Anybody else want anything to drink?"

"I'm fine, baby," Nana said.

"I could take a piece of that cake," Miss J responded.

Naomi returned to the kitchen, glad that the women suspected nothing and hoping that the police would arrive quickly. She waited until the conversation had resumed, moving plates and uncovering pots and pans more loudly than needed. She placed a plate full of food in the microwave.

"Five minutes," she said as she crossed the living room to the bathroom. "I'll be right back."

Once inside the bathroom, she turned on the faucet and dialed 9-1-1.

"Nine-one-one, what's your emergency?"

"I'm being held hostage by a man with a gun and have snuck into the bathroom to call you." She gave the operator their home address. "He's crazy. Please hurry. Come now!"

There was a knock at the door. Naomi jumped. Her phone almost fell in the toilet.

"Naomi! What are you doing?"

"Just washing my hands, Rodney. Give me a minute!"

"Let me in!"

"Hold on."

Naomi hurriedly looked around, then silenced her phone and slid it inside her pants and between her legs.

"Open the door!"

She did. "What is wrong with you!"

Rodney stormed past her and into the room. "Where's your phone?"

"In my car, why?"

"Food's ready," Nana called from the living room. "I just heard the microwave go off."

Naomi left the bathroom but instead of turning left toward the kitchen she headed straight for the door and the sound of sirens that could be heard in the distance.

Rodney reached her but too late, she'd already opened the door. She ran into the yard as the phone dislodged from her panties and slid down her leg.

"You'd better run, Rodney," she panted.

The sirens grew louder.

"You called the police?" he asked.

"Yes, and I gave them your name, told them that if anything happened to me . . . you did it!"

The wailing grew louder. Both turned to the sound of a car speeding down the block.

"Bitch!" Rodney said, and took off running. He darted between two houses and disappeared.

The police car stopped in front of her home. Naomi ran to the officer and collapsed in his arms. Rodney had always been weird. Now he appeared to be crazy, or on drugs, or both.

35

How did one go from the headiness of feeling
that life was a chess board where you knew all the
plays, to one where your queen may be holding
court with a pawn? That's the question Marvin
asked himself as he lay on the couch in the family
room, idly flipping channels. Several days had
passed since crazy had shown up at Naomi's front
door and interrupted dinner with her and her
grandmother. She'd called less than an hour after
he'd left with an explanation as crazy as the dude's
sudden appearance. Could he really have threatened Naomi, made her kick Marvin out because
Rodney said he had a gun? Possible, Marvin con-
cluded, but unlikely. Stuff like that happened in
movies, not in real life.

Thinking about what may or may not have
happened had given him a headache. Where was a
dead-end job when you needed it? Where you
project your bad mood onto the boss and spend
ten hours over a flame so hot it burns up your

thoughts? When his phone rang a few minutes later, he was glad for the distraction.

"Hey, bro."

"What up, Marvin Gaze?"

"You got it, Dougie Not-so-fresh," Marvin said, reverting to the childhood names they called each other. "What's going on with you?"

"Jan and I are sitting here hungry, thinking about heading to the Spot, but only if you're cooking."

"That would be a negative. I don't work there anymore."

"What happened?"

"Got tired of working two positions, mine and Don Jr.'s."

"The owner's son?"

"Exactly. He said the wrong thing at the wrong time, and I quit." Marvin gave him a brief recap of his equally brief and anticlimactic exit from the Soul Spot.

"It doesn't matter. You're getting ready to be your own boss."

"That's what's up. I'd planned to wait until the finals aired, but . . . I had to go."

"You sound a little down, bro. Is that why? You need anything?"

"No, man. I'm good."

"Where's your girl?"

"What girl?"

"Marv, are you high? Naomi."

"Yeah, about that."

"Uh-oh. A little trouble in paradise?"

"Man, I almost went to jail yesterday."

"Hold on a sec."

Marvin rolled off the couch and walked into his bedroom.

"Yo, Marv?"

"What?"

"Jan's going to do something else right now. Why don't you come over to the Indian Palace and grab a bite with me?"

"Indian food?"

"You always were bright. The title kind of gives it away, doesn't it?"

"Man, forget you. I'm just surprised you're going for Indian food at this time of the morning."

"It's going on ten thirty. That's almost brunch. Besides, Indian breakfast food is some of the best."

"Said the postal worker to the chef."

"I'm heading out now. You're meeting me, right?"

"Yes, I'll see you in about fifteen or twenty."

Marvin entered the Indian restaurant and was immediately pleased with Doug's dining choice. Hints of curry, cumin, coriander, and cloves tickled his nostrils. He inhaled deeply, looking across the dining room. Seeing Doug, he waved away the hostess and crossed the room.

He clamped a hand on Doug's shoulder. "Hey, bro." He slid into the booth seat across from Doug. "Good choice. I haven't eaten Indian food in a while."

"It's one of Jan's favorite restaurants. If left up to her, we'd eat here every other day."

Marvin picked up a menu. "Then you probably have a good idea of their best dishes."

"I've had almost all of the chicken dishes, a few of the lamb ones. Jan often eats off of the vegetarian menu. Personally, I don't think you can go wrong."

The guys took a few moments to make their selections and place their orders. Doug handed his menu to the server and relaxed against the booth's cushioned back. "What's this about, you almost needing bail?"

"Man." Marvin shook his head. "The situation was crazy. So I decided to go over to my girl's house the other day, Sunday."

"Naomi?"

Marvin nodded. "We hadn't seen each other much since the contest ended. I thought it would be nice to, you know, put together a nice little meal for her and her grandmother."

"Sounds like a good move."

"I get over there, nobody's home."

"You didn't call first?"

"I'd called, but she hadn't answered or returned the call. But we'd talked about getting together the day before, the day I came over for the meeting. You'll remember I didn't leave your house until late. That's another reason I wanted to do something nice for her, because we'd talked about maybe getting together. Then you guys called the meeting. By the time I called she'd copped a little attitude and didn't answer the phone. So anyway, yeah, I went over without calling, but no big deal, right? I mean, it's just dinner."

"I don't know, man. You go over to a chick's house without calling, no telling what you'll get."

Marvin huffed.

"Is that what happened? You went over there and somebody else's feet were already under the table?"

"Not at first."

Marvin told Doug what happened. "She called me later and explained why she asked me to leave," he finished. "Said the dude threatened her with a gun."

"You went up against bullets and steel, my brother?"

"I never saw a gun. I'm not sure she did either."

"You don't believe her?"

"I don't know what to believe."

"Who was the guy, did she tell you that?"

"Rodney something or other, an ex—according to her—who she hadn't dated or seen in the past few years."

"He just showed up all this time later?"

"She said she ran into him at a party the night before, the night her and I were supposed to get together. She told me all they'd done was dance. He made it sound like way more happened, and acted that way, too. How many men would act that possessive over someone they just danced with?"

Doug sighed. "I don't know. Somebody crazy, maybe?"

"That's what she said."

"How'd he know where she lived?"

"He knew her grandmother, who's lived in that house for years, decades. Plus, Naomi said he followed her and the friend she rode with, and once she got in her own car believes he followed her home."

"I don't know, Marv. It sounds too crazy, like a bunch of bullshit I'd be crazy to believe. Dang, you were really digging her. I liked her, too. The whole family did."

"Yeah, but sometimes what looks like a meal to keep you full is just a snack to tide you over until the next plate comes along."

"Only a cook would have come up with a metaphor like that." The server delivered their first dishes. "Has she lied to you before?"

"Not that I know of."

"And you haven't seen her since it happened?"

"For what?"

"What did she say happened after you left?"

"She said she called 9-1-1 and the fool ran away. He looked like a coward, so that I can believe."

"I admit what happened sounds crazy, but stranger things have happened, bro. It's hard to find a good woman these days. I get that vibe from Naomi, from what I've seen in the short time I've known her. Don't be so quick to throw something special away."

"Who's talking trash?" Marvin saw Doug look beyond their booth just as Byron punched his arm and Barry slid into the booth next to Doug.

He turned as Byron reached them. "What are you doing here?"

"Came to talk to you about the Carter Collective."

"The who?" Marvin asked.

"Carter Collective," Bryon replied. "The name of our newly formed corporation."

After giving each brother a fist bump, Byron sat down. "We're leaving here and heading over to an attorney friend's office. Leimert is heating up, brothers. Folks are snatching up properties like Monopoly houses. I don't want us to miss out on a golden opportunity because we're too busy overthinking when we should be making a move."

Marvin caught Doug giving him a knowing look that had nothing to do with real estate.

36

Turns out that Marvin quitting the Soul Spot was perfect timing. He spent the next week in a crash course on real estate and looking at properties, mostly with Byron, but occasionally Doug or another brother would join them, too. When they walked up to a three-bed, two-bath gem hidden behind two palm trees, Byron and Marvin looked at each other and before even opening the door knew they were on to something. Once they stepped inside, it was a done deal. They'd called the other brothers while standing in the living room. Nelson was working and Barry was out of town, in Vegas. But Doug finished his bus route a couple hours later and gave the place his thumbs-up. While not closing the door to a commercial location, they all agreed this home was one they couldn't pass up. They called the Realtor that night and made an offer that the seller couldn't refuse.

Because the brothers paid cash for the house, the deal was closed in three days. An interior designer was hired. The brothers decided that until they agreed on how they wanted to profit on their investment, that Marvin and Barry would live there. For Marvin, the chance to move came right on time and gave him somewhere else to place his focus besides Naomi. They'd talked a few times since the incident, but conversations were stilted and he hadn't seen her since then. Everything about what happened with Rodney, the way Naomi had reacted, had been out of character. Or maybe it wasn't. How did he know? He'd barely known her, what, three months? And most of that while competing head-to-head. Maybe the other Naomi had been the imposter and the real one just came out. He'd never given her a reason to doubt him, or feel insecure about her place in his life. But she'd acted suspicious when told he'd spent the entire evening with his brothers. Only for him to find out that she'd gone to a party and did something that caused a man to believe he could show up at her house. *Like you did?* Yeah, like he did. Again, he was thinking too much about Naomi when he should be thinking about his parents, and the conversation he was about to have with them.

Liz, dressed in a satiny caftan, sat with her back against the headboard, reading a magazine. She looked up when he entered. "Good morning."

"Good morning, Mom." He gave her a hug.

"You headed out to see Naomi?"

"No."

"Whoa, that answer came quickly. Y'all having problems?"

"You could say that."

"There isn't a relationship out there that's problem-free, son."

Marvin turned toward the walk-in closet. "I wondered where you were, Dad. Good morning."

"Mornin'."

"I like Naomi," Liz said. "What did y'all get into it about? Another woman?"

"Why do you assume that I'm the culprit? Why wasn't the question 'another man'?"

"Because most of the time it's another woman."

"Most of the time isn't all of the time." Marvin walked over and sat on a large wooden chest at the end of the bed. The sound of items tumbling and hitting the floor came from the closet. "What are you doing in there, Dad?"

"Looking for a piece of my army gear that I put at the back of this shelf. Told your mother not to mess with it, but she didn't listen. Now neither one of us can find it."

"Wasn't enough room in that closet for items that were not being used. I told you it's out back, in the storage shed. Why does it take telling a man something three times before he hears it once? Never mind that. What's on your mind, son?"

"It's about the house that we just purchased. Barry and I are going to move in."

Willie responded first. "Don't move that girl in with you if you want to keep track of what's yours."

Marvin laughed. Liz ignored him. "I thought that was going to be investment property to be used as a rental."

"It might be, eventually. We're not going to live there forever."

"You haven't mentioned moving before. I like having you here and thought you liked being here."

"You like having a chef at your fingertips."

"Does the reason matter as long as you're wanted?"

Willie's slow, melodious laughter floated into the room.

"Y'all might be fighting now, but Naomi is why you want to move. Is she pressuring you?"

"Nobody's pressuring me to do anything. This move back home was always temporary."

"How can something always be temporary? Son, you're not making sense. That girl's got you twisted. One look at all that badonkadonk and your brain stopped working."

"This move is not about Naomi, Mom."

"I admit she's loud and likes telling you what to do. I am too. Women like us want to share our opinions. But we're not bossy."

Willie came to the door of the closet, took a long look at Liz, a glance at Marvin, then turned and resumed his hunt.

"I know you're not calling me bossy!" Liz hollered.

"Loud either," Willie calmly responded.

Liz grabbed a decorative pillow off the bed and

threw it into the closet. "I'm not bossy, I'm the boss. There's a difference."

She refocused on Marvin. "What happened, baby?"

Any other time, and any other woman, and Marvin would have been happy to share all with Liz. But in the moment, Doug's words came back. About how he should give Naomi the benefit of the doubt, know the whole story before cutting her out of his life. Liz was a Carter to the core and could cut a person out in a minute. If she thought Naomi had put his life in danger, getting back in her good graces would be a steep mountain for Naomi to climb.

"Couples fight, just like you and Daddy," he finally said, standing. He walked over and gave his mother a hug. "I'm going to leave y'all to handle your business, while I go handle mine."

"Did you call Marvin?"

Naomi continued to scroll the internet, and said nothing.

Nana took one step inside the room. "I know you're not ignoring me, Naomi Renee, so the only thing I can figure is you've lost your hearing. Next, I'll find something to throw upside your head, see if your sight is gone as well."

"I've been the one calling, Nana. I'm not going to anymore."

"Why not? On second thought, never mind about that. Keep ignoring him like you did me just now, sleeping in that bed with pride for a partner. That's a good young man—thoughtful, respectful. Hope you figure that out before it dawns on another young lady. You'll look up and uh-oh will be too late."

Delivered quietly, calmly, the words splashed across Naomi's mind like cold water on a just woke face, and continued to taunt her.

Keep ignoring him like you did me just now . . .

She went back to reading, or tried to. Except now, instead of the face of the hero Brenda Jackson had described in her novel, all Naomi kept seeing was Marvin's face.

. . . sleeping in that bed with pride for a partner.

He's the one with pride, she countered with the argument in her head. What was she supposed to think when he went all this time without calling her, or asking to see her? Besides, he had nerve pointing the finger. She'd never have gone to the party had he called as they'd planned. So what, a man came over. She told Marvin that Rodney was an ex. That she didn't know he was coming over. That he forced her decision by saying he had a gun, for God's sake! If one was in the wrong, they both were.

That's a good young man—thoughtful, respectful.

Played that role in front of Nana. Nana didn't know him. She'd known him only briefly herself. Could be a serial killer, for all they knew.

Hope you figure that out before it dawns on another young lady.

Naomi tossed her tablet aside and lay on her stomach. Maybe the connection they shared was heightened by spending so much time together, having the contest in common, and experiencing the excitement that comes with all new love. Maybe now she was finding out who he really was. She wasn't sure if she liked it.

You'll look up and uh-oh will be too late.

Nana was right. If she saw someone else hugged on Marvin right now, she'd want to take off her earrings and smear Vaseline on her face. Naomi rolled over, reached for her phone, and tapped his number.

"Hey."

"Hey." Silence. He wasn't going to make this easy.

She took a deep breath. "They must have you really busy with that food truck win. You haven't called at all."

"I've been busy."

"Sounds like you're still upset with me."

"I'm still processing everything that you told me. You have to admit that it was a lot to think through."

"You assumed that there was something going on with Rodney and me, when there wasn't."

"If you'd been over to my house when another woman came over and I asked you to leave, wouldn't you have assumed the same thing?"

"No."

"Whatever, Naomi. Look, I've got to go."

"Wait, Marvin. You're right. I wouldn't be okay with you doing that at all. But I already told you why I did what I did. He said he had a gun, and as crazy as he was acting, I feared he was right. I thought he was high, you heard me ask him that. But if I were

in your shoes, I don't know if what I've told you
so far would be enough to convince me either,
which is why I want us to get together and talk,
face-to-face. For me to answer every question you
have, erase every doubt from your mind. I want
you to be as sure as I am about what happened, why
I asked you to leave, and why I'm now asking you to
meet me. Can we get together, Marvin . . . please?"

"We can do that," he softly said.

Just four words, but they sounded like a love song
and made Naomi's heart sing.

37

Out of the four hundred and eighty minutes that were in an eight-hour day, there may have been five when Marvin wasn't on Naomi's mind. Every part of her body wanted to see him, but as she drove down Crenshaw Boulevard to where they'd agreed to meet, the fear of how the conversation might play out caused her to almost drive past the mall. Her desire to straighten things out between them was bigger than her fear. A few minutes later, she was out of the car and heading to the restaurant.

It was the dinner hour, but not very crowded. Naomi looked around but didn't see Marvin at any of the tables. The first thoughts that popped up were negative, but she refused to go there. Doing so was partly to blame for creating the rift between them. She took a deep breath and scanned the room again. There he was, sitting casually at the bar, talking with the bartender. Naomi headed toward him, determined to be herself, the large, in-charge sister he met at the convention center. She had no idea how the evening would end, but it had started with the sight of him making her heart skip a beat.

The bartender must have said something because he turned around before she arrived. His gaze traveled the length of her body. He smiled, sort of, and slid off of the bar stool.

"Hey, Marvin."

"Juicy."

He moaned, soft and low as she stepped into his arms. It felt like coming home. His rapid heartbeat let her know that he was just as uncertain as she was.

She pointedly looked around and asked, "What is this going to be, a one glass of wine conversation?" Marvin looked at the bartender, who shook his head and chuckled. "It's been a little rough, but we can't find enough small talk to get through a salad? And if still speaking by then, maybe order dinner?"

Marvin eyed her with a serious expression. "Girl, it's been quiet without you."

Everybody laughed, including the bartender.

"You want dinner?" he asked.

"Let's start with a drink, and then we'll see."

They got their drinks and then sat on the last two stools away from the crowd, and spent a moment just looking at each other.

"Where do you want me to start?" Naomi asked.

"At the beginning," Marvin quickly responded. "How do you know that guy?"

Naomi took a long swig from her glass of wine. "I met Rodney in middle school. Actually, I met his brother first. Rodney was two years younger. He was goofy, funny, made me laugh. There was a group of us who all hung out together. Eventually we started messing around, nothing serious at first. Then he asked me to be his girlfriend, and I said okay."

"How long did y'all date?"

"On and off, for several years. It started in high school, both of us too young to commit to anything besides growing up. It was cool at first, but then he started to get possessive, and more controlling. We'd break up, make up, until I started seeing weird behavior that scared me."

"Like what?"

"Kind of like what you saw that Sunday, like maybe he was on drugs or psycho, something."

"Does he do drugs?"

"Just weed, or so he claims, but it's more . . . got to be."

"What happened at the party?"

"One of our high school friends threw it. There were a lot of people who I hadn't seen in years, including my friend Zena, who's just moved back to LA from Arizona. Once there I drank too much, too fast, and forgot I hadn't eaten. When I saw Rodney, I was already on the dance floor, having a good time. I admit to having fun with him, maybe flirting a little. But we were all acting silly, jamming to our old faves—Usher, Monica, Chris Brown, the lineup. We went down the soul-train line together. Harmless fun, I thought. But obviously not. Looking back, I shouldn't have given him the time of day. I knew better."

"What do you mean?"

"When I finally put my foot down with Rodney and let him know we were over for real, he went off. He wasn't violent, at least physically, but he cursed me out, issued subtle threats, I even felt like he stalked me for a while, like several months. I was living somewhere else, then. A roommate and I had an apartment in the Valley. She got engaged and moved in with her boyfriend. Around that same time, Nana had a few health issues, so it made sense for me to move back with her. That was more than two years ago. I hadn't seen him since then. But that night . . ."

Naomi paused, remembering the signs she'd seen that Rodney was stalking her and how quickly she dismissed them.

"What about that night?"

Naomi had told him on a phone call before, but reminded him how Zena had seen Rodney behind them at the fast food drive-through, and how the way he'd stalked her in the past had gone through her mind.

"It was so long ago," she finished. "I thought we were way past all that. I thought we'd moved on."

"But he hadn't. He was still stalking you."

"Yep." Naomi finished her drink and pushed it aside. "He commented about where I worked. I didn't think anything about it, although it should have been a huge red flag since that wasn't where

I worked when he and I were together. Obviously he'd kept tabs on me for a while."

Naomi reached out and placed a hand on Marvin's arm. "I should have known better, and to think you or Nana or even Miss J might have been harmed . . ."

"He had a gun, for sure?"

"That look I saw in his eyes that day made me not want to find out." She reached into her purse and pulled out a stack of papers.

"What's this?"

"The police report I filed the day after dialing 9-1-1. They didn't catch him, but I wanted what had happened to be put in writing. Beneath that is the restraining order that was requested and approved. If he comes closer to me than the length of a football field, he's going to jail."

Marvin laid the papers on the bar and pulled her hand between his. "I'm sorry, baby. I hate that you went through that."

Naomi hadn't shed a tear over what had happened with Rodney, but the tenderness in Marvin's voice pushed them precariously close to her eyelids.

"I never should have gone to that party," she said harshly, creating an emotional dam to stanch the flow that threatened. She glared at him. "It's your fault."

"Ha! How do you figure?"

"I was mad at you because you didn't call."

"You make it seem as though I was out with some female. I was with my brothers!"

"I know. My going to that party wasn't your fault.

And that I wasn't sure I believed you wasn't your fault either."

"I'm glad you said that. I couldn't understand why you were tripping."

"There is no understanding it, except to say that earlier that day Kristy pushed a button I thought I'd dismantled years ago."

Marvin frowned. "What button was that?"

"I'm almost ashamed to say it." Naomi actually felt embarrassed at what she'd allowed to stick in her craw. "She suggested that since you won . . . with your newfound business owner status, you'd go after a different type of woman."

Marvin's frown deepened. That he was genuinely confused blessed Naomi's heart.

"You know, the skinnier women society deems beautiful. Thinking back, that's why I even took issue with Abbey and her skinny, khaki-wearing behind."

"You're kidding, right?"

"I should be, but babe. There's not a woman out here, no matter how beautiful, who hasn't at one time or another dealt with insecurities that threatened her self-esteem. For a thick chick, I can guarantee you that's doubly true. When it comes to the standard displayed for beauty, by and large—no pun intended—big women get no love."

Marvin stood then, eased her into his arms and slowly wrapped his meaty ones around her and pressed in for a kiss, nice and easy, in a way that made her know he felt all of what she was working with and liked every pound.

He finished kissing her and grabbed a chunk of her ass, right there in front of God and everybody. "Don't ever doubt how beautiful you are, mouth and all, inside and out. There's not a woman in the world that can compete with this. Do you understand me?"

"I do now." Naomi's eyes sparkled as she eased back on to the bar stool. She may have loved Marvin before, but in this moment the feelings went to another level. She was in love with him.

"How are we doing over here?" the bartender asked, wiping down the counter as he approached them.

Marvin looked at Naomi. "Do you want to head to the dining room?"

Naomi nodded. "I could eat."

Marvin's eyes narrowed. He looked at her mouth. "Me too."

Clearly, he wasn't talking about food.

They walked to the hostess stand and were promptly seated in the dining room, and given menus.

Marvin picked his up, looked over it at Naomi, and chuckled while shaking his head. "I never would have thought that about you," he said. "Lacking confidence, especially where I'm concerned."

"I know."

"No, you don't."

"What?"

"I had a conversation about you . . . with Abbey."

"Oh, that's one I don't know and probably don't want to know."

"It was interesting."

"When? Why?"

"A couple days after we got called in over those trumped-up allegations. I was angry and trying to figure out who did it. Remembered you thinking it could have been her, and given how she'd treated you, I thought you might be right. So I asked her, straight out. Did she do it? Did she report us to them?"

"And let me guess. She denied it."

"Yes, but it was the way she denied it that I wasn't expecting. I called her out on how she treated you and said it was clear that she didn't like you. She said that it wasn't that she didn't like you. It was that she envied you."

"Stop."

"I'm serious. And so was she, Nay. She explained how everything you are is everything she isn't. She wanted to be like you, or the 'you' she saw. The strong, confident persona that most people see, the one I know.

"I asked if I could tell you and at first she said no because she was embarrassed. But I told her what she said was really nice, and I thought you'd like to hear it."

"And now you know that I needed to hear it. Taking care of me before you even knew what was wrong."

The waiter returned. They placed their orders. Naomi looked at Marvin with regret in her eyes. "I have to say something."

"Okay, but why are you looking at me like some-body died?"

"Probably because when Rodney acted a fool and you left my house, a little of me did die. I know I apologized for his crazy behavior, but I still feel so bad. I want to—no, have to—apologize. I shouldn't have gone out that night, shouldn't have talked to Rodney, and shouldn't have opened the door when he came by. I should have known he brought trou-ble just by the look in his eye. I'm sorry, Marvin. Will you forgive me?"

"Of course."

And just like that, the Marvin and Naomi love train was back.

38

Labor Day weekend arrived and that Sunday, the day the Food Truck Bucks finale aired, Marvin was in his element. Word spreading about his appearance on the televised show had resulted in an impromptu block party. A one-hundred-inch projection screen had been mounted on the side of Liz and Willie's home, ready to capture Marvin's image in full HD. All of his brothers were on the scene, along with their wives or dates, except Jan, who'd been called away to do a private show. Nelson, who because of his work schedule missed many family-held evening events, had traded with another employee to be there. Everyone speculated about the Latina he had on his arm, the first of his women the family had met in a while. People had been encouraged to BYOB and bring their own lawn chairs, but Marvin felt it only right that he handle the food.

Two hours before the show was set to start, Marvin was in his element, basting ribs, steaks, chicken, burgers, and dogs across multiple grills. Old-school music blasted and he'd had a couple Coronas, but that wasn't why he was in such a great mood. The smile that seemed glued to his face came courtesy of his sous chef, Naomi, the one who since she'd apologized and they'd rekindled their romance hadn't missed a beat, who along with his mama and Janet had whipped up an array of complimentary sides including macaroni and potato salads, coleslaw, and baked beans. When Nana asked what she needed to bring, Marvin had assured her to just bring herself, but there were three large sheet cakes and two commercial-sized pots of greens swimming in fatback that had come courtesy of the women at Morningside Baptist Church. Their little group sat in comfy lounge chairs on the safety of the concrete patio, armed with throws against the slight evening chill that had been forecasted. Once the patio filled up, others took their chairs and their chances by placing them in the grass. An hour before the broadcast, Marvin took a bullhorn and made an announcement.

"Food's ready!"

After that a steady stream passed from the food tent to the drinks table and back to their chairs. Five minutes before showtime, Liz took the horn.

"Excuse me, everybody." The din quieted a little. "May I have your attention?" More people heard her and the noise decreased further, but not enough for Mama Liz, who cleared her throat and bellowed, "I'ma need all of y'all to shut the hell up!"

This brought on more whooping and laughter, and left only a couple minutes for her to say anything before the show began.

"I want to thank all of y'all for coming over and showing support for our son Marvin. Many of y'all helped raise him. He grew up on this block, learned to cook on this block, and when he went on this show, he represented Inglewood and let the world know that lots of good came from the hood!"

"Yes!" someone shouted.

"That's right!" another agreed.

"Now, when there's a commercial, everybody can talk and laugh, eat, drink, and be merry. But when my son is on that screen? I want to be able to hear a mosquito pee on grass."

"It's on, Mama, shut up!" one of her sons yelled.

This brought on a huge guffaw, which turned into cheers the moment Marvin's face lit up the side of the house. When Naomi was introduced, Nana shouted, "That's my baby!" which caused Liz to take to the horn again.

"I'm sorry, y'all, for breaking my own rule and yapping, but I've got to recognize Marvin's girl-friend, who he met on the show. Y'all give it up for Naomi!"

Marvin squeezed Naomi's hand. "It feels weird seeing us on there," he whispered.

"I know, huh?" she answered. "Seems like that happened so long ago."

They continued talking—heads together, voices low.

"Or not at all. That looks like somebody else's life right there. I can't believe I entered the contest, let alone made it to the televised finals."

"We made it, baby," she replied, and kissed his cheek, not talking about the contest at all.

When the show ended and Marvin was crowned the winner, the party went up another notch, poised to last well into the night. But just after midnight, Marvin and Naomi slipped away to give her grandmother and friends a ride home. Naomi drove Nana's car. Marvin followed behind in his SUV. Once they'd bid all of the ladies good night, Naomi slid into Marvin's front seat. He began to drive, but in the direction opposite his parents' home.

"Where are you going?" she asked.

Marvin looked over and smiled. "I want to show you something."

"What?"

"It's a surprise."

They drove down Crenshaw, less than two miles, before Marvin turned from the commercial boulevard onto a residential street, pulled into the driveway of a quaint stucco home, and shut off the engine. Naomi looked at the house in front of them, over at Marvin, and back at the house. At one time, it was probably lovely. Like the ones to either side of it, the home was a bungalow style with a Spanish tile roof. Its dull yellow paint was peeling, and the front window was cracked. Shoddy brick foundations supported four columns that framed a large porch. A set of steps led to the front door, another down to a dilapidated carport. The yard

wasn't maintained and the sidewalk was buckled.
Every place her eye landed needed work. There
were no lights and on top of that, security bars
were everywhere.

"Who lives here?"

Marvin smiled. "I will, in a minute. Do me a favor
and grab the flashlight out of the glove box."

He hopped out of the car and came around to
open her door. Naomi didn't move. "Come on!"

Naomi shook her head. "This looks like the type
of place a crazy ex would hide." She looked at the
house. "With an ax," she added.

Marvin reached for her arm and the flashlight.
"Come on, girl."

He pulled out a set of keys and after searching
through them found one to open the gate. A short
sidewalk led to a narrow, heavily secured porch.
Marvin unlocked the heavy steel door and then the
front door. Before stepping inside, he turned on
the flashlight.

"Watch your step. There's debris and a couple of
the boards are loose."

Naomi's steps were tentative as she stepped over
the threshold. "Who would rent out a place that
looked like this?"

"Nobody. I bought it."

"You did not buy this house."

"It doesn't look like much now, but in a month
or so . . . it's going to be hooked up."

"I'm not talking about the shape it's in. I'm talking about the price. My grandmother's home is

worth over four hundred thousand. In this location, this has got to be around five."

"Look at you! Knowing a little something about LA real estate. I see you, girl."

Naomi now viewed the room through new eyes. The living room was larger than expected, with high ceilings, a fireplace, and large windows that in the daytime she imagined let in tons of light. The dining room flowed directly off from the living room with a galley kitchen beyond it and a brick back wall. Two bedrooms took up the left wall with a bathroom between them. A larger bedroom was on the right.

Marvin, who'd been quiet during the walk-through, pointed at the room across from the last bedroom. "This is going to be reconfigured to add another bathroom that will hold a stackable washer/dryer, and turn this bedroom into a master suite. There's enough room in the back to add a small deck and possibly a storage shed."

"This is nice, Marvin."

"Ha! That's not what you said when I drove up here. You were looking for my crazy ex or Freddy Krueger's cousin.

"The place is in pretty bad shape. But it's got potential. I don't know if I would sink all of my winnings into it, but I think in the long run it will definitely pay off. Not that it's my business.

"It isn't just me. It's all my brothers. We formed an S corporation to purchase investments. That's what we were talking about the day that you called. Byron had done a lot of research and provided valuable information. Explaining it was complex and generated a ton of questions. The discussion on how to proceed was fairly intense. That's why I turned off my phone, so that its ringing wouldn't disturb the group."

"You are so lucky to be in this family."

Marvin eyed her with a look that was intense and unreadable.

"What's that look for?"

"Nothing. Let's go back to the party."

As they headed back to Inglewood, the streets were quiet. Once on the Carters' block though, it was still all the way live. They strolled back to the patio hand in hand.

"There you are," Liz said to Naomi, coming to pull her away from Marvin. "I want you to tell my neighbor here what you put in those baked beans . . . besides your foot."

"Ha!"

Marvin laughed as he watched Naomi walk away with his mom, their heads together as he imagined Naomi spilling culinary secrets.

Doug came up to him, handed him a beer. "Congratulations again, brother. Glad to see you got your smile back."

"I'm just glad it isn't a secret anymore. Not revealing I'd won the contest was the hardest thing in the world to keep from the whole family."

"Everyone knows you won the contest. I wasn't talking about that, though. I was talking about your girl."

He nodded toward where Naomi held court,

surrounded by a group of women. She was smiling, animated, and made a comment that sent the entire circle into laughter.

"She fits, doesn't she," Marvin observed.

"Just like family," Doug agreed.

His older brother had given Marvin confirmation. Earlier, Naomi had mentioned how lucky he was to be a Carter. Soon, if Marvin had anything to do with it, she'd be lucky, too.

39

Marvin couldn't believe it was almost Halloween. *What the heck happened to the rest of October?* Between keeping up with the Leimert property renovation and finalizing plans for Slice, he felt overwhelmed, almost to the breaking point. But the renovations were almost finished. The plans for his truck were coming together. Naomi had a lot to do with that. They talked every night, discussing details and exchanging ideas.

Yesterday, the show had called and scheduled an appointment when he'd meet with the designer who'd create the logo and wrap for his truck. The truck was getting ready to be hooked up from the outside. But it was what needed to happen on the inside that was currently on Marvin's mind. He looked at the clock and reached for his phone. A groggy voice answered.

"You asleep?"

Marvin imagined Naomi either frowning or rolling her eyes. "Really?"

"I know it's late, but I had to call you. It's about the truck."

"What about it?"

"I have an appointment to meet with the designer this week and wanted to bounce a couple of ideas off of you. I need to make a final decision on the name."

"I thought you were going to call it The Perfect Slice," Naomi said.

"I was leaning more toward The Savory Slice."

"The name I came up with for what was supposed to be my truck? No, you can't use that name."

"Is it trademarked?"

"Yep."

Marvin chuckled. "You're lying. Besides, that's a common phrase. There are probably pizza trucks already using it."

"Can we talk about this tomorrow?" Naomi asked amid a yawn.

"That's what I wanted to ask, if you'd meet me to talk about work on the truck."

"The design, right?"

"Yes, and maybe more."

"More like what?"

"Like being my sous chef, girl. Can't nobody burn beside me the way you do."

"Are you saying I can light a fire under that booty?"

"Baby, you can light a fire anywhere you want."

"You're silly," she said with a flirty laugh. "Call me tomorrow."

Naomi hung up. Marvin smiled.

* * *

The next day they sat at a Starbucks—heads together, conversation low and intense.

"I'm thinking stark white for a color, with different kinds of slices all over."

Naomi shook her head. "People will take one look and think of pizza, without even seeing your menu. I think it needs to be a bright color. Like red."

They looked at each other and said, "No."

"No red, no blue," Marvin repeated.

"I do think it should be a bright color, though. Something that stands out. Especially here, the food truck capital of the world."

"What about orange?"

"It would depend on the shade. Maybe a turquoise, or lime green."

"That will never happen."

"Is this guy designing your logo, too? He must be, because you definitely need one."

"Have to lock down the name first." He looked over at her.

"No . . ."

"Slice has got to be in the title, but for some reason the word *perfect* doesn't sound right with it. Imagine someone saying, *Hey, where are you going, man? I'm going to the perfect slice.*"

Naomi laughed at his humorous delivery. "Not when you say it like that."

"You know what I mean though. It needs to be a

name that just rolls off the tongue, something with a rhythm."

Naomi placed her chin in her hand. "The tasty slice."

Marvin shook his head. "That's only one letter off from the nasty slice."

Naomi cracked up. "Only you would think about that."

"Don't get me wrong. Sometimes a brother wants a nasty slice."

"A good slice."

"Boring. What about the spicy slice?"

"Ooh, that's kind of cool." Naomi repeated it a few times with different inflections. "Except what if a person doesn't like spicy food? And what about the sweet slice dessert ideas you've created?"

Marvin sighed. "It's going to be almost impossible to find a name that matches everything on the menu."

"Maybe not," Naomi replied. "But the name of your business can make it or break it."

"I've got to get this right." Marvin stopped. Snapped his finger. "That's it."

"What? Get it right?"

"No. The Right Slice."

"I don't love it." Naomi thought for a second. "What about just Slice?"

"Just slice?"

"No, just one word—Slice."

Marvin pondered the idea, slowly nodded his

head and let the word roll off his tongue a couple times. "Slice. Girl, I think you just named my truck."

They high-fived.

"Now, on to the menu."

Over the course of several days they solidified a menu that they felt was varied enough to have wide appeal yet simple enough to be rapidly executed. Because Naomi cooked almost exclusively on the savory side, she came up with most of those ideas. They decided to have ten choices of each—savory and sweet—at any given time, swapping out for seasonal and holiday flavors. A few slices would be permanent, including the pork slice Naomi used in the contest and a salad slice for vegans, on a crouton crust. The breakfast slice—a deconstructed omelet with choice of sausage or bacon on a biscuit dough would be served all day, and all of the sweet slices. Both Janet and Ricky wanted to work with him but needed full-time paychecks, so Marvin reached out to Tat and Zen, who both agreed to help out part-time. It took Marvin a week to construct the shopping list. On the evening before Thanksgiving, Marvin and Naomi spent four hours buying food, then returned to the home he'd just moved into last weekend. While organizing the groceries on the galley kitchen's huge, granite-top island, they talked about operations.

"What time are Tat and Zen arriving?" she asked.

"Seven o'clock."

"You think that's enough time?"

Marvin nodded. "I'm going to start some of the

meat tonight, let it go low and slow. The way we've compiled the menu items, everything else gets done on the spot. It's a lot of work, but if we stay organized, we should be well able to handle the flow."

"What about orders? I think Zen would work well at the window. He's calm, just like the nickname you gave him. Even if it gets busy up there, no one will see him sweat."

Marvin walked over, gave Naomi a kiss and began to rub her shoulders. "Zen would look okay there. But when people walk up to my window, I want the first thing they see to be the best my food truck has to offer. And that, Naomi, is your pretty face."

"Ah. Even though I'm tired as hell, you're getting some tonight!"

"Ha!"

"After this though, we should take a vacation. Maybe go to New York, as I've always dreamed."

"You keep saying that. What's so special about the East Coast?"

"Are you serious? It's the foodie capital of the world!"

"I've been there," Marvin replied. "It's overrated."

"Humph. Let me go and be the judge of that."

"No more judging," Marvin declared, as the last of the food items were put away and they made their way to the bedroom. "Time for some loving."

Naomi followed behind him. "Agreed."

* * *

Six months had passed since Marvin declared himself the cook who would take it all. From that day, he'd dreamed of being able to quit working at the Soul Spot and be his own boss. He wanted a brand that he could be proud of and to have Naomi as his assistant. As she lay sleeping and cuddled against him in one of two identical master suites, while he was wired with excitement, he mouthed a silent thank-you to the Universe. He'd believed and received, and now the day he'd dreamed of was finally here.

It was Saturday, just after nine o'clock on Thanksgiving weekend. Marvin, Naomi, Zen, and Tat stood in Marvin's driveway, staring at the brightly colored food truck emblazoned with SLICE, the name Marvin and Naomi had created together, spelled out within a clip-art pic of the same. Having spent the past twenty-four hours in heavy prep, the trio should have been exhausted. But they weren't. Instead of blood, excitement ran through their veins.

For Marvin, the moment was surreal. Over the past week, he'd been in that truck more than he'd been in his house. And he'd loved every minute.

Naomi leaned against him, in awe of the moment, too. "Are you ready?'

Marvin nodded. "I've waited on this moment for a long time."

"Now it's here," Tat said, rubbing her arms as a cloud covered the sun. "You're doing everything right. Debuting on the biggest shopping weekend of the year. Alerting the masses through social media and marketing cards. Setting up in a killer location with two of the best cooks with whom you could ever share a kitchen." She and Naomi fist-bumped. "What more can you ask for?"

"Nothing," Marvin said. He slid an arm around Naomi's waist and squeezed. "I've got it all."

He took one last look around. "It's time to head out, y'all. If I know my family, some of them are already up there wondering where we're at."

After quick hugs, Marvin and Naomi got into the food truck while Tat drove Marvin's SUV, which had been wrapped to match the truck. Travel from his home to the Leimert Plaza Park, where the truck would be set up, took all of five minutes. Byron had been right. The Carter Collective purchasing that home had been a wise move.

The truck got attention from the moment it pulled up. Marvin jumped down from the driver's side and, as he figured, saw his dad, Nelson, and Barry strolling over to greet him.

"Why are you starting so late?" Nelson asked. "At least five hundred dollars have passed by this area just since I've been here."

"Good looking-out for me, brother. But we'll be fine."

Marvin was right. When they opened the window just twenty minutes after parking, there was already a line. It formed and never ended. Nelson had to work, but Barry was instantly recruited. Texts went out for extra hands, and later, extra food. For all of their planning, the on-the-job lessons came fast and furious. Still, with Naomi on the window and Tat and Marvin executing, they emptied the truck. When they shut down just eight hours later, they'd moved every type of slice prepared. Nothing was left. Not even a lettuce leaf.

Back at the house, Marvin and Naomi walked straight through the living and dining room area, entered the bedroom, and collapsed on his brand-new, king-size bed.

"Ooh, baby," Naomi said, as she reached out and touched him. "I've never had this feeling before."

"What, the feeling of running your own business?"

"No, the one where every part of my body hurts."

"Oh, my poor baby. Come here and let me kiss your booboo so you'll feel all better."

"Ooh, no, baby. I'm funky. Let poor baby take a shower first."

"Ha!"

Marvin laughed as Naomi slid off the bed, removing clothes as she entered the master suite. He went to his chest of drawers, pulled out an envelope and set it on a pillow, then stripped and joined her in the shower.

Bubbles slid down her ample globes as she turned to face him. He rubbed himself against her, using the suds on her body to soap his own.

"Here, give me that." He took the bar of fruity-smelling soap from her and began slowly gliding it over every inch of her body. "Spread your legs."

She did. He ran the soap between her legs and along her folds, smiling at the hitch that caught in her breath when his finger followed the path of the soap bar before sliding inside her.

"Ooh, baby," she cooed, pressing his favorite body part of hers against him, grinding her booty against his rapidly hardening flesh. He reached for the loofah and sponged both of their bodies, even as she turned in his arms and slid her tongue into his mouth.

"Give it to me," she whispered, while capturing Marvin's dick between her thighs.

In the moment all of the pain must have been forgotten as a surprisingly limber Naomi leaned against one shower wall and hoisted her leg up against another one. Marvin's eyes fluttered as he walked toward her, shaft in hand, and guided it into her warm, waiting heat—slowly, in, out, again. He thrust. She swiveled. It didn't take long. Their climax was hard and simultaneous. They finished showering, donned towels, and headed back into the bedroom, both prepared to do it again.

Naomi brought a bottle of lotion into the bedroom. She got ready to lotion herself, but Marvin took the bottle away.

"Get on the bed, sexy," he ordered.

She complied, noting the envelope as she did so. "What's this?"

"Your check for working today."

"Check? On top of the cash you already gave me? You going to pay me twice?"

"Only one way to find out."

Naomi continued looking at him while her hands worked to unseal the envelope. She pulled out stationery with a travel agency's logo on top. She saw two words, New York, and screamed.

"We're going to New York?"

"You said we'd need a vacation after weathering the holidays. I thought New York would be a great getaway. Do you think you'll have quit work by then?"

"I don't think so, Marvin."

"Why not? You saw how much money we made in one night. Once word gets out, we'll do six figures easy, and I'm talking more than a hundred grand. More like two or three, maybe more."

"I know, and I believe in you one hundred percent. The one thing that has me hesitating is the expense of getting my own insurance. Okay, and maybe the assurance of a steady paycheck, too. Give me a little time, okay, before I ride-or-die with you, which you already know I will. Meantime, I'll get these days off for sure. If they don't let me have them, I'll quit."

"What's your boss's name?"

Naomi frowned. "Why?"

"I want to call her and make sure she doesn't give you those off days. I need you full-time, Naomi Carson. Not just in my truck . . . in my life."

40

Naomi's face was pressed to the airplane window. Her eyes shone like a kid's. It was her first trip to New York City, and that she was experiencing it with the man sitting beside her was thrilling beyond words. A three-day weekend was hardly enough time for all the city had to offer. But Naomi planned to see as much of it as she could.

"Babe, when was the last time you were here?" Naomi asked.

"I think it's been three or four years ago, something like that. A friend of mine's wedding. They got married in Central Park."

"That sounds so romantic. Will we have time to go there?"

"Maybe," Marvin drawled. "But we won't have time to tie the knot."

The plane landed. They got their bags. Marvin used a ride-share app to order a car. When it was less than five minutes away, they exited the airport to the sights and sounds of the city near LaGuardia Airport.

"I'm in New York!" Naomi squealed.

"I'm cold," Marvin responded.

Because it was Naomi's first time, Marvin wanted to stay in Manhattan. Byron's wife, Cynthia, had suggested they book through a house-sharing website instead of staying in a hotel. She assured them that not only was it cheaper, but they'd have a more authentic experience staying in a home. When Naomi had balked at the idea, Cynthia offered to handle the reservation herself and take full responsibility for their living experience. Naomi budgeted for a hotel room, just in case. They arrived to an elegant one-bedroom apartment just blocks from Times Square. Naomi vowed to never book a hotel again.

Marvin suggested a little lovemaking to take off the chill, but Naomi wasn't having it. She was ready to hit the streets.

"Times Square is just blocks away! I want to see where they drop the ball."

"We'll hang out down there tonight. It'll be better then. How about we take a subway to Harlem, check out the Apollo and a few other sites, and then grab lunch at Red Rooster."

Naomi gasped. "Marcus Samuelsson's place! Yes! Let me freshen up."

There was Alice in Wonderland and there was Naomi in Manhattan. She was in awe of everything—buildings, traffic, billboards, people—even the plethora of pigeons and trees. The subway ride was fascinating and somewhat scary.

"It looks just like the movies! Think of everything on top of us, all of those tall, heavy buildings, and millions of people!"

Marvin had replied, "No, let's not think about that."

When they arrived in Harlem and came up out of the subway, Naomi couldn't help but pinch herself. When she saw the Apollo sign, she almost cried. Took pictures of it from every angle. She hugged the imitation tree of hope that sat in the lobby. Marvin had to almost bear hug her to prevent her from ignoring security and running up to the stage. She grew up watching *Showtime at the Apollo*. With the mirror as her audience and a brush for a mike, she'd regularly slayed the competition and wowed the masses. In her mind, she'd been on that stage a thousand times.

The weekend was a whirlwind of wow, and food accompanied almost every experience. Warm nuts, hot pretzels, and hot dogs all sold on the street. Gourmet-quality pizza sold by the slice in shops no bigger than Naomi's closet. One could walk a city block in certain locations and take a trip around the world—Middle Eastern gyros and lamb kabobs, Chinatown's rice noodles, and Trinidadian roti filled with beef, veggies, and rice. Naomi hadn't eaten any of those dishes before and wanted to try them all. When Marvin surprised her with dinner in Brooklyn at Butterfunk Kitchen, one owned by a man she'd watched on *Top Chef*, she could have kissed his sock. They saw a Broadway show, and took a ferry ride to the Statue of Liberty. They spent time in Times Square, a voyeur's dream. Every adventure-filled day ended with love-filled nights—their laughter unending, their love real. When the trip ended, and they boarded a plane bound for California, Naomi turned to him with teary eyes.

"Thank you so much for bringing me here, babe. This was the best trip ever, one I'll never forget."

Back in California, Marvin and Naomi settled into an effortless groove. She finally made the appointment and got on birth control, and after both were tested, enjoyed regular lovemaking skin-to-skin. Three weeks after Marvin's food truck, Slice, opened for business, news of their truck and the delicious menu continued to spread like wildfire. Naomi took a leap of faith and quit her job to work with him full-time. They were able to hire permanent part-timers. Tat and Zen continued to help with prep and peak-time service. Naomi even created part-time work for Kristy, who despite her earlier prediction was now noticeably with child. Since her cousin's cell phone was an extension of her hand and she navigated social media like a fish did water, Kristy handled their social media blasts announcing locations where they were set up. The internet was a godsend. Customers were often standing in line waiting when the Slice pulled up.

Life was so busy that with turkey and stuffing barely digested, Naomi blinked and Santa was headed their way. On Christmas Eve, she found

herself again in Venice Beach at a sit-down dinner
with the entire Carter clan. It was a family affair,
but Cynthia had stipulated that dress attire was required and that the rule would be strictly enforced.
Thirty people occupied three round tables set up
on the home's heated rooftop, which twinkled with
lights and boasted decorated Christmas trees that
were ten feet high. After casual mingling during
the cocktail hour, the guests were seated. This visit
was even more special than the first time, when she
first met her idol Jan. This time, to her right was
the love of her life, and to her left was Nana.

"Are you okay, Nana? Having a good time?"

"I'm fine, baby. This is all so lovely. Marvin has a
beautiful family." Nadine leaned and whispered, "I
think you've got yourself a good man."

As uniformed waiters began service, Naomi looked
across the table and caught Jan's eyes on her.

"I don't mean to stare at you," Jan said. "But you
have such a pretty face and your skin is flawless."

"Thank you, Jan!"

"I meant to tell you that the last time Doug and I
came to the truck. What do you use?"

"I don't wear foundation."

"No, I meant what cleanser?"

Naomi shrugged. "Whatever's on the Dollar
Store's shelf."

The woman next to Jan chimed in. "Then you
need to thank your parents, because they've passed
on some very good genes."

"Which means y'all will have some pretty babies,"
Jan teased.

Marvin, who'd been talking to Doug, sitting beside him, caught the last comment. "I think so. A little Carson, a lot of Carter . . ."

Nadine leaned forward. "Watch it now!"

Amid the laughter came a tinkling sound. Cynthia stood, ringing a crystal bell. Conversations quieted.

"Good evening, family. As service begins, I just wanted to thank everyone for coming and for dressing so nicely." The comment drew the intended chuckles. "Byron and I are thrilled to have all of the people we love celebrating this, my very favorite holiday, with us. Most of you know my parents, but a few of you haven't met them, so I'd like to acknowledge my parents, Mr. and Mrs. Carlton Hall, and my brother Jeff, my son Jaylin, and of course the reason my heart beats, Doug Carter."

She held out the mike, but he shook his head.

"Who would like to offer a toast?"

All of the Carter brothers except Nelson began to rise. "I got it first," Byron said, laughing at Barry, who was right behind him.

"Good evening, family. Tonight I'm in a celebratory and thankful mood, especially mindful of gifts that keep on giving. Most of you know that just a few months ago my brothers and I incorporated to do business as the Carter Collective. We . . ." Byron paused as the room applauded. "Thank you. It was a very deliberate move to own, invest, and accumulate wealth that can continue to sustain this family for generations. The market value in South LA continues to climb, and we believe it will be that way for years to come. That's where we focused for the group's first purchase. That home, a bungalow that has been completely renovated, is just south of Leimert Park. It's currently being occupied by America's newest food truck owner, and one of the best chefs to ever pick up a pan."

"I really am," Marvin called out, to various reactions.

"He won first place in Food Truck Bucks, and along with a nice cash prize was given a food truck. Along with his lady, Naomi, Marvin's truck, Slice, has already become a must visit for people coming to Leimert Park. They're on course to go deep into six figures their first year out. He already knows how proud we are of him. Thanks, bro, for helping the Carters shine."

Byron held up his hand to do the toast, but Marvin stood. "I know everyone is ready to eat, but I just wanted to add something to that real quick. A couple things, actually. One, is that the meat dishes you'll eat tonight were prepared by a woman who was once my competition, Naomi Carson." He nodded. She smiled and waved to light applause. "Two, the dessert is all me. And three, I really wanted to emphasize the value that this woman sitting next to me has brought to my business and to my life. She gave me a run for my money on the show . . ."

"I'm still giving him a run for his money," Naomi said, to the delight of all the women and most of the men.

"She tries," Marvin replied. "But seriously, it was her idea to brand the business as one where everything is served as a slice, and having that unique twist is one of the reasons people drive to wherever we are to get . . ."

Several people joined him in finishing the sentence, "The right slice."

"We clicked from the very first day of the competition, so first I asked her to come and just brainstorm with me about the name of the truck and the menu. And she did. Then I asked if she would help me out in the truck, at least part-time, while I was getting everything up and running. She said yes. Business went crazy and three weeks later I asked if she would take a chance and quit her job with benefits to work full-time for one who doesn't have benefits set up yet. She did that, too. Which goes to show that she's crazy."

He laughed and dodged her punch.

"And now, tonight, I have another question for her."

A low murmur spread across the room as Naomi met Jan's widened eyes, saw Doug's knowing smile, and felt Nana's pinch beneath the table.

"Naomi Carson, would you stand, please."

Butterflies turned flips in Naomi's stomach. She willed her legs to stop shaking as she stood next to him.

Marvin turned and faced her directly.

"From the first day I met you, there was a connection." He looked around. "No, y'all, there was a literal connection because I accidentally bumped her butt."

The room roared. Naomi blushed.

"She got with me like my mama would, and I immediately thought, I like this girl." He looked at her again, and reached for her hand. "You have competed against me, stood beside me, and got behind me and my dream. You were one of the first people who told me that you knew, without a doubt, that my business would be a success." Marvin's eyes became bright, his voice raspy. "You don't know what that does to a brother, baby. To know your woman not only believes you but believes in you."

He picked up the linen napkin near him and dabbed the trickle of tears now coating Naomi's cheeks.

"I love you for that, and so much more."

Again, he looked around. "By now, y'all probably know where this is going, right?"

It was a welcome breath of levity in a room where almost everyone was in tears. He reached into his pocket and pulled out a ring with a stone that could clearly and easily be seen from across the room. "You're my partner in business. I'd like to make you my partner for life. My knee might curse me out tomorrow but . . ." He kneeled. "Naomi Carson, will you change the last three letters of your name and take mine? Will you have the baby who's going to look just like me . . ."

Naomi play-punched him.

"Our stomachs are growling, bro."

"You're not a preacher and this ain't a church. Wrap it up!"

And into the silence a petition from Nadine. "Jesus, take the mike."

"Naomi, I love you. Will you marry me?"

There was a pregnant pause. She placed a finger to her lip as if pondering the question. "Ummm . . ."

Joyous, boisterous reactions ensued, almost drowning out her clear and certain yes.

Two weeks later, when Naomi hadn't gotten her period, she called the doctor.

"That's to be expected," the doctor said. "It sometimes takes up to eight weeks for the cycle to regulate. Don't worry. You're fine."

Even though Naomi knew she wasn't pregnant, the doctor's reassurance was still a relief.

The following week she and Marvin were shoulder to shoulder, prepping chicken and onions for a fried chicken slice.

"Ugh, cutting up so much chicken is making me nauseous."

Marvin nodded. "You, too? The skin and that metallic bloody odor. Nasty!"

Three days later she was cuddling with Marvin when she felt her stomach bubbling. She raced to the bathroom and a round of dry heaves.

She rinsed her mouth and rejoined Marvin in bed.

"You alright?"

"Probably not. Both auntie and Kristy were sick with the flu last week. God, I hope I'm not getting it."

"I love you, honey, but . . . ." Marvin put a couple feet of distance between. "No need of both of us going down."

She smacked him with a pillow. "Whatever, dude. Thanks for the compassion."

Later that morning she called Kristy and thanked her for the germs. Two hours later, Kristy showed up at the truck.

Naomi stepped out of the truck, gave her a hug, and patted Kristy's belly. "You didn't say anything about coming down here."

"Didn't know I had to announce myself."

"What can I get for you, cousin?"

"I want two breakfast slices, sausage, and two Southern pecans." Kristy reached into her purse. "And I also came down to give you this."

Naomi looked around before snatching the package from Kristy and putting it in her pocket. "Girl, why are you bringing me a tampon?" she hissed between gritted teeth.

"It's a pregnancy test."

"Why? I'm not pregnant."

"Did you get your period?"

"No."

"Is food still making you sick?"

"Not really. And I don't have the flu. You just want a playmate for your child."

Naomi hopped back in the truck and promptly forgot about Kristy's assumption. Unseasonably warm weather had people out in droves, a fact that hadn't been anticipated. Less than eight hours after opening for business, Marvin and Naomi packed up the truck and headed home.

She went to use the restroom. Only then did she feel the plastic and remember what Kristy said. Her hand hovered over the wastebasket and then she thought, *Why not?*

Quickly reading the instructions on the wrapper, Naomi took care of business, set the applicator on the counter, and washed her hands while waiting to see the one line she knew would be there.

Except there were two.

"Marvin!"

Turns out the New York trip was indeed unforgettable. A constant reminder of just how amazing it had been would be delivered seven months later. Sweet.

Zuri Day turns up the heat with three sexy page-turning tales of unexpected love and introduces the Morgan men, three fine brothers who have it all—except what their mama wants most for them: wives . . .

Meet Michael Morgan in
Love on the Run

In the world of sports management, Michael Morgan is a superstar. But his newest client, Shayna Washington, may be his most lucrative catch yet. The record-breaking sprinter with the tight chocolate body has a talent and inner light Michael knows he can get the world to sit up and notice. He's certainly paying attention—and suddenly the sworn bachelor finds his focus changing from love of the game to true love . . .

Meet Gregory Morgan in
A Good Dose of Pleasure

When artist Anise Cartier leaves Nebraska for LA, she's finally ready to put the past and its losses behind her. She's even taken a new name to match her new future. And she soon finds a welcoming committee in the form of one very handsome doctor, Gregory Morgan. Their attraction is instant. So is their animosity . . .

Meet Troy Morgan in
Bad Boy Seduction

Gabriella is a triple threat—singing, acting, and dancing—and has always lived the life of a princess. Now, her father is determined to marry her to someone who can help expand her brand and the Stone empire, not some ordinary Joe. Of course, Troy Morgan is anything but ordinary. But can bad boy Troy take a backseat to someone with more money, more fame, and more of just about everything than him?

**Available wherever
books and ebooks are sold.**